D1580300

L ONG EVITY PARK

ZHOU DAXIN

Translated by
James Trapp

SINOIST

Published by
Sinoist Books (an imprint of ACA Publishing Ltd)
University House
11-13 Lower Grosvenor Place,
London SW1W 0EX, UK
Tel: +44 20 3289 3885
E-mail: info@alaincharlesasia.com
www.alaincharlesasia.com
www.sinoistbooks.com

Beijing Office
Tel: +86(0)10 8472 1250

Author: Zhou Daxin
Translator: James Trapp

Paperback ISBN: 978-1-83890-520-0
Hardback ISBN: 978-1-83890-529-3
eBook ISBN: 978-1-83890-521-7

A catalogue record for *Longevity Park* is available from the National Bibliographic
Service of the British Library.

经典中国国际出版工程
China Classics International

LONGEVITY PARK

ZHOU DAXIN

Translated by

JAMES TRAPP

SINOIST BOOKS

GRATEFUL ACKNOWLEDGEMENTS

This book draws on conversations with several scientists and on the results of their previously published research. It also uses some journalists' reports of scientific advances. At this point, I would like to record my warmest gratitude to all these people. If there are any errors in my representation of this material, the fault lies entirely with me.

PROGRAMME FOR THE MAIN EVENING ACTIVITIES IN LONGEVITY PARK

MONDAY EVENING
Promotional event for Miss Weiwei, the robot nurse
Entry to the event only on production of identity card. Restricted to those aged 65 and above. Free gift, one only per attendee.

~

TUESDAY EVENING
Promotional sale of Lingqi Longevity Pill
Identity card required for purchase. Over 65s only; sales restricted to three boxes per person, male or female. Preliminary evidence shows that one box can extend your life by one month and seven days.

~

WEDNESDAY EVENING
Virtual Rejuvenation Experience
Entry to the event only on production of identity card. Open only to those aged 70 and above, and restricted to one turn per person at a cost of Rmb300. Participants must bring a photograph of themselves aged around 20.

~

THURSDAY EVENING
Lecture series – "The Future of Human Lifespan"
Lead lecturer, by special invitation from New York – Lin Xinhan, Chinese Deputy Director of the Human Longevity Research Institute. The lectures will address the latest news in the study of human longevity. Because of limited space at the venue, admittance only to those aged 30 and above, or born before 1987. Entry only on production of identity card. After the lecture, free gift of

the latest electronic blood pressure, blood sugar or blood cholesterol monitor – only one type per attendee.

~

FRIDAY EVENING
Discussion of experiences nursing the elderly (Part 1)
Entry restricted to certified caregivers of Beijing households; registration of name and certificate number required. Not open to the general public. The discussion leaders have requested anonymity in advance but are well worth listening to; the audience is responsible for maintaining this anonymity.

~

SATURDAY EVENING
Discussion of experiences nursing the elderly (Part 2)
Entry requirements as above.

~

SUNDAY EVENING
Discussion of experiences nursing the elderly (Part 3)
Entry requirements as above. At the end of the event, every attending caregiver is entitled, on production of their registration certificate, to a free home first-aid kit worth Rmb880. This event is sponsored by the Yida Corporation.

~

All the above activities will take place in the semi-covered theatre in the southern section of the park.

SENIOR CITIZENS, hello!

To begin with, I would like solemnly to inform you all that your coming to attend this event today is an opportunity for you to extend your lives beyond those of anyone who is not here. Thanks to the computer technology of our Biquan Nursing Home, we now have Miss Weiwei. Rigorous testing and evaluation by worldwide authorities on the care of the elderly have shown that people who enter our nursing home can live an average of three to five years longer than those who are looked after at home!

Three to five years! Those are not small numbers!

I have some more good news for you: at the end of this promotional event, each one of you senior citizens here today can go to Table #2 to collect a valuable free gift. For gentlemen, this is a heart attack warning device which is triggered fifteen minutes before the onset of a heart attack. For ladies, it is a stroke warning device, which is triggered thirteen minutes before the onset of a cerebral stroke. Both of these devices are the products of work by our dedicated medical research experts, and each is worth more than Rmb800. This clearly demonstrates to you all the high levels of both our scientific research and of our financial strength.

Now, on behalf of the board of directors of the Biquan Nursing Home and all its workforce, I solemnly welcome you to this promotional event. What we are presenting to you today is the finest, most beautiful robot nurse in the world: Miss Weiwei. Let us welcome her onstage, in all her glory, with a warm round of applause.

Miss Weiwei is 1.58m tall, with an oval face, long, shapely eyebrows, alert eyes and slightly dishevelled hair. She is wearing a well-fitting qipao. The mechanisms concealed in her head make it a little larger than normal, but it is still within the limits of what men might find attractive. Her legs and backside are very neat and shapely. Her legs are a little thick because they have to support the weight of her workings, and we ask you to forgive us this shortcoming. Weiwei's research team have come up with a solution, and the next stage of development will result in legs that are pale, smooth and elegant. You ladies and gentlemen seated in the front row can reach out and touch Miss Weiwei's skin and tell us how good it feels. Our research team has already demonstrated that they will soon be able to use even more refined materials for Miss Weiwei's flesh and skin, and if you were to feel her again then, it would be as soft and yielding as if you were touching a real girl. What is more, she will also have that fragrance unique to a virginal young girl.

Miss Weiwei's intelligence is already at the level of an eight-year-old girl, and she can understand everything, and perform every task that an eight-year-old girl can. Our research team is very confident that they will soon advance this to the capabilities of a sixteen-year-old, at which point Miss Weiwei will have become an attractive young woman.

Miss Weiwei was truly born at our Biquan Nursing Home, and her mother and father are our scientific experts. The home is to be found at the foot of Beijing's beautiful Qingquan Hills. It is situated in an environment of hills, trees, bamboos and vines. Inside its grounds are broad green lawns and flower gardens; it has natural mountain springs and hot springs, and an artificial drainage system; it has viewing pavilions with panoramic vistas, and its limpid air is filtered by the surrounding greenery; in every season of the year, you can hear the singing of birds and the tinkling of flowing water.

Now we also have Miss Weiwei, we truly believe we can create a paradise on Earth for the elderly.

At the Biquan Nursing Home, we have top-quality medical and nursing teams. In the medical team, we have the country's most famous gerontologist, Mr Fang Jiazhen, who has had the retired presidents of many countries around the world as his patients. Our nursing staff includes a recipient of the internationally recognised nursing award, the Nightingale Medal: Nurse Lin Yunyuan. Our team are ready to treat any sudden medical emergency successfully. With the birth of Weiwei and her addition to our team, we will be able to advance the quality of our nursing to a new, higher level. Weiwei can wake you whenever it is time for your medications; she can take your pulse and collect a urine sample; her touch is as soothing and comforting as if your own granddaughter has come to look after you. Although she only has the intellect of an eight-year-old, her height gives her an illusion of maturity, so gentlemen take note: you had better not take liberties with your hands, as she is able to shoot video and send it back to the central control room. (The audience laughs)

At the Biquan Nursing Home, we have the most modern exercise equipment for the elderly, and Miss Weiwei can supervise you on all of them. She can assist you with any activity: walking, running, dancing, helping reach things down from shelves and cupboards. Whether you want to go swimming, bathe in the hot springs, play croquet, tennis, badminton, ping pong, indoor golf, snooker, she can give you expert assistance with all of these activities. You can look on her as your close friend and companion.

At the Biquan Nursing Home, we also have the most up-to-date leisure facilities. Miss Weiwei can accompany you to a film or play, or take you to the supermarket; she can play Go with you, or battlefield chess and Chinese checkers. We regret that, at this time, she is still unable to play Chinese chess with you. When you watch a film or a play, or listen to music, she can snuggle into your shoulder, like a little bird, giving you a warm, comfortable feeling. When she is playing chess with you, if she happens to bemoan a wrong move, you should treat this as a charming little temper tantrum, and not be angry with her.

You will be amazed how many books we have at the Biquan Nursing Home, as well as tea clubs, little bars and coffee rooms; Miss Weiwei can sit beside you and wait on you when you are reading; when you are drinking wine or coffee, she can liven things up by singing and dancing for you. Her repertoire covers many popular songs from the 1930s, 40s, 50s, 60s, 70s, 80s and 90s. If you don't like a particular song, you can just shake your head or gesture with your hand, and she will change to a different one. Although her dance moves may not be complicated, they are elegant and beautiful, and we are sure everyone will be pleased by them. She can only discuss a few of the most basic family matters with you, like a son or daughter who doesn't come to visit often, or like a teenage girl who can't be bothered with anything, or a rather distant son. I'm sure you get the idea. Although you may not be completely satisfied with this, you should forgive her as she is really just a big girl.

At the Biquan Nursing Home, we have many little snack bars serving food from Beijing, Sichuan, Hunan, Shanghai, Huaiyang, Shandong, Henan, Shaanxi and so on, so Miss Weiwei can go and buy you anything you fancy to eat and bring it to your room. She is quite able to open and close doors, go up and down stairs and use an elevator.

At the Biquan Nursing Home, we have classes in sculpture, painting, calligraphy, weaving, pottery, angling, patio design, bonsai art and many other subjects. For any craft or skill you wish to study, Miss Weiwei will be your patient companion.

At the Biquan Nursing Home, we have three types of bedroom. Type 1 is the standard room you can see in this photograph, which is for single occupancy. We have two thousand of these rooms. As you can see, it contains the most modern therapeutic bed with a headboard that houses the most up-to-date care equipment. When you lie on this bed, there is an automatic digital display of your blood pressure, heart rate and blood oxygen saturation; it can be inclined to any angle, and it is also equipped with an automatic massage facility. If you sleep in this bed, you are guaranteed to be free of bedsores. There is a bathroom in the room, with a bathtub and a sit-down shower, and a toilet specially designed for the elderly with limited mobility. You can see in the photograph the furniture and electronics with which the room is equipped: there is a cupboard, a refrigerator, a television, a sofa and a dining table. Type 2 is the double room shown in this photograph, suitable for an elderly couple. We have another two thousand of these rooms. It is rather larger in area than the single room, with two therapeutic beds. In every other respect, it is the same as the single room. Type 3 room is the luxurious suite in this photograph. We have one thousand of these for the use of the more affluent elderly. They have a separate living room and a small kitchen. After the occupants move in, we can provide a chef according to their preference to prepare their favourite dishes. These rooms are equipped with a safety sensor system, an emergency alarm system and infrared security detectors. A Miss Weiwei is on duty twenty-four hours a day in each room to serve the occupants. Of course, in addition to Weiwei, there is one real human nurse on duty for every three residents. As well as seeing to her ordinary duties, this nurse is responsible for checking the power levels of several Miss Weiweis, cleaning them, changing their clothes and updating their computer care programmes. Each Weiwei has a serial number for easy identification. If there is a Miss Weiwei standing in front of you, and the name badge pinned to her chest shows the serial number 106, you can call her Weiwei 106.

Because the Biquan Nursing Home has not been in operation for very long, at the moment we still have vacancies in all three types of room, and we invite each of you, in your own time, to approach us for an application form. The fees for each type of room are fixed and are shown on this display board. As a mark of our appreciation of your making the effort to come to this evening's lively and crowded promotional event, we are making a special offer of a one per cent discount to everyone who takes an application form today. And when Miss Weiwei is looking after you on a daily basis, she may well also give you a specially warm kiss. (The audience laughs)

We would also welcome it if anyone wishes to buy a Miss Weiwei to take home. Prices differ according to the material and style of Weiwei's clothes, and the price list can be found on the display board in front of Table #3. If you pay in full today, we are also offering a one per cent discount.

After you have taken your Miss Weiwei home, our after-sales team will fix a time to come and give instructions on her care and operation so that she will be guaranteed to provide a complete service every day. I would like to take this opportunity to state categorically that in no circumstances can Miss Weiwei cause any harm or injury to the user. Our design team have incorporated three fail-safes into her design. The worst she can do in response to her user is go on strike. Her aspect when on strike is one of anger, looking at you with pursed lips, one hand on her hip, her body motionless. (The audience laughs) Isn't that quite adorable? If the user encounters this situation, all he or she has to do is phone our helpline number, and the problem will be fixed.

Yes, sir, the old gentleman with his hand up: what is your question? Can Miss Weiwei supervise bowel movements? I regret that, at this time, she is unable to perform this function, principally because she lacks the finesse of touch for cleaning the bodies of elderly people, and cannot respond precisely enough to a request for help with defecation. Perhaps at some time not too far in the future, when her technology has been upgraded, she will have this capability. Would you like us to inform you when that time arrives? Very good, please leave us your name and contact details. Your name is Fu Xiao? OK, and your cell phone number is 17799999089. May I ask if this young lad is your grandson? What? He's your son? Good heavens! You look as though you must be in your eighties, and you still have such a young son? Congratulations to you!

Now, may I ask any of you who are interested to form a queue in front of Table #1 where our customer advisers will give detailed answers to any other questions you may have...

NURSES, gentlemen, everybody – good evening!

My name is Zhang Jingyang, and I am the lead researcher on the Lingqi Longevity Pill development team. Before we start the sale of Lingqi Longevity Pills, I would like to give you a brief introduction to how they came about.

As we know, almost everybody on Earth wants to prolong their time here to some extent, although there are, of course, a few exceptions. If we look back on the growth and development of human existence, we can see that, as the standard of living rises, especially with the advent of advanced medicine, this has indubitably caused a continuous rise in life expectancy. In Bronze Age Europe, the average life expectancy was around 18 years, and by the time of the Romans it had advanced to 29. In Renaissance Europe, it reached 35. There is a line in the writings of Alexandr Pushkin that reads, "An old man of about 30 years old entered the room", which is a comment on the life expectancy of that period. In his novel *Eugene Onegin*, the 36-year-old mother of the heroine is referred to as "an old woman". In Dostoyevsky's novel *Crime and Punishment*, the "old woman" murdered by the hero is just 42. It was only in the 19th century that European life expectancy reached 45. In the 1950s, thanks to the abundance of supplies and the appearance of a plethora of life-enhancing drugs, life expectancy rose almost at a stroke to 68. Currently, their average is around 78. According to the deductions of scientific experts, in China, life expectancy was 18 in the Xia dynasty, and 20 in the Qin and Western Han. In the Eastern Han it was 22, in the Tang and Song, 30, rising to 35 in the Ming and Qing. During the Republic, there was no advance, and it remained at 35. After the establishment of the People's Republic, thanks to the rise in standards of living, advances in medicine and the discovery of new life-extending medicines, the current life expectancy is about 76. In a number of big cities and particularly favourable areas, it has already risen as high as 78-80. History shows us that the power of life-extending drugs is indeed enormous, and there is much hidden potential for human life still to be explored.

So, just how far can life be extended?

Currently, there are several ways of predicting the limits of life expectancy. The first is calculated according to period of growth. I'm sure some of you know about "Buffon's Lifespan Ratio". Buffon was a French naturalist who reckoned that a human's natural period of growth was 20-25 years, and that the mammalian lifespan was 5-7 times this growth period, giving humans a total potential lifespan of 100-125 years. The second way is to use the age of sexual maturity. Humans are considered to reach sexual maturity at the age of 14-15, regardless of gender. If the mammalian lifespan equates to 8-10 times the age of sexual maturity, then this means humans should live to 110-150. The third way is calculated by the number of times a cell divides under in vitro conditions. In America, there is a Dr Hayflick, who conducted experiments under laboratory conditions which showed that in vitro human fibroblasts divided approximately 50 times before the process ceased. For this reason, 50 is known as the human cell's "generational number", and is also called the "Hayflick Limit". Thus, if the generational cycle of a cell takes 2.4 years, human lifespan can be calculated as 120 years. The fourth way is by calculating from the human life-cycle. The Russian scientists Mussorgsky and Kuzmin believe that the first period of the cycle is the peri-natal phase, which, assuming a normal pregnancy, lasts 266 days. The second phase is 15.5 times 266 days, which equals 11 years. If you then multiply 11 by 15.5, you get 167. Thus, they believe 167 is the limit of human longevity.

No matter which of these methods one follows, potential human lifespan is clearly much longer than the present average, and for this reason we must continue to discover new life-enhancing drugs to extend our life and release its full potential to the benefit of all humankind. At this time, every country in the world is making advances in the research into and production of life-extending medicines. A 2006 edition of the Russian newspaper *Komsomolskaya Pravda* reported that researchers at Moscow State University have discovered a kind of powerful antioxidant; if this can be used internally on humans, it could guarantee a life expectancy of 150 years or more. In 2010, British scientists said they had recovered bacteria from a thousand-year-old glacier which could allow people to live to 140 if it can be manufactured into medication. It is this latter process that is currently presenting difficulties. Also in 2010, at the Albert Einstein College of Medicine in New York, a small research team has demonstrated that they have already discovered three types of gene that could unlock the development of gerontology, and medicines based on these discoveries could ensure that the majority of people live to a hundred. In China, we too have many scientists working night and day on research into life-extending medicines. The Lingqi Longevity Pills my own research team has brought along here today are not the result of formal research into internal medicine but the product of private enterprise through the work of an independent group of experts in Chinese medicine. They have been developed and manufactured based on the miraculous drugs given to us by the gods in ancient times.

All of you in the audience are my seniors, and many of you will be very familiar with the history of the Han dynasty; you will know how interested the Emperor Wu, Liu Che, was in the arts of prolonging life. Of course, this is quite understandable, as everyone is interested in living longer, but how many can rely, like Emperor

Liu Che, on having fine food every day, on always having beautiful clothes to wear, or on having beautiful women to embrace every night. Of course, he didn't want to die. This is why he found many ways to try to extend his life, and why, when he sent Zhang Qian to the countries of the Western Regions with instructions to liaise with all the countries there on how to resist the Xiongnu, to open up future trade routes with them, and to expand the market for the silk and tea of the Han dynasty, he also gave him a secret mission: to seek the elixir of youth of the Western Regions. For this reason, he incorporated one of his imperial physicians, a man called Yao Mingsheng, into the armed party that accompanied the mission, specifically to take care of this matter.

We will leave the story of how Zhang Qian opened up the trade routes to the Western Regions to the historians. What I want to talk to you about today is what the imperial physician Yao Mingsheng did on his journey to the west. Every time he entered one of the countries of the Western Regions, he would carry a pack full of silk and tea leaves, employ a local who could speak Chinese, and explore the highways and byways, enquiring among the ordinary people for the famous local doctors and places where people lived particularly long.

In the ancient kingdom of Loulan, he learned from a white-haired old doctor that all the doctors there used the plant called dogbane along with several other local herbal remedies to make a kind of longevity pill for the king, and when the king took it, he felt his health greatly improved and believed it prolonged his life. But because of the rarity of its ingredients, the doctors could only make three pills every month, all of which were handed over into the control of the king. Yao Mingsheng relayed all this to Zhang Qian, and the next time Zhang saw the king of Loulan he immediately raised the suggestion of exchanging the dogbane pills for the very highest quality silk. The king thought long and hard about this, keenly aware of the need not to antagonise the all-powerful emperor of China. In the end, he handed twelve of the pills over to Yao Mingsheng, telling him that the emperor should take one pill every month. As he continued his journey westwards, Yao

Mingsheng learned from a famous doctor among the Greater Yuezhi that a decoction of the roots of the desert poplar could be used for prolonging life; and in the kingdom of Dayuan, he discovered that hairs from the mane of the precious "sweat blood" horses could be soaked in boiling water and the water then used for the same purpose. In the kingdom of Qiuci, he heard an astonishing report that you could take dogbane, hairs from the mane of a "sweat blood" horse and certain local medicinal herbs, and boil them in precise proportions. Then you had to add the liquid from a soup made with an unnamed fruit kernel, and leave it out under the moon at midnight for four hours. After that, it was ready for use, and three spoonfuls could add six months to your life. Yao Mingsheng secretly exchanged silk and tea leaves for these medicinal ingredients, and although he could not get very much of any of them, he did obtain the complete recipe. However, when he finally made his roundabout way back to China, because he was unsure of the authenticity of the samples, he did not dare tell Emperor Liu Che about them, and only presented him with the twelve pills given to him by the king of Loulan. The emperor was delighted by the pills and began to take them immediately, and from then on many times sent envoys with gifts for the king of Loulan to exchange for more of the pills. The pill caused Emperor Liu Che to live to the age of 71, thus becoming the first emperor of China to exceed 70 years of age. Today, 71 is not an age to raise any eyebrows, but, in the Western Han, when average life expectancy was only 20, this was a very great age indeed.

But let us turn away from Liu Che and concentrate on Yao Mingsheng. After his return to the Han court, he secretly began to experiment with the dogbane, "sweat blood" horsehair, unidentified fruit kernels, miscellaneous herbs and thousand-year desert poplar root. Doctors at that time didn't have the laboratory mice and volunteers of today to test their medicines on, and could only take them themselves and observe the results, very much as the sage Emperor Shennong did. Yao Mingsheng tasted as he worked, and gradually began to discover that he was becoming more and more alert and vigorous. At the time, he was fast approaching 60 years of age and had been struggling to lift anything that weighed more than twenty or thirty jin; but now he gradually found he could carry loads of medicinal materials weighing more than a hundred jin; teeth that he had formerly lost grew back again; his skin became incomparably soft and supple, and he started having morning erections again. Secretly amazed, he realised this was all the result of his taking the medicines, but he thought to himself: Since no one else knows about this, why should I feel obliged to offer it up to the emperor? There's no point in going looking for trouble, so I might as well keep it for my own use. By this means, he went on to live until he was 99 years old. At the time, his longevity was a cause of great amazement at court, and of course no one knew what lay behind it. Just before his death, he wrote down the formula for his longevity medicine on a bamboo scroll and gave it to his son. In order to protect the secret, he added a number of random, meaningless characters, thereby encrypting it, as we would say today. His son did not enter the court as an imperial physician but practised his medicine among the people, and because the ingredients of the formula were uncommon ones, he was never able to make up the longevity medicine, and he just left the scroll in a wooden chest. By the time several generations had passed, no one was able to decipher its contents. Later on, after the fall of the Western Han and the establishment of the Eastern Han, Yao Mingsheng's descendants moved east to Luoyang and continued to practise medicine as before, but their skill and reputation never again reached their former heights.

One day, one of Yao's descendants read a book called *Shanghan Zabing Lun*.[1] He thought it was very well written, and went on to ask around about where the author, Zhang Zhongjing, lived. When he discovered that Zhang lived in Nanyang County, he determined to go and visit him. Sadly, when he got there, he found that Zhang was seriously ill and not strong enough to give him any instruction. As he was about to leave, Yao's descendant produced his ancestor's bamboo scroll and asked for Zhang Zhongjing's help reading it. Zhang was a doctor of great learning, and recognised immediately the meaning of what was written on the bamboo slips; he wrote down the names of the ingredients to be found in China that could be substituted for the dogbane, "sweat blood" horsehair, the unnamed fruit kernels and the roots of thousand-year-old desert poplar. This meant that this method of extending lifespan could continue to be used in the country. Yao's descendant was delighted, and when he returned to Luoyang, he began using Zhang Zhongjing's altered prescription to make up the medicine. After he had been taking it for a while, the results were extraordinary: his appearance was particularly youthful, his white hair grew black again, his wrinkles diminished and his stamina increased. To start with, use of the medicine was limited to the family clan, but later on they began to use it on any ageing invalids who came to consult the Yao family doctors. Because of the undoubted rise in life expectancy of people treated with the medicine, the reputation of the Yao family doctors rose once again. On the back of this formula, generations of the Yao family continued to practise medicine in Luoyang right through to the Anshi Rebellion[2] in the Tang dynasty.

As everyone knows, during the Anshi Rebellion, after An Lushan took Luoyang, on Lunar New Year's Day of the fifteenth year of the Tianbao reign period (756 CE), he proclaimed himself emperor, calling himself Emperor of the Great State of Yan. Three years after he ascended the throne, the emperor of Yan learned that the Yao family in the city possessed the formula for a life-extending medicine, so he ordered his men to bring them to him in chains, and demanded that they hand over the medicine. They did not dare disobey, and began to treat An Lushan with the medicine. Sadly, he was not destined for that kind of longevity, and soon after was assassinated by his son, An Qingxu. Later on, the Yao family were taken by force to Fanyang, modern-day Beijing, by the forces of Shi Siming, and obliged to become doctors to him and his family. After the Anshi Rebellion was quashed, they remained working as doctors for the ordinary folk of the Fanyang area. Although the Yao family were continuously on the move, they never lost the secret formula, which was passed on from generation to generation. The story goes that, in the Ming dynasty, when Ming Chengzu, the third Ming Emperor Zhu Di, moved the capital to Beijing in 1421, he heard members of his court talking about a family of doctors called Yao who were highly skilled and possessed a formula for a life-extending medicine that could prolong someone's life by many years. So he sent men to search everywhere for them and bring them back to act as court physicians. Because he had access to the Yao family's life-extending medicine, Zhu Di, on whom constant campaigning had taken a severe mental and physical toll, doggedly managed to live to the age of 65. This was the greatest age attained by any of the Ming emperors. After the Qing vanquished the Ming, the Ming court physicians were scattered, and the Yao family returned to doctoring the ordinary people. It is common knowledge that, at the end of the Qing dynasty, the Empress Dowager Cixi set great store by prolonging her life, and sent out her medical superintendents to make secret inquiries of famous doctors all over the empire, hoping to discover the secret formula for longevity. In the end, they discovered the Yao family, doctors for so many generations, and once again they were brought to the Forbidden City, this time to serve the Empress Dowager. And indeed it was because of the Yao family's secret formula that Cixi, who had long suffered from venereal disease, still managed to live to the age of 73.

After the fall of the Qing, the Yao family once again returned to doctoring the ordinary people. Yuan Shikai and Zhang Zuolin both sent men to seek out the Yao family, but they were well aware of the perils of tending to emperors and high officials. They secretly fled to a village deep in the Yan Mountains, and made their living by treating the people of the mountain villages and gathering medicinal plants. In the present day, in the course of our researches into longevity pills, we at the Shuntian Longevity Company chanced to discover the whereabouts of the Yao family. The president of the company went in person to pay a formal visit to them, and, for the enormous price of Rmb10 million, bought the secret longevity formula that has been passed down so many generations. Since then, we have followed the results of modern medical research, and enhanced the formula one step further, resulting in the Lingqi Longevity Pill that I have brought here today.

Contemporary medical science holds that there are seven causes of human ageing: number one is degradation of the genes, which increases with the advance of age as the processing capability of the body's cells diminishes and causes genetic atrophy; number two is the areas of infection and inflammation of the body's tissues and organs, which increase steadily with advancing age; number three is the increase in the physiological stress of oxidisation caused by free radicals, and its effect on the orderly function of bodily processes; number four is the functional decline of the cells and tissues of worn-out heart, brain and muscles etc; number five is the growing imbalance between saturated and unsaturated fatty acids in the body; number six is the insufficiency of digestive enzymes and the chronic slowing down of the digestive process; number seven is the dysfunction and imbalance caused by calcification, which causes calcium build-up in the walls of the blood vessels, the heart valves and the brain cells. In the course of our researches into the Lingqi Longevity Pill, we have paid particular attention to the resolution of these problems.

Our Lingqi Longevity Pills have currently been taken by 1,555,668 people over the age of 65. They are all still alive, the oldest being 101 years and five months, and the youngest now 82, giving the pills an efficacy rate of a hundred per cent. Our statistical calculations show that taking one box of pills increases your life by one month and seven days. The rarity of the ingredients means that our production is small, and I have only brought a limited supply today, which means that, on production of your ID card, each of you can only buy three boxes at a cost of Rmb999 per box. Some of you may feel this price is a bit of a nuisance and would be more convenient if it was an even one thousand, but we have chosen the figure deliberately for luck – what could be luckier than three nines? Now, all of you, please form an orderly queue first in front of Table #1 to pay the money, and then proceed with your receipt to Table #2 to collect your pills. Once you have them, you can take your first pill this very evening: there is no room for delay in the quest for longevity; you must pursue it night and day. Please don't push, ladies and gentlemen; form an orderly queue. The old gentleman in the wheelchair, please be careful you don't run over anyone's foot. What's that? You want to buy four boxes? The rule is three boxes. You have difficulty getting about, so you want to buy an extra box? I'm very sorry, but I can't set that precedent, or the others might have something to say about it...

WEDNESDAY
EVENING

GRANDPAS, grandmas, welcome one and all to this evening's Rejuvenation Experience.

I am sure you all know the story behind the saying "turning back the years": King Liu An of Huainan (164-122 BCE) sent men all over the kingdom to seek out the secret of staving off old age. Then, out of the blue, eight white-haired, silver-bearded old men came seeking an audience with him, saying they had the secret of "turning back the years" and wanted to present him with the elixir of youth. Liu An was delighted beyond measure with this news, and hastened to open his doors to welcome them. But when he saw the old men, he couldn't help laughing out loud and saying:

"How can you claim to have the secret of eternal youth, when you all look so old? Clearly you are all frauds!"

He was about to order his guards to throw the old men out of the palace, when the eight of them all burst out laughing, saying:

"You accuse us of being old, do you? Well, look carefully at us again!"

And with this, they all suddenly turned into young men.

I am sure some of you grandpas and grandmas will remember that, in 2008, the American film director David Fincher released a movie called *Turning Back the Years*, starring Brad Pitt and Kate Blanchett. It told the story of strange events that took place in

Baltimore in 1919, and how Benjamin Button reversed the laws of nature, being born as an old man and turning back time as he grew younger every day.

The Chinese saying "turning back the years" and the American movie of the same name both reflect a common wish of humankind that once they have grown old, they might return to their youth and live their life over again. Sadly, of course, such a wish can never be fulfilled in real life. However, today's scientific advances have allowed us to think up something that at least partly makes up for this, and that is to use modern imaging technology, artificial intelligence and fashion techniques to create a new environment. After the elderly enter this environment, they are swiftly transported back to the time of their youth, to experience, for a short while, the beautiful sensation of reliving those years. My team and I are currently performing this operation, and up to yesterday we have already enabled 128,903 people to have this experience. Every one of them has said it was a miraculous and wonderful thing. According to the statistics from our follow-up survey, people who have undergone this experience lose an average of two years from their psychological age.

Everybody knows a person's age can be expressed in three different ways. One way is their natural age, calculated from the day, month and year of their birth; another is their physiological age, which can be calculated from the functional capabilities of the body's organs using data from clinical examination. Then there is psychological age, which can be calculated according to changes in psychological state and mental ability. What this rejuvenating experience we have developed affects is the psychological age, and when a person's psychological age is reduced, it can bring about a corresponding reduction in physiological age, naturally extending one's life. I am sure everyone also knows that the number of old people on Earth is gradually increasing. Statistical analysis of the elderly population in America shows that, in 1900, over 65s made up 4.1 per cent of the population; in 1940, it was 6.8 per cent; and in 1975, it was 8.9 per cent. By the year 2000, it was 11.7 per cent, and it is projected to reach 16 per cent by 2050. According to the statistics here in China, at the end of 2016 there were 230 million people aged over 60 in the population, and in the future that number will increase by 10 million every year. By 2050, one in three of the population will be over 60. It is for this reason that it has become a duty of us younger people to find ways to serve our elderly, to reduce their psychological age so that they may extend their physiological and natural lifespans. The aim of this experience we have brought to you today is to change your psychological age. We have had numerous requests from venues for us to run our event, and we have come here this evening at the third time of asking by the management of Longevity Park.

Now I am going to explain the method and process of our experience. Each one of you should hand over the photograph of yourself aged around 20 at Table #1. Then, after you have paid the fee at Table #2, you should proceed to the cordoned-off Zone A where you put on the equipment we have prepared for you. Next, you move on to Zone B, where you will find our large-scale, super-high-definition surround-screen display, on which you will see your white hair gradually turning black again, your hairline returning to where it was twenty years ago, and the wrinkles on your face smoothing out until they disappear. The bags under your eyes will vanish, your skin will turn white and soft, the gleam will come back into your eyes, lost teeth will reappear, pearly white and complete, and you will be restored to the height you were twenty years ago. At the same time, the men among you will feel your penis thicken and stiffen, and you women will feel your vulva tighten and grow moist. By the end, you will have turned into the person you were in the photograph you brought along. As you watch these transformations, you may also feel your energy increasing and a sudden desire to dance or shout or laugh. Next, our staff will lead you into Zone C where you will see yourself on the extra-tall, super-high-definition surround screen, and it will be the image of you in your youth, three-dimensional, waving and kicking and completely true to life. Here you will find a number of youngsters, the same age, both boys and girls, who can chat and joke with you about the kind of things that young people are interested in.

Perhaps there will be a boy or a girl who fancies you, who will move closer, throwing flirtatious glances. Most likely, if you are a young lad, after five minutes or so, a pretty girl will come up to you and ask you to go for a walk in the nearby woods. If you are a girl, maybe a handsome young lad will come over and ask to go for a stroll along the river. You shouldn't hesitate, but boldly take their hand and go along with them, as you may be sure that we will not allow anything to happen that can't be sorted out. When you go into the woods with them, or along the riverbank, you can kiss them, but it is best if you don't get more intimate – although, of course, there is nothing wrong with thinking about it. But hugging, caressing, kissing long and hard, that is all OK. Of course, as you go deeper into the trees, or along the banks of a little stream, just when you want to find a secluded spot to be alone together, that is when you arrive at Zone D. At this point, you will discover that you have already returned to old age, and are back to being your current self. This may seem a little cruel, but it is as far as modern science can take us. Perhaps, not too far in the future, our scientists may allow you to go further, into a Zone E, where you can get married, and once again enjoy the springtime of your youth. As I speak, I can see a number of you grandmas and grandpas shaking your heads, thinking that this is all wild talk and some kind of trick. I am not a scientist myself, but recently, on WeChat, I saw a popular science article written by a physicist. So, hot off the press, I am now going to read you an excerpt from it.

At present, the newest discoveries by scientists may have profound effects on the survival of humankind. Recently, there have been two important and eye-catching discoveries, namely dark matter and quantum entanglement. Let us take dark matter first. We already know that the form of the universe is dependent on gravity to maintain itself. Heavenly bodies are held in attraction to each other across the distances between them by gravity, and their rotation is swift but orderly. But when scientists came to calculate these distances between heavenly bodies minutely, they discovered that their gravitational pull is far from sufficient to hold together a complete galaxy. If there is only the pull of their currently known mass in operation, then the universe could not exist in its present form, but could only be inchoate like a tray of loose sand. That is to say, for the universe to preserve its current order, there has to be some other matter operating on it. So far, however, humankind has not been able either to see or to uncover this matter, which is why we call it dark matter. Pursuing their calculations to the next level, scientists have worked out that for the universe to maintain the order of its movements, dark matter must exist in quantities five times greater than the matter we can currently see.

Now, turning to quantum entanglement. In their study of matter, as scientists progressed through the levels of atoms, molecules, quantum particles and other minuscule entities, they discovered an extraordinary phenomenon: quantum entanglement. That is to say, two unconnected masses in separate positions can display identical behaviour as if they were completely connected. For example, with two quantum masses separated by a great distance without any conventional connection between them, if one displays a change in form, the other almost simultaneously displays the same change. Moreover, this is not simply a coincidence but follows rules of behaviour that have been demonstrated by repeated experiments. These scientific discoveries have overturned the existing understanding of the laws of physics. Our existing theories of physics are all founded on the belief that nothing can exceed the speed of light, but, according to new evaluations, the speed of connection in quantum entanglement is at least four times faster than the speed of light. This presents a challenge to our current understanding of the world. At present, the matter that we recognise is only a part of the universe, and a very small part at that, perhaps only five per cent. Since the greater part of the universe is formed of matter we know nothing about, who would dare assert that this matter may not have influence over the survival of humankind, or may not extend the limits of human life? Perhaps it may allow us to turn back the years. If two quantum masses can mysteriously develop a connection, why also should human lifespan not be mysteriously extended? Why should the two states of youth and old age not mysteriously be reversed? Anything is possible!

So, just wait, dear grandmas and grandpas sitting here today; perhaps, not too far in the future, within this mysterious universe of ours, our scientists will be able to send you back to your youth; send you back to live in that youth where you can once again enjoy its splendour!

Never give in to pessimism! Just think: a thousand years ago, how could humans ever have thought that their descendants would be able to sit in a high-speed train travelling at more than 300 kph, or in an aeroplane at speeds approaching 1000 kph?

Right then, let us return to today's experience.

Dear grandmas and grandpas, I guarantee that today's experience will be something entirely new to you, something that will benefit you enormously both physically and mentally. Now, when we start the experience, five people can be admitted at a time; five people can start the experience at the same time in Zones A, B, C and D respectively. Please start up the magical music!

Yes, sir? The gentleman on crutches. You have your hand up to ask a question? Can you go through the experience twice in succession today? No, I'm sorry, but you can't; see for yourself how many people there are in the queue. How about this, though? Tomorrow evening, we will be running the experience in Lotus Flower Park, and you could go through it again there. Your name is Lian Fafu? Very good; I'll remember you, and I will most certainly let you go through the experience again tomorrow evening. Now, the first group of five, please proceed to Zone A...

GOOD EVENING, everybody!

I am delighted to be able to come here to Longevity Park today to give you all a lecture on predictions for the future of human life expectancy. I am very grateful to the management of Longevity Park for their gracious invitation that allows me to hold my lecture for the first time in one of Beijing's free public parks, especially on such a beautiful evening as we have tonight.

Many people are making predictions about what the future of humankind will be like, about how long people will live, about what the limit might be to life expectancy. Professor Yuval Noah Harari of the Hebrew University of Jerusalem in Israel predicts in his book *A Brief History of Tomorrow* that, as humankind reduces famine, pestilence and war, it may set itself a new target to aim for, which could be to overcome old age, defeat death and attain eternal life and happiness.

I am very interested in this prediction, and feel that there is more than a grain of truth in it. Researchers studying one aspect of humanity, life expectancy, are taking together the current state of scientific development and the possible directions it may make in the future, and making their own predictions about the future of humankind, in particular the question of life expectancy. Of course, there is no guarantee that my own predictions are completely accurate, but they may open a window for you all to catch a glimpse of what the future of humankind may look like.

First of all, I must make it clear that my discussion of this topic today cannot be very detailed, as to go into detail would take too much time, and would also require specialised conditions and equipment.

My overall prediction is that, in the future, humankind will be able to take advantage of all manner of scientific techniques to extend our lives as this is one of our innate capabilities. In the future, we will surely never be satisfied with any level of life expectancy, no matter how long, or cease our quest to extend it; our natural insatiability will undoubtedly always assert itself on this matter. Once on the road to longevity, humans will never erect a finish post. Or, to put it another way: the road to long life is never-ending.

My prediction is that average life expectancy will successively leap up four levels. The first level will be 120 years of age. At present, there are only one or two individuals who reach this level. In China, I know that there are people who have reached it in the regions of Hainan, Guangxi, Henan and Xinjiang. For example, in 2013, Ms Luo Meichen from Bama in Guangxi passed away at the age of 127; currently, Alimihan Seyiti, who lives in Xinjiang, is 130 years old; Zhu Zhengshi, from the Shengliu district of Chengdu in Sichuan, has already passed her 117th birthday, so is fast approaching this level. As things stand, however, the numbers of people actually reaching it are still too few, but in the future, 120 will be just the first stage that our average lifespan attains. The second level is 150. According to our research institute, currently no one in the world has reached this level.

The third level is 180. People who lived to this age are only to be found in the historical records of a few countries. The fourth level is 230. In popular Chinese folktales, there is indeed one person who lived to this age, but only as a figure of legend. In other contexts, the numbers 120, 150, 180 and 230 are nothing remarkable, but put them in the context of life expectancy and they are huge and astonishing figures, beyond anything our predecessors even dared think about. Even now, the majority of people don't dare believe them. I think that in the audience here today, many of you will certainly be sneering at my predictions, thinking they are the ramblings of a madman. I don't expect to be able to change that at a stroke. All I want to do at present is reaffirm a tenet common to all humankind: that human life is sacred beyond measure. The preservation and prolonging of human life is something that corresponds with the value systems commonly held by all humankind.

The reason I predict that human life expectancy can ascend these four levels is because I believe that, in the future, human life will no longer be a question of individuals running their course alone, or of a lonely battle against the advances of old age and death; rather it will become a process based firmly on scientific and technological progress; a systematic progress through life based on the collaborative efforts of scientists across the whole world. With the strenuous efforts of these scientists, this systematic progress will be refined day on day, with a corresponding continuous rise in efficacy.

To start with, I would like to talk about the question of the future of human reproduction. Birth is the starting point of human life, and the circumstances surrounding this start have a major effect on longevity. I would like to inform you that future scientific and technological advances may bring about a revolution in human reproduction. We all know that, in the past and at present, the fundamental model of human reproduction has relied on successful copulation between the sexes. The male sexual organ enters the female reproductive organs in order to transport male sperm into the female's uterus, where the ovum can be fertilised. The fertilised ovum can then slowly develop into an embryo, allowing the infant finally to be born. But perhaps it won't be too long before the birth of a child no longer requires copulation between male and female, since, as a result of the maturing of the processes of artificial insemination and in vitro fertilisation, and especially with the advances in stem cell research, the collection of sperm and egg sooner or later may no longer be necessary. At Capital University in

Japan, there is a professor who can take human skin cells and turn them into embryo stem cells. When the time comes, if a man and woman want a child, they will be able to go to a clinic, where all they will have to do is provide tiny specimens of skin. The clinic will take stem cells from the female specimen and convert them into a mature ovum, and take stem cells from the male specimen and convert them into a mature spermatozoon. They can then be brought together to form a fertilised ovum from which the embryo can develop. This would be implanted into an artificial uterus, and the child can be born.

In Germany, not long ago, a news agency announced that the New Mankind Company at 8 Schandegen in Berlin has already used an incubator to produce two healthy children, a boy and a girl, for a couple called Hoffman from Dresden. What is more, the process only took six months, although, of course, on this occasion, they used real human ova and spermatozoa. More importantly, genetic modification could be carried out on the fertilised embryo, using gene editing to filter out genes that might give rise to hereditary diseases. Effectively, this means that, in future, people will be able to design the baby that they want.

The most recent development around the circumstances of birth is the supplementary fertilisation technique of mixing three or more people's DNA, and this is beginning to show successful results. A child has already been born using this technology – in Mexico in 2016. A few days ago, a hospital in the Ukraine announced that two childless, infertile women had become pregnant using this technique. The parents of these children do not conform to the traditional model of a male-female couple. Humankind's method of reproduction has already been turned on its head. Sexual intercourse will soon no longer be about the function of reproduction but will become purely a leisure activity. Women will no longer have to worry about having children ruining their figure; they will no longer have to suffer the discomforts of ten months of pregnancy; nor will they endure the vomiting, constipation, bloating and weight gain that goes with it; and especially they will be spared the agonies of labour and delivery.

This method of reproduction can provide a solid foundation for the extending of human life expectancy.

There may be considerable differences between what humankind eats today and what we will eat in the future. We all know that we rely on food for our energy and to sustain life: the better we eat, the longer we live. When considering what humankind may eat in the future, we may see three changes. Firstly, there is the addition of new kinds of foodstuff. At the moment, there are certain things that are considered inedible, but rapid scientific advances may unlock their nutritional value. Take insects for example: their protein content is even greater than that of meat, and a market for them as comestibles may well develop. There are also many varieties of algae, and some wild plants and leaves that are hiding great nutritive value, and which, once processed, may also become viable foodstuffs. Another thing is the increase in artificial foodstuffs. Veal with a high nutritional value is already being produced in Petri dishes. Single-celled proteins produced by non-agricultural methods, so called "man-made meat" is a kind of micro-organic food, and its production by fermentation processes can result in an abundant supply. Medical science already knows that over-consumption of meat is one of the causes of nutrition-related illness. High blood pressure, high blood cholesterol and high blood sugar are all connected, at one level or another, with eating meat, but the consumption of man-made meat can prevent the appearance of these conditions. What is more, our food processing and storage techniques may also undergo great changes. In particular, traditional cooking methods such as frying and roasting may gradually be supplanted by steaming, clear-stewing and boiling, and by cold dishes and raw salads; vacuum packing will become widespread. As well as a refrigerator, households of the future will all be equipped with a vacuum sealing machine. If people eat well and eat healthily, their life expectancy will naturally increase.

One topic I particularly want to talk to you about today is the future of sex. Other than food, this is the most important subject from a human point of view, and one intimately related to the matter of longevity. All of you in the audience who have children are adults, and will not be embarrassed by my raising this topic. In the past, many people had their lives cut short because they did not pay proper attention to this matter, thereby reducing average human life expectancy. In the future, in order to satisfy human sexual needs, other than encouraging even more men and women to fulfil their sexual desires through the free association of the sexes, science can offer two further ways of making sex more convenient. The first is to solve the problem of how a couple can have sex when they are in different places. At present, two people have to be in the same place to have sex, in a room, on a bed or a table or on the carpet: that is to say, they have to be together. Naturally, the pain of separation or living apart in this context can have an adverse effect on any increase in life expectancy. But in the future, this no longer has to be the case: advances in virtual reality technology and high-quality realistic sex robots will make long-distance sex a possibility. When its time comes, virtual reality technology will transport the complete physical forms and personalities of lovers separated by thousands of miles, and transfer them into the bodies of realistic sex robots standing right in front of you. It will be just as though your real lover has been whisked across all that distance to stand there. It will be so realistic to sight and touch that you will see every swish of hair and blink of eye, and every change of expression. Even your sense of smell can come into play as you will be able to smell the perfume of their skin and hair; you will be able to hear their gentle breathing, and be able to hug and kiss the sex robot just as if you were hugging and kissing your real lover. As your desire surges, you will be able to make love to the robot and achieve the most satisfying of sexual highs. The second step is the question of the production of these realistic sex robots and how they can completely solve the problems of the difference in size between men and women and of couples in unhappy marriages. If a man can't find a wife, or a woman can't find a husband, or if a man is married but at loggerheads with his wife and there is no affection between them but they can't separate, then all you do is go and buy or hire a realistic sex robot. Making love to a realistic sex robot is almost exactly the same as making love to a real person, and a person's sexual urges can be completely and utterly satisfied. When that time comes, things like rape and sexual molestation will no longer happen. Of course, when these realistic sex robots roll off the factory line, they will each carry a warning notice: *Please don't talk to me about feelings; I am not a real person.*

So, just how realistic can a realistic sex robot be? I know an American scientist who has done specialist research in this area, and he tells me that, the way he sees it, they will reach the point where you can't tell one from a real person unless you open up its body or head with a scalpel and reveal its hidden microchips. Its blood and bodily fluids will be exactly the same as a human's; if you were to break its skin, it would bleed just like a real person; if its labelling was removed, and it got mixed up in a crowd, you wouldn't be able to identify it without detecting equipment. Just yesterday, one of our own Chinese scientists researching this matter told me that, in his view, the sex robots of the future will be tall, short, fat or skinny according to an individual's sexual preferences; the physiognomy and expressions of male ones will have categories such as masterful, handsome and open, dissolute and so on. The female ones could be charming, dignified or sexy. Every existing desirable male characteristic could be incorporated into the software of a male robot, and the same for female robots.

In the future, when a man buys or hires a female sex robot, it will be as tender and gentle as can be, and when a woman buys or hires a male sex robot, it will be as protective and considerate as can be. Between owner and machine, there will be no such things as reproach, anger, verbal or physical abuse, frigidity, weeping and wailing, quarrelling or separation. Thus, people's mood will be improved, and their life expectancy will naturally increase. After production of these realistic sex robots commences, all the time and effort people waste trying to persuade their partner to have sex will be dramatically reduced; the sexual violence between partners that ends up with one of them in jail will disappear, as will all the emotional pain and distress. Of course, this will demolish yet another barrier to human longevity. However, with the gradual virtualisation and mechanisation of the physical side of human sexual activity, the emotional aspect will also decrease. Couples will no longer whisper sweet nothings to each other as they make love, and the basic animal instincts of the sexual urge will reassert themselves. This is a problem that demands our close attention.

In the future, our treatment of illness and disease will be very different from now. Currently, if we develop pathological changes in a particular organ, our first response is to take medicines; if those medicines are ineffective, or there is a tumour that doesn't respond to drug therapy, then we turn to surgery. Both of these options can cause a lot of pain and discomfort. Drugs can have harmful side effects on other organs; surgery can often fail with destructive consequences. But, in the future, our ways of treating disease will change completely as there will be a simple method of growing organs from stem cells, and, in addition, all organ transplant surgery will be controlled by computer, and analgesia, haemostasis and suturing will all be performed by robotic operatives. It will all be quick and safe, and recovery time will be very rapid. If, one day, you discover harmful changes to one of your organs, you will be able to go to the organ shop on the main street and use your own stem cells to order a new one. Then you go to the organ transplant room in your local hospital, lie down on the operating table, and either you or the surgeon can start the robot. In no time at all, you will have a new organ, and the whole process will be practically pain-free. I have just received news today that the University of Sydney in Australia, Harvard University in the US and our own Northeastern University have cooperated in the recent manufacture of a kind of elastic protein gel, which, if layered over an open wound, closes the wound in rapid time. They are presently preparing human trials, and it may very soon be in use in hospital operating theatres. Just think: with this kind of gel available, in the future, will there still be any pain involved in organ transplant surgery? Of course, brain transplants are not possible, as after such an operation, the patient would no longer be the same person. However, it won't be long before scientists can put a large number of nanorobots in your brain to repair your cerebrum or destroy any tumours there.

Yes, sir! My friend in the wheelchair; you have your hand up. What do you want to ask me? Can we transplant half an old person's brain? Ah, that is a question I cannot immediately give a definite answer to because questions about the brain raise the problem of a person's self-recognition. I can't say for sure what the result would be of changing half a brain. Would Old Number Seven Wang suddenly become Old Number Eight Han? How about this? I'll pass your question on to our specialist pathologist who is researching the future of the brain, and he will be able to give you a clear answer. What is your name? Yan Shenglong? And what is your cell phone number? 12001131918. Very good, you will get a call from him within the week. Now, let's get back to our original subject.

The rapid changes and advances in the elimination of disease offer even more important guarantees of the extending of human life.

In the future, a portion of humankind may be able to benefit from hibernation and cryonics technology to increase their life expectancy. At the moment, a number of doctors of internal medicine are already using low body temperature therapy: over a period of several days, they reduce the patient's body temperature by a certain number of degrees to treat wounds, brain damage, epilepsy and other such conditions. There are also scientists experimenting with putting patients into a sleep-like state for a period of several days, even extending it to a matter of weeks, and then bringing them back round in conditions that avoid any unwanted side effects. Other doctors are obtaining the consent of patients whose conditions are currently incurable and placing them in an experimental state of deep freeze in order to revive them when medical science has discovered a cure for their disease. In the future, this kind of experimental research will expand even more rapidly and more widely. Perhaps within a few decades, or a century, when the weather is bad or they're feeling grumpy, for the sake of their longevity, people will say to their family members or friends: I'm going into hibernation; remember to wake me up next spring. Then you would just take a pill and go to sleep for the next couple of months or half a year. In the future, every city or township community will have a purpose-built human cryonics unit. Anyone who develops a condition for which there is currently no cure, some kind of blood condition for example, can simply go to the community cryonics unit, fill in a form on the computer, including the name of their condition, with instructions that they should be revived when a cure is found. Then they lie down on a bed in the unit, a member of staff will turn on the refrigeration, and they will enter into a state of deep freeze. Of course, this use of technology to extend one's life costs money, so those old people who are rich enough to use their money to extend their life will have to assess the value of this extension to their existence.

In the future, people will have even more opportunities for pleasure and enjoyment, which will also benefit life expectancy. The first thing that should give them pleasure is how quickly they will be able to travel to any place on Earth for a holiday. Within a hundred years there will be high-speed trains capable of 1000 kph, and a dozen or so years after that their speed will be up to 6500 kph. People will be transported at enormous speed in hypobaric tubes; a trip between New York and Beijing will only take two hours, and a trip around the world will be completed in four. We will soon have cars powered by hydrogen cells that can travel by land and in the air continuously for more than 2000 km. In 120 years, there will be aircraft carriers in the sky, and the seaborne type will be a thing of the past. The second thing that should give people pleasure is that, in about 220 years, they will be able to break out of the constraints of the human sleep mechanism. They will be able to stay alert and even-tempered twenty-four hours a day, only having to rest once a month and sleep for just a few hours to recharge their energy levels. Led by technology, the limits of human potential will be continuously exceeded, and the human body will continue to improve. There will be contact lenses with sensors and computers embedded in them, quite possibly permanently implanted in the eye, giving people improved night vision and X-ray vision too. Prosthetic limbs with connections between the skeletal system and the brain will return normal movement to disabled people and allow them to walk up mountains as if they were flat surfaces. The third thing that will make people happy is that intelligence-enhancing drugs will raise human mental capacity even higher. If an intelligent person's current IQ is between 120 and 140, in the future, the average IQ across the population will be higher than that. Genius level is currently 141 and above, but in the future, there will be numerous people with IQs over 150, so everybody will have a genius in their immediate environment. In only 250 years' time, people will have organic microchips implanted in their brains and mechanical learning will be a thing of the past. A traditional education taking a dozen or more years may be compressed into a few weeks by implanted learning, with the result that schools may completely disappear. If you want to learn something, you will just plug in a transducer, and that's it. This kind of life will greatly increase people's pleasure and enjoyment, with a corresponding benefit in life expectancy.

In the future, as transport becomes faster and more convenient and human contact becomes more frequent, the world will become like a village; intermarriage between different ethnic groups will become more common, and thus differences in racial characteristics will disappear. This will all create conditions favourable to the dissemination of life-extending technology, and will naturally have a beneficial effect on life expectancy. In October 2010, a group of British scientists offered a prediction of the new form humans will present a thousand years in the future. Bringing together their prediction and the results of my own research, I believe there will be only one human type across the whole globe, which will differ in six respects from how we are today. Number one is that head and body hair will have reduced even to the point of total disappearance. This will be because of continuous advances in the technologies of central heating and heat-retaining clothing, which will mean that humans' natural heat retention systems will largely decline, so head hair, armpit hair, body hair and pubic hair may gradually disappear. Number two is that our stomachs may become smaller and more concave. This will be due to the appearance of weight-loss foods and our fear of fat: our intestines will gradually become shorter to avoid the over-absorption of lipids and sugars. Number three is that our fingers and arms will grow longer. This will be due to the more widespread use of touchscreen electronic devices which will require more complex hand-eye coordination. Number four is that our heads will become smaller. This is because many tasks requiring mental effort and memory will be taken over by computers and other electronic devices, making such a change inevitable. Number five is that our mouths will become smaller. This will be due to the nature of the food we will be eating in the future, which will be more and more finely processed and softer and softer. It will be possible to get much of our necessary nutrition in liquid or tablet form, so we will need fewer teeth, our lower jaws will become more recessed, and small bud-shaped mouths will become more common. Number six is that we will grow even taller. This will be due to the continuous improvement in our nutrition. The average American is now 2.54 centimetres taller than in 1960, and if this rate of change continues, in a thousand years' time, everyone will be between 1.82 and 2.13 metres tall. If you all look at the picture on that display board, you will see a depiction of what the future human form will look like. How do you think it compares to how we look today? It certainly hasn't become any better looking, and it might even be said to be rather strange and ugly, mightn't it? That is certainly the case if we judge it by today's standards of beauty, but you should be aware that those standards change along with changes in society, so by that time they will certainly not be the same as today.

In the future, the external appearance of old people as they age will not be the same as today, and as a result their psychological age will get younger. Let me illustrate this with statistical data: at present, the median age in China is 36.7; that is to say, already fifty per cent of the population are aged over 36.7, which means that China is currently an upper-middle-aged society. This has never been the case before throughout its history. There is a statistically-proven phenomenon after people enter upper-middle-age, which is that the wrinkles on their faces increase, doubling in number and depth with every ten years. About half the people in our society have wrinkled faces, which is not something we feel good about. Why do people's faces develop wrinkles as they get older? It is because the fat cells in our skin disappear with age. It is this lack of fat cells that causes the wrinkles to form. At the moment, the research team led by Professor George Cotsarelis of the University of Pennsylvania in America has already succeeded in regenerating fat cells, and it may not be too long before this technology can be used in humans. That is to say, if fat cells can be regenerated in the skin of old people with wrinkles, their faces and necks can be returned to a smooth and blemish-free state. Just think about it: after you have turned seventy or even eighty, your face and body will be just the same as your children's and grandchildren's, not a wrinkle in sight and your skin smooth and glowing. How much will that cheer you! Other than this, although in the future your skull won't change, your eyes, teeth and ears will. That is to say, the strength of your vision, the power of your bite and the acuity of your hearing will all be the same as a young person's, so what will you care how old you actually are? All this will remove many psychological barriers from the elderly. In the past, society used to denigrate the elderly by saying to the young: I was once you, and you will one day be me. In the future, the elderly may be able to say: I was once you, and in the future I am still going to be like you. If the elderly lose the psychological fear of being old, this can only increase their life expectancy. In the future, humankind and a host of intelligent robots will together enjoy the life of the global village. In the course of my discussion of other matters, I have already mentioned intelligent robots on many occasions, but now I would like to focus on the subject. In the future, the numbers of these intelligent robots will be enormous, and they will be present in every corner of society.

People will hand over all manner of work to robots. There will be robots not just in the city, in offices, hospitals, markets, factories and restaurants, but there will also be a host of them in the fields, the woods, the seas, the air and on battlefields. Just recently, here in China, robots have also started operating express delivery services. In the future, it could be that all manual labour is handed over to robots. Humankind will have to build, live in and enjoy a society that works in collaboration with robots that are almost as intelligent as itself. We will have to set their scope, their rest periods, their accommodation, and their eventual resting place at the end of their usefulness. Moreover, we will have to give careful thought to areas where robots and humans come into conflict or contradiction. When I go home after this trip, I am going to take a special look at a particular courier company to see how their "little orange men" robots operate in the field of logistics, where their presence causes no little astonishment. Three hundred and thirty robots, moving autonomously round the warehouse, can sort and select small packages of less than five kilograms, handling eighteen thousand per hour with exceptional accuracy, thereby reducing the human workforce by seventy per cent. This is just one area of work for robots in the field of logistics; in the future, fields where humans completely hand over the work to robots are only going to increase. This shows that, in the future, people will no longer have to do the dirty, tiring hard work to make their living, but will be able to lead much easier, more comfortable and carefree lives. This will be another major contribution to human longevity.

In the future, some portion of humankind may move to other planets, and these interplanetary migrants may experience an even greater range of improvement to their life expectancy. The question of humans colonising other planets has already been discussed for many years, but in recent years, the prospect has become much more likely; so much so that it is practically a certainty. At an open symposium in the American city of Houston in April 2015, scientists from the US Space Agency said they firmly believed that humankind was not alone in the universe. They reckon that since there are so many astonishing seas and oceans in our galaxy, there must certainly be the possibility of organic life forms in our own solar system. It is not a question of whether we will discover them, but when. Most recently, humans have discovered many heavenly bodies that are concealing water within them. Underneath the frozen surface of Jupiter's moon, Europa, there may be an enormous ocean; on Saturn's moon, Enceladus, there may be sedimentary hot springs; on Jupiter's largest moon, Ganymede, there are certainly saltwater oceans. Apart from these, there are numerous satellites and dwarf planets containing precious water capable of supporting life. This proves that our solar system is a wet place, where the environments of fixed stars and huge planets form a continuous stretch of space capable of supporting life. Perhaps within ten years, we will discover clear evidence of extraterrestrial life, and within twenty years we will have definitive proof. In December 2016, researchers at McGill University in Montreal used West Virginia's Green Bank Telescope to investigate radio pulses emitted five times by the Auriga constellation. Each pulse lasted a few milliseconds at a frequency of two gigahertz. Investigations at the Arecibo Observatory in Puerto Rico measured them at 1.4 gigahertz. From these beginnings, they ended up registering seventeen radio pulses. The researchers believe these repeated radio pulses are not a chance, one-off phenomenon, but could be a signal being sent from a particular neutron star. I myself believe it is an intelligent life form there making contact with our planet. According to a public announcement from the San Francisco headquarters of the Messaging Extraterrestrial Intelligence programme, they expect to be able to report that they have opened several dialogues using radio pulses or lasers by the end of 2018. All that is needed is for us to find a planet capable of supporting life, and humankind will have a guarantee of being able to implement interplanetary migration. What then remains are preliminary exploratory missions, planning for mass migration, and the manufacture of the means of transport. Of course, this will take a very long time.

I have some other news for you: in around sixty years' time, scientists may have established the first city on the Moon. Larger scale human migration may need a few hundred years. In the most recent news, Tesla's CEO, Elon Musk, has said that, beginning in 2024, he plans, in stages, to send a million people to Mars and to establish a completely sustainable society there as a back-up plan for humankind. If a proportion of the Earth's population does indeed move to another planet, and proper attention is paid to that planet's environment from the outset, those migrants' life expectancy will naturally improve enormously. There has long been a popular saying among us Chinese: Living in heaven for one day is like living on Earth for a year. If such a thing happens, the improvement to the migrants' life expectancy may bring about even greater improvements to the average life expectancy of the whole of humankind. Now I have finished talking about my own predictions, I would particularly like to inform you all of the predictions of Google's director of engineering, Ray Kurzweil, about the future of humankind. He has said: "With the help of technology, in 2029, humankind will achieve the possibility of eternal life, and that possibility will be realised in 2045." I have heard that this prediction is already circulating on WeChat here in China. It is even bolder and more optimistic than my own predictions.

Ray Kurzweil is a man I admire greatly, and I have often attended conferences held by his organisation. One after the other, he invented a reading machine for the blind, a music synthesiser and a speech recognition system, and he is acclaimed as a modern-day Thomas Edison. He has been awarded nine honorary doctorates, and twice received presidential honours; the Massachusetts Institute of Technology has named him Outstanding Inventor of the Year, and he is chancellor of Singularity University. His power of prediction is almost magical: in 1990, he predicted that by 1998, a computer would defeat a chess grandmaster, and in 1997, IBM's Deep Blue computer did indeed defeat the international chess champion, Gary Kasparov. In 1999, he predicted that, in ten years' time, computers would be operated by voice command, and that became reality even before ten years had passed. In 2005, he predicted that within five years, the evolution of online technology would allow simultaneous translation, and foreign languages could be translated into your mother tongue and simultaneously be displayed on a screen in your glasses. This is now a reality. His most famous achievement is his discovery of the Law of Accelerating Returns which states that the rate of technological innovation increases exponentially, and that humankind is on the crest of an accelerating wave, where even more things that exceed even further our imaginings will be realised.

The reason he has asserted that, by 2029, humankind will have the possibility of living forever is that he believes that, at the moment, there are limits on the capabilities of the human brain, which works at least a hundred times slower than a computer. But once we are able to introduce nanorobots woundlessly into the cerebrum through our capillary blood vessels to interact with our cerebral cortex and connect with the Cloud, our intelligence will increase exponentially. After this enlightenment, advances in medicine will be earth-shattering, our outdated human programming will be upgraded, and the microprogramming of our 23,000 genes will be fundamentally changed. This genetic adjustment will free humankind from disease and ageing. By 2029, we will have reached a critical point at which medical advances will mean a year can be added to our life expectancy for every year we live. Moreover, by 2045, further advances in medical science will have extinguished all disease and will provide never-ending vitality to our bodies' systems and organs, and all the barriers to eternal life that have preoccupied humankind over the millennia will be removed!

If Ray Kurzweil's predictions do come true, then I will withdraw all my own predictions and simply say that humans really will live forever!

I really do hope that Ray Kurzweil's predictions do come true, as then I too will be a beneficiary and become an immortal.

If eternal life is achieved, then regional, societal and world government, and many other tricky problems and areas of dispute will naturally come under the scrutiny of politicians, sociologists, economists and ethicists.

My friends, I do hope that you will manage to live until 2045, or at least until 2029! If you do, you may be present at the birth of a new world!

But suppose his prediction does fail – and the chances of failure are indeed great because it goes against many scientific and human laws and conventions. Many people will not see the world he describes, but they may have the chance of seeing the world I have just described. And that world of the future is just as beautiful and optimistic. The future is worth waiting for!

At this time, I would advise you to be particularly on your guard against accidents, especially car accidents, air crashes, shooting incidents and crowd tramplings; and say particular prayers that you don't get caught up in a terrorist incident. At present, car accidents claim countless lives in every country across the world. Here in China, the rate of accidents is very high, with many deaths resulting. According to my calculations, most victims of car accidents around the world are aged between fourteen and forty. This naturally has a marked downward effect on average life expectancy, but, more importantly, it is a senseless way to die.

Staying alive is a specialised, full-time job; it is a subject we must study in the university of life, and I hope that each one of you will give careful thought to it every time you leave the house. What dangers to my life might I have encountered when I went out of my door? So, we must cultivate a mindset in which we are constantly on our guard. Thus, if you treat staying alive as your speciality, you give yourself the best chance of living a long life.

Miracles absolutely can happen!

I wish you all well!

FRIDAY
EVENING

AUNTIES, older sisters, younger sisters, everybody: good evening! My fellow carers for the elderly, I must tell you at the outset that I don't have any special skills or techniques in the care of the elderly. I have never given any kind of class or lecture before, and I really don't know what I should talk to you about today. But Aunty Han of Longevity Park insisted that I come to meet you all and give you a little talk, so I am going to tell you the story of my career as a carer. If you feel what I have to say is interesting, then stay and listen; but if you are not interested, then please just get up and leave, and don't sit there getting bored.

I am originally from the countryside around Nanyang in Henan, and it was only by chance that I came to Beijing to work as a carer in a private household.

My grades at senior high school were not very good, so my top option in the *gaokao*[1] was the Nanyang Medical College, specialising in nursing in a three-year professional degree course. After I graduated, I came to Beijing. To tell the truth, someone with a professional degree qualification like mine shouldn't really come to Beijing, since there are many, many people with better qualifications here, and competition is very fierce. But at the time, I was in love. He was my fellow student and classmate, Lü Yiwei, who lived in the neighbouring village of Lüjiazhaung. In the *gaokao*, he had got into the Beijing University of Aeronautics and Astronautics, and when I graduated from my three-year course, he still had his fourth year to go. He said he wanted to go on to do a postgraduate degree, but I knew that his family was very poor: his mother and father both worked on the land, and it was very hard for them to make ends meet, not like my family. My dad is a bricklayer, and always has work building houses, and my mum weaves straw mats, so they don't have the same problems earning money. I thought I should come to Beijing, as he would need to pay his university fees, and if I found work here, I could give him some financial and material support. Please don't laugh; I was a real innocent at that time, and I thought our love was the most precious thing in the world. A long, long time afterwards, I finally realised what a fool I was then, and that the most enduring thing in the world is certainly not love. Love is just a candy that tempts adolescents and disappears as soon as you put it in your mouth. It sparkles and glitters like a diamond but is no more permanent than a drop of dew: as soon as the wind blows or the sun comes out, it's gone without trace.

It was only when I got to Beijing that I discovered that it is as difficult for a professional degree graduate to find congenial work here as it is to sprout wings and fly. Everywhere I looked, I ran into a brick wall. In the end, I decided to look for a nursing job in a private clinic, but the starting salary was only two thousand six hundred yuan. I rented a basement for six hundred yuan a month, my food bill was another six hundred, and I had to spend a little on clothes, so, if I was going to send anything to my boyfriend and his parents out of what was left, I was certainly going to have to make some very strict economies. This was going to make it very uncomfortable for me if I stayed in that job. Luckily, I was on a government website one day, and I saw an advertisement for a job as a nurse-cum-housekeeper in a private household. It read: *Nurse-cum-housekeeper required in a family household; female, aged 20-45. Responsibilities include the care of a 73-year-old elderly gentleman; food and accommodation included. Starting salary 4500 yuan per month, to be reviewed in the light of level and quality of care provided. Experience preferred*. This advertisement raised my spirits. I felt it was an opportunity I had to seize. With food and accommodation included, the salary of four thousand five hundred yuan per month was worth more than six thousand. If I could get this kind of income, it would be much easier for me to help my boyfriend complete his degree, and also give some assistance to his mum and dad to support his little brother and sister in their studies. So I contacted the advertiser on the internet.

On my way to meet my prospective employer, I still had some doubts. I was worried about three things in particular. The first was that the advertisement didn't specify whether the elderly person needing care was able to look after their own basic needs or not; if not, then the workload could be very heavy, and I wasn't sure if my constitution was strong enough. The second was that there are no guarantees with personal ads from this kind of private home services provider as to whether the employer will actually pay the wages or not. The third was that as a single woman living in a male household, would I get any trouble from harassment by the men living there? After I had met with the advertiser, all my worries went away. As it turned out, the household consisted only of the father, his daughter and her husband. It was the daughter I met, who looked to be in her thirties, and was called Xiao Xinxin. I called her Older Sister. Older Sister Xinxin said that her father had no major illnesses but only slightly raised blood pressure, blood cholesterol and blood sugar, and haemorrhoids. His daily routine was very regular and normal, but the three raised blood readings were a risk factor, and on top of that, he was already seventy-three years old, which is an age that needs careful watching. That is why he needed twenty-four-hour care. Older Sister and her husband were well off and could bear the expense, so she would pay my wages promptly on the twenty-eighth of each month. Her mother had died three years ago, so her father was usually on his own after she and her husband went to work. Neither of them could return home at lunchtime, so they needed someone to come in and cook for her father. I asked her how many rooms there were in her apartment, and she told me there were three bedrooms and two living rooms, and an area of more than one hundred and thirty square metres, so I could have my own room. It all sounded pretty good to me, and I felt I could accept the post, so I signed the contract on the spot. It was then that I discovered that Beijing has a standardised contract for home carers and their employers that is commonly used in these circumstances.

The day after we met was a Saturday, and, as agreed, I arrived at the Xiao home with my single suitcase. As soon as I was in the door, I could see that this was a family with a good standard of living and some culture: there were spotless white walls, wood floorboards, a very handsome leather sofa, a huge television, deep-red lacquered furniture, and pictures hung on the walls. Older Sister Xinxin led me into a bedroom and said: "This will be your room."

As I put down my suitcase, I heard the sound of a man's slipper-clad footsteps approaching the door. Before I could even turn round, there came a cold, harsh voice asking: "What's going on here?" "Dad, this is the carer I've found for you. Her name is Zhong Xiaoyang. She studied nursing and has a professional degree." I realised immediately that this was the Mr Xiao Chengshan I was going to be looking after, so I quickly turned to face a middle-sized, rather fat, old man with raven-black hair. I bowed and said: "Good day, Great Uncle!" "I'm not old, and I don't need a nurse! Tell her to go away at once!" So, there I was! Mr Xiao stretched out his two hands, and, with a little swishing noise, turned a three-hundred-and-sixty-degree circle, before coming smartly to a halt and asking me: "Am I old?"

He certainly seemed pretty nimble, and he looked a lot younger than any seventy-three-year-olds in my village. "Come on now, Dad!" Older Sister didn't let me reply, but went over and took her father by the elbow, leading him into the other room. The two of them spent a long time in conversation behind the closed door, most of which I couldn't hear clearly. Of course, I wasn't deliberately listening because, even though I was new to caring, I still knew it wouldn't do to eavesdrop on my employers. I only heard a couple of sentences. One was when Older Sister said in a loud voice: "The two of us both work a long way away, outside the Fourth Eastern Ring Road, and if anything, heaven forbid, happened to you, even if the traffic wasn't snarled up, I couldn't get back in time. And that doesn't even take into account the times we have to make business trips..." The other was Uncle Xiao raising his voice and saying: "You two get on with your jobs, and go on your business trips. I'm not old yet, and I can look after myself. If you've got four thousand five hundred yuan to spare, why don't you give it to me so I can go out and have a few decent drinks..." But apparently, in the end, Older Sister Xinxin talked him round. After a while, she came back in, all smiles, and said quietly to me: "It's all right, it's all settled. The main problem is he won't admit that he's getting old, and thinks he's still a young man. He has forgotten the old saying, 'At seventy-three and eighty-four, Yama blocks your way.' Aiya! I should wash my mouth out with soap for talking like that..."

Older Sister talked about her father's daily routine, and what he particularly liked to eat and drink; she told me which medications he took for blood pressure, cholesterol and blood sugar, what haemorrhoid treatment he used, showed me his blood sugar monitor, and described what clothes and underclothes he wore. She also showed me on a map where the nearest hospital was, as well as the nearest supermarket, farmers' market and department store. She took me round the kitchen and then showed me on the computer the park where her father liked to stroll and practise *taiji*. This turned out to be Longevity Park, where we are today. She wrote down her work address for me, along with the landline and her cell phone number. She was also very careful to tell me that her father used to be very fond of drinking *baijiu*, but his doctor had told him that, given his state of health, he should give alcohol up completely. The most he was allowed was one glass of red wine a day, and I was absolutely not to buy him any *baijiu*. If he bought some for himself, I was to make no bones about confiscating it. I was to ignore it if he got angry, and wait for her to come home to handle it. The last thing she said that day was: "Xiaoyang, starting from today, apart from at weekends, my husband and I both get up very early to go to work, and I am expecting to hand the running of the household over to you. I hope you won't let me down in what I expect of you! So, let's get the unpleasant stuff out of the way at the start. If you are not conscientious in your work, or do anything that does not correspond with your duties as nurse-cum-housekeeper, then don't expect me to be polite about it! I have a photocopy of your ID card, and if I have to, I can easily find where your parents live and complain to them. I want you to know that my father is a retired judge, my husband is a lawyer, and I have also studied law, as well as construction and landscaping. But I really hope we don't ever have to resort to the law in our relationship."

I remember feeling uncomfortable at the time; you city folk are very fierce about protecting your own interests. We all know the principle: If you employ someone, trust them; if you don't trust someone, don't employ them. But I needed the job, and I couldn't afford to push back, so I just smiled and said: "Don't worry, Older Sister. I'm not as well-educated as you, or as experienced, but I know how to behave, and you'll find out what kind of person I am as we go along."

In the afternoon, the same day, Older Sister told me her husband had gone to Datong in Shanxi on a case, and that she had to put in some overtime on a project plan, so she was going into the office. As she was leaving, she whispered to me, in rather embarrassed tones, that her father's haemorrhoids were quite serious, and often bled; if I was to see any streaks of blood on the toilet paper in the basket, then I was to remember to urge him to change his underpants. I nodded, thinking to myself what a filial daughter she was to take such pains – much better than me. Probably because my mother was still alive, I didn't pay much attention to my father's health. So, starting from that afternoon, I began to take my duties very seriously.

To start with, my relationship with Mr Xiao Chengshan was not a happy one. He probably thought that his daughter was wasting money spending four thousand five hundred yuan on me, so he was very rude to me. He was also suspicious of my nursing knowledge. When I took his blood pressure and told him the reading, he frowned and said: "Is that right? Have you taken a blood pressure before?" When I measured his blood sugar, he asked, disbelievingly: "Is that reading accurate?" When I gave him the correct dosage of his medications, he asked: "Are you sure you've got them right? It would be terrible if my drugs are wrong!" When I put antiseptic cream on a graze on his hand, he asked, searchingly: "Why does it sting like that? Are you sure it's the right cream?" I didn't know whether to laugh or cry, so I just said with a wry smile: "These are things nurses do every day. There's no chance of me making a mistake. I have a professional degree in nursing, I'm not a know-nothing country bumpkin, so you can just stop worrying." But when I wanted to see to his haemorrhoids, he waved his hands agitatedly and refused: "No, no, no! I'll do it myself..."

He still kept his eye on me. When I was cleaning his bedroom, he would stand in the doorway, watching me, as though he was afraid of me moving his personal things; when I folded his clothes, he stood in front of the wardrobe as if he was afraid I was going to make off with his clothes; when I dusted his bookshelves and strongbox, he absolutely forbade me, saying: "The safe doesn't need dusting." When I came back from shopping at the supermarket, he wanted to check the use-by dates on every item, as though he was worried I would deliberately buy out-of-date goods. This all made me rather unhappy. When he went out for a walk or to do his exercises, according to Older Sister Xinxin's instructions, and according to the rules of the nursing profession, I had to go with him. But he wouldn't allow it, saying it was going too far not to let him have his own exercise space and it was an infringement of his liberty. He asserted that he could walk sixty *li* a day without breaking sweat. So I told him that accompanying him when he went out was written into my contract, and his daughter would stop my wages if I didn't do so; moreover, if his high blood pressure caused any mishap, I would have to pay compensation. It was only then that he grudgingly agreed that I could follow him at a distance. If ever I got too close to him, he would glare at me. In the end, wherever we went, it looked as though I was trailing him.

The park he went to most often was this one, Longevity Park.

He wanted to come here every morning to practise *taiji*, but his wasn't ordinary *taiji*, it was a combat form that used very extreme movements. I didn't really know about *taiji*, so I couldn't tell what the form was called, but later, I learned from a neighbour it is called Grab Fist Combat Form. In the past, the Xiao clan had been bodyguards in the imperial palace, and over the generations its men were all skilled in martial arts. When he was young, Mr Xiao had acquired some skill in unarmed combat, and as an adult, when he worked as a bailiff, he practised wrestling, so he was a man who had no need to be afraid of anyone. I was surprised to find that, even in his seventies, he was still an irascible and belligerent man. There was one day when I went to the market with him to buy some stuff, and there was a tap-dancing demonstration going on in the square in front of the main gate of the market. Three girls and three young lads were dancing very well, and drawing quite a crowd of spectators. Uncle Xiao and several other old folk, along with me, all stopped too, and everyone was enjoying watching the show. At that point, a young lad, leading a group of young girls, suddenly appeared in front of us and said to Uncle Xiao: "Can you old folk get out of the way, please, and let these girls stand at the front so they can watch and learn?" Uncle Xiao wasn't very happy about this and asked coldly: "Why should we give way?" The young lad replied rather rudely: "Can't you see? This is a young people's dance; do you think you could do it?" Uncle Xiao shot back: "You've got no legal right to ask us old folk to give way when we're watching the dancing. Even if we can't do it, we can still watch it, can't we?" The young lad shouted back angrily: "Pah! So you still think you can throw your weight around, do you, you old bastard. I tried to be respectful, but you weren't having it, were you! Old folk today won't give way even when they're asked!" And with that, he reached out to shove Uncle Xiao out of the way. To his surprise, Uncle Xiao suddenly punched him on the shoulder, and the blow sent the young lad staggering backwards. Humiliated, the lad flew into a rage and attacked Uncle Xiao with both fists raised. I immediately cried out in alarm: "Help! Help!" I was afraid the lad might knock Uncle Xiao down. Uncle Xiao had high blood pressure, after all, and there could have been serious consequences. But, to my surprise, when the lad rushed Uncle Xiao, once again he was knocked down by a blow from him. As the lad rolled around on the ground, howling, the dance performance came to a halt. Another three lads from among the dancers came running over and surrounded Uncle Xiao, looking as though they were about to beat him up. It turned out they were all part of the same gang. Luckily, two policemen, who had arrived on the scene, heard my cries and came running over; otherwise, the situation could have turned really serious. Afterwards, as I was pulling Uncle Xiao away to go back home and telling him off for provoking the youths, he was still fuming and said: "I hate that kind of discrimination. It seems to me that when you get old, you can't do anything right. You're not even supposed to watch some dancing. All I did was defend myself; he started it, so I don't have any legal responsibility for…"

Not long after, I came here to Longevity Park with him so that he could have a stroll, and he got into another argument with someone, which again descended into fisticuffs. You all know there's a set of a dozen or so steps just as you come into the park by the west gate. They're not very wide, just enough for two people abreast. There were lots of tourists coming into the park at the time, and there was a music performance going on which people were hurrying over to listen to, so the stairs were rather crowded. When Uncle Xiao was about to start climbing the stairs, a young guy gestured at the people either side and called out: "Make way, everyone, and let this old gentleman up first." Of course, this was a very courteous and considerate request, but Uncle Xiao flew into a rage and glared at the young guy: "Who are you calling old?" The young guy was quite taken aback and replied with a grin: "What's that? Is the old gentleman trying to impersonate a youngster?" Of course, he was just joking, but Uncle Xiao just got even angrier and yelled: "You should wash your mouth out? What do you mean 'impersonate'? That's a legal term, and you shouldn't just bandy it around!" This contrary reaction didn't just leave me feeling put out, it astonished all the other people on the steps too. The well-intentioned young fellow also began to lose his temper and muttered to himself: "What an ungrateful old sod!" He turned, and was about to go up the steps first, but in the blink of an eye, Uncle Xiao charged forward and grabbed the youngster by the collar, yelling at him: "Don't you dare swear at me!" Swept up in the anger, the lad yelled back: "And what are you going to do about it if I do, you stupid old sod?" And he poked Uncle Xiao with his finger. Aiya! That really did it for Uncle Xiao, and he suddenly swung his fist at the youngster, knocking him to the ground. The lad seemed to have been taken by surprise by the fact that Uncle Xiao could actually strike him, and, losing his temper completely, he scrambled up, rushed headlong at the old man, knocked him down with one blow, and sat astride him, raising his fists to pummel him. Luckily, several other men stopped him and pulled him away. In normal circumstances, I should have reprimanded the young lad, and even reported him to the police, but I didn't do anything like that; I just wordlessly helped him to his feet. To tell the truth, this time I was on the side of the young lad, as I could tell that he had been well-intentioned and was only trying to be polite. I couldn't understand why Uncle Xiao had reacted so unreasonably and let things escalate to such a mess. Fortunately, he wasn't hurt that time. I helped him up, and he turned to leave the park in a huff, without bothering about his exercise. His unreasonable behaviour left me feeling baffled and confused.

By the evening, he had calmed down completely, and, as I gave him his medications, I couldn't help asking him gently: "Why did you fly off the handle like that at the park gates this morning? The young lad only meant well." He paused for a moment, then replied: "I really hate other people calling me old, and that young lad broke the taboo. You don't think I'm old, do you? Just because I've got a few wrinkles on my face? There aren't very many of them, anyway! Besides, I didn't go beyond the bounds of justifiable retaliation!" I couldn't stop myself giving a wry smile and saying: "Heavens above, you're seventy-three already, and you still hate people calling you old?" Now I finally understood why he would brush my hand away when I stepped forward to support him going upstairs: he didn't want anyone to think of him as old. I found myself a little bit in

sympathy with him. I began to notice that he went to great lengths
to eliminate any signs of physical ageing. I could see how distressed
he was at his hair going grey, and he was constantly dyeing it, at
least every twelve or thirteen days. Trying to be helpful, I once told
him: "Most hair dyes have got lead in them, and even those that
don't have got amines. If you use them too often, it could be bad for
your health." But he didn't take any notice. The fourth time I told
him, he stared at me coldly and admonished me angrily: "I know, I
know. You're not old enough to be this irritating. Do you think
you're a scientist now too?"

Gradually, his eyebrows began to go grey too. When it came to
dyeing them, I made sure that he used an old toothbrush which he
dipped in the dye, and when he was finished I washed it repeatedly.
I was particularly worried that the dye might get past his eyelids
and into his eyes, where it could cause damage to the eyeball, but I
didn't dare bring it up in case he got angry. Later still, the body hair
on the back of his neck began to go grey too, and that was clearly
irritating him a great deal, so he took an electric razor and shaved it
all off in the mirror. He couldn't see the hairs at the very back, so he
got me to help him with them. As he furiously tried to get the
better of all the grey hairs on his body, I couldn't help laughing to
myself and thinking: What's the point?!

Other than this, it wasn't long before I became acquainted with
his other major failing: his craving for alcohol. Older Sister Xinxin
had told me at the outset that I must absolutely never buy her
father *baijiu*, and he was strictly forbidden from drinking it, but I
hadn't paid too much attention at the time. Then, one day, we were
passing the door of a little local restaurant, where we saw a waiter
throwing some rubbish into a garbage van. A bottle of *erguotou* fell
out of the rubbish and onto the ground; there was about twenty-five
millilitres of spirit left in the bottom of it.

The waiter was about to pick the bottle up, but Uncle Xiao
nimbly bent down and snatched it away. He wasted no time
opening it up and smelling it, before saying: "There's still some in
here – wouldn't it be a shame to throw it away?" The waiter replied
with a laugh: "The customer's finished with it; who'd want it now?

It's only fit to be thrown away." "Waste not, want not – I'll drink it!" The words were no sooner out of his mouth before Uncle Xiao had indeed tipped back his head and drained the bottle of those last few drops. I was dumbfounded. What was the world coming to? Such shameful behaviour! A retired judge, on the street, drinking the dregs of a bottle a restaurant was going to throw away! What would people think if the story got spread around? I grabbed him by the hand and hurriedly pulled him away. I remembered Older Sister's instructions as we walked, and finally realised that he really was an alcoholic. When we were halfway down the street, I glared at him and said angrily: "Your state of health makes it imperative you don't drink *baijiu*; you know that, don't you? What do you think you're doing drinking other people's dregs?" He looked very put out and unhappy, and walked on, head down in embarrassment. After that, I understood the extent of his addiction and began to take the task of keeping him away from alcohol very seriously. When I bought cooking wine, I even made sure to keep that in a locked cupboard.

One morning when I went to take his blood pressure, I caught a really strong smell of alcohol. I was astonished: where could such a smell be coming from this early in the morning? Taking another careful sniff, I realised it was coming from his mouth, so I asked him straight out: "Have you been drinking?" At first, he shook his head vigorously, but when he saw me beginning to search, he hurriedly took a bottle of *baijiu* out from under his quilt and said in a low voice: "This is mine; I bought it yesterday. You can't take it away." I told him, furiously: "You shouldn't be drinking at all, let alone first thing in the morning. Don't you know that wine in the morning and tea at night are the two things old people should most avoid!" Older Sister Xinxin heard my shouting and came running in. Without a word, she snatched the bottle out of her father's hand. She was clearly not happy, and glared at me, saying: "You meddlesome wretch. Even if you didn't buy it, you can't pretend you didn't know about it. What is it? Too much work for not enough money, for you?" I pretended not to hear, and left the room, ignoring her.

As we were thrown together morning till night, Uncle Xiao's attitude towards me began to change, perhaps because, in his heart of hearts, he knew I was genuinely looking out for him. The one thing he was really happy with me about was my cooking. His family came from Weinan in Shaanxi, where they are used to eating flour-based foods and especially like noodles. This corresponded very closely with the food Nanyang folk like too. From when I was little, I had learned from my mother how to make rolled noodles and hand-pulled noodles, and they were always just as chewy as you would want them. Whether I made soup-pot noodles or braised noodles, they were all delicious. The first time he nodded in approval at me was after he had finished a bowl of my soup-pot hand-pulled noodles, when he said: "Mmmm, these noodles you made were all right..."

Uncle Xiao's work-and-rest schedule was pretty regular: every morning after breakfast, he would usually sit at his desk for a couple of hours, reading or writing, and then he would go for a walk and do his *taiji*. I didn't feel that this regime was particularly good for him at his age, so I suggested: "Uncle Xiao, why don't you just have a little sit-down for twenty minutes after breakfast, and then go out for your walk and exercises. When you get back, then you can sit at your desk with your reading and writing." Rather to my surprise, he looked very displeased and said: "You don't need to get so involved in my affairs. Do you know what I am doing? I'm getting ready to write a book. I used to be a famous judge. Now I'm retired, I want to become a famous academic lawyer. Do you know what that means? To be an academic lawyer, first you have to have written books. I'm going to write at least three books, and then I'll be widely recognised as an academic lawyer. Do you understand? I don't suppose you do! My free time is very valuable, OK?" "I certainly don't understand why you have to become an academic lawyer." "Haha! There's too much background to give you, so I'll keep it simple: my duties as a judge disappeared very quickly after my retirement, but the title of academic lawyer will stay with me for the rest of my life. Even after I'm dead, my reputation as an academic lawyer will stay with people for a very long time." I nodded to show I understood: "If you become an academic lawyer, your name will be remembered for a very long time." "This is the proof of the value of a man's life!" he said, taking the explanation one step further. I asked him what three books he was going to write, and he perked up a bit, but then went back to his normal, serious self as he waved a hand and said: "These three books of mine have to be major legal works, belonging on the shelves of original works. The title of the first book is *An Examination of the Motives of Male Offenders*; the second is *An Examination of the Motives of Female Offenders*; the third is *A History of Human Criminality*. Each book is going to be eight hundred thousand to one million words, making a total of 2.4 million to three million words. When these three books are published, they will create quite a stir in legal circles, and provoke a lot of discussion everywhere. I will be the person everybody is talking about, and all the news reporters working in legal circles will want to interview me." "How long will it take to write three million words?" I asked him. "Fifteen years, at most, but it might take up to twenty if things don't go right" "Good heavens! That long?!" "That's just the project plan. If things go right, it won't take anywhere near that long." "And you've absolutely got to become an academic lawyer?" I asked. "A man must have a target to strive for! What? Don't you think I can do it? Well, let me tell you, in my life, I have succeeded in every target I have set myself. Bailiff? Been one! University? Graduated! Judge? Done that! Beautiful wife? Married one! Beautiful daughter? Got one!"

Wow! I stared at him, amazed at his total self-belief and steely determination.

Older Sister Xinxin's husband, Older Brother Chang Sheng, had come back home from a trip. His normal routine on getting home was to go straight to his bedroom, and he seldom spoke to anyone. On this particular day, however, Uncle Xiao and I were making rather more noise than usual, and he came hurrying out of his room. He asked Uncle Xiao: "Dad, have you taken my copy of *A Compendium of Criminal Case Law*? I need it now." Uncle Xiao looked at him coldly and replied: "I took it to look at yesterday. In fact, here it is; take it if you want it." He rather grudgingly pushed the book over to the corner of the desk. As Older Brother came over and took the book, then left the room, I saw Uncle Xiao curl his lip at his retreating form.

In fact, I hadn't been with the Xiao household long before I could see what the problem was: Uncle Xiao didn't think very much of Older Sister's husband, and there was some kind of ill feeling between father-in-law and son-in-law. I could sense that the conflict between them wasn't just over something trivial. If Older Brother Chang Sheng ate at home, Uncle Xiao would sit at the table in total silence, but if he wasn't there, Uncle Xiao would chat away and joke with his daughter quite happily. When Older Brother was at home and discussing some case or other of his, Uncle Xiao would listen with a slight sneer on his lips, but not make any comment. Whenever Chang Sheng came into the same room, Uncle Xiao couldn't stop himself frowning slightly. The two of them very seldom spoke, and Chang Sheng almost never called him "Father" or "Dad". If something came up that they had to discuss, the two of them spoke through Older Sister Xinxin. They were seldom in the same room, and even when they were, they hardly looked at each other.

Actually, Older Brother Chang Sheng was a very handsome man; he was about 1.8 metres tall, always dressed in Western-style clothes, and he looked very classy. He had a lawyer's panache of the kind that really caught a girl's eye. I could tell that Older Sister Xinxin was very much in love with him. Every day, when he left for work, she would make sure she gave him a goodbye kiss, and the first thing she asked when she got back from work was always: "Is Older Brother Chang Sheng home yet?" If he was, then she was really happy, but if he wasn't, she always looked disappointed.

I didn't know what had gone wrong between father-in-law and son-in-law. I could see that Older Sister loved both of them, and the fact that she couldn't find any way of bringing about a reconciliation between them caused her a lot of distress. One evening, around nine o'clock, when Uncle Xiao had gone to his room, Older Sister, Older Brother and I were watching television in the living room. Older Sister wanted to watch a soap opera, and Older Brother wanted to see a special documentary called *The Two Sides of the Taiwan Strait*. Neither one would give way, but it was the kind of light-hearted argument that young couples have, with Older Sister acting the spoilt little girl. I smiled at their squabbling, which ended with Older Brother snatching away the remote control and putting on the programme that he wanted to watch. Older Sister pretended to be upset, and berated him for being a petty tyrant. It really was just a light-hearted tiff between husband and wife, but, to everyone's surprise, Uncle Xiao suddenly threw open his bedroom door and shouted at Chang Sheng: "Why don't you do what Xinxin asks you to, Chang Sheng? She is your wife, isn't she?" Older Brother Chang Sheng's face fell when he heard this, and he threw down the remote control and retreated to his bedroom. Older Sister was initially too surprised to speak, but then she shouted at the old man: "Why don't you just stay out of our affairs, Dad!"

One day, after breakfast, Chang Sheng said to Older Sister: "I've got to go to the detention centre today, Xiaoxin, to see a suspect. I'm really tight for time, so if I don't drive you to work, will you be all right to go by bus?" "Yes, yes, I'll be fine. Hurry up and get going!" Older Sister replied immediately. Out of the blue, Uncle Xiao piped up: "Why don't you drive Xinxin to work first, and then go on to your meeting? What's so urgent about seeing a suspect? How can you be so offhand about making Xinxin go by public transport? Are you really not worried about her being crushed and jostled on the bus?!" Older Brother looked a little embarrassed at this, as Older Sister hurriedly tried to smooth things over, saying: "Don't worry, Dad, there's no problem with me taking the bus to work. Chang Sheng's very busy, so let's just let him get a move on and take the car." And with that, she pushed her husband out the door.

One afternoon, when Older Sister Xinxin came home from work, the architects she was working for had given her a sack of rice and a giant can of peanut oil. She hired a taxi to bring them home and phoned me from downstairs to get me to help her carry them up. Uncle Xiao saw us carrying the stuff upstairs, and at the sight of Xinxin huffing and puffing as she carried the giant can of oil, he asked, concernedly: "Couldn't you have called Chang Sheng to drive over and bring you home?" Older Sister replied: "He's got a banquet this evening, and he's not coming back till later. It was more convenient for me to get a taxi." Uncle Xiao's expression really darkened at this. That evening, as soon as Older Brother Chang Sheng came through the door after getting back from his banquet, Uncle Xiao said coldly: "All you cared about was filling your own stomach, and you didn't give a damn about Xinxin, letting her struggle home with all that heavy stuff." As Older Brother look stunned and discomfited, Older Sister came running out of the bedroom as she heard what her father said: "It wasn't any problem for me bringing those things home, Dad. And anyway, Chang Sheng's banquet this evening was to do with work." With that, she took Chang Sheng's hand and led him into the bedroom. I knew that Uncle Xiao was genuinely concerned for his daughter, but I felt the way he went about showing it was rather unsatisfactory. Leaping to his daughter's defence over every little thing was only going to upset his son-in-law. One day, when I was accompanying him to Longevity Park for a walk, I said quietly to him: "I don't want to talk out of turn about your household, Uncle Xiao, but us Henan countryfolk have a custom I'd like to tell you about; but I don't know whether you're willing to listen or not." "What custom?" he asked. "Well," I said, "what we say about being a mother-in-law or father-in-law is that the best way of showing concern for your daughter is to show concern for your son-in-law. If the in-laws are good to the son-in-law, the son-in-law will be good to their daughter." He grunted at this, and seemed to understand what I was saying, but he went on to say: "I don't approve of that Chang Sheng; I don't think he's sincere, and I think he's messing Xinxin around. I don't trust him." I didn't say anything more, as to do so might have brought me into conflict with his personal opinion, and that wouldn't have been good for my standing as a nurse. On the next two-day weekend,[2] I was making dumplings in the kitchen, and Older Sister Xinxin came over to help. I said to her quietly: "You must try and persuade your father to be a little nicer to Older Brother; otherwise, the relationship between the two of them will just get worse and worse, and it will be really hard for you being stuck in the middle." Older Sister sighed and said: "Ai! There are three reasons my father has no respect for Chang Sheng. The first is that when Chang Sheng was first courting me, in order to get my family to agree to the relationship, he said that he was from Xuzhou City, but my father found out that he was actually from a township twenty or thirty *li* from Xuzhou City. So, although that was in the Xuzhou municipality, Chang Sheng wasn't really from Xuzhou City. My father counted this as a lie and thought that he was being dishonest. The second reason is that while he was my boyfriend, but we weren't yet married, I had two abortions. My father was furious when he found out. Two months after we were married, I fell pregnant again, but Chang Sheng was worried that because he had been drinking when we slept together, that might badly affect the child's health, so he made me have another termination. When my father found out, he was even more furious. He thought that Chang Sheng's willingness to harm my health like that was evidence that he was too irresponsible. The third is that Chang Sheng ignored my father's urgings, and acted as defence lawyer for a corrupt official. That official had a really terrible reputation, and although Chang Sheng argued very well on his behalf in court, in the end the man was convicted. My father believed Chang Sheng should never have represented that official. Now, neither of them has any faith in the other, and I'm caught in the middle, with troubles on either side. I love both of them very much, and I don't dare open my mouth to criticise either of them..."

So then I had the whole picture. I thought at the time that when you grow old, if you don't take the initiative to resolve any conflicts in the household, you can end up causing a lot of problems. The way things developed only served to justify my prediction. It wasn't long after this that Older Brother Chang Sheng began openly to argue back, and it ended with him deciding to move out and rent an apartment elsewhere, as he was determined not to live there anymore. The cause of all this was Older Sister Xinxin falling pregnant again. There was one morning when she had just got up to go to the bathroom to freshen up, and she began to vomit. To start with, she thought it was just a stomach upset, but then, after breakfast, she brought up everything she had just eaten. Uncle Xiao advised her: "You'd better go to the hospital to get yourself checked out, and see if there is any problem with your stomach." After he finished breakfast, Older Brother drove Older Sister to the hospital, where the tests showed that she was pregnant. This made everyone in the household, including me, very happy, since, at her age, the pregnancy really should end successfully.

No one expected that, only two months into the pregnancy, Older Sister Xinxin would have a miscarriage. It happened around midnight one night: I was suddenly woken by the sound of Older Sister crying and wailing. I ran out into the living room, where I saw Uncle Xiao standing there in his pyjamas. We looked in alarm towards Older Brother Chang Sheng and Older Sister Xinxin's bedroom, not knowing what was going on. A moment later, we saw Older Brother carrying an ashen-faced Older Sister out of their bedroom. As he hurried over to the front door, he blurted out a single word: "Miscarriage." Uncle Xiao gestured to me to go with them, so I followed them down the stairs, and we drove to the hospital. Fortunately, it was just a miscarriage, with no complications. We stayed at the hospital for several hours that night while they did tests, and sometime after dawn we returned home. As soon as we got there, one look at Uncle Xiao's face told me the affair wasn't over yet.

Indeed, at dinnertime that day, when I was bringing in the food and Older Brother had just sat down at the table, Uncle Xiao burst out: "Are you determined to torture my precious daughter to death, Chang Sheng?" Chang Sheng, who had just picked up his chopsticks to start eating, was frozen to the spot for a moment, then got up and left the room without a word. Older Sister Xinxin was sitting up in bed at the time, eating the food I had taken in to her. As I took in the scene, I hurriedly urged Uncle Xiao: "Let's all eat first! Let's all eat first!" But he was too angry to contain himself, and he slammed his chopsticks down on the table and continued: "What kind of man can watch his wife miscarry not once but three times? Doesn't the sight of her blood upset you at all? Don't you have any kind of sympathy or compassion?" Older Sister heard this and wailed from her bed: "You can't blame Chang Sheng for this, Dad! Stay out of it!" But Uncle Xiao was even more incensed by his daughter's objections and shouted back: "If I can't blame him, who am I supposed to blame?" This time it seemed Older Brother Chang Sheng lost his temper too, as he came a few steps out of the bedroom and shouted back at Uncle Xiao: "Do you think I wanted Xinxin to miscarry? Haven't I always wanted her to have a baby? How can you blame me for this?" "If I don't blame you, who should I blame? After Xinxin's mother died, she's the only person I'm close to in the whole world; I have her clutched to my heart, and I'm terrified of dropping her. But as for you, you clearly don't cherish her if you mistreat her like this even when she's pregnant!" Uncle Xiao had leapt to his feet, pointing a finger accusingly at Chang Sheng, whose face showed blank astonishment, as he shot back: "What makes you think I'm mistreating her? How am I mistreating her?" Uncle Xiao began to shake uncontrollably as he said through clenched teeth: "Do you want me to spell it out to you? Well, since her mother is no longer with us, I'll say it plain: if you hadn't had sex with her, how could she have got pregnant?" Older Brother went almost purple in the face, and even I felt embarrassed. I heard Older Brother roar at him: "That's crazy talk! You can't come out with any nonsense you like, just because you're her father!" He turned on his heel, went back into the bedroom to pick up his coat, then stormed out the door, slamming it behind him. Choking on her sobs, Older Sister cried out from the bedroom: "Why can't you just keep your nose out of our business, Dad?!" The perfectly good dinner I had made went uneaten because of Uncle Xiao's outburst. What is more, his anger sent his blood pressure sky-rocketing, and he clutched his forehead, exclaiming that his head was aching. This greatly worried me, and I helped him to his bed to lie down, as I maintained constant pressure on his *quchi* and *sanyinjiao*[3] acupressure points.

I originally thought that Older Brother Chang Sheng had just gone out to find somewhere to cool off and would come back during the night, but, to my surprise, he didn't come back that night, or the next day, or the day after that. On the morning of the fourth day, Older Sister Xinxin told me to help her put together Older Brother's clothes and other daily necessities, which she said she was going to have sent over to him. That's when I discovered he had rented a two-bedroom apartment between the Fourth and Fifth Eastern Ring Roads, and had decided not to come back home. Crying as she packed the items, Older Sister Xinxin said: "The two of them are both too pig-headed, and I can't see any way of reconciling them…"

As I watched Older Sister carrying her husband's suitcase downstairs, I said quietly to Uncle Xiao: "Older Brother isn't coming back here, and Older Sister is taking him some of his clothes." Still angry, Uncle Xiao shouted: "If that Chang fellow knows what's good for him, he'll never come back! This is my apartment, after all, and I'll feel a lot more comfortable if he's not here." I tried to talk him round: "The two of them are both grown-ups, and maybe you should stay out of their private life." But Uncle Xiao just glared at me and said: "When a family lives together, they share their lives together, and there's no difference between private and public. I've only got one precious daughter, and I didn't have her until I was over forty; I kept it to myself, but I was always afraid of her changing. How could I stand by and let that Chang person hurt her? With her mother dead, who else is going to look after her affairs? Tell me, who?"

As I listened to this string of "I"s and "me"s and saw how tightly clenched his hands and jaw were, I thought better of saying anything more, lest his blood pressure go too high for his heart to cope with.

To put him in a better mood, I didn't say anything for a while, and then turned to one of his favourite subjects: "Have you started writing your first book yet, Uncle Xiao?" The dark clouds finally began to disperse from his face at this question, and he replied: "I've got pretty much all my data together. I got a lot of case records for male offenders from my old law firm, and I discovered three constantly recurring main causes of male offending. The first is loss of control over desire. Loss of control of sexual desire often results in rape; loss of control of material desire often results in fraud and embezzlement; loss of control of desire for power often results in bribery and corruption. The second cause is mental instability. If a man is still not cured of his illness even after he has slipped the doctor a red envelope, he may lose his mental equilibrium and attack the doctor; if a man sees other people spending money like water when he doesn't even have enough to eat, he may resort to robbery and vandalism of other people's property, public and private. The third is loss of honour and dignity. A man sees his honour and dignity as the foundations of his status in the world, and if he loses them, it may lead to male offending: it might turn the victim of such a loss of dignity into an aggressor himself. If the loss is caused by an individual, the victim might try to frame him for something, or attack him, even possibly murder him. If the loss is caused by a group, or an organisation or by the government, the victim might take even more extreme action to avenge it..." Once I had diverted him onto this new subject, Uncle Xiao's mood gradually began to improve.

After Older Brother Chang Sheng moved out, Older Sister stayed living in the apartment by herself for a week. One morning, after that week had gone by, she called me into her bedroom and said quietly: "Xiaoyang, Chang Sheng isn't coming back here, but he doesn't know how to cook, and getting by on fast food is not good for him; over time, it could ruin his digestion. So, this is how it's going to be: starting today, I'm going to move out to live with him over there. It's best if we don't live together with my father and avoid him and Chang Sheng always bickering and getting angry with each other. So I'm handing over all the running of the household here to you, and you must make sure you take good care of my father. I'll be able to come back from time to time to see you both, and I'll make sure your salary is paid on time." What could I do, except nod my head in agreement and say: "Yes, yes, Older Sister, don't worry."

After Older Sister had finished giving me my instructions, she went back into the living room and said to Uncle Xiao: "I've been thinking about it, Dad, and now Chang Sheng has rented an apartment, I think I should go and live there. This way, you and he won't keep on upsetting each other. You'll have Xiaoyang here to look after you, and I'll come back to see you whenever I've got time. Take good care of yourself, and if there's any problem, give me a call."

It seemed that it hadn't occurred to Uncle Xiao that Older Sister might move out, and he was stunned into silence momentarily. But then he waved his hand and said: "You go then! But remember to ask for two days off to give yourself time to recover. When your mother was alive, she used to say that when a woman has a miscarriage, she needs to behave as if she actually had a baby; otherwise, she can undermine her constitution." Older Sister nodded and said: "Don't worry, Dad, I'll make sure I..."

After Older Brother and Older Sister left, what had originally been a household of four when I joined it, suddenly seemed rather empty. As Uncle Xiao looked around the empty apartment, he said: "Very well then, since those two have broken up this household, I'm going to set up a new one. I can't believe I don't have a home." At the time, I didn't really understand what Uncle Xiao meant by this, and I thought he was just being grumpy. It was only after a few days that I worked out from his manner and his actions what the true meaning was.

About a fortnight after Older Sister and Older Brother moved out, Uncle Xiao's behaviour became rather odd. Over the next few days, he wouldn't let me accompany him when he went out to take his exercise. When I raised with him the obligation the rules of nursing put on me to go with him, he just glared at me and said: "I'm not going to die on you. You just wait for me at home." When

I saw he was getting worked up and wasn't going to stand for any argument, I didn't dare push it any further. But after he had been out alone for two days running, I began to get worried: he was an old man, after all, and if anything should happen to him while he was out, Older Sister Xinxin might question my responsibility, and even stop my wages. There were always reports in the news about some old person collapsing in the street with a heart attack. I had to be prudent, so I telephoned Older Sister and told her what was going on. She shared my concern that something might happen to him while he was out, especially since he was an old man with elevated blood pressure, blood cholesterol and blood sugar. So she suggested: "Let's handle it like this. If he goes out, you tail him secretly, and don't let yourself be seen by him unless something does actually happen, so he doesn't get upset again." I didn't have any option but to go along with this plan.

So, according to Older Sister's instructions, whenever Uncle Xiao went out, I shadowed him like a spy in the movies, not getting too far behind him, but never allowing him to see me. When I'd been doing this for a few days, I discovered something unexpected: the places Uncle Xiao visited most often were marriage agencies. If it wasn't one agency, it was another, and he spent a long time in all of them. Light dawned on me: Uncle Xiao was looking for a new partner; he wanted to get married again. When I remembered his words about "setting up a new home" I realised that he was saying to Older Brother Chang Sheng: "Off you go if you want to! There's nothing special about you – you don't frighten me! If worst comes to worst, I can just set up a new home!"

In that short period of time, Uncle Xiao visited seven or eight marriage agencies; it seemed that he was trying to find out which was the most trustworthy, as he searched for the most suitable partner. In the end, he appeared to find someone compatible through the "Great Destiny in Old Age" agency, as he spent longer and longer in there. As he was waiting inside, I took cover in a department store on the other side of the road and watched the activity in the agency through the store window. I was content just to wait as long as I didn't see any excitement across the road. Ai!

It's really not an easy job being a personal nurse! It's normally described as looking after a person's daily needs, but in fact it's more like learning to live together. If you're not able simultaneously to deal with every need and desire, and every complex relationship, then you can easily find yourself with problems. This situation continued for ten days or more, but then Uncle Xiao stopped going out; instead, he usually stayed at home, using the landline to make phone calls. My suspicion was that Uncle Xiao had already established phone contact with his intended and was making more detailed arrangements. With him not going out, the difficulties of my duties lessened considerably. At home, I could listen in on the telephone conversations and knit my boyfriend, Lü Yiwei, a sweater at the same time. Although I couldn't hear all of the conversations completely, I did work out that there were three women in contact with him: one was a divorcee, and the other two were widows. This told me that he was still casting around and had not yet definitely settled on a marriage partner.

After another few days, he appeared to make his final choice, as he was only having lengthy phone calls with one of the three, and the other two gradually disappeared from his telephone routine. I couldn't work out how old the woman was, nor what she looked like, but judging by the way Uncle Xiao spoke to her, she had to be younger than him. When he spoke to her, his normally rather forceful manner of speech became more careful and thoughtful, and his tone of voice even sounded coaxing and placatory. From all this, I reckoned that the woman must be quite comfortably off; that he was happy with her; that he was courting her good opinion; and that he was definitely her suitor.

When he was on the telephone, his voice involuntarily got louder, suggesting he wasn't thinking I might overhear him. I got to hear quite a lot about his youth from what he told this woman about himself in the course of their conversations: he went to primary school when he was eight, and it was there that he met a PE teacher who was a martial arts expert; he had done some studying at home too, from a young age, and this was how he got his own expertise in martial arts. He trained with the teacher in fist forms and staff forms, and he once came first in a tournament in his hometown. Later on, he was recruited by a law firm in Xi'an to be a bailiff; after he had signed up, because his martial arts skills had caught the eye of the examiner, he passed the necessary exams without a hitch. After he had qualified as a bailiff, there was an occasion when his law firm was prosecuting a hardened criminal accused of murder. The criminal reckoned that he was heading for a capital sentence, so he decided to escape while he was being escorted to the court for trial. The man had made careful preparations in advance and had improvised a key that could open his handcuffs and leg shackles. On the way to his trial, he secretly opened the cuffs and shackles, then jumped the three bailiffs who were escorting him. Uncle Xiao was one of those three, and when he found himself suddenly upended by a kick from the criminal, he rolled back up to his feet, jumped out of the prison van, and ran hell for leather after the murderer who was disappearing into the woods at the side of the road. He said he chased his adversary for a dozen or more kilometres through the woods before he finally tackled the exhausted man to the ground. He handcuffed him as tightly as possible and dragged him back to the roadside to wait for the other bailiffs to catch up with him. Finally, they managed to deliver the criminal to the courthouse. He said that, on the back of this incident, his reputation rose considerably in Xi'an's legal circles, and later on, the court sponsored him to go to study at the Beijing Institute of Politics and Law. After graduating, he stayed on in Beijing and joined a law firm there. While he was working in Beijing, he was ordered to interview many officials with gang connections and black-market bosses; in the course of these investigations, he received many threats from gang members, even receiving bullets and knives in the post to try and intimidate him. But he paid no attention to any of this and simply saw the cases through to their conclusions, receiving much praise and many rewards from his superiors...

I'm not sure what the woman on the other end of the phone made of these stories by way of introduction, but for my part, I felt he was being rather too bullish and, of course, enjoying boasting about himself; I also knew that there was a lot of "padding" in what he said. That said, I understood that if a man wants to gain the favour of the woman he has his eye on, he has to big himself up a bit. When Lü Yiwei was first trying to win me over, he did the same.

After spending most of the day on the telephone, it seemed that the woman agreed to meet him to talk in more detail, as I heard them set a meeting place. Following Older Sister Xinxin's instructions to inform her of any major developments, I hurriedly passed on what I had just heard to her. She had already understood her father's intentions and said bitterly: "Let him do what he wants. If he really does want to find a suitable wife, it takes some of the burden off me. And if we're not living with him and he has an experienced wife to look out for him, then I can stop worrying. I'm sure that my mother, on the other side, will look tolerantly on him..."

On the day he went out to meet this woman, I trailed him as before. The site of their assignation was a grove of trees in Yuyuantan Park. I took up my observation post at a distance, and I wasn't going to show myself unless Uncle Xiao had some kind of medical emergency. Because I was a long way away, I couldn't see well enough to make out her age and appearance, but from her outline, she was a shapely woman.

Not long after this, I heard Uncle Xiao on the telephone, inviting the woman to come over for a meal. But for some reason I don't know, the woman refused. On another day, I then heard him on the telephone to a member of staff at the marriage agency, making a complaint: "Is this Ji woman you introduced me to reliable or not? I've been talking with her for a long time now, and she's not come to any kind of arrangement with me. I need you to help me find out what she is up to and whether she's going to come to a decision or just keep sitting on the fence, making me more and more agitated. You can tell her from me that I'm keeping my options open, and I'm not putting all my eggs in her basket!" I could tell he was getting a bit impatient, as the other party hadn't come to a firm decision. I'd seen it said on the television that there were several obstacles to old people getting married: established lifestyles and habits; sons and daughters; the other party's health; their financial circumstances, and so on and so on. I wasn't sure, for the moment, which one of these my couple were stuck on. It may be that the marriage agency talked the woman round, or urged her to come to some kind of reconciliation, but one evening, a few days later, Uncle Xiao told me, very seriously: "When you go to the supermarket tomorrow morning, buy some extra fruit, vegetables and fish. You need to make six dishes for lunch tomorrow – three vegetable and three meat; we have a guest coming, and we must put on a warm welcome." I understood immediately: the woman Uncle Xiao had his eye on was finally coming on a visit of inspection, and her appearance indicated that a wedding in the household had moved a step closer.

I immediately made the most conscientious of preparations. To start with, that evening after dinner, I swept everywhere thoroughly and made sure the whole place was clean and hygienic. After breakfast next morning, I went shopping and bought lots of delicious food; at ten o'clock, I went into the kitchen and started cooking. Of course, I hadn't forgotten to relay this seismic event to Older Sister. When she had listened to my report, she laughed and said: "Well then, I must make a trip home and see just what kind of woman wants to be my stepmother..."

When Uncle Xiao finished his breakfast, he went to a local barber to have his hair freshly dyed and his beard shaved. On returning, he put on the most up-to-date of Western suits, with a red necktie, and changed his sandals for a pair of leather shoes. Once dressed, he sat bolt upright on the sofa in the living room, reading a newspaper. He looked like someone waiting for a VIP client. At the first ring of the doorbell, he straightened his tie and signalled for me to open the door. When I did so, it turned out to be Older Sister Xinxin. Uncle Xiao clearly hadn't expected her to return at this point, but he only looked a little surprised and indifferent. He glanced at me and then said: "This isn't a two-day weekend; how have you got the time to come back here?" Older Sister grinned mischievously: "What's the matter, Dad? Aren't I welcome? I heard there was some change for the good in the air for our family, so I hurried back to find out what's going on." Uncle Xiao smiled back and said: "Your arrival is very timely; there is something I was just getting ready to tell you." With that, he pointed to his bedroom, indicating that Older Sister should go in and listen to what he had to say. I bustled off to the kitchen to make myself busy. The second time the doorbell rang, it was Older Sister who went to answer it. I heard her say warmly: "Welcome to our home, Aunty Ji!" I hurried out of the kitchen to have a look, and saw a lady in her sixties, very tastefully dressed, and very poised. She looked very much the intellectual. At this point, Older Sister introduced her to me as "Aunty Ji". Then she introduced me, saying: "This is my father's nurse companion, Miss Xiaoyang." Aunty Ji nodded politely to me. Uncle Xiao was standing legs together at attention in the living room, like a bailiff waiting for inspection. I noticed that as soon as he saw Aunty Ji come into the room, Uncle Xiao, who was normally pretty easy-going at home, became unusually flustered. When he was drinking his tea, he even dropped his teacup, so porcelain shards scattered across the floor. I tried to guess Aunty Ji's status as I tidied up the mess: Was she an administrative official with a history degree? Was she a researcher in a scientific institution? Was she a retired executive from a major company?

It was time for lunch. When Older Sister had finished laying out the tableware, she told me to bring the food in. Halfway through the meal, Older Sister came into the kitchen and whispered to me: "Aunty Ji's name is Ji Yingmei, and she was an associate professor in a teacher training college. She is sixty-two, her husband is dead, and she has one son. Her son is a high school teacher. Her status is fine. I approve. That's right, my old dad still has a good eye; he hasn't disappointed me." She nodded contentedly. "So, you're satisfied with her?" I asked. "It doesn't matter whether I'm satisfied or not; what matters is whether my father is satisfied. Just look how serious he is! If these two really do get together, then we can live elsewhere with peace of mind; in fact, your Older Brother Chang Sheng wants to go to America to study for his doctorate. If he does make up his mind to go, then I'll have to go with him to support him in his studies; if Aunty Ji is with my dad, then that will be just perfect." "What!? The two of you are going to America?" This was the first I'd heard of this news. "You don't need to worry. No matter whether we go or not, we'll keep on employing you as my dad's nurse. After all this time you've just spent keeping my dad under surveillance, I'm really happy with your work," Older Sister said, patting me on the shoulder. Lunch that day went all right, and as I worked away in the kitchen, the three of them sat at the table, talking and laughing in a very harmonious atmosphere. After lunch was over, Uncle Xiao once again fell into conversation with Aunty Ji. Their voices sounded less cautious than before, and their talk seemed to be much freer. My guess was that the meeting between Uncle Xiao and Aunty Ji had been a great success; Aunty Ji certainly had a different attitude now, and relations between the two of them had taken a step forward.

One morning, a few days later, at the time he should have been relinquishing the telephone, I was very surprised to see Uncle Xiao was still pacing around the living room. Then, not long after, out of the blue, Aunty Ji knocked on the front door. I hurriedly made her some tea, then retreated into my own room and listened to the sounds coming from the living room. To be honest, before this, I had thought only young people fell in love, and I'd never heard old people talking about getting married. If the old people in my village, both men and women, lost their partner after they were in their fifties, none of them would dare think of remarrying. If anyone even mentioned the possibility, they would drown in the scorn of the village and be called "dirty old reprobates" or "ageing sex-maniacs". Their children, too, would rain curses on them. I really wanted to hear what the two of them said to each other when they were alone.

I remember the first thing I heard Aunty Ji say was: "We shouldn't be in a rush to make a decision; let's take a little more time to get to know each other and see whether we're suited. After all, we're both already carrying a fair burden of life's baggage, and we're quite set in our ways, so it's not as easy for us to get used to each other as it is for young people." She spoke in a very refined manner, just like an associate professor; that's the impression I got at the time. Uncle Xiao replied: "Very true, very true, but the most important thing is that my daughter Xinxin intends…" Aunty Ji wasn't pleased at this and said: "You mean to say you don't want us to go on discussing this?" "No, no, no, that's not what I mean. I agree with what you just said; neither of us is young anymore, and we already have a lot of health issues…" Aunty Ji interrupted him: "I don't have any major health issues; I'm quite well. At my last health check, not long ago, all my readings were quite normal. Perhaps you'd better tell me exactly what health issues you have!" Uncle Xiao realised he had put his foot in it and hastily backtracked: "Oh, there's nothing serious wrong with me, just a little haemorrhoid trouble, everything else is fine." Aunty Ji just grunted and said: "Well, haemorrhoids aren't serious; nine out of ten people have them, and they're nothing to worry about. I'd like to make it quite clear again that I decided to remarry in order to improve my quality of life and enjoy the time that is left to me. I'm certainly not looking for an invalid to look after. You need to be quite clear about that." "I understand, I understand, I understand completely!" Uncle Xiao agreed immediately. Aunty Ji continued: "There is another basic principle I want to establish: if, at some later date, we decide to live together, whatever material wealth we have, including real estate, remains the property of the individual, and is not included in the marriage agreement. We both have children, and we will want to leave everything to them. Any common assets we have once we are married will only comprise whatever pensions we receive after that event. If we do, indeed, get married, I want these terms formally documented." Uncle Xiao seemed rather taken aback, but he replied, promptly enough: "Yes, yes, we'll do as you say…" At the time, I thought this conversation very novel and unusual. I had never thought old people's courting would be as different from young people's as this, and that they would discuss things as dispassionately and rationally as this. Every time my boyfriend Lü Yiwei and I met, we would immediately start hugging and kissing, and we certainly had no time for such potentially hurtful talk as this. Once, he asked me what I thought about us living together, and I told him quite openly: "Everything I have at the moment and everything I am going to earn in the future is yours..."

After Aunty Ji had left that day, Uncle Xiao said to me, with deliberate indifference: "Xiaoyang, anything to do with matters of my health is just between you and me; no one else must know." Of course, I knew exactly who he meant by "no one", and I hastily nodded in agreement: "Yes, Uncle, don't worry." I knew by now that Uncle Xiao had really taken to this woman; that is to say, he'd fallen in love.

I think it was a day later that Aunty Ji came to visit again. By the looks of it, their affection had grown after their last meeting. This time, she brought two bottles of disinfectant, which she gave to me as soon as she arrived, saying: "Give the bathroom a proper clean, and, after you've cleaned the toilet bowl, flush it through twice with this disinfectant; otherwise, I won't be able to use it." I wasn't very happy about this: I was a specialist nurse, so of course I knew to clean and disinfect the bathroom. She'd only been here once, so it was a bit much for her to tell me I didn't know my job. Of course, I didn't let this show, and just nodded and said: "Yes, you don't have to worry." And I kept my temper because this was the woman Uncle Xiao had set his heart on.

This time, as before, Aunty Ji and Uncle Xiao sat talking in the living room, while I eavesdropped as I pretended to be busy in the bathroom. I heard Aunty Ji ask: "Do you remember your paternal great grandfather, Lao Xiao? How old was he when he died?" Uncle Xiao thought for a moment, then replied: "I'm not too sure, I was very young when he died. I vaguely remember my father saying that his grandfather was well over sixty when he passed away." Aunty Ji continued: "What about your great grandmother?" Uncle Xiao thought for longer this time before replying: "I think she was in her fifties. She got some kind of serious illness." Aunty Ji sighed: "Ai! Your great grandparents didn't live very long. Do you think it's genetic? How old were your grandparents when they died?" Uncle Xiao thought again and said: "My grandfather was sixty-five, and my grandmother was sixty-eight. I'm sure that's correct. I was very close to my grandparents." Aunty Ji sighed again: "Ai! So your grandparents weren't very old either. It's likely to be something genetic. How old were your mother and father when they passed away?" This time Uncle Xiao replied very promptly: "My father was seventy-one, and my mother was seventy-four. I organised both their funerals, so I'm very clear about all this. I can even tell you the time they died. My father passed away at 3.46 in the afternoon, and my mother at 11.21 at night. Ai! Both my parents had a hard life…" Aunty Ji sighed even deeper this time: "Ai! So your parents didn't live to any great age either. That makes it certain there's some genetic problem in your family. You need to watch out!" "Why?" Uncle Xiao seemed to be quite concerned by this warning. Aunty Ji replied: "Since the two of us are looking to get married, we must know everything about each other. A person's genes are very important; if his family genes are good, as an adult the chances of him getting a serious illness or having an incurable condition are much less, and he may live to a better age. That is to say, a person's life expectancy is largely dependent on heredity. Judging by your family history over the generations, your hereditary genes are not that strong." "What?" This was the first Uncle Xiao had heard of this, and he looked very taken aback. Aunty Ji went on: "I can tell you quite truthfully that my parents, grandparents and great grandparents all lived until they were eighty-five or over, so my family's genes are excellent!" When I heard this, I gasped to myself, thinking it was most inappropriate for Aunty Ji to be talking like this. Quite apart from the boastful tone of what she said, the main thing was how much it might scare Uncle Xiao. Anxiety is the worst thing for old people, and wasn't what Aunty Ji was saying guaranteed to stress out Uncle Xiao? My feelings were proved correct, since, as the two of them kept talking that day, I could hear that Uncle Xiao's emotions had been all twisted up, and his replies all sounded rather preoccupied. It seemed as though all he could think of was his family's genetic problems. I felt that as a nurse, it was my duty to relieve him of this psychological burden. When I was at nursing school, a teacher told us that a nurse had to look after not just a patient's physical health but also their emotional well-being, and pay attention to their psychological state. So after Aunty Ji had left that day, I made haste to tell Uncle Xiao: "Genes are only one of the things that determine a person's life expectancy; their future life circumstances and environment are the most important factors. When I was at nursing school, a teacher told us a person's life expectancy is forty per cent dependent on heredity, and sixty per cent on their future conduct. You mustn't let the question of your family genes weigh too heavily on you…" Uncle Xiao began to cheer up slowly under my encouragement. He said, mocking me gently: "So what Aunty Ji had to say put the wind up you, did it?"

The next morning, just after eight o'clock, Aunty Ji knocked on the door again. It seemed that their morning meeting had become a habit. I opened the door and made Aunty Ji some tea. Then I went back into my own room. Today, Uncle Xiao, a man not given to compliments, started, completely out of character, by admiring what Aunty Ji was wearing: "What a beautiful outfit." Surprisingly, Aunty Ji rebuffed the compliment, saying: "Do you mean my outfit yesterday wasn't beautiful?" Somewhat embarrassed, Uncle Xiao hurriedly regrouped: "Everything you wear is beautiful." Aunty Ji finally deigned to smile at this, saying: "Yes, you're quite right about that. Now we're on 'the last pleasure-seeking stage' we must make sure we live every day the best we can, including making sure we dress beautifully. Every day, I choose the clothes that please me most." Uncle Xiao asked: "What do you mean by 'the last pleasure-seeking stage'?" Aunty Ji replied very clearly, emphasising each word like a schoolteacher in class: "'The last pleasure-seeking stage' is the term a famous British doctor uses in his books for one of the phases of human life. This British doctor believed that a person's life after they retire can be divided into three stages: last pleasure-seeking, preparing for death, and the onset of death. The last pleasure-seeking stage represents the last period of time a retired person can move about freely, inside and outside the home. It is the most splendid of the latter stages of life, and one of the most beautiful of life as a whole. During this stage, the restrictions the outside world imposes are greatly reduced, and a person's inner longings contract, so that the pursuit of pleasure and enjoyment becomes a person's most important consideration. The stage of preparing for death, however, begins when a person's mobility gradually decreases: they may still be mentally agile, but they are physically confined to the house. This is when they must begin preparing for death: making sure their will is in order, for example, appointing a solicitor and naming executors, settling any serious disputes that might arise after their death, making disposal of property that needs to be done while they are still alive, summoning people they need to see to their bedside, disclosing what had formerly been secret to relatives, imparting to friends such secrets as can only be revealed after their death, and so on. After this comes the onset of death, the last stage of a person's life. For some, this is very short: no more than ten minutes or so. For others, it can be very long, dragging out over ten years or more..." What I heard that day was all new to me, and I thought how wise this associate professor was.

Uncle Xiao had clearly not expected any kind of reply like this, and it was a while before he spoke: "It seems you are even more widely-read than me..."

The next time Aunty Ji came, I poured her some tea, and was about to leave, when she stopped me: "You sit down too, Xiaoyang. You are the nurse and housekeeper here, and today we should have a talk about the question of diet." I was rather taken aback, and I looked meaningfully at Uncle Xiao and asked: "Would it really be proper for me to sit in while the two of you are talking about wedding matters?" Uncle Xiao smiled weakly: "Since Aunty Ji has asked you to sit down, you'd better sit down." So I had no choice but to sit there while Aunty Ji talked about diet.

She began: "To start, I'd like to tell you which foods are suitable for old people to eat, so you'd better get a notebook to write it down. The first is sweet potatoes: sweet potatoes contain eight per cent dietary fibre, most of which is soluble fibre, so they're very good for bowel motility. Li Shizhen[4] said that sweet potatoes increase longevity and reduce illness. The second is potatoes. Potatoes' carbohydrate content can be as high as fifteen to twenty-five per cent, and they are rich in vitamin C, sodium, potassium, iron and so on. Every one hundred grams of potato contains five hundred and two milligrams of potassium, which is particularly good for old people's hearts." As I wrote, I exclaimed in amazement at how good Aunty Ji's memory was. It wasn't surprising she'd been an associate professor. The third was garlic. Aunty Ji said: "Garlic is the healthiest food in the world. It can help control high blood pressure, low blood pressure, high cholesterol and coronary heart disease. Within two to four hours of you eating it, it can help protect your body against free radicals, and eliminate the body's naturally-occurring cancer cells. Within five to six hours, it can burn body fat, and in seven hours it can neutralise poisons in the body. In eight to ten hours it protects the body's cells against oxidisation, and in eleven to twenty-four hours it performs a deep clean on the human body, regulates cholesterol levels, adjusts blood pressure either way, and eliminates any heavy metals that have entered the body." The fourth was chestnuts. "Chestnuts can regulate kidney function, and if there is weakness below the waist, they promote healthy kidney *qi*, they strengthen the stomach and intestines..." The fifth was onions... Almost without taking a breath, she spoke for more than twenty minutes about the foods suitable for old people, wanting me to memorise them, and incorporate them into my shopping and cooking. As I wrote it all down in my notebook, I thought to myself: This aunty is not going to be easy to work for once she marries into this household. When the time comes, my best plan is going to be to leave and look for another family that needs a nurse... After this, Aunty Ji basically came over every day.

One day, it was raining, with sizeable raindrops, and Uncle Xiao said: "Your Aunty Ji will certainly not be coming today, so I think I'll take an umbrella and go for a walk in the park." But the words were hardly out of his mouth before we heard Aunty Ji's knock at the door. Having braved the rain, she began to talk to Uncle Xiao specifically about physical deterioration with age. From my room, I heard her slurp a mouthful of tea, then ask Uncle Xiao: "Well, Lao Xiao, what do you think about the problem of physical deterioration with age?" Uncle Xiao clearly didn't have any thoughts on the subject to hand, so he replied, in some embarrassment: "It's not something I've given much thought to." Actually, it was an honest reply; he wouldn't even admit that he was old, so why would he think about physical deterioration? Thereupon, Aunty Ji started another lecture: "If you want a definition of physical deterioration with age, it is the normal gradual downward trajectory of the functions of a person's skeletal and organ systems. This deterioration manifests itself in the nervous system as a decline in memory and concentration; in the musculoskeletal system as the atrophy of muscles and in osteoporosis; in the respiratory system as reduced lung capacity and weakness in coughing; in the integumentary system as thinning of the skin, loss of hair, reduced sweating and increased shivering; in the circulatory system as hardening of the arteries and reduced blood supply; in the endocrine system as a reduction in hormones; in the urinogenital system as a loss of libido and a weakness in elimination; and in the blood system as uncontrolled blood sugar. In the past, it was thought that physical deterioration with age was a phenomenon of the later stages of life, whereas, in fact, it begins when you are in your teens. The biologist Professor Lawson of Harvard University says that when a person is born, they have fourteen billion brain cells; these cells are incapable of division, so they never increase in number. Rather, they begin gradually to decrease as age advances. From the age of twenty-five, several tens of thousands die off every day, with a corresponding loss of brain mass. Different people's brain cells die off at different rates, but the fastest rate can result in dementia at the age of sixty. The Japanese gerontologist Professor Kunio Ota believes that after males and females reach sexual maturity in their teens, their production of the disease-reducing hormone thymosin begins to decrease, and the process of deterioration has begun. Starting at the age of nineteen and a half, women develop their first wrinkle; at twenty, the body's vital capacity begins to decline, and hair shows its first sign of deterioration as its growth rate slows; at twenty-five, muscle strength begins to weaken; at thirty, the skin's elasticity begins to decline, and fine lines appear; the gap between the vertebrae then begins to shrink, and women begin the descent from their sexual peak; beginning at the age of forty, physical deterioration becomes obvious, as grey hairs appear; at forty-five, there is a marked fall in the number of cancer-destroying lymphocytes; from fifty to fifty-five, the speed of deterioration increases as wrinkles appear in men, and women lose their reproductive ability; from fifty-six to sixty, the speed of deterioration becomes acute as brain cell function drops, muscle tissue atrophies, and the amount of semen decreases in men; from sixty-one to seventy-one the rate of deterioration is relatively slow, but height decreases, the sense of taste is blunted and vital capacity has halved from where it stood in youth; once past seventy-three, the rate of deterioration speeds up again..."

At this point, I began to wonder why Aunty Ji was telling us all this. Was she trying to frighten Uncle Xiao? Indeed, I then heard him ask: "I'm seventy-three this year. How am I going to deteriorate more quickly?" Aunty Ji said with a laugh: "If you're seventy-three now, you're still in the period of comparatively slow deterioration, so you don't have to worry. What is more, there are some researchers in the field who have demonstrated that if a person over seventy-three has a companion of the opposite sex, that can reduce the rate of deterioration too." At this point, I gradually began to relax a little, as I finally understood the meaning of what Aunty Ji was saying. She was finding a different way of telling Uncle Xiao that she wanted to spend her later years with him. I knew that after going through a period of getting to know him, Aunty Ji had fallen for Uncle Xiao...

Although Aunty Ji came across as very efficient, she also seemed very genuine, and Uncle Xiao had obviously been smitten by her. But, whether through embarrassment or nervousness I don't know, there had been no physical intimacy between the two of them. They limited themselves to sitting talking quietly and peacefully in the living room, not touching each other. I worried a little about them because of this. When young people today get together, they don't waste time on empty chatter, do they! I felt Uncle Xiao should take the initiative. One evening after Aunty Ji had left, when I went to take his blood pressure, I said, conversationally: "Uncle Xiao, I read in a book that going for a walk is very good for the health. Next time Aunty Ji comes, you could go for a stroll with her, and chat while you walk. A nice relaxed mood will help deepen the feelings between the two of you." Uncle Xiao was probably not expecting me to give him advice, and he looked a little surprised when he said: "Thank you for your concern. The trouble is, this is a very small neighbourhood, and almost everybody knows me. If they suddenly see me walking out with a strange woman, it will attract an awful lot of attention..." As he said this, his normally serious countenance actually looked a little bashful. So, even though he really wanted to set up a new home, he was still afraid of what other people thought.

Older Sister Xinxin phoned to ask: "How far have they got with this business now?" I laughed and replied: "They're still just sitting talking in the living room, and most of the time it's Aunty Ji giving Uncle Xiao another lecture." Older Sister began to laugh uproariously, and when she had finished, she said: "I'm going to give you a mission, Xiaoyang: you have to find a way of getting those two married as quickly as possible. Your Older Brother Chang Sheng has already made the arrangements for him to go and study in America, and I've agreed to go and support him. Since my father has decided to remarry, I'd like to be at the wedding before I leave. That way, I can relax a little when I go, knowing that he'll have Aunty Ji for company." I promised that I would give it a go, but it was not an easy mission, and I didn't really know where to start. Judging by my own experience with my boyfriend Lü Yiwei, all that was needed was physical intimacy for talk to turn directly to the question of marriage. So the first thing I had to do was create the circumstances for physical intimacy for them. The next day, I used the excuse of having to clean the living room, to shift them into Uncle Xiao's bedroom for their usual conversation. I also left the apartment, saying I had to buy a few things, thereby giving them both the time and the space. It was a shame, then, that when I came back I found Uncle Xiao still wearing his neat Western-style suit, sitting meekly in his bedroom, listening to Aunty Ji expounding on all the problems of getting old. It went on like this, day after day. Every day he felt obliged to dress in sombre-coloured Western clothes with black shoes, but he did add a colourful necktie and made sure his shoes were polished till they gleamed. Then he would sit there, bolt upright, waiting for Aunty Ji to arrive and start the day's lesson. Another ten days passed. One evening, Older Sister Xinxin came over and called me into what was formerly her bedroom, where she asked quietly: "How are they getting on? Have they made any progress?" I knew what was behind the questions, and I replied truthfully: "The two of them are just still sitting there every day chatting, or if not that, Aunty Ji is delivering one of her lectures. It's all very proper." "So Aunty Ji hasn't stayed the night even once?" I hadn't expected her to be so direct, and my face flushed with embarrassment as I hurriedly shook my head and said: "No, Aunty Ji usually leaves after they've had dinner." Older Sister sighed and said, as she paced up and down agitatedly in front of me: "This won't do at all; we'll have to think of something else!" "Is it urgent that we solve this problem quickly?" Older Sister replied, in a low voice: "Our departure date for America is already set. If my father and Aunty Ji are still just chatting with no concrete result, how can I go with any peace of mind? I won't be able to stop worrying." I could understand her concern, so I suggested: "Why don't they go on a trip? Don't the books say that travel is a great aphrodisiac, and it would make it easy for them to get together." Older Sister clapped her hands, saying: "Ha! That's an excellent idea! Let's get them to go on a trip together! But with two old people like them, and my dad's high blood pressure, cholesterol and blood sugar, what do we do if something happens?" She muttered to herself for a moment or two, then she clapped her hands again and said: "I've got it! You can go with them, Xiaoyang. I'll pay all your expenses, so you'll be making the trip as my representative." All I could do was nod my head and say: "All right, I'll do as Older Sister says. Where shall we go?" She lowered her head in thought for a moment, murmuring to herself: "Yellow Mountain? No, they're not up to climbing mountains. Qingdao? No, swimming in the sea is not really for them either. Lhasa? No, the altitude wouldn't be good for them. Li River? No, the flight down there is too long for them..." Seeing her frowning in thought, I couldn't stop myself suggesting: "We should go to my hometown, Nanyang! It was the secondary capital of the Eastern Han dynasty, and one of the six biggest cities in the country at the time. It's got lots of historic sites and scenic spots. The countryside is lovely, and there are lots of places to visit. Besides, it's not far at all from Beijing. We can go by plane or train, and it won't be too tiring for them." Older Sister grinned in delight at this suggestion and clapped me on the shoulder: "Great idea! The most important thing is that you know the place, so you can be their tour guide, and if the need arises, you'll have friends who can help you look after them. Now we've settled on the destination, the next thing is for me to go and drum up their interest in going..."

Two days later, Older Sister called me on my cell phone to tell me that her father and Aunty Ji had agreed to go to Nanyang, so she was going to book the flights today. She wanted me to get a move on with making all the nursing preparations for travel. I should go with her father to the medical insurers to identify a hospital, stock up on his usual medications, and she particularly instructed me to make sure that I took some of his heart pills, just in case.

I was really happy. I'd already been in Beijing quite a long time, and of course I'd been homesick. I hadn't dared go back because I was trying to save my money, and I'd never expected a chance to go home for free to drop in my lap like this. It was also more than I'd ever dreamed of to be going home by aeroplane. On the same day, as I was supervising Uncle Xiao taking his pills, he asked me: "Are you happy to be going home to Nanyang, even though you've got the trouble of looking after me?" "Of course I'm happy," I said, then asked him in return: "Are you happy to be taking a trip to Nanyang?" He laughed and said: "Of course I am! I've got your Aunty Ji coming with me, and with a guide who knows the place as well as you do, we're bound to have a very enjoyable time." I grinned with delight at him being so pleasant to me. Three days later, we set out.

Although Uncle Xiao and Aunty Ji were both well-travelled people, they had never been to my little city of Nanyang before, so, once we were off the plane and into a taxi, everything was new to them. They kept up a constant barrage of questions, which I answered, one after the other. I knew everything there was to know about this little country city where I had studied for so many years. The beautiful buildings on either side of the road, the source of the White River, and the bridges across it, all the sculptures and carvings in the district, I expounded on all of them as if they were my own precious household treasures. When we reached the Plum Tree Stream Hotel, following Older Sister Xinxin's instructions, I requested two identical, adjoining standard rooms. Just before we left, she also instructed me, when we reached the floor our rooms were on, to direct Uncle Xiao to one of them, then to go to my own room, but to stay out of the question of which one Aunty Ji chose to enter. I did as I was told, and when, as she walked along the corridor, Aunty Ji saw Uncle Xiao and me each going into our own room, she evidently hesitated for a moment. Although I didn't turn back to look, I sensed that, first off, she took a step towards my room, but then she turned and made for Uncle Xiao's. Only when I heard the door of their room close, did I turn round and shut my own. Once inside, I heaved a sigh of relief: it seemed that Older Sister's plan had worked.

As we were having lunch, I asked them whether they just wanted to rest that afternoon, and save the sightseeing for the next day. Uncle Xiao said: "I'll leave the decision to Aunty Ji." Aunty Ji said: "It was only a short flight and I'm not tired. Let's go into town this afternoon to see some of the sights." So, after lunch, I hired a taxi and took them to the Wuhou Temple on Wolong Ridge. The two of them were very familiar with the story of Zhuge Liang and showed great interest in the place where he lived when he went into seclusion for ten years, tilling the land, and the memorial temple, first built in the time of the Wei and Jin dynasties, and subsequently restored many times. I led them in through the main gate to the main hall of worship, Zhuge's Thatched Cottage, the Ancient Pine Pavilion, the Wild Cloud Shrine, the Till the Fields

Pavilion, the Half Moon Terrace, the Little Rainbow Bridge, the Hug the Knee Rock, the Old Dragon Cave, the Tilling Field, the Ningyuan Tower, the Guan Zhang Hall, the Three Visit Hall, the Book Study Terrace and on down out of the temple precincts. The two of them chatted as they walked, and they seemed very intimate; to an outsider, they must have looked like an old married couple. This sight made me even more content, and I hurried to send Older Sister a text from my cell phone reporting: *Situation excellent – not just good, excellent!* Older Sister immediately texted back: *You'll definitely get a bonus if you're successful!*

After dinner, as Aunty Ji went for a stroll in the hotel courtyard, I took the opportunity to supervise Uncle Xiao's medications and take his blood pressure and blood sugar. Thanks to the drugs he was on, both were within the normal range, which reassured me. Tonight was effectively to be Uncle Xiao and Aunty Ji's wedding night, so I needed to be sure that he was going into the wedding chamber in good health. Although I myself wasn't married at that time, my boyfriend and I had already tasted the forbidden fruit, and I knew what a man and a woman's first night together was like, so I had given it all very careful thought. The most important thing was that no one else knew what was going on.

After I'd watched them go into their room, I relaxed and shut my own door, then started to call my family members on the telephone in the room. Nanyang was a prefectural-level city, and calls from the hotel within the Nanyang district were free, so I was feeling very free and easy as I made my calls. I told my dad that I was back in Nanyang, and, in a few days, I'd have some free time to visit the whole family. My mother was so happy I was back, she started crying down the phone; my younger brother and sister fought over the phone to talk to me, and before I knew it, more than half an hour had slipped by. After I'd finished my calls, I went to have a wash, and by the time I was finished, it was already ten o'clock. I knew that Uncle Xiao usually went to bed at nine thirty, and was pretty well asleep by ten. I didn't want to think too closely about what might have been going on this evening, but I did have a little smile to myself as I got into bed to go to sleep. I was young then and fond of my sleep; what is more, I'd been making preparations for the trip for the last two days, and I was quite tired, so I drifted off pretty quickly. I was startled awake from my dreams by a continuous knocking on my door. The instant I woke up, I was frightened: who could be knocking on my door at this time? Could there be some ruffian on this floor of the hotel who had seen that I was a lone woman and was planning some kind of outrage against me? Or could it be the security police looking to catch hotel guests using prostitutes? My heart racing, I threw on my gown and went over to the door. "Who is it? Who are you looking for?" "It's me, Xiaoyang. Open the door!" It was Aunty Ji's voice, and my fear evaporated. Even so, I was still startled as I unfastened the lock. Why was she knocking at my door at this hour when she should be lying safe in the arms of Uncle Xiao? Could something have happened while they were making love? When I opened the door, I saw Aunty Ji standing there in her dressing gown, looking very unhappy. I had just opened my mouth to ask what was going on, when she had already slipped past me into the room and was pulling back the quilt on the other bed from mine, and beginning to get undressed. "What's the matter?" I shut the door and hurried over to her bedside. Events were certainly not unfolding as I had anticipated. "I had no idea he had habits like these!" Aunty Ji was looking intensely unhappy. "He wanted to get into bed without even washing. He was filthy. The worst thing was the stink of his feet; I could even smell them from the other bed."

I groaned because I immediately understood what the problem was. Uncle Xiao was a Beijinger, and he wasn't accustomed to washing before bed every day; he normally only washed if he thought he was dirty. But Aunty Ji was from the south of China, and she had washed every day since she was a little girl, so when, tonight, she saw a man getting into bed in the same room as her without washing, she was inordinately alarmed. Yes, I should have warned Uncle Xiao! I thought I'd taken care of everything, but I hadn't anticipated our great plans coming unstuck over a little thing like this. I reproached myself bitterly that night, but I still couldn't help thinking that Aunty Ji was making a bit of a meal of this: if she genuinely fancied Uncle Xiao, presumably she wouldn't even have minded rolling on the floor with him, so would she really still care whether he washed or not?

The next morning, when I went to check Uncle Xiao's blood pressure, I quietly asked him: "Why didn't you wash last night?" He looked taken aback and said: "I washed the night before, and yesterday we only had a two-hour plane ride and a visit to the Wuhou Temple, and I didn't sweat a drop. Why should I wash every day if I'm not dirty?" I laughed and replied: "You missed out last night because you didn't wash. Do you get my meaning?" Uncle Xiao looked a little embarrassed and even seemed to blush. He sighed and said: "Isn't she being a bit too pernickety?"

In the course of the second day, I took them to the Xixia Dinosaur Relics Park, where the two of them showed great interest in the dinosaur remains from the Cretaceous Period. They exclaimed in amazement at the fossilised eggs of fifteen species of dinosaurs from eleven families in eight genera. They were as excited as schoolchildren as I led them through the tunnel containing the exhibit of the site where the fossilised eggs were originally buried. An enormous quantity of eggs of many different kinds were excavated over a wide area, in an excellent state of preservation, and they were astounded by the experience. They both said to me: "Thank you for showing us this wonder of the world, Xiaoyang." At the time, I thought to myself: My real aim certainly isn't to show you fossilised dinosaur eggs, it's to get the two of you together, married and making a new household! That evening, as I watched them happily following me in through the doors of the hotel together, I thought that tonight must surely be the night they got together properly. Uncle Xiao certainly seemed to have learned his lesson from the night before, and when I went to take his blood pressure and supervise his night-time medication, he was sitting on his bed, already washed and changed into his pyjamas. I grinned to myself, and made myself scarce just as soon as I'd finished my duties. When I got back to my own room, I saw Aunty Ji taking out her nightclothes before going to wash, and I said casually: "Uncle Xiao has finished in the bathroom, Aunty Ji; why don't you go over there to wash, and leave the bathroom here for me?" She seemed surprised for a moment, but then, without a word, she picked up her clothes and left. I was over the moon and immediately texted Older Sister Xinxin the message: *Success!*

I locked my door, had a leisurely wash and did a little laundry, thinking to myself that I was going to sleep really well that night. To my absolute astonishment, not long after I'd fallen asleep, I was woken up by a knock at the door. After the initial shock of waking, I wasn't at all alarmed this time, reckoning that it must be Aunty Ji again, so I didn't hurry going over to open the door. Standing outside, there indeed was Aunty Ji. Nothing showed on her face as she came in and went straight over to the bed she had slept in the night before. "What's up?" I asked cautiously. As she got undressed, she said: "Farts." I was stunned into silence for a moment, scarcely believing my own ears. Had I really heard that word? Even us young country girls hardly ever used it. I hurriedly asked: "What farts?" She pursed her lips censoriously and went on: "Too many farts! Non-stop farts! I can't stand it!"

Ai! I was hard put to it not to burst out laughing. Was she really so angry about a little thing like this that she couldn't sleep? What had happened to all the sweet talk about weddings? It was just like playing house with a pair of little kids! When Older Sister Xinxin had first given me my instructions, she had mentioned that Uncle Xiao had a little intestinal problem, a slight blockage of the passage of air, and she told me to make sure that every day he ate foods that helped with gut motility. Back in Beijing, where I did the cooking, I could take care of this, but for the last couple of days we had been eating out, and I hadn't been able to. Perhaps that was the cause of the problem. A young lad probably wouldn't dare fart in front of a girl, and would hold it in, but Uncle Xiao was an old man, and presumably didn't think he was doing anything wrong: if he felt a fart coming, he would just let it out, and this must be what Aunty Ji couldn't take. Yes, that was it: although Aunty Ji was an old lady, she was still like a young girl when it came to men and what she expected of them.

But what could I do about it? It wasn't a problem I could talk directly to Uncle Xiao about, as it might hurt his dignity. But, if I didn't say anything, Aunty Ji clearly wasn't going to put up with his little shortcoming. It was then I understood: when girls are young and in love, they are more tolerant of a boy's faults, but when they grow old, they become a lot more picky.

The next morning, when I went to give Uncle Xiao his medications and check his blood sugar, I thought I might find him out of sorts and not having slept too well. To my surprise, he was the same as normal, in good spirits, and apparently not much troubled by Aunty Ji's midnight desertion. In fact, he turned the tables on me by asking: "Do you know what upset your Aunty Ji last night?" I didn't dare tell him directly, so I tried making a joke of the situation: "Perhaps you haven't been taking enough of the initiative in showing your feelings." Uncle Xiao seemed to have lost any of his embarrassment as he replied: "I don't dare take the initiative in case she turns me down again. That would be just too much to bear!" I didn't dare go into any further detail, so I quickly made an excuse and left.

While I was having breakfast, Older Sister sent a text in reply to my situation report of the night before: *I've bought you a gown as a reward for your success. You can try it for size when you get back.* I made haste to reply: *It was a premature report; please take back the reward.* Older Sister didn't seem to be cross, and replied, with equanimity: *Be patient, and take the opportunity when it comes.* Over the next few days, I kept to our original travel plans and took the two of them to Dengzhou to visit the Baihuazhou Academy founded by Fan Zhongyan; we went to Xichuan to see one of the biggest water storage areas in Asia at the Danjiangkou reservoir which was being built to provide water for Beijing; and we visited the Water Curtain Cave and Water Curtain Temple in Tongbai County. They were amazed to hear that Fan Zhongyan wrote his *Memorial to Yueyang Tower* at the Baihuazhou Academy; they were delighted to discover that in the future, Beijing folk will be drinking clear water from the Danjiangkou reservoir; and they were amazed to discover that the Water Curtain Temple is one of the four great temples of the Central Plain, along with the Daxiangguo Temple in Kaifeng, the

White Horse Temple in Luoyang and the Shaolin Temple in Dengfeng. But however good the two old folk were at being tourists, they still didn't manage to make any progress in their intimate relations, and remained in separate rooms.

In no time at all, the return journey was on us, and my only remaining hope was in my going home to see my mum and dad. Perhaps, with me out of the way, the two old folk would feel less pressure, and might share the same room again. I didn't arrange any activities that afternoon, and I agreed with them in advance that I would be going home to visit my parents, and would stay the night there. They were both all in favour of this, and Aunty Ji insisted on giving me a pot of her face cream which I was to be sure to give to my mum. She said it was the best thing for getting rid of wrinkles. I gave a slightly wry smile as I thanked her, thinking to myself: How's my mum ever going to use something like this? When does she have time to worry about her face being wrinkled?

Before I left that afternoon, I carefully separated out and boxed Uncle Xiao's medications for that evening and the next morning, and said pointedly to him: "I won't be here tonight, so you must take the initiative and go to Aunty Ji's room to look after her. I don't think she will want to be all alone there." He took my meaning and replied grumpily: "All right, all right. But you're still just a kid, and you should stay out of other people's business a bit more..."

I got home before dinner and gave my parents some of the money I had earned. Then I rode my bicycle over to the neighbouring village where my boyfriend, Lü Yiwei, lived, and gave his parents some money too. The rest of the evening, I spent with my mum, dad, little sister and little brother, answering their questions about what it was like working in Beijing. At eleven o'clock, when Uncle Xiao and Aunty Ji should be asleep, I used my cell phone to call the telephone in my room at the hotel in Nanyang. My aim was to find out whether Aunty Ji had gone to stay in Uncle Xiao's room or not. The phone rang three times without anyone picking up, and I was just becoming convinced that they were indeed together, when, to my surprise, someone answered. Down the line, I heard Aunty Ji's sleep-fuddled voice saying: "Who is it?" I didn't dare reply, and just quietly cut the call. So, Older Sister Xinxin's and my carefully laid plans for Nanyang had been foiled, and all I could do was go back to Beijing with them.

When I saw Older Sister after our return, I was filled with guilt: she had spent a lot of money on this trip to Nanyang without anything to show for it. In particular, money she had lavished on me had been a very poor investment. I gave her all the tedious details of the whole affair, and accepted all the blame. After she had heard me out, Older Sister laughed and patted me consolingly on the shoulder: "It's not your fault. All this just means that their feelings for each other haven't come to the boil yet. What we need now is not self-criticism, but some way of stoking the fire underneath them." She still insisted on me trying on the dress she had bought me, but I wouldn't have it: "I can't accept a reward for failing in my task, I simply don't deserve it." Smiling, she tapped my head with her finger and said: "Silly Little Sister! I was only joking when I called it a reward. It's just something I picked out for you when I was out clothes shopping for myself. When you joined our household, it was as a nurse-cum-housekeeper to my father, but in fact, you've really had the role of a daughter to him, and I look on you as my little sister. I just want to show you how I feel about you!" Hearing the sincerity in her voice, what choice did I have but to put the dress on? As soon as I put it on, I felt a rush of genuine emotion: grown up as I was, because I was the oldest child, and our family was poor, I'd only ever had the clothes my mum got for me, and no one outside the family had ever bought me anything. My boyfriend, Lü Yiwei, had said he was going to buy me clothes, but he never had the money. Also, I had to admit that Older Sister Xinxin was a city girl, born and bred, and cultured to match, so the clothes she bought were not run-of-the-mill. The dress she had bought me didn't just fit well, more importantly it was the height of fashion, and in exceptional taste. As soon as I put it on and stood in front of the mirror, I felt I had become beautiful; I felt I had become a real big city girl. On the Sunday, when I wore it to visit Lü Yiwei at the Beijing University of Aeronautics and Astronautics, he stared at me for a long time, almost as though he didn't recognise me. When I asked him what the matter was, he said, with a wicked grin: "You've got more beautiful; so beautiful I want to eat you all up!" Then, without any thought for how many people there were in the school grounds, he pulled me into his arms, and his hands certainly forgot their manners...

I took Uncle Xiao's blood pressure when he got back to Beijing, checked his blood sugar, and drew some blood to send to the hospital for testing. They all showed that there had been no changes from before he went to Nanyang. After I explained everything to Older Sister, she instructed me: "Since everything is fine, give Aunty Ji a call, and invite her over to lunch tomorrow for dumplings. I'll come too." When Aunty Ji took the call, she was silent for a long while before saying: "All right then." She didn't sound as warm as she had done previously on the phone.

I hurried to make my preparations. Older Sister's idea was that I should buy quick-frozen machine-made dumplings from the supermarket, but that didn't seem respectful enough. Since we were specifically inviting Aunty Ji over for dumplings to restore good relations, it seemed to me that hand-made dumplings would be much more appropriate. I bought chives, pork meat and onions, minced the meat myself and rolled out the wrappers, then stuffed a hundred dumplings. I reckoned that with four of us in total, including Older Sister, twenty-five each would be enough.

Aunty Ji was a little late arriving, and she wasn't smiling as much as she had in the past. Nor did the conversation between her and Uncle Xiao flow very freely as they sat opposite each other in the living room. I began to be a little worried for Uncle Xiao, but he was just the same as before, sitting there in his Western-style suit, waiting attentively on his guest.

When Older Sister arrived back at noon, she went straight into the living room and greeted Aunty Ji. It all came down to Older Sister's way with words; as soon as she saw Aunty Ji, she said: "Your complexion is looking wonderful, Aunty. I bet it's the good water and clean air of Nanyang that has done it. Your skin tone is at least fifteen per cent better than it was before you went. You look years younger!" Aunty Ji's face broke into a happy smile at this, and she put her hands up to feel her cheeks as she said: "Really? Is it as good as you say? I did think my skin had got softer..." The atmosphere in the apartment immediately began to lighten. When Older Sister came into the kitchen, she looked at the hundred dumplings I had made, and she pinched my cheek happily: "Excellent! These dumplings you've stuffed are works of art; they're bound to sit comfortably in our stomachs." Then she said to me, confidentially: "Make a few more dishes; we're going to need some drinks to lift the mood. We've got to get the two of them happy." I nodded my understanding, and hurriedly set about frying, steaming and boiling. When the dishes were done, I put them on the dining table and called Uncle Xiao and Aunty Ji over. Older Sister said with a smile: "To celebrate Dad's and Aunty Ji's happy return from their trip to Nanyang, let's eat dumplings and drink yoghurt." Uncle Xiao said, unenthusiastically: "I can't drink yoghurt; it's got sugar in it." Older Sister smacked her forehead: "Of course, Dad! You can't drink sweet things. What do you want instead?" Uncle Xiao replied, casually: "Wine, of course, if it's up to me. A cup of wine would hit the spot." Older Sister hesitated a moment, then turned to Aunty Ji and asked: "I think Aunty Ji must decide whether Dad can have some wine today." Aunty Ji laughed: "Why should I make the decision?" "We've been following your advice in the household for a while recently," Older Sister replied. "So, if you say he can have some wine, I'll pour it for him. If you say not, he can't have any even if he wants it." Aunty Ji shot a glance at Uncle Xiao and said: "Then let him have a cup of wine. A cup can't do any harm..." Because of Older Sister's presence, the atmosphere during the meal was excellent, and whatever discontent there had been swirling around Uncle Xiao and Aunty Ji was blown away by the happy conversation and laughter. After everyone had finished eating, Aunty Ji addressed me with the voice of the mistress of the household: "Make sure you give the toilet in the bathroom an extra good clean, Xiaoyang." As I nodded in acknowledgement, I thought to myself: It looks as though she and Uncle Xiao aren't at war anymore.

After this, life returned to as it was before we went to Nanyang. Every other day or so, Aunty Ji would come over after breakfast, Uncle Xiao would greet her at the door as usual, and then lead her into the living room where they would sit and talk. As before, my job was to make the tea and then retreat into my own room. Sometimes they discussed ways of staying healthy in old age, sometimes it was what foods old people should eat or the prevention of bone fractures. Usually, it was Aunty Ji doing the talking and Uncle Xiao listening, although occasionally the latter would voice an opinion. They would always talk then fall silent, then talk some more, and as the time ticked slowly by, I gradually lost interest in listening to everything they said, so I sometimes pretended I needed to go down to the supermarket for something, and just went for a stroll on the street.

One day, after breakfast, Aunty Ji arrived carrying a very large object in a hard case. I hurried over to take it from her. Rather out of breath, she handed it over, and I took it and put it down very carefully. Uncle Xiao looked at it in surprise and asked: "What's this then?" "Guess!" Aunty Ji replied. Uncle Xiao looked at the case, went over and poked it, shook his head and said: "I can't." Aunty Ji laughed and said: "It seems you don't know your musical instruments. It's a *gu zheng*. That's an ancient type of stringed instrument. They had them back in the Warring States period." Uncle Xiao was clearly rather surprised, and he asked: "Can you play it?" Aunty Ji smiled: "I learned to when I was a young girl, but after I got married, I was busy with children and work, and I stopped playing. My son was sorting out our box room, and rooted it out. I thought I'd try it out and see if I can still play anything." I was delighted to hear this, as, although I didn't know anything about musical instruments myself, I really liked listening to music on the internet. If I could have the chance to listen to Aunty Ji playing live, that would be splendid. Uncle Xiao also seemed to be interested, and helped Aunty Ji to set up the instrument. When Aunty Ji produced a string of notes from the *gu zheng*, Uncle Xiao and I exchanged looks, as much as to say: Not bad! Very pretty. Aunty Ji cleared her throat and said: "I haven't played for a long time, and I'm really out of practice. You must forgive me if I don't play very well. First I'm going to play you an ancient tune I used to play a lot when I was a girl. It's called *The Fishermen's Song at Dusk.*" With that, she began to play, and as we watched her right hand plucking, damping, striking and picking, and her left hand pressing, sliding, rubbing and vibrating, the beautiful tune filled the whole room. Uncle Xiao and I stared wide-eyed as her hands danced across the strings of the *gu zheng*. "How was it? Did you get the real flavour of the song?" Aunty Ji asked Uncle Xiao when she finished. Rather uncomfortable, he looked at me: "I'll let Xiaoyang say." I was caught off my guard and said hurriedly: "It was really lovely." Aunty Ji smiled widely and went on to explain: "It's a song about the life of a fisherman, and it's based on a line in the poem *Tribute to King Teng's Tower* by the Tang dynasty poet Wang Bo: 'At dusk, the fishermen sing their evening songs, their voices drifting as far as the banks of Poyang Lake.' It uses simple language and music to portray the beautiful riverside scenery of the lakes and mountains of the South in the setting sun, and the delightful world of the fishermen singing as their boats return for the night. As you must have heard, the song is in three parts: the first is slow, lyrical and melodious, setting the tone of the song; the second is faster, swift and lively with a briskly moving rhythm; in the third, the rhythm is more fickle, moving to and fro, full of warmth and enthusiasm…"

I didn't really understand what she was saying, and Uncle Xiao was looking a bit blank too, so it seemed as though he was in much the same state as me. In the course of that morning, I came to understand that there was nothing accidental about Aunty Ji's status as an associate professor – she was the real thing. If you could have said that previously I only respected Aunty Ji for Uncle Xiao's sake, it is certain that from that morning onwards that respect was genuinely for her as a person, even though I didn't always like everything she said and did. Ever since I was a little girl, I have always respected people who have genuine talent.

After that day, Aunty Ji often took pleasure in playing a few tunes on the *gu zheng* for Uncle Xiao and me. To this day I still remember some of the tunes she played: the quiet, gentle beauty of *The Lotus Rising from the Water*; the honest simplicity of *High Mountains and Flowing Water*; the charming emotion of *Jackdaws Playing in the Water*; the intangible magic of *Drums Echoing on Incense Mountain*. Of course, I relied on Aunty Ji for the descriptions of these songs. Although Uncle Xiao didn't really understand music, I gradually noticed that, as he studied Aunty Ji playing the *gu zheng*, his eyes became very gentle. If previously he had only looked at her as a man might look at a woman, now there was an extra layer of admiration and respect. One afternoon, after Aunty Ji had left, he said to me: "Let's make a trip to the shopping mall, Xiaoyang."

I was delighted at the suggestion because, even though I didn't have any money, I really loved window shopping at the mall. "Great!" I replied eagerly. As I called a taxi to take us there, I wondered to myself: Uncle Xiao normally hates the mall, so what's going on with him today? It was only when we got there that I discovered he wanted to buy a necklace. He went up to one of the jewellery counters, pointed at a twelve-gram gold necklace and said to the salesgirl: "I'll take this one." The girl took it out and handed it to him. He passed it on to me, asking: "What do you think?" I immediately shook my head: "I don't know about this kind of thing." That was nothing but the truth: in all my life, it was the first time I'd handled a gold necklace. Neither my father nor my boyfriend had ever been able to buy me any kind of jewellery, and I'd never had the courage even to look at a jewellery counter. At this point, the salesgirl opened her mouth: "If you're buying a necklace for this young lady, Uncle, might I suggest a different style? This one you are looking at is a bit sedate and would suit an older woman better." I hurriedly interrupted: "He's not buying it for me; it's for an older aunty."

When Aunty Ji arrived the next day, Uncle Xiao solemnly handed her the necklace in its box, saying: "This is for you." Aunty Ji was dumbstruck for a moment, then, when she realised what was going on, she opened the box, took a look and said modestly: "What are you doing spending so much money?" Then she put the necklace on and went over to the mirror to look. "It's beautiful!" I chimed in, going over to stand next to Uncle Xiao in front of the mirror. Aunty Ji laughed and said: "This carer of yours is no fool, always loyal to her employer."

I felt that the *gu zheng* and the necklace had brought about a change in the relationship between Uncle Xiao and Aunty Ji and pretty much closed the rift that had opened up between them on our travels. The two of them seemed seriously to want to advance the relationship. I telephoned Older Sister Xinxin to tell her about what I had seen and what I thought it meant. Of course, she was delighted and asked: "So, in your opinion, can we now be certain they are going to get married?" I said I wasn't sure and the key thing was whether Aunty Ji would agree or not. My own feeling was that she was very wary of the marriage, and I wondered whether raising the matter precipitately might not put her off. Older Sister muttered to herself for a moment, then said: "You may be right. It may be enough just to get them living together for the moment. Once they're doing that, the wedding should be a natural progression."

But Aunty Ji was showing no desire to stay over. I kept a very careful eye on her, and if she were to show any sign of staying, I was ready to spring into action. Every time she came over, after dinner she would rinse her mouth out, wash her hands, and say to Uncle Xiao: "Good night, Lao Xiao!" Then she would pick up her handbag and leave. She seemed quite happy to be in no hurry over this old-age love affair, and to take her time talking it through.

One day, when Older Sister had come over, she said anxiously to me that everything was all set for her husband to go and study in America; the plane tickets were reserved, and he would be off in two months. She was worried that, with her father's remarriage still up in the air, she wouldn't be able to go with him. I tried to reassure her: "If you let your husband go and get on with his studies, and you stay behind here, maybe it won't be more than six months before this thing between Uncle Xiao and Aunty Ji is settled." She said with a sigh: "Ai! You've never been married, so how can you understand? If you had a handsome young husband, would you dare let him loose on his own in America? It's a very liberal country, and who's to say, if he's there by himself, he might not let his eye wander onto some pretty young American girl. And mightn't you be worried about those female students going to study abroad with him. Can anyone guarantee they wouldn't stir his interest? How many marriages have been broken up in foreign parts away from China? I'm never going to rest easy if I don't go with him!" I was very taken aback by Older Sister's words. I'd never have thought that a well-established, successful woman like her could have such doubts over her husband, and over the stability of her marriage. It was all very different from us countryfolk. When a man and a woman from the countryside get married, in general it means they'll stay together their whole lives. Of course, there are some divorces, but even so, the strength of their marriages is far greater than Older Sister's. Up to this point, I'd always been very envious of her life, but now, for the first time, I actually felt superior to her. I was quite sure that, when my boyfriend, Lü Yiwei, and I eventually got married, we would do much better than this!

But even though I wasn't overflowing with sympathy and understanding, I remained upset for Older Sister. After giving it some thought, I still felt that travel was the only way of getting Uncle Xiao and Aunty Ji together and speeding up their marriage; yes, it was still only travel that could provide that opportunity. I told Older Sister my thinking, and after considering it for a moment, she said: "I think that's right. So if we send them off on their travels again, where should they go?" She paced the room for a while, then clapped her hands: "They should go to Jinan. It's not far from Beijing, so the travelling won't tire them out. It's an easy journey and doesn't take very long. The only thing is, I'm going to have to trouble you with another mission for me and get you to go with them again. Of course, the travel isn't the main object, and just like before when you went to Nanyang, I'll pay for your tickets and food and accommodation." Of course, I was delighted, and nodded eagerly in agreement. I'd never been to Jinan, and how could I refuse an all-expenses-paid trip like this? We divided the preparations between the two of us: Older Sister was to go and persuade Uncle Xiao and Aunty Ji to make the trip to Jinan, and buy the train tickets; I was to get ready all the medical and care necessities for the two old folk.

The first time I heard anything about the city of Jinan was when I was in high school. When our history teacher told us about famous figures from Jinan, she mentioned Tie Xuan and how he was born in Dengzhou in Nanyang district. He was highly valued by the first Ming emperor, Zhu Yuanzhang, and given the courtesy name Dingshi. He held high political office in Shandong and commanded the defensive garrison in Jinan. He was further promoted to a high-ranking post in the Ministry of War for his resistance to the rebel army of the Prince of Yan.[5] His resolute defence of Jinan forced the Prince of Yan to divert his advance south, so later, when Zhu Di took Nanjing and declared himself emperor, he sent his army back to attack Jinan. This time, Tie Xuan's defences could not hold out, but, although he was defeated and captured, he would not kneel to Zhu Di. Even when his ears and nose were cut off, he still refused, and after he was executed by the death of a thousand cuts, Zhu Di ordered that his body be cooked in boiling oil. Later generations venerated Tie Xuan for his refusal to yield even in the face of death, and later a shrine was erected in his memory on the shores of Daming Lake in Jinan. Even though I am a woman, I have always admired and respected history's tough guys, so ever since I learned about Tie Xuan, I had wanted to go to Jinan and worship at the shrine of this iron-willed fellow countryman of mine. How could I have expected this aspiration to be so easily achieved?

It was midday by the time Uncle Xiao, Aunty Ji and I reached Jinan. We stayed in the Thousand Buddha Mountain Hotel. Following Older Sister's instructions, once again I asked for two standard rooms, and we followed the same plan of Uncle Xiao going ahead and taking one room, while I followed behind and took the other; then it was up to Aunty Ji to choose which one she would go into. Just as I had imagined would happen, she once again hesitated for a moment between the doors of the two adjoining rooms, and then went into Uncle Xiao's. Although this was exactly as Older Sister and I had planned, I didn't celebrate too early but waited to see what the night would bring. Although this all felt a little sneaky, I held onto the fact that this was what Older Sister was paying for, and that the client I was looking after wanted to marry Aunty Ji, and, even though she still had some doubts about Uncle Xiao, I still considered that this was something it was right for me to be doing at this time.

That afternoon, I took the two of them to Daming Lake. We went there first, not just because I wanted to visit the shrine to Tie Xuan but also because I had found out on the internet that the Daming Lake scenic spot was mostly flat, so was not too taxing on the strength to visit. I had realised that this was an important consideration, as Uncle Xiao was going to need to conserve his energy for the coming night. It was only once we were in the park that Aunty Ji announced she had been there before, and she eagerly took on the role of our tour guide. Pointing at the jade-green waters of the lake, she told us they were supplied by the confluence of numerous springs within the city, and that the lake had a surface area of fifty-eight hectares; she pointed out the black tiles, red columns and tiered eaves of the octagonal Lixia Pavilion, and even recited two lines from the poem written by Du Fu when he visited the spot: "To the right of the lake stands this ancient pavilion; Jinan has produced many fine scholars." She took us to see the North Pole Temple, pointing out the frescoes on either side of the main hall depicting the Daoist practices of the Lord of the North, which were of great artistic merit; she took us to visit the Little Rippling Wave Pavilion, the zig-zag covered walkways and the lotus ponds, and told us to look at the famous couplet written in the Qing dynasty extolling the scenery of Jinan: *Lotus flowers on four sides and willow trees on three; a city of mountain scenery and half a city of lakes.* Finally, she told us to rest our feet in the shrine to Tie Xuan. I took advantage of the pause while Uncle Xiao and Aunty Ji rested and had a drink of water, to stand in front of the bronze statue of Tie Xuan and bow deeply to it, as I said to myself: Xiaoyang has come to see you, my old countryman; I am just a young girl, but I admire your great integrity...

When Aunty Ji suggested we have dinner that evening in a restaurant on the shores of Daming Lake, of course Uncle Xiao and I both agreed. She ordered everything, and the dishes I remember included chicken slices with lake vegetables, and cattail root in white sauce; the former was made with chicken breast meat and water bamboo from the lake, and the latter with cattail roots from the lake, a kind of flowering broccoli and shitake mushrooms stewed in pork bone broth. We had lotus flower congee made with long-grain rice and dried lotus flowers, and baked sesame seed cakes; and we drank "jade cylinder wine" out of cups made from lotus leaves. Aunty Ji said this way of drinking wine started in the Wei and Jin dynasties and became fashionable in the Song and Tang. I didn't normally drink wine, but Aunty Ji insisted I try a cup, and it did indeed have an intoxicatingly pure and fragrant taste. Uncle Xiao's eyes lit up when he saw the wine, and he exclaimed in delight. But Aunty Ji only poured him one cup. When he had drunk it down, he clearly wanted more and smacked his lips as he looked at his empty cup, but Aunty Ji had no intention of giving him any more. He didn't show any disappointment, or voice any discontent. The two of them seemed to be getting on very well on the way back to the hotel and were chatting away very merrily in the taxi. I was secretly delighted, thinking to myself that everything was going to plan. I clasped my hands in prayer: "Gods willing, please may tonight be a success, so Older Sister Xinxin need not worry about going to America with her husband." After a hasty wash, I sat on the edge of my bed reading a nursing book, with one ear cocked for any sound of activity next door. Excellent, everything quiet, right through to half past eleven. I was confident there wouldn't be any problem this time, so I relaxed, turned off the light and went to sleep. I slept very soundly, not because I was tired but because I was young. I was startled awake from my dreams by an urgent, persistent banging noise on the wall. As soon as my head cleared enough to realise the banging was coming from the wall between our two rooms, I gave a great shiver of alarm, as I was sure it could only be something very serious that would make them alert me like this. I jumped out of bed, and, not even stopping to put on my slippers, snatched up my travelling first-aid kit and ran out of the room. The door was flung open at my very first knock. Great heavens! Aunty Ji, normally so prim and proper, was standing there in just a pyjama top, her bottom half naked. She gestured desperately to me, pointing at the naked body of Uncle Xiao sprawled face down on the bed: "Quick... quick quick... quick..."

In that instant, there was a kind of explosion in my head, and my hands began to shake. Fortunately, I had already seen a few emergencies when I was still studying at the hospital, and I was able to compose myself very quickly. I rushed over to the bed and checked Uncle Xiao's pulse: it was all right, his heart was still beating. I swiftly realised he had only fainted, and I immediately employed the series of measures I had been taught. Thank heavens, under my ministrations, Uncle Xiao gradually let out a long breath, slowly opened his eyes, and looked at us blearily. Only then did I take the time to pull up the quilt, and cover his naked body. It was probably this that made Aunty Ji recover from her agitation enough to remember that she too was naked from the waist down, and she hastily snatched up her pyjama bottoms. As soon as she had them on, she also adjusted her pyjama jacket, and finally heaved a long sigh.

There was no need to ask: even to someone as inexperienced in intimate human relations as me could see what had caused the emergency here: in the middle of having sex, Uncle Xiao's blood pressure had shot up because of the combination of physical and emotional excitement, and he had briefly passed out. To spare her embarrassment, I didn't dare look Aunty Ji in the eye again. All this time, Uncle Xiao was breathing through the miniature respirator I had brought with me, and blinking his eyes. Gradually, his memory came back to him. I could see a deep blush of embarrassment suffuse his cheeks, and he closed his eyes. I continued to check his heart rate and blood pressure until they returned to normal, and only then did I take off the oxygen mask and turn off the respirator. I hunted out his pyjamas and put them on his bed, then quietly left the room. As I stood in the empty corridor and took a long deep breath, I realised that, with the emergency now passed, it was already two o'clock in the morning. I went back to my own room and lay down, but, for a long time, I was too shaken up by what had just happened to go to sleep. Really! Something like that shouldn't happen to a man and woman when they get it together. It offended all my own experiences and the beautiful imaginations I had about intimate human relations. That this was the sort of prospect old people faced, for the very first time made me genuinely apprehensive about growing old. Was it really possible that one day this could happen to my own boyfriend Lü Yiwei? The thought made me shudder... After the events of that night, I was afraid it was going to be very difficult for things to continue between Uncle Xiao and Aunty Ji, but what was I going to say to Older Sister? She had spent so much money on this affair, put so much thought into it, and had so much hope invested in it...

As I was having these ultimately useless thoughts, I heard two light taps on the room door. I immediately assumed that Uncle Xiao had had a relapse, and, in some agitation, I jumped out of bed and ran over to the door. When I opened it, I saw Aunty Ji standing outside, clutching her gown to her chest. Before I could open my mouth to say anything, Aunty Ji whispered: "He's fast asleep, but his snoring is so loud, I can't get to sleep myself." On hearing this, I hurriedly stood aside to let her into the room. At the same time, I took the key card she was holding and went along to the other room. Almost certainly, Uncle Xiao had been exhausted by the night's commotion, and he had fallen into a very deep sleep and was snoring thunderously. He didn't stop, either, when I picked up his wrist to take his pulse. I stood beside the bed for a while, making sure that he had just gone sound asleep and nothing else was amiss, and only then did I relax and go back to my own room. "Do you want to go straight to sleep, Xiaoyang, or will you listen to what I have to say for a bit?" "It's all right, Aunty," I hurriedly replied. "I'm not tired, so please go on." "Your Uncle Xiao isn't working!" she suddenly blurted out. I had no answer to that. I didn't really understand what she meant. That she and Uncle Xiao weren't going to get it together again? "He was working at it from past ten on." "Working at what?" I was even more confused, and had no idea what she was driving at. "Working at me!" Aunty Ji was too embarrassed to look at me, and was staring at the ceiling.

Suddenly, like a gust of wind blowing away the clouds, I realised what she was saying, and my face flushed bright red. Luckily, my face and upper body were shaded from the lamplight. "But he didn't get anywhere at all," Aunty Ji continued. I didn't dare say anything; in fact, I had absolutely no idea what I could say. All I could do was listen. "At first I thought he'd been incapacitated by over-excitement, so I reassured him and told him to have a little rest and try again. After a short while, I began to stroke him to help him along, but still nothing..." As I pictured the scene Aunty Ji was describing, I could feel my cheeks burning. "In the end, he put in a big effort and turned me to and fro. It wasn't very comfortable, but I didn't dare say anything. I went along with everything he did, but I could tell from the sound of his breathing that he was getting angrier and angrier. Then suddenly, his noises stopped, and his body slid off mine. I knew something was wrong, and I shouted at him, but he didn't reply. I put my hand to his nose and couldn't feel any breathing. I was so scared, and my hand was trembling so much I couldn't even ring your cell phone, so I just banged on the wall..."

The reason Aunty Ji was telling me all this in such detail was that she wanted me to understand it wasn't her fault. I said softly: "I understand, Aunty Ji..."

The next morning, after I got up, I took both of their blood pressures and checked their heart rates. I found that both measurements were significantly elevated in both of them, and that neither of them wanted to go down to the restaurant for breakfast. I realised that they were too embarrassed to meet, so I ordered room service for them both so they could eat separately. I knew that trying to continue our tour under these circumstances would just make things worse for the two of them, so, while they were eating, I went down to the lobby and gave Older Sister Xinxin a call. Naturally, I couldn't give her the whole story of the previous night over the phone, as it would only embarrass her, especially as she was Uncle Xiao's daughter. I just said that, probably because of tiredness, both his and Aunty Ji's blood pressures were not too stable, and suggested that, to be on the safe side, we should come straight back to Beijing and look for an opportunity to resume our travels later on. Older Sister heard me out and immediately agreed to book our return tickets, as the two old folks' health was paramount.

The two of them were going to have to meet to pack their things and go to the station. When Aunty Ji went into the room to pack her own stuff, I noticed that Uncle Xiao stepped forward without a word to help, but he didn't dare let their eyes meet. For her part, Aunty Ji kept her gaze on the stuff she was packing, and didn't let it rest for an instant on Uncle Xiao. The atmosphere in the room was very fragile, and I didn't dare say a word in case I set off something unexpected. I was very thankful that the seats on the train that Older Sister had booked were together but spread across three rows, so the two of them didn't have to sit together and could avoid the awkwardness of having to talk to each other.

Once out of the station back in Beijing, Aunty Ji hailed a taxi, saying: "I'm going home now." I didn't dare suggest she come back to Uncle Xiao's place for something to eat, and just watched her get in the taxi. Uncle Xiao went over to the taxi window and waved to her, a look of deep apology and regret on his face. As we were waiting for our own taxi, Uncle Xiao came close to me and suddenly said, in a low voice: "When we get back, remember to tell your Older Sister that Aunty Ji and I stayed together and everything was fine." I nodded and stole a glance at him. An expression of shame and embarrassment flitted across his face.

Not long after we got back home, Older Sister arrived. Departing from his normal practice, this time Uncle Xiao didn't sit quietly in the living room, waiting for his daughter to make her greetings, but was the first to speak: "Our trip to Jinan and back went very smoothly. Your Aunty Ji had been there before, so we came back a bit early." Older Sister smiled and said: "I'm glad it went smoothly. Xiaoyang told me that your and Aunty Ji's blood pressure was up a bit; you need to take care." Uncle Xiao shot me a meaningful look and replied: "It was nothing, it's back to normal now." Older Sister clearly still had her doubts, and after we'd eaten, she came specially to my room and asked, in a low voice: "So nothing out of the ordinary happened, Xiaoyang?" Of course, I knew that Uncle Xiao wanted nothing more than to keep the real story secret and save Older Sister from further worry, so I backed up his pretence with a smile: "No, nothing; everything was fine!" "So did the two of them share a room in Jinan?" She asked the one question she was most interested in. I nodded and said: "Yes." "And everything was OK the next morning?" I nodded again: "Of course." "That's excellent!" Older Sister clapped her hands in relief. "Mission accomplished! I couldn't have done it without you, Xiaoyang!" I hurriedly turned away on the pretext of tidying up the table, so she couldn't see how uncomfortable I looked. "Just wait there a moment." She ran gaily out of the room, and was back in a moment carrying a shawl. "Your Older Brother Chang Sheng bought me this the day before yesterday, and now I'm giving it to you as your reward." I pushed her hand away, saying: "That's not right: I can't accept something your husband gave you as a present." "Silly girl! After he gave it to me it became mine, so why shouldn't I pass it on to you? Look, it's pure silk. It will make you look really beautiful! When your boyfriend sees you, he'll think you look really glamorous. Come on, let me show you how to wear it." Without waiting for me to reply, she arranged the shawl on me, and that left me really conflicted. I knew quite well I was helping Uncle Xiao trick her, but I still wanted this reward...

Since parting at the train station, Aunty Ji hadn't come to visit, or even telephoned. Uncle Xiao stopped going into the living room to wait for her but resumed his habit of going out to the park for a walk. I reckoned he knew that, the way things stood, any further talk of marriage was off the table. Although I didn't notice any obvious changes when I took his blood pressure, ECG and other measurements, I was worried that his mood was low, he was eating less and his appetite was suppressed. I was well aware of his urgent desire to set up a new home, in the hope of using it to show his son-in-law, Chang Sheng: You see, I don't need you to look after me in my old age, and it doesn't make the least difference to me if you move out or even leave the country. He also wanted to show his daughter that, with this new household, she didn't need to worry about him in the future. This unexpected setback in his plan had certainly hit him very hard, and, naturally, this psychological blow could well have a negative effect on his physical health, but there was nothing to be done about it. All I could do was to watch over him even more carefully, make my food even more appetising, talk to him a bit more on his walks in the park, and, at home, help him listen to more of the solo *erhu* tunes he liked so much, all in the hope of lifting his mood as quickly as possible.

As the day of Older Sister's departure got closer, even though she was busy with preparations for the trip, she didn't forget about Uncle Xiao and Aunty Ji. She came over, one evening after dinner, and as soon as she saw me, she asked: "Xiaoyang, has Aunty Ji been living here all the time recently?" I was shaken by the question but immediately came up with a story to fob her off with, and said, blushing but straight-faced: "Aunty said she had some important things to see to at her place, and would probably be back in a few days." I winked at Uncle Xiao, who was sitting in the living room, and saw him nod slightly in return. Older Sister just grunted in reply, then turned to Uncle Xiao and said: "Dad, wouldn't it be best if you and Aunty Ji got the marriage ceremony done and dusted? If it's all settled before we go, I'll be able to relax. How about it?" Uncle Xiao didn't say anything for a moment, perhaps because he hadn't thought Older Sister would be so careful in her planning, but he quickly recovered himself and said: "What do we need with a ceremony at our age? Let's keep it low-key. The less fuss the better with this kind of thing. Everyone in this little district knows me, so why give them more fodder for gossip at a wedding banquet?"

But Older Sister wasn't giving up: "We don't have to make a big fuss, and we can keep the occasion simple, but even so, we'll still have to invite Aunty Ji and her son over here for a meal together, won't we? That way will be just as good as doing everything in public, and it will show that our two households are genuinely united. Then I'll be able to stop worrying completely." "I... er... let me think about that for a bit." Uncle Xiao could probably see the sense in what Older Sister was saying, and knew that any further refusal on his part would arouse her suspicions. "I'll wait for your decision then, and once you've fixed on the day, I'll make all the arrangements." Older Sister rubbed her hands together happily.

Once she had left, Uncle Xiao sat dumbly in the living room, sipping continuously at his tea, a worried look on his face. I was considerably agitated myself, as I knew that this kind of anxiety was bad for his health. But what could I do about it? Tell Older Sister what the real situation was? That would be deliberately going against Uncle Xiao's wishes, and cause Older Sister to be leaving the country in high anxiety. What is more, it would almost certainly make Uncle Xiao feel he had lost face in the eyes of Older Brother Chang Sheng. I really wanted to help resolve this situation between father and daughter, but I couldn't see what I could do. After Uncle Xiao had been sitting there without speaking for more than an hour, he suddenly called out: "Come here a moment, Xiaoyang." I went over to him and waited quietly for him to speak. He swallowed hard, then said, with some difficulty: "I need you to go somewhere for me, Xiaoyang." I knew where he meant, but what did he want me to say when I saw Aunty Ji? I just had to wait and find out. "You are to tell her I need her help to act out a little play for me, so Xinxin can be comfortable about going to America with her husband." "Ah, so what do you want her to do?" I hadn't really understood what he meant. "Ask her to come over here with her son to have a meal, and pretend that everything is settled between us." "So that's it, just to have a meal. Hmm, do you think that's the kind of thing Aunty Ji will agree to?" "You've been with us for quite a while now, Xiaoyang, so you've probably noticed that I have certain opinions of Chang Sheng. Chang Sheng himself is not at all satisfied with me; in fact, I'd go so far as to say he hates me because I opposed his marriage to Xinxin from the start. I criticised him a lot after they got married, so he decided the further away from me he was, the better. His decision to study in America now is probably partly him going off in a huff. I can see that your Older Sister Xinxin going with him is the right thing for her to do: she loves him, she's married to him, and going with him will be good for their marriage. That's why I'm not going to put any pressure on them over it; otherwise, Chang Sheng might think I was secretly working against him, and he might take out his hatred for me on Xinxin. So I have to find a way of letting him and Xinxin go off to America together free from worry. Do you understand?" I nodded. Of course I understood; my own mum and dad disapproved of me going out with Lü Yiwei because they thought he was a bit of a snob, and I might not fare too well with him as time passed. Because of this, he would sometimes be a little tetchy and disrespectful towards my mum and dad, but it only took a look from me for him to stop. It seemed that Older Sister did not have the same kind of control over Older Brother Chang Sheng. All I said on the telephone was that I wanted to come and see Aunty Ji. Although she must have had her doubts and suspicions, perhaps because of the way I had treated her in the past, she just replied: "You'll be very welcome!"

At ten the next morning, I found the address Aunty Ji had given me. Her place was pretty much the same as Uncle Xiao's, except the rooms were even neater and cleaner, all the furniture and fittings in their proper place, and everything so highly polished you could see your face in it. Aunty Ji poured me some tea and said: "Xiaoyang, I think you already know that there's no way your Uncle Xiao and I can live together." I hadn't expected Aunty Ji to be quite so direct, but I still summoned all my courage and said to her what Uncle Xiao had told me to. Aunty Ji didn't reply for quite a while. I thought to myself: That's it! I've got no chance of success. But, to my surprise, Aunty Ji said: "Getting me to bring my son along to help act out this charade is not a good idea: for one thing, I don't want to involve him in such an embarrassing affair, nor would he agree to it. For another, it is very difficult to be convincing in hiding the truth in this kind of thing, and I find dissembling very distressing. Nonetheless, I understand your Uncle Xiao's intention, and I would like to help him. But rather than arranging a fake wedding banquet, I think it would be better if the three of us went on another trip, to Luoyang. I've heard all about the Peony Festival there, and I'd like to see it. Only this time, I'll pay my own travel expenses. You can tell your Older Sister that we will be travelling as a couple, just as though we were actually married; we've already been on two trips together, so making another one won't raise any eyebrows. It doesn't matter what anyone else says, we just need to hoodwink his daughter until she is on her way to America, and that will be enough."

I found myself agreeing with her, so I went back to Uncle Xiao and explained what she had said. When he had listened, Uncle Xiao nodded and said: "That's good, that's good; this way it will be easier to hoodwink them. I'm grateful for her consideration." Later on, he telephoned Older Sister Xinxin, and it wasn't long before she jumped in her car and drove over. She was delighted: "Let's do what you and Aunty Ji suggest. I'll give Xiaoyang some money to make sure you can spend this honeymoon in style." Then she went on to instruct me: "Take all the nursing and medical stuff you need, and make sure the food and accommodation are just so, to guarantee them a happy honeymoon!"

Following Uncle Xiao's intentions, we arranged for the three of us to set out the day before Older Brother and Older Sister left for America, so Older Sister could relax completely. The evening before our departure, Older Sister brought Chang Sheng over for dinner, and this was the first time he had been back since he moved out. He clearly wasn't there by choice. Once inside the apartment, he nodded to Uncle Xiao, handed him the wedding gifts they had brought, then sat down on the settee, leafing through old magazines and newspapers. Afraid that the atmosphere was getting too stiff and uncomfortable, Older Sister thrust two heads of garlic into Chang Sheng's hands, saying: "Get on and peel these." I could see that Older Sister's eyes were full of love and affection as she looked at her husband. He was wearing an Italian-label lounge suit, which, because of his height and good build, just served to make him even more handsome. It couldn't be denied, he was the kind of good-looking fellow who made a girl's heart flutter at the sight of him. I could see why Older Sister loved him. But to tell the truth, I didn't like those eyes of his. He always narrowed them as he looked at people, his gaze darting to and fro, as though he was always on the look-out for something. There was something furtive about it all, that made you feel as though you were being spied on. Maybe this was because he'd been a lawyer for so long, and perhaps he had become this way because he was always dealing with suspects and criminals, and had to probe and weigh them up.

Following Older Sister's prior instructions, I had made a good few dishes and opened a bottle of Great Wall red wine. As Older Brother and Older Sister had come to say farewell to Uncle Xiao and Aunty Ji, they were going to have things to talk about, so once I had served dinner, I withdrew back into the kitchen. But perhaps because she was so excited, Older Sister was talking very loudly, and you couldn't help hearing her no matter what. I heard her say: "You don't know how happy I am today, Dad. From now on, you have someone in your life to look after you, and Chang Sheng's ambition to go and study in America is being realised. The two people I most love are both getting what they most want. It makes my heart so happy. Come on, Dad, let's drink a toast..."

Chang Sheng naturally spoke very little over dinner that evening, and all I heard him say was: "Here, Dad, let me drink to the happiness of the newly-weds!" In the past, when Chang Sheng was at the dinner table, Uncle Xiao never spoke, but this evening, he seemed to have a lot to say. As I took the food in, I heard him saying: "Chang Sheng, Xinxin, now you're going to New York, you're going to be in a new country where there are going to be lots of things that will be unfamiliar and problematic, and you'll need to be mentally prepared for the difficulties and setbacks. And then there's the language barrier: Chang Sheng, your English is passable, and I'm not too worried about you, but Xinxin, you've only got a little simple conversational stuff, and you're bound to meet with a lot of problems in day-to-day living and in your studies. It's going to need a lot of patience, which isn't usually your strong point. You'll need to watch out for that. And then there's the question of your safety, as I know that American law allows the individual to carry weapons. I've heard on the news that there are lots of shooting incidents in their cities and schools, and you'll have to beware that. Avoid the streets where there are a lot of muggings, and go out at night as little as possible. Of course, you two will have to watch out for each other, but if anything tricky turns up that you need to talk about, or if there's something that can be handled back here, then you are to telephone me. You, Xinxin, will have to drop your bad habit of acting too impetuously, and moderate your voice so you talk to people quietly and thoughtfully. You're going over there to support Chang Sheng in his studies, so you have to make sure all the household affairs are looked after and he can concentrate properly..." As I listened, I sighed to myself: These things Uncle Xiao is telling Older Sister should be coming from a mother's mouth! I don't know what emotions were going through Uncle Xiao's heart, but I do know that his light remained on until late into the night.

The next afternoon, the three of us went to Luoyang. Because this trip had a very definite purpose, everything was much better organised. Uncle Xiao, Aunty Ji and I each had our own room, so no one was suspicious of anyone's motives and there was no awkwardness. Aunty Ji had said that she was going to cover all her own travelling expenses this time, but how could I permit that? I pretended that Older Sister had paid in advance online for the travel and accommodation, and that put an end to her protests. When we had settled into the hotel and had a little rest, Aunty Ji announced she wanted to go out to view the peonies; after I had checked Uncle Xiao's blood pressure and heart rate, I asked him if he wanted to go too. He nodded and said: "All right."

It was my first time in Luoyang, so I wasn't sure where to go to view the flowers. I was about to go over to the reception desk to ask for directions, when Uncle Xiao said: "I've been here once before; I'll be your tour guide." He told the taxi driver to take us straight to

Wangcheng Park. Once inside the park, I gazed around me, wide-eyed in wonder. Heavens! It really was an ocean of peony blossoms! Everywhere they were in full bloom: red ones, white ones, pink ones, yellow ones, green ones, purple ones, blue ones, purple-black ones, lilac ones, crimson ones. Huge blooms of every kind in amazing colours, almost too much for the eye to take in. It was the first time I had seen so many beautiful peonies, and the joy of it was almost too much for me to contain. I just wanted to dance and shout. Of course, I did neither, as I was still mindful of my responsibilities as a nurse and carer, and I kept my eye firmly on how the two old folk were bearing up. When I was training, our teacher told us that some old people, when confronted with scenes of exceptional beauty, could be overcome by the spectacle and develop heart problems. But everything was all right, and I could see that they were both fine. Uncle Xiao had found a quiet spot to enjoy the spectacle, but Aunty Ji was busy taking photographs of one bloom after another, and from time to time, she would stand in front of one she particularly liked, and get me to take her picture. It was probably seeing Aunty Ji so happy, and because he was grateful to her for helping him out, that made Uncle Xiao step forward and launch into an introduction: "The cultivation of peonies in Luoyang started in the Sui dynasty and began really to flourish in the Tang. By the Song, it was one of the glories of the Empire. Just as the poem says: 'The *fengshui* of Luoyang is most propitious for flowers and its peonies are a wonder of the world.' When you compare the peony to other flowers, it is more graceful, sumptuous and luxurious in its appearance." On hearing this, Aunty Ji relaxed the rather serious demeanour she had been showing Uncle Xiao so far, and said, with a little laugh: "So true! Even Liu Yuxi was moved to declaim: 'Wild peonies grow with exuberant colours. Pond lotuses are pure and free of passions. Only red peonies epitomise the essence of beauty, whose blooming presence decorates the capital city.' It is truly a cause of lifelong regret if you don't come to see the peonies of Luoyang at least once…"

At that moment, as I saw their relaxed and intimate air, my heart gave a little jump: wasn't there still a chance the two of them might become husband and wife? For his part, Uncle Xiao genuinely wanted to create a new home, and for her part, Aunty Ji still fundamentally approved of Uncle Xiao. The biggest stumbling block was what happened when Uncle Xiao tried to make love last time in Jinan, but maybe that was a one-off, and if he was given another opportunity, everything would be all right. I would once again have to try my hardest, and create that opportunity for him. If I could do this, it would be a very good thing from several points of view: one, it would be a great help to the two of them in finding a settled and peaceful old age; two, it would put Older Sister Xinxin's mind at rest once and for all; and three, it would mean that this trip wouldn't become another occasion on which I had to deceive Older Sister, and I wouldn't have to keep feeling guilty about her. But how was I to bring this about? I came up with one idea after another, but none of them really seemed to fit the bill. I knew that I was faced with two very worldly-wise old people, and if my plan was too obvious, they would see through it and all would be lost.

Entirely unexpectedly, as the three of us were leaving Wangcheng Park by the main gate, a furtive-looking man gave me a brilliant idea. It was early evening, and the tourists who had been admiring the peonies were streaming out of the main gate, bathed in the fragrance of the flowers. As I was following Uncle Xiao and Aunty Ji out of the park, a vulgar, sly-looking man stopped me. I was about to get away from him, when, to my surprise, he whispered to me: "Hey, lady! Do you want to help your parents live longer?" As he spoke, he was pointing at Uncle Xiao and Aunty Ji's retreating forms, and he had clearly taken me for their daughter. I didn't bother to put him right, and just asked coldly: "What do you think you're on about?" "I have a secret recipe handed down through generations. You only have to use it once, and I guarantee it will add ten years to their lives. Of course, no one can use it more than once because if you use it again it becomes a poison." "Oh yes? What secret recipe is that?" I asked mockingly, as I was quite sure he was just another snake-oil salesman out to swindle people. "It's these two things." With the speed of a magician, he pulled two glass bottles out of his backpack. I took a look, and saw that one

contained tree peony petals, and the other, a clear liquid of some
kind. "You see? This one contains petals from the black tree peony
that I picked before dawn from a ten-year-old tree. And this one
contains yellow wine that has been steeped with the skin of the
root of the purple tree peony, which is called 'peony skin' in
traditional Chinese medicine. If you crush the black peony petals
and add them to the 'peony skin' wine, then, within three hours,
massage the body with it, working it into the skin all over, one
application is guaranteed to add ten years to an old person's life."
"How miraculous!" I said with a sneer. "Perhaps the young lady
doesn't believe me. Well, how about this? I won't say any more
because I need to guard the secret of the way the medicine works,
but I will just tell you that in 1972, a tomb from the early Eastern
Han dynasty was excavated in Baishu Village in Gansu's Weiwu
Prefecture, and they found bamboo slips with the medical formula
for using tree peony to cure stasis of the blood. Look, here's a
newspaper report about the excavation." With one hand he stuffed
the two bottles inside his jacket, and with the other pulled an old
newspaper out of his backpack, and handed it to me. I didn't want
to listen to any more of his bullshit, and turned to leave. But at that
moment, a light suddenly went on in my brain, and an inspiration
came to me about how to get Uncle Xiao and Aunty Ji together
again. I turned back to the man and asked: "How much for those
two bottles?" "Best price is two hundred yuan!" he said firmly. "And
that's a special price because I can see how devoted you are to your
mum and dad." I didn't want to haggle with him, so remembering
how much money Older Sister had given me for the trip, I just
pulled out two hundred yuan and shoved it into his hand. When I
caught up with Uncle Xiao and Aunty Ji, carrying the two bottles,
they asked in surprise: "What have you been buying?" "A magic
potion!" I said mysteriously, and only explained further when we
got back to the hotel.

   At the dinner table back in the hotel, I laid it on with a trowel in
retelling the huckster's tale, and when I came to the bit about
massaging the potion all over the body to add ten years to your life,
they both exclaimed: "Heavens! Do such magical things still exist?"

But it was Uncle Xiao who first expressed doubts: "Can it really be true though? If it is, wouldn't our leaders have bought it all up?" I didn't want this feeling of doubt to have a chance to take root, so I said hurriedly: "There have always been a lot of wise men out among the people; you don't have to believe everything you hear, but you can't dismiss it all either." "That's true! There's always been an element of magic in traditional Chinese medicine, and it can do many things that Western medicine can't!" Aunty Ji came in on my side. "The man told me that once the contents of the two bottles are mixed together, the potion has to be used within three hours, and, with the massaging and rubbing in, it has to be a man and a woman doing it to each other; that's the only way the potency of the medicine is brought out." I put a lot of emphasis on this last part because it was the inspiration I had had for getting the two of them back together. It certainly rendered them silent when they heard it, and I thought to myself: Maybe it's going to work!

When we were going to our rooms after dinner was over, I resumed the subject very directly: "I'll wait until you two have both finished washing, then I'll make up the potion. After that, I'll trouble you to massage it into each other, and we'll see what happens. If, by any chance, you do live an extra ten years each, that will be quite a result. And, if not, I don't suppose it will have done your skin any harm." Neither of them replied either in acceptance or refusal, so I decided this amounted to a tacit agreement. Indeed, after I checked Uncle Xiao's blood pressure and heart rate when he had finished washing, I put the pre-mixed peony potion down in front of him. Without a word, he picked it up, stood up and made for Aunty Ji's room. Aunty Ji opened her door without a murmur and let him in. I felt a surge of elation and was very proud of myself for coming up with this idea.

After I returned to my room, I sat watching the hands of my watch, and listening carefully for any sounds from next door. Three hours passed, and Uncle Xiao had still not come out of Aunty Ji's room. I was happy about this, but I didn't let my hopes run away with me. I still lay on my bed fully dressed, listening out carefully, afraid there might be a repetition of what happened last time. As the time passed and we moved deeper into the night, I became more and more sleepy and muddle-headed, until I finally slipped into dreamland. By the time I woke up, it was already full daylight, and as soon as I returned fully to my senses, I leapt agitatedly out of bed, and ran out into the hall. First I had to make sure Uncle Xiao was all right. There was no reply from his room when I knocked on the door. Had something happened to him? As I was standing anxiously outside his room, the door to Aunty Ji's room opened, and I saw Uncle Xiao coming out slowly, still wearing his pyjamas. I hastily explained why I was standing outside his room: "I was just thinking it was time to take your morning blood pressure and so on, Uncle." "Ah! Come back when I've had a wash." He yawned and went into his room. My happiness expanded: the two of them, a man and a woman, spending the whole night together in the same room? Wasn't that proof of the success of my plan? Haha! Well, Older Sister, I haven't let down the trust you put in me! You haven't spent all that money in vain! I've earned my pay after all!

My breakfast tasted particularly good that morning, and the two old folk also ate very heartily. When we'd finished, Aunty Ji took it on herself to come to my room, and I thought she wanted to compliment me on my efforts. To my surprise, what she said was: "Xiaoyang, I am very grateful to you for your good intentions, but I'm afraid I have to tell you that your Uncle Xiao is not the right man for me. You mustn't repeat this to anyone else, but he's not in working order. He tries hard in bed, but he's not functional, and I'm not willing to live the rest of my life without sex. Last night, after he tried everything else he could, he fumbled about in the pocket of his pyjamas, took something out, put it in his mouth and swallowed it. I didn't pay it much attention, thinking it must be some kind of calmative, but, to my surprise, not long after, he suddenly lay down on the bed complaining of feeling really dizzy. I jumped up to go and call you to look after him, but he stopped me, saying: 'Don't worry; I just took a Viagra, and my blood pressure must have dropped a bit. I'll be all right in a moment.' My Lord! If he's crazy enough to take that kind of thing, what would I have done if something had gone wrong? It was only after he'd been lying there half the night that he stopped feeling dizzy; it all made me very nervous. You tell me: if the two of us were really to get married, what would it be like if he always relied on taking Viagra? Wouldn't it quickly take its toll on his body and threaten his life? So he and I can be friends, but we can never live together. Please don't spend any more time and effort on it." I listened to her wide-eyed and open-mouthed...

That morning, I stuck to our original plan and took the two of them by taxi to the Longmen Grottoes. On the way there, I didn't dare catch Uncle Xiao's eye. But, in fact, he seemed just as he always was. As soon as we had got out of the taxi and were making our way to the main gate of the grottoes, my cell phone rang. When I saw it was Older Sister Xinxin, I hurriedly told her our sightseeing itinerary for the day, but was surprised when she said: "There's no need to give me all the details of your travels. I'm quite sure you've got everything under control with the honeymoon. I was just ringing to tell you that Older Brother Chang Sheng and I are already onboard our plane for New York, and we'll be taking off any minute. Once we're gone, those two old folks' lives together and their health are going to be in your hands, so you've really got to be on the ball. I'll make sure your salary goes into your account on time at the end of every month, so you must absolutely live up to your responsibilities." "Yes, yes, Older Sister. Please don't worry!" She continued: "Now give the phone to Aunty Ji, I've got a few things to say to her." I hastily passed the phone to Aunty Ji, who was standing next to me, and whispered: "It's my Older Sister Xinxin. She wants a word with you."

I saw a moment's hesitation flash across Aunty Ji's face, but she immediately held her hand out for the phone and said: "Hello, Xinxin!" When Uncle Xiao realised it was Xinxin that she was talking to, he looked a little nervous, as if he was afraid Aunty Ji might give the game away; but everything was fine, and she sounded completely natural. Because we were all very close together, the voice on the other end of the phone carried quite clearly, and I heard Older Sister say: "I want to wish you and Dad a happy married life together!" Aunty Ji grunted an acknowledgement and said: "And, Xinxin, I wish the two of you bon voyage, and I hope everything goes smoothly for your studies in America!" Then she handed the phone to Uncle Xiao, and I heard him say: "Don't worry, Xin'er, everything's going to be fine!" Older Sister's final words floated down the connection: "The plane's about to take off, Dad, I'm going to have to turn off my phone. Call me immediately if anything happens..." Uncle Xiao gave me back the phone, saying, as he let out a long sigh of relief: "Finally, the play is over."

Only then did we go into the Longmen site and look at the stone carvings of the Buddha that densely covered the slopes of Dragon Gate Mountain and Fragrant Mountain on either side of the Yi River. They were started during the reign of the Emperor Xiaowen of the Northern Wei dynasty, and work on the grottoes went on continuously for more than four hundred years; its multitude of shrines and niches and the splendours of its Buddha statues are a constant source of wonder to those who view them. Even for someone like me, who had no understanding of sculpture, was stunned into silence at the sight when we entered the Fengxian Cave Temple. That is one of the grottoes excavated in the Tang dynasty, and its central figure of the Vairocana Buddha is enormous: its ears alone are 1.9 metres long...

The three of us spent three days in Luoyang visiting the Guanlin and White Horse Temples, and going to see the former residence of Bai Juyi. On the way back to Beijing on the fourth day, I got a text from Older Sister: *We are well settled in New York, so no need for you to worry. Hope you've had happy travels!* I showed Uncle Xiao and Aunty Ji the text separately, and neither said a word. I looked down and texted back: *Uncle Xiao and Aunty Ji are both well and happy, and send their best wishes to you and Older Brother Chang Sheng.* When I looked up again after sending this, I noticed that a teardrop had gathered in the corner of Uncle Xiao's left eye... This time when we got back to Beijing, Aunty Ji told me to have the *gu zheng* sent back to her place, and after that, she didn't come round anymore. This was the formal declaration of defeat in Uncle Xiao's strenuous campaign to remarry and build a new home.

⧖

Time flew by, and in the blink of an eye, it was high summer. The heat in Beijing in high summer is close to intolerable, a continuous succession of days like saunas concentrate the pollution in the atmosphere, making it hard to breathe. Watching the completely motionless branches of the trees and listening to the ever louder chirping of the cicadas have a dulling effect on a person's emotional well-being. Uncle Xiao was at a low ebb: his daughter was far away, Aunty Ji had left him, and all that remained for him was an empty apartment and unending loneliness. This emotional distress led to the rupture of his daily routine of work and rest, and he spent every evening on the sofa listlessly watching soap operas on the television, and not going to sleep till very late. In the morning, he didn't get out of bed promptly when he woke up, but just lay there, unmoving. During the day, he didn't go to the park anymore, but just sat at home, staring blankly out of the window. I was beginning to get worried, as his emotional state could also drag down his levels of physical immunity and cause other health problems. I tried desperately to think of some way of lifting his spirits, and suddenly remembered the three books he had talked about writing to establish his reputation as an academic lawyer. I reminded him of this: "You haven't done a thing about those three books you said you were going to write. It's best not to let the grass grow with that kind of thing. Back then, you told me about the content of the first book, but what about the second one? Have you given it any thought? When are you going to get writing again?" As he listened to my enquiry, a little life came back into him. He sat up straight, thought for a moment, then said: "The second book is called *An Examination of the Motives of Female Offenders*. Over the last few years, the number of female offenders has been on the rise, and in the book I am going to analyse the psychological motivations of female offenders, as I believe that while, of course, females are motivated by money and power, for the majority of offenders it is actually one of the following three reasons: one, they inflict harm on a male because that male has cheated on them and they are taking their revenge out of anger and resentment; two, they are violated in an incident of domestic violence or some other situation, and rage drives them to retaliate, even to the extent that they kill their violator or attacker; three, when someone deliberately damages their reputation, out of hatred for that person, they may look for an opportunity to harm them, sometimes even throwing acid in their face. I am planning to write three sections for each of these, explaining the deepest layers of psychological motivation in female offenders." "So are you ready to start writing soon?" I asked, trying to get him re-involved with this project. "And when have I had time to write anything recently, when I haven't even had time to read my source material, and have been wasting all my efforts on that Aunty Ji of yours? Ai! A total waste of effort that ate up all my writing time!" He managed to make everything Aunty Ji's fault, and was beginning to get angry. I hurriedly distracted him by asking: "Have you got the notes ready for your first book?" "I've got the notes done, but I haven't started writing the text yet. That's the next thing I've got to get on with, not using up all my energy on some woman; that was just a waste of my time." He became more animated as he spoke. "If you start writing properly, how many characters can you write in a day?" I asked, redirecting the conversation again. "At least three thousand a day. Back in the day, when I was writing court reports, I was up to ten thousand a day. And that was before we had computers, and were scribbling away by hand!" "I bet you were the best writer in the court when you were young, Uncle!" I said, deliberately flattering him to try and cheer him up. At this, his expression relaxed completely, and he said: "That's very true. Sometimes, the president of the court wanted me to write the end-of-year report for him. At the court general assembly, he always looked forward to seeing my work as it was always rational, accurate, logical and meticulous, and the language could serve as a model of elegance!" "I bet all the other youngsters in the court really envied you!" I said, still trying to take him out of himself. "Of course they did! The director of the court office specially arranged for me to hold a class on Friday afternoons to teach the youngsters the principles of writing legal and other official documents. There were a lot of those youngsters, including quite a few pretty girls, who all came to listen to my classes." "There were pretty girls in the courts then?" I asked deliberately, leading him on. "What? You think there were only old men in our courts? Let me tell you, not only were there pretty girls, they were pretty, unmarried girls with law degrees." "But I bet they weren't as pretty as Older Sister Xinxin's mother!" I said, pointing at the family photograph he had hung back up on the wall. "There's no comparison." He grinned, and, at that moment, I was sure he had completely forgotten all the troubles Aunty Ji had brought him. "And did any of these beautiful girls flutter their eyelashes at you in class because of your brilliance, or show they fancied you?" I kept trying to bolster his mood. "Listen to you, girl!" he said with a chuckle. "I can't say there weren't any at all." "So there were some?" I pushed him further. "You're too young to remember, but back then we were very conservative about sex. If anything happened, you could be very severely disciplined, so no one dared overstep the mark." "I didn't ask if you overstepped the mark, I asked if any of these beautiful girls fluttered their eyelashes at you in class because of your brilliance, or showed they fancied you." "Haha! Well, if I've got to answer, the answer is yes." Uncle Xiao couldn't help laughing. I had clearly succeeded in lifting his mood. I originally thought that from now on he could forget about the whole business with Aunty Ji, but, out of the blue a few days later, something new happened.

One Friday, after breakfast, he told me he was going to visit friends in Changping. I was all in favour of this, as going to see family or friends is an excellent way of cheering oneself up. I said I'd call a taxi and go with him, but he shook his head and replied: "The taxi is fine, but you're not coming with me. It's not appropriate to have you with me when I go to a friend's house for a chat. I'll be back after dinner at the latest. I'll keep my cell phone turned on, so we can easily be in contact if anything happens. Besides, Changping isn't very far away, and there's a hospital there if I really do fall ill. Anyway, I'm in excellent health at the moment, so there's nothing at all for you to worry about." I thought he was probably right, so I didn't make a fuss, but just put the medications he needed for the day in his bag, called a taxi and let him go.

The day passed peacefully. I rang him twice in the course of it, once in the morning, when he said he was sitting chatting in his friend's house. The second time was in the afternoon, when he told me his friend was insisting he stayed for dinner, and he would come back after that. These two conversations reassured me, so I went out for a stroll, and to buy an outfit for my boyfriend, Lü Yiwei. I ate my dinner alone, did the washing-up, then, just at the time I reckoned Uncle Xiao should be getting back, my phone rang. I saw it was Uncle Xiao's number, and I had just answered it and said "Hello, Uncle Xiao..." when, to my surprise, I heard a very fierce woman's voice saying: "Is your name Zhong?" Dumbfounded, I asked back: "Who are you?" "Don't worry about who I am," the woman replied. "You just bring two thousand yuan out to Changping to pay your old man's compensation and get him back." There was something like an explosion in my head when I heard this: Great heavens! What had happened? What kind of thing was it that needed compensation? The woman grew fiercer and more insistent. "You've got to let me talk to the old man," I said. I was really worried for his safety. Had he been kidnapped or something? I began to regret not going with him. I heard Uncle Xiao's voice down the phone: "It's me." Then the woman came on the line again, insisting: "Be quick about it, or I'll hand the whole thing over to the Public Security to deal with." I knew from that it wasn't a kidnapping, but I still couldn't work out exactly what was going on. I was so flustered, I even forgot to pick up my front door keys: what could it be that would involve the Public Security? I hurriedly asked for the address, distractedly counted out two thousand yuan from my purse, flew downstairs out onto the street, ran down a taxi, and headed towards Changping with all speed.

All the way there, I was trying to guess what it was that Uncle Xiao had done that involved paying a fine to avoid involving the Public Security. Had he broken something valuable in a shop? Had he gone somewhere he wasn't allowed? Given his familiarity with the law, he couldn't have done anything too outlandish, could he?

At my urging, the taxi driver sped to Changping and found the address the woman had given me. Ah! It turned out to be a foot-washing salon. I looked at its advertising sign: *Pretty Girl Foot-washing Salon*. My heart gave a lurch: although I'd never been in such a place myself, I knew from things I'd seen on the internet that this was just the kind of place you could easily get into trouble in. When I went in, I saw Uncle Xiao sitting in a corner, with a middle-aged woman glaring truculently at the door. As she saw me come in, the woman scowled and asked: "Is your name Zhong? Have you brought the money?" I nodded and asked quietly: "What's it compensation for?" She replied angrily: "This is my little place, and there's only me and a girl who works for me here. We run a decent business here, foot washing and foot massage, but he took advantage of me being out in the late afternoon to proposition my girl. He negotiated a price of two hundred yuan, and the two of them did the deed in my shop. In fact, that old man of yours is quite something, and he yelled at my girl, bullying her into doing it twice. Luckily, I came back in time; otherwise, someone else might have heard what was going on and reported it to the local police station; I might have had my shop shut down and my business ruined." I went pale when I heard this, and went over to Uncle Xiao, hoping he might refute her claims and tell me what really happened; but he didn't say a word. In fact, not only did he not explain, he wouldn't even look at me, but just stared at the wall, and said, in great embarrassment: "Just give her the money." What could I say? He had as good as admitted the truth of the woman's accusations. I handed over the money. The woman counted it deftly, then gestured at me: "Take him away! And keep a better eye on him in future; men's sex urges get stronger as they get old, so don't let him out to get into more trouble! You two were lucky you met with a decent person like me today, or your reputation might have been destroyed." My guess was that Uncle Xiao was being ripped off here: hadn't Aunty Ji told me quite clearly that he wasn't sexually functional? So how could anything like this have happened here today? I led him out of the shop, and once we'd turned a corner on the street, I asked him softly: "Do you want to go home now, or shall we find somewhere here to talk about all this? Should we go to the Public Security Office?" Uncle Xiao still wouldn't look at me, and just said: "Home."

On the way back into the city, the presence of the taxi driver stopped me enquiring further, and Uncle Xiao didn't say a word. It was already after eleven o'clock at night by the time we got home. As soon as we were in the apartment, he went to his bedroom, fished out a bundle of banknotes and handed them over to me. At that point, I couldn't help asking: "So, what exactly happened?" "That woman explained it to you, didn't she?" he said mildly. "And was she telling the truth?" I asked, looking hard at him. He nodded. Not a moment's hesitation. "Oh!" I looked at him as though I'd never seen him before. "And what's so surprising about that? I'm not that old, am I?! I can..." I was angered by his lack of concern, and said, almost yelling at him: "But you're a retired judge! What do you think you're doing visiting a prostitute? Aren't you afraid of losing your good name? If an ordinary man got caught doing this, he wouldn't dare show his face in public again, so what do you think would happen if word got out about you?!" "There's no need to make a mountain out of a molehill! I don't care who you tell about this. You probably ought to tell your Aunty Ji; give her the whole story so she knows for sure she did the right thing not marrying me. In fact, I think you should phone her tomorrow!" With that, he retreated to his bedroom and went to sleep, leaving me standing dumbfounded in the living room. Wow! I'd never come across anything like this before! If his son-in-law Chang Sheng found out, wouldn't he give him a really hard time about it! And as for Older Sister Xinxin, if she didn't die of anger, she'd die of shame!

Of course, I didn't ring Aunty Ji. How could I? But from then on, my regard for Uncle Xiao diminished, and I felt he no longer deserved my respect. Visiting a prostitute! I ask you! A retired judge too! It was too demeaning! If he had been taken to the Public Security Office, it would have made the news across the whole of Beijing! Then, a fortnight or so later, I received a text from an unknown cell phone number: *I'm the owner of the Pretty Girl Foot-*

washing Salon in Changping. I'd like to talk to you at your convenience. As I read it, I recalled how fierce the woman had sounded, and I wondered what it could be she wanted to talk to me about. Was she going to demand more money? I was going to ignore the text, but, in the end, curiosity got the better of me, so I went downstairs and called the number. She started apologising as soon as she answered: "I'm so sorry, Miss Zhong. I was very rude to you that evening. I've been feeling really uncomfortable ever since I took that two thousand yuan off you. I've been struggling with the whole thing until today, when I decided to call you and return the money." My heart gave a start: what new game was she up to? I replied cautiously: "Why?" She gave an embarrassed laugh: "The fact is, that old man of yours didn't do anything in my shop that night. I was by myself there when he came in, and he offered me two thousand yuan to act out a little charade with him. That was what you saw that night. Business had been slow that day, and in the end, greed got the better of me, and I agreed to it. I thought he must be venting his anger on you or some other girl, and he wanted to prove he wasn't too old for it and was still a man. But I've decided I can't profit by an old man's psychological troubles, and that's why I'm talking to you now..." I stood rooted to the spot in amazement. Then the light dawned on me, and I finally understood why he had specially told me to call Aunty Ji and tell her the whole story: he wanted her to know how strong and virile he was with another woman, and that he wasn't the least bit worried about not being able to perform with her. Great heavens! Was he really that concerned about such things?! He was actually willing to spend that money to regain his manly reputation in my eyes and those of Aunty Ji. He must have known Aunty Ji had told me about his incapacity that night, and thought that the two of us would look down on him for it.

Once I'd got the whole picture, I quickly told the woman: "You don't have to worry – you earned that money. You agreed to help him with the way he had chosen himself to find some psychological comfort and peace of mind. It was an act of charity, and I'm very grateful to you..."

After this phone call, my opinion of Uncle Xiao revived again, and I also recalled that I really should telephone Aunty Ji to tell her the story, or Uncle Xiao's two thousand yuan would have been wasted. To tell the truth, deep down, I was also a little annoyed with Aunty Ji for her superior attitude back then. So, one morning, I phoned Aunty Ji, and after exchanging greetings, I told her the full story of Uncle Xiao's version of what happened in Changping, hoping it would annoy her, and maybe bring her down a peg or two. But you'll never guess what she actually said…

OK, OK – Aunty Wei from the park authorities is signalling to me that it is getting late and we will have to finish here. I'll come back tomorrow evening to continue the story…

GOOD EVENING AUNTIES, older sisters and younger sisters; I'm flattered that you have all come back to listen to the rest of my meanderings.

Let me pick up from where I left off last night. But before I do, I have a request to make. Since what I am talking about involves certain individuals' private affairs, I would ask you to treat it with a caregiver's confidentiality, and not spread it around outside this setting. So, have you guessed what it was Aunty Ji said at the end of our phone call? She said: "Your Uncle Xiao must have been taking Viagra; he was lucky his blood pressure didn't drop so he got all dizzy again. You should tell him that the worst side effect of Viagra is blacking out; statistical studies have proved this. All American men are aware of it. You should tell him he'd be better off not taking it." Ha! With that reply, I ran into a brick wall and had no comeback.

I think it was after this that Uncle Xiao finally decided to let matters rest with Aunty Ji, and his speech and behaviour began to change. It started with the children on the street: when they called him "Grandpa", he would actually reply. In the past, he would stop and talk to them with a smile if they called him "Uncle", but if they called him "Grandpa" or "Old Grandad" he wouldn't turn to look at them, let alone stop, as if they hadn't even called out. What is more, when he went to the park, he was keen to join the groups of elderly folk who gathered there, sometimes going over to listen to them singing, sometimes standing watching them playing chess, and sometimes sitting down and joining in their sporadic conversations. In the past, he had completely avoided them, considering that he didn't belong with any group of old people. The final thing was that when we went out and used public transport, he was happy to follow my instructions, and, leaning on my arm, go quietly and sit down on the seats specially reserved for the elderly and infirm. One day, when we were having lunch, he said to me, out of the blue: "It doesn't matter how many times a person gets married, if you outlive your partner, you are going to end up living alone. Loneliness is one of life's flavours that everyone tastes a little of; it's nothing to make a fuss about." At first, I didn't understand what he meant, or why he was saying it now, but then I understood: he was telling me that he had come to accept what had happened with Aunty Ji, and he wasn't thinking about setting up a new household anymore.

After this affair was all done and dusted, I thought he would surely be a bit more relaxed in his life, but I hadn't reckoned with the reawakening of his concerns about the relationship between Older Brother and Older Sister. I remember that, as we were having lunch one day, he suddenly put down his chopsticks and asked me: "Tell me, Xiaoyang, how do you think Xinxin and Chang Sheng have been getting on together since they've been in America?" I immediately replied with a laugh: "I'm sure they've been absolutely fine! They got married of their own free will, and they love each other. Just before Older Sister left, she told me that she and Older Brother had discussed it thoroughly, and they were going to stop using contraceptives when they got to America, and when they had the baby, she was going to look after it and study English at the same time." Uncle Xiao fell silent for a moment when he heard this, then said: "I hope that's the case. It's just that I didn't treat Chang Sheng at all well in the past, and I remember one occasion when he took on a case which was being heard in the court where I used to work. The presiding judge used to be one of my juniors, and Chang

Sheng wanted me to introduce him to him, saying he wanted to discuss with the judge a certain way of considering the evidence. Of course, that is quite permissible. But I balked at this and didn't make the introduction. Do you think he could still be holding a grudge because of that?" I knew immediately what he was getting at, and I dispelled his worries with a smile: "Impossible! How could one family member hold a grudge against another like that? You can stop worrying; Chang Sheng isn't petty enough to do anything of the sort." At that, he picked up his chopsticks and started eating again.

After that, I noticed how he always asked after Chang Sheng whenever he made an overseas call to Older Sister, and I realised he was making a big effort to repair his relationship with Chang Sheng and had recognised that his previous behaviour towards him had not been correct. This was quite a step, coming from a no-nonsense man like Uncle Xiao, who was so firm and proud in his family dealings. I just didn't know whether it was going to do any good.

A little while later, Uncle Xiao went and took some books out of the National Library, and he began to spend a lot more time at home, reading and researching on the internet. I asked him if he was about to start properly writing his three books, and he said: "That's right. I'm not going to be distracted by any more women, and I'm going to use my time properly. Other than some time for physical exercise, I'm going to concentrate solely on my writing, in the hope I can finish the three books sooner than planned. Once I've held the news conference announcing the publication of the three volumes, I'll start on something else." Seeing how determined he was, I asked him which book he was going to write first, the one about male offenders or the one about female offenders. He replied: "First I'm going to bring together the material for the third volume, *A History of Human Criminality*, then I'm going to start the actual writing of *An Examination of the Motives of Male Offenders*. Once I pick up my pen, I'm not going to stop, and I'll write it all in one go."

I made many trips to the National Library with him as he gathered his material. I didn't know anything about law, and even less about writing a book, so I wasn't really much help. Every time we went there, while he searched for his material, I sat by the main entrance knitting a sweater, or looking at my cell phone. Once, when he emerged from his researches looking pleased with himself, I asked if he'd been particularly successful, and he nodded and said that he'd stumbled upon a book by a young law professor that had a lot of interesting things to say about the history of human criminality. The author believed that the history of human criminality is intertwined with the development of humankind. Property theft developed at the same rate and to the same level as did capitalism, and it only became possible with the arrival of private ownership. Sex crimes only arose after the arrival of communal marriage and polygamy. Crimes involving corruption only began when power and profit became intimately linked. Crimes of honour began when humankind started paying attention to reputation, particularly after death, and fame became a preoccupation...

About three months after he started these researches, Uncle Xiao announced that he was going to start writing properly. He told me his writing time would be after breakfast from eight thirty to eleven o'clock, and every afternoon from two o'clock to five o'clock; during these times, I was not to go into his bedroom, which was now doubling as his study, so as not to disturb his writing. I felt that five and a half hours writing a day was too much, and might not be good for his health; he was well into his seventies, after all. But he wouldn't listen to me, saying: "I've got to work while I'm still alive, and I won't be happy until I've finished what I've got to do." There was nothing more I could say in the face of his stubborn determination, so I just made sure I cooked him good food to give him the strength for his writing.

From then on, he put this daily work schedule into operation; he stopped visiting friends and relations, didn't go on any more travels, greatly reduced his exercise time, and immersed himself in writing his legal volumes. One morning a month or so later, a bit after ten, I heard a sudden noise from his study-cum-bedroom that sounded like a book falling to the floor. I gave a start and looked at my watch: it was still forty minutes before he was due to stop work for the morning. I thought about opening his door to have a look, but I was afraid he would be angry if I interrupted his writing. There had been a number of occasions before when I had gone in to top up his tea, and he had been very displeased. He looked at me indignantly, saying I had broken his train of thought. As I hesitated, wondering whether to go in and look or not, I heard a plinking noise which sounded very like a water glass falling onto the wooden floor. I decided there really must be something wrong, and I rushed over to the door, calling out: "Uncle Xiao!" There was no reply. My heart in my mouth, I forgot my other concerns and pushed open the door. The moment I did so, my spirits sank. Heavens! There was Uncle Xiao, his eyes shut, fallen to the floor. One hand was clutched to his head, his face was deathly white, his face was covered in sweat, and there was blood on his forehead. A heart attack! I made the diagnosis almost instantaneously, and hurried over to him. Using my first-aid training, I started to try to revive him. I laid him out flat, then, first, I took out of my pocket a glyceryl trinitrate tablet I carried against just such an eventuality, broke it into pieces and put it under his tongue. I took a pillow from his bed and put it under his feet, then turned on the portable oxygen bottle we had in the apartment to help him breathe. Finally, I put three hundred milligrams of aspirin in his mouth, then telephoned 120 for an ambulance. Thank heavens, by the time the ambulance arrived, Uncle Xiao had already slowly opened his eyes, the colour had returned to his face, and the pain had passed. The ambulance men and I escorted him to hospital, and after the cardiologist had given him a thorough examination, he told me that Uncle Xiao had had a serious heart attack and it was fortunate that I had used my specialist first-aid knowledge to give him prompt and expert attention; otherwise, he might not still be alive now. Even so, I remained fearful for him.

The hospital wanted to perform bypass surgery. I asked the now fully conscious Uncle Xiao whether he agreed or not. Thoroughly scared by the experience, he reeled in his habitual stubbornness, and immediately nodded in agreement: "Very well, I'll do as they suggest." At this, I immediately made a suggestion: "Should I tell Older Sister Xinxin what has happened so she can get home as soon as possible? It wouldn't do for her not to be here when you have an operation like that." My main concern was that it would be awful if I had to take responsibility if anything went wrong. Uncle Xiao didn't reply immediately but pressed the call button to summon the doctor. When he came, Uncle Xiao asked him how great the risks were with this kind of operation. The doctor said: "Heart bypasses are now routine cardiac surgery, and the risks are very small, although that is not to say there aren't any at all." Uncle Xiao waited until the doctor had gone before saying to me: "Since the risk is so low, it's not worth getting Xinxin to come rushing back. Quite apart from the expense, the main thing is they are not properly settled in America yet, and time is precious to them. The return trip would take Xinxin at least a month before she could get back and start settling in again. How about we do it this way: before the operation, I'll write out an affidavit making it clear that you are signing on behalf of my daughter, so if anything should happen, it won't be your responsibility." Seeing how his mind was made up, I couldn't see any point in persevering. But on the morning of the operation, I still thought I should telephone Older Sister; after all, it was her father having heart surgery, and if, by some chance, anything did happen, she might never see him again. I had punched in the first few digits when I stopped. I thought to myself: The operation is just about to start, and if I tell her about it now, it will only intensify her worry, and what purpose would that serve? I'll just have to risk it!

After Uncle Xiao had gone into theatre, my heart was in my mouth. If, by some chance, something was to happen, although it wouldn't be my responsibility, there was no doubt Older Sister would be angry with me for not calling her. Heavens! I really should have called her! Thank the gods, the operation went smoothly. It seemed that Uncle Xiao's underlying health was really pretty good. After the operation, he stayed in hospital for a short time, and he

returned to the same state of health he had been in before he had
been taken ill. After he left hospital, I really wanted to warn him
against going back to writing straight away, and tell him he should
take a break and then we'd see. But before I could even open my
mouth, he took matters into his own hands by picking up all his
notes and other material from where they were piled up on his
desk, and stowing them in a trunk. He said to me: "Look here, the
first thing I've got to do is start counteracting the effects of ageing;
otherwise, they're always going to be getting in the way and
stopping me finishing my books. As long as I can do something
about that and extend my life, then I can start talking about getting
the work done." I could tell from what he said that this incident
had put the fear of ageing and illness into him, and he was willing
now to admit that he was getting old. He began to put his health
first. After breakfast, he would wait for me to finish tidying up the
kitchen, then get me to go with him to the park for a walk and to do
his exercises. After his siesta, in the afternoon, he would go to the
park again, and join in with a group of old folk doing callisthenics.
He spent most of what was left of the day on the internet,
researching ways of counteracting the effects of ageing, and looking
for material about extending one's life expectancy. One evening, I
was cooking in the kitchen when he rushed in, calling out excitedly:
"Xiaoyang, it says on the internet that in the past there was a
Chinese man who lived to be two hundred and fifty-six years old!"
"What?" I laughed. "And you believe that?" He nodded his head
solemnly: "Of course I believe it! I've already looked it up in a book.
A man called Li Qingyun died in Kai County in Sichuan Province in
1933. He was born in the sixteenth year of the Emperor Kangxi in
the Qing dynasty; that's 1677. In 1777, when he was a hundred
years old, he was rewarded by the Qing government for his
achievements in the field of traditional Chinese medicine. In the
sixteenth year of the Republic, 1927, the Sichuan warlord, Yang
Sen, invited him to Wanxian to teach the ways of maintaining good
health. He was two hundred and fifty years old then. At the time,
the Sichuan Photographic Institute exhibited a photograph of him
wearing a long black gown. He lived another six years after that,

and died in 1933, at the age of two hundred and fifty-six." "Do you think the records could be wrong?" I asked with a laugh. "How could anyone have lived to that age, given the state of medical knowledge at the time?" "Perhaps he had some secret, not known to others, for preserving life. In 1492, in the hope of achieving eternal life, Pope Innocent believed that he could absorb a young man's youthfulness by swapping blood with him; he died after receiving three such transfusions. In 1868, when the American from Kentucky, Leonard Jones, ran for president, he announced that he had sought eternal life through prayer and fasting, and had found the secret of denying death. He died of pneumonia at the end of that same year. In 1956, at Cornell University, a famous gerontologist called Clive McCay conducted an experiment: he took a healthy young rat and an ailing older rat, and sewed their stomachs together so their blood supplies were interconnected. After a short while, the older rat began to show signs of rejuvenation, and the younger rat showed signs of age-related degeneration. These results occasioned a lot of interest, and it is a shame that McCay changed his field of study and didn't pursue them. In 2004, a researcher at the Harvard University Stem Cell Institute called Amy Wagers repeated Clive McCay's experiment and obtained the same results. Wagers then isolated the proteins in the older rat's blood to try and determine what it was that caused the rejuvenating effect. In the course of this work, she discovered that it was a protein called GDF-11 that appeared to be responsible. It was able to preserve the life of stem cells. With the advance of age, a person's GDF-11 levels drop quickly, the ability to protect stem cells weakens, and the speed with which damage is repaired slows down, thereby causing the body to age. However, even if the GDF-11 levels drop even further in extreme age, the stem cells are not destroyed; the GDF-11 causes them to enter a dormant state. Wagers' experiments showed that when the old rat received a transfusion of young blood containing a large amount of GDF-11, this reanimated the dormant stem cells, reviving and revitalising the body's vital systems, and causing a rejuvenating effect. If, one day, we can infuse an old person with young blood containing this protein, it could reanimate the dormant stem cells in the old person's body, gradually renewing all the organs and vital systems, and inducing rejuvenation." "Is that so?" I was amazed by his clear and logical exposition. "How can we not be convinced that this is the secret of extending human life expectancy?!" he concluded.

A few days later, he told me that he had been listening on a longevity website to a certain Master Fei Wen, who had the power to help people avoid calamities and extend their lives. This man came from the Dabie Mountains, and, at the age of seventeen, he had chanced to enter a mountain cave where he saw a huge black shadow, from which he received the mysterious ability to help people avoid calamities and extend their lives. Now, he had established a centre in the Beijing suburb of Shunyi where he concentrated on performing good works concerned with extending people's lives. So far, he had succeeded in helping more than two thousand people, and currently was being consulted by many heads of industry and stars of film and television, who hoped he would help them avoid calamities and extend their lives. Uncle Xiao said he had already put in an online application to meet the Master, and it had been approved, so he wanted to go out there as soon as possible. I was completely dumbfounded and asked: "Does he charge?" "Master Fei Wen says he is accumulating merit through good works and has no interest in money. It is for those he helps to decide whether they want to pay or not. If someone wants to give money, the amount is unimportant; if someone doesn't want to pay, that is fine, and he won't apply any pressure." "So, do you want to pay?" I asked Uncle Xiao.

"If he helps me as he says he can, then of course I'll pay. I've got ten thousand yuan to take with me, and I'll decide at the time, depending on what happens." Seeing how determined he was to see this Master Fei Wen, all I could do was put together the things we needed for the trip. Since his heart attack, whenever he set foot outdoors, he wanted me with him, and this time was no exception.

One fine bright morning, we took a taxi to Master Fei Wen's Longevity Centre in Shunyi. The driver took us to the address Uncle Xiao had got from the internet, and the journey took two hours.

The place turned out to be a beautiful compound set in a patch of woodland; it had a main building and two subsidiary ones, all Western-style two-storey lodges, with a huge flowerbed and fountain in the middle. I hadn't expected there to be so many people coming to consult Master Fei Wen; there were at least twenty of them in the waiting room on the ground floor of the left-hand side-building. Uncle Xiao went up to the female receptionist and gave her his appointment number. She politely told us to sit on a sofa at one side of the room to wait. The waiting room was very well provided, with tea, soft drinks, snacks and fruit, which people could help themselves to. I sat with Uncle Xiao waiting for him to be called, and after a while I began to take notice of the large framed colour photographs that filled the walls. They all showed the chubby figure of the fifty-something-year-old Master Fei Wen with people he had helped avoid calamities and extend their lives. Among them, I recognised a very important government official, the chairman of a very well-known real estate development company and the celebrity female lead in a television soap opera. This cheered me up, as I thought to myself that if important government figures, captains of industry and soap stars came here, then Uncle Xiao was surely right to do so too.

Our turn did not come up in the course of the morning, and at midday the receptionist told everyone still waiting to go over to the buffet on the first floor of the right-hand side-building. The buffet was very lavish with lots of vegetarian and meat side dishes, five or six main dishes, and three or four soups; the tableware was top quality, and all the bowls, plates, glasses and cups had gold edging. Everything else was excellent too: real wood dining tables, brilliant white tablecloths, snowy napkins and fresh flowers in little vases. The fact that they provided such excellent food for the people waiting, even though they were complete strangers, gave me even more confidence in Master Fei Wen. It was three o'clock in the afternoon by the time a very polite young lady came and called out Uncle Xiao's name. She led us to a large room on the upper floor of the main building. There were thick net curtains drawn across the windows, making it a little dark, but we could see that there, sitting

at a rosewood desk in the middle of the room, was the man I
recognised from the photographs as Master Fei Wen. Our guide told
me to sit down on a bench beside the door, and Master Fei Wen
indicated that Uncle Xiao should sit down on a round stool in front
of his desk. There was a click as he turned on a switch on the desk
in front of him, and six spotlights came on, suddenly illuminating
Uncle Xiao where he sat, from all sides. They were all focused on
Uncle Xiao, so he was enveloped in a pool of light. At the same
time, black window blinds descended with a *whoosh*, plunging the
room into darkness. In the whole room, Uncle Xiao was the only
thing to be seen. The bright lights and the darkness alarmed Uncle
Xiao, and they startled me too. I had been to many hospitals and
clinics when I was training, but I'd never seen a consulting room
like this. The room was completely quiet for maybe ten minutes,
with only the slight buzz of an electric current. Master Fei was
apparently conducting a careful visual examination of Uncle Xiao,
while also using some kind of apparatus to examine his body. Just
as I was wondering how long the silence could last, Master Fei's
voice suddenly came out of the darkness: "Mr Xiao Chengshan,
have you quite recently suffered a potentially fatal incident?" Uncle
Xiao was already looking startled, and he was even more astonished
when he heard this; he looked towards me where I sat, as though he
wanted to share his amazement with me. On the way there, I had
asked Uncle Xiao, and I knew that he hadn't given Master Fei any
other information about himself apart from his name and his age.
So how did he know that Uncle Xiao had experienced a sudden
onset of heart disease? Had he found it out from his visual
inspection and the other mystery examination? Uncle Xiao replied:
"Yes, I had a heart attack." "Do you think you are out of danger
now?" Master Fei asked. "I haven't been feeling unwell recently,"
Uncle Xiao replied. "Well, let me tell you the results of my
examination just now," Master Fei said. He flicked the switch on his
desk with another *click*, and the spotlights trained on Uncle Xiao
went out. At the same time, the black window blinds suddenly
rolled upwards, and the room returned to the state it was in when
we entered. "There is still a black poisonous snake coiled around

your body, and it may well bite you again within the next three months, and this time it will put you in your grave." "What?!" Uncle Xiao leapt to his feet in fear. "Is that true?" Shocked by this diagnosis, I jumped up too. Master Fei motioned to Uncle Xiao to sit down, then stood up himself and came round the desk, so he was standing beside him. He said: "Before you say whether you believe me or not, I am going to wrest that snake from your body so you can see it with your own eyes." Uncle Xiao and I glanced at each other, exchanging a dumbstruck look: how was it possible to pull a snake out of someone's body?

Master Fei walked around Uncle Xiao several times, looking closely at him. He picked up his pace, then suddenly we saw him reach into Uncle Xiao's breast and there in his hand was a black snake, wriggling and rearing its head. Neither Uncle Xiao nor I could suppress a cry of surprise and alarm. "Do you see it?" Master Fei held the snake out towards Uncle Xiao, who recoiled in alarm. Master Fei continued: "Now I'm going to send the snake away, which is the same as taking away the threat to your health. You will live at least another twenty-eight years. You are now seventy-five, so another twenty-eight years will take you to one hundred and three. This is what I can do for you at present. Although it is not extending your life very long, it is the full extent of my powers, so do you agree or not?" Uncle Xiao immediately nodded his head eagerly: "I agree, I agree!" On hearing this, Master Fei slowly walked to the rear window, opened it, and muttered the incantation: "Begone! I give you your life, and you must give him his. Let there be no grievances from past generations, and no revenge in future ones. If you give him twenty-eight years, you can ascend to the heavens, and my heart will be at peace..." As he spoke, he released his grip, and the snake immediately crawled over the windowsill. Uncle Xiao and I were both rooted to the spot in amazement. We were speechless for a moment, just staring at the window. Then Master Fei gestured to us, and said, in a low voice: "Go now, Mr Xiao. That poisonous black snake was the symbol of the illness that afflicted you, and all I did was make it temporarily take shape to you. The process of avoiding calamity and extending your life is now complete, and I trust you will now live peacefully past a hundred." At this, I hurried forward and took Uncle Xiao by the arm, as he asked excitedly: "Excuse me, Master Fei, but where should I go to pay?" "There is no need, but if you truly wish to pay, then tell Ms Lu to take you there." He nodded towards the young lady who had brought us there. She indicated for us to follow her, and led us to a door on the first floor labelled *Donations*. "This is the Donations Office." Uncle Xiao and I went inside, where we saw a middle-aged man pushing a box towards us. On the box was written: *Donations – Minimum amount 10,000 yuan*. The man said: "Put the money in here and leave!" I looked at Uncle Xiao in surprise, and whispered, drawing his attention to the notice: "Heavens! Minimum amount ten thousand yuan!" He just laughed and said: "If it's ten thousand it's ten thousand! It's worth it to live another twenty-eight years!" And with that, he stuffed the ten thousand yuan he had brought with him into the box.

Uncle Xiao was in high spirits when we got home that day, and he told me happily: "It's very hard to believe things like this happen unless you witness them yourself. I've just spent ten thousand yuan to add twenty-eight years to my life; for me to chance on such a wonderful thing as that really is a miracle. With those twenty-eight years, at the same time as writing my legal volumes, I can search across a much wider area for other ways of extending human life, so I can live even longer. What it comes down to is that a man's life expectancy is simply how long his physical body can remain on this Earth. Extending the limit of your life simply means extending the survival of your physical body. There are bound to be other ways of extending life apart from Master Fei's, so the most important thing is for us to go and search them out..." I was happy for Uncle Xiao too. If I hadn't seen what happened with my own eyes, I would never have believed it.

One day not long after all this happened, a text from an unfamiliar number appeared on Uncle Xiao's cell phone. It read: *Dear Mr Xiao*

Chengshan, we know that you are already advanced in years, and because of our earnest desire to be of service to the aged, we would like seriously to recommend to you a set of exercises to prolong your life. If you master these exercises, you will live to a hundred years of age. If you wish to learn these exercises, please get in touch with us. Uncle Xiao showed me the text and asked dubiously: "Who do you think sent me this? It's very odd that they know my name and how old I am!" I replied: "In this day and age, it's easy to find out someone's name, age and telephone number. If you don't recognise the number it has come from, just ignore it." But Uncle Xiao was worried that his number might have been given out by some well-intentioned individual or friend, and it would be rude to ignore the text, so he dialled the number. He immediately discovered that it was a well-known company called Tiancheng that provided health services for the elderly and was offering home visits to teach a set of patting exercises that promised to extend the participant's life. They claimed the exercises had undergone scientific tests that showed that if an old person followed the programme every day for a year, they could live an extra four months. The cost of a home visit from a trainer, including both time and tuition, was five hundred yuan. Uncle Xiao was delighted by this: "Only five hundred yuan to learn a set of exercises that can extend your life! That's good value!" He gave them his address, and the company arranged for one of their representatives to come round the next morning to teach the exercises.

At the time, I thought to myself: Well, it's not that much money, and if Uncle Xiao wants to learn the exercises, let them come. Even if the results aren't everything they claim, it's no big deal. At nine o'clock the next morning, as agreed, there was a knock at the door. I opened it and saw that the newcomer was a woman in her forties, looking very neat and efficient and holding a laptop. She said her name was Pang Ren'ai and she was the representative of the Tiancheng Company who had come to teach the life-extending patting exercises. On hearing this, Uncle Xiao came hurrying over eagerly, saying: "Welcome! Welcome!" First, the woman plugged in her laptop and started playing some relaxing music. Over the music, she said: "Dear Mr Xiao, let me first tell you the story of the famous patting exercise programme: this programme was invented by a certain lady called Kuang Xiuhua. In 1902, Ms Kuang was born into the household of a wealthy merchant in Handan City. In the autumn of the year she was twelve, which was 1914, her parents took her two younger brothers on a business trip to Tianjin, and she was left behind at home with her grandmother. One day, as they were having lunch, her grandmother's chopsticks suddenly fell from her hand, and the grandmother herself slowly slid to the floor from her chair. One corner of her mouth drooped downward. This terrified Kuang Xiuhua: what was wrong with her grandmother? At that time, there was no 120 emergency telephone number, nor any ambulances. The handful of household servants all stood around in front of the grandmother, waiting for the twelve-year-old Kuang Xiuhua to come up with a plan; at that moment, the young girl realised that it was up to her alone to save her grandmother. But all she had ever been taught were drawing and painting and other feminine skills, and she had no knowledge of medicine or first aid. In the midst of her panic, she remembered how, if she felt ill or uncomfortable, her grandmother would always pat her with her hand. She patted herself now, and began to feel better, so then she began to pat her grandmother with both hands. Her grandmother was lying on the floor, so she used the palms of her hands to pat her arms. As she patted, she heard her grandmother start breathing, and saw her eyes slowly open. At this, she increased the force and speed of her patting, and her grandmother's drooping mouth began to straighten out. Delighted, she went on to pat her shoulders, chest, waist, legs, feet and hands. As she patted her grandmother's whole body, over and over, the old lady, at last, slowly sat back up from the floor and gradually returned to the state she was in before she was taken ill. Kuang Xiuhua was overjoyed and burst into tears, hugging her grandmother and saying: 'Thank the gods for protecting you!' A doctor who was summoned later told Kuang Xiuhua's grandmother: 'You had a major stroke. If your granddaughter hadn't continuously patted your arms, you might have been confined to your bed, never to rise from it again. Your granddaughter has saved you!'

That was how Kuang Xiuhua discovered the method and importance of patting the body. From then on, she decided thoroughly to understand the therapeutic action of patting the body; she undertook extensive reading of traditional Chinese medicinal texts and sought instruction from traditional doctors across the country. Later, she successfully took the examinations to enter the National Yanjing University of Medicine. Gradually, she began to work things out for herself and ended up by formulating this system of life-extending patting exercises. This set of exercises consists of sixteen types of patting. The first type is called patting both ears, in which you use the palms of your hands to pat both ears; the second is called patting the forehead, in which you gently pat the forehead, alternating left and right hands; the third is call patting both cheeks, in which you pat both cheeks lightly using left and right hands simultaneously; the fourth is called patting both shoulders, in which you pat left and right shoulders alternately like this; the fifth is called patting the upper arms, in which you first use the left hand to pat your right upper arm, then use your right hand to pat your left upper arm; the sixth is called patting the lower arms, in which you first use your left hand to pat your right lower arm, then use your right hand to pat your left upper arm; the seventh is called patting the ribs, in which you first use your left hand to pat the ribs on your right-hand side, then use your right hand to pat the ribs on your left-hand side; the eighth is called patting the lower abdomen, in which you use both hands lightly to pat the lower abdomen in a circular motion; the ninth is called patting the back, in which you first reach back with your left hand to pat your back and then reach back with your right hand also to pat your back; the tenth is called patting the buttocks, in which you reach back with both hands simultaneously and pat your buttocks; the eleventh is called patting the thighs, in which you bend at the waist and use both hands to pat alternately all around both thighs; the twelfth is called patting the lower leg, in which you bend right down and alternately pat all round both your lower legs; the thirteenth is called patting the instep, in which you sit on a low stool and, using both hands, simultaneously pat both insteps; the fourteenth is called patting the soles of the feet, in which you take off your socks, sit on a stool and first rest your right foot on your left knee and use your left hand firmly to pat the sole of your right foot, then rest your left foot on your right knee and use your right hand firmly to pat the sole of your left foot; the fifteenth is called patting the backs of your hands, in which first you pat the back of your right hand with your left, and then you pat the back of your left had with your right; the sixteenth is called patting your palms, in which you pat the palms of your hands together, and the louder you clap, the better. With this sixteenth move, no matter where you are, you must do it at least thirty times, and it is best if you clap until your palms grow hot. And now we will ask the venerable Ms Kuang Xiuhua herself to give you a demonstration."

At this point, Ms Pang tapped the keyboard of her laptop, and an old lady appeared on the screen, performing the tapping exercise routine. Ms Pang said: "Look at this, Mr Xiao! This is the one-hundred-and-six-year-old Kuang Xiuhua: see how smooth, self-possessed and confident her patting is. Look how energetic, assured and precise her movements are. This venerable lady leads a normal daily life, eats ordinary home-cooked food, uses ordinary household equipment; she doesn't take any health supplements but relies on performing the patting exercises on a daily basis. At the age of more than a hundred, she is still robust and healthy, her mental faculties are still sharp, as is her eyesight; her teeth are strong, her hair is only half grey, and all this is proof of the power and efficacy of the patting exercise routine." It has to be said that the old lady on the screen did look exceptionally healthy. Ms Pang continued: "Mr Xiao, I would also like to inform you of an extraordinary and inspiring event that took place in Xi'an in Shaanxi Province, where an eighty-year-old lady performed the patting exercise routine, and, as she finished the sixteenth move, her body suddenly levitated half a metre from the ground, and she was surrounded by a white mist. Onlookers saw her slowly rotate in this mist, and after the mist dispersed and she returned to the ground, they were amazed to discover that her previously shrivelled and shrunken breasts had become full and plump again, just like a twenty-year-old girl's. The crowd was astonished, and the lady herself was quite startled. Two of her friends who were there thought she must have fallen victim to some sudden strange illness, and they rushed forward to loosen her collar. What they discovered was even more surprising: the old lady's two breasts were now high, firm and white. When she was asked if she had felt anything, she said there had been no uncomfortable sensation at all. This incident caused a sensation in her neighbourhood. As someone who came along afterwards to study the phenomenon explained: there exists, in our universe, including, of course, this world we inhabit, a kind of mysterious force. In the course of their observations, scientists have discovered that the universe has not only not stopped expanding, the expansion is actually accelerating. This means that new energy is continuously being added; otherwise, that expansion couldn't happen. But what is this energy? Scientists are not sure yet, so they have called it dark energy. Normally, we cannot feel this dark energy, but perhaps that old lady in Xi'an, in patting different parts of her body and different acupuncture points, unconsciously triggered some kind of connection with the dark energy that surrounds us humans, which caused the miraculous effect on her two breasts. At the moment, we cannot prove whether this explanation is true or not, but this whole affair does tell us that, as well as the observable physical effects of our system of patting exercises, it may very possibly also have other inexplicable benefits."

Uncle Xiao was beaming with delight at Ms Pang's presentation, and she proceeded to take him, hands-on, through the exercises. I stood beside them, following the instructions too, and thought to myself that if I could study this programme now for free, when I went home, I could teach it to my mum and dad.

That morning, amidst the relaxing music, Uncle Xiao and I practised the exercises until almost eleven o'clock. I have to say, they were very easy to learn, and both of us had mastered them within two hours. As agreed in advance, Uncle Xiao paid five hundred yuan to Ms Pang. As she was leaving, Ms Pang said: "Providing instruction in these exercises is the main business of the

Tiancheng Company, but they also consider themselves to be doing good works, for would it not indeed be an act of charity to enable every old person to live beyond a hundred? If you have any friends who would like to learn the exercises too, please give them my telephone number so they can get in contact." Uncle Xiao nodded eagerly in agreement: "Surely, surely!" The result was that, after three days, he had introduced Ms Pang to three other judges who were his contemporaries, and she had arranged to go and teach them too. Even I introduced a couple of elderly acquaintances from Longevity Park to her, and they became her students.

Uncle Xiao was unusually excited after learning the patting exercises, and he told me: "If I persist in doing these exercises daily for thirty years, then I can extend my life by one hundred and twenty months, which is ten years. If you add that to the extra twenty-eight years Master Fei gave me, that makes thirty-eight years in total. I'm seventy-five now, so, if you add thirty-eight years to that, it takes me to one hundred and thirteen. In that time I can write 2.8 million characters of my legal texts, which means establishing myself as an academic lawyer will be no problem at all. I'm so happy! And at the same time, in those thirty-eight years, I can search out more ways of extending my life…" From then on, as well as doing his daily exercises, he did indeed start thinking about going off in search of other ways of prolonging his life. To this end, he often went to the Beijing Book Building to buy books: new publications about cytology, molecular biology, DNA analysis, gene technology, neurology and so on. I didn't understand a single one of them, and I just went with him to help carry them back. If he did have a spare moment, he went online looking for new material on extending life and immortality. The websites he visited most often were concerned with life science, biology, artificial intelligence and medicine, fervently hoping that he could hunt down on the web even more material on life expectancy and prolonging life. Some evenings when he sat down at the computer, he stayed there for several hours.

⏳

When Older Sister Xinxin rang from America, I told her all about his visit to Master Fei and his study of the patting exercises, including the recent changes in him. After I had finished, she gave a few exclamations of surprise and said: "He's an old man now, so let him follow his inclinations and do what he wants, just so long as it makes him happy." She told me that, over in America, she had seen some stuff about prolonging one's life on the television and on the internet but had never checked it out to see if any of it was real or fake. Even though it was an overseas call, I could hear that her voice sounded a bit harsh and dry, not mellow and rich as it used to be. Of course, at that time I did not know about the serious changes that had happened in Older Sister's life. When she first got to America, everything was fine. She would usually phone home once a week, and the calls were full of her tinkling laughter. When she was talking to her father, she was sure to enquire in detail how he was eating, how he was sleeping, what he was doing for relaxation, how his bowels and waterworks were functioning, how his overall health was, how his mental health was, how things were going with Aunty Ji and so on and so on. After she had finished talking to him, she would always want a few words with me, asking about his blood pressure, heart rate, blood cholesterol and blood sugar, checking that he was taking his medications and whether there were any changes in his weight and so on. Then she would ask me how things were going with my boyfriend, Lü Yiwei, check that my salary had reached my account OK, and ask if I had anything I needed to say. She really was meticulous and considerate in every possible way.

Of course, at that time, the questions Uncle Xiao and I had most difficulty answering were those about Aunty Ji. This was not something we could keep covered up for very long. Several times, Older Sister asked to talk to Aunty Ji, and Uncle Xiao and I were hard put to it to keep coming up with reasons she could not come to the phone. Finally, there came a time when Uncle Xiao said: "There's something I've got to tell you, Xin'er: Aunty Ji and I found that we aren't suited to living together, and we've already split up. You mustn't worry about this, and you mustn't try to contact Aunty

Ji; I'm just not suited to remarrying. I've got Xiaoyang as my carer, and we're getting by very well. You just concentrate on making sure you and Chang Sheng make a success of your time in America..." When she heard this, Older Sister fell silent for a while, then said with a sigh: "Very well, you just do things however you want to do them." Later, she spoke to me in solemn tones: "Well, Xiaoyang, it seems that the whole burden has fallen on you. I hope I have not been mistaken about you. For the time being, you must be like a daughter to me, and if you keep a careful eye on my father for me, I will be sure to repay your efforts. From now on, I'm putting your salary up to five thousand five hundred yuan, and that's the amount you'll find in your account every month." I hurried to make it clear where I stood: "You needn't worry, Older Sister, I'll perform my duties as a nurse and carer to the very best of my ability, and make sure Uncle Xiao keeps safe and happy. There's no need for you to raise my salary like that, it just puts an extra burden on you..." But Older Sister was a woman of her word, and from then on, my monthly salary went up to five thousand five hundred yuan. I immediately used the extra salary to help my boyfriend, Lü Yiwei, with food, school fees and spending money. He was taking his postgraduate exams at the time, and I needed to make sure he was well fed and watered for his studies!

Not long after this, the frequency of Older Sister's telephone calls increased to roughly twice a week. She was clearly worried about her father. Uncle Xiao would urge her: "You must economise on your phone bill; these are long-distance calls after all. I'm not really that old, and my health is fine. Besides, I've got Xiaoyang to look after me, so there's really no need for you to worry." I don't know whether Older Sister listened to Uncle Xiao's urgings, or whether it was because her English studies were becoming more pressing, but after that, her phone calls gradually decreased again. It must have been about a year after she left for America that her calls became quite rare: sometimes three weeks could go by without us hearing from her. At the time, Uncle Xiao was thoroughly immersed in his researches into extending life, and he didn't really pay any attention to the falling off of Older Sister's calls. If he didn't worry about it, I worried even less. Just so long as I kept receiving my salary on time, and I continued to perform my duties conscientiously, I didn't give it another thought. As it was, Lü Yiwei's postgraduate studies were going very well, and he had formally promised that as soon as he passed his exams, he was first going to marry me, and then go on to do his doctorate. The thought that one day I was going to be the wife of a doctor of science meant that I spent every day bathed in a rosy glow of happiness.

On the second New Year's Eve I had been with the family, I got a text from Older Sister that read: *Hello Xiaoyang. I'm very sorry that I haven't been able to come home for New Year. The reasons are all rather complicated, and I'll explain properly next time we meet. I really hope that you will be able to stay in Beijing over the New Year period to look after my father and make sure he is not left on his own over the holiday, in case something happens to him. And because of this, I am going to give you a two-thousand-yuan holiday bonus. I know that the money can't make up for you not being able to go home for the New Year, and I can only ask for your forgiveness. I look forward to your reply.* To be honest, I was not at all happy about this text. She had said ten days before New Year that she was going to come back to spend the holiday with her father, and that I could go home to see my mother, father, little sisters, little brother and grandmother. I really cared about having my New Year holiday because, after all, what more important festival is there? I had already found time, over the last few days, to go out and buy presents to take home to give to my friends and family, and I had already reserved the train tickets to go back together with Lü Yiwei. So what was I supposed to do now? Could I refuse and leave Uncle Xiao all alone in Beijing over the holiday? It's hard on old people psychologically to find themselves in second place, and what would I do if he got taken ill? But if I agreed, I would feel really bad about dashing the hopes of all my family just because she was buying me off with those two thousand yuan. I hesitated for a long time, before finally forcing myself to send a one word reply: *Fine!* I rather thought she would be able to read into that single word, my unhappiness and unwillingness. And she did indeed reply very quickly: *I'm so grateful to you, and I'll send another thank you present in a while.* I didn't reply again, as I was very unhappy about the way she was using money and gifts to buy off my opportunity to see my friends and family.

Only after she had received my agreement did Older Sister call Uncle Xiao to tell him she wasn't coming home for the holiday, and it was me who would be celebrating it with him. When the call was over, Uncle Xiao urged me to go and confirm my train tickets home, saying: "You just concentrate on going home to be with your family over New Year. Supermarket dumplings are more than good enough, and I'll just go and buy some to cook and see in the New Year with." I wasn't happy about it, but I had to think up a good excuse for not being able to go home for the holiday; otherwise, Uncle Xiao would be upset. So I said my boyfriend, Lü Yiwei, couldn't go home and wanted me to keep him company. Uncle Xiao nodded in acknowledgement and said: "Very well, very well." Later, I urged Lü Yiwei not to go home himself, but to send all the New Year presents the two of us had bought, back home by KuaiDi express courier. He wasn't very happy about this, but in the end he was no match for my determination. And I did hint that he could come and see me any time he liked over New Year.

On New Year's Eve morning, Uncle Xiao said: "Give your Yiwei a call, and tell him to come over and spend New Year's Eve with us." I didn't stand on ceremony, and called Yiwei immediately, urging him to buy some flowers for Uncle Xiao on his way over. I was cooking in the kitchen when he arrived, so it was Uncle Xiao who opened the door to him. Yiwei thrust a bunch of flowers into his hand, which delighted the old man, and I heard him say, with a laugh: "Ha! Yiwei, you know your etiquette: you've really done your research! Thank you!" Uncle Xiao didn't normally smile very much, and he laughed even less, so I could tell he was genuinely happy. The New Year's Eve dinner was very jolly. I had told Yiwei in advance why we couldn't drink alcohol, so the two of us toasted Uncle Xiao with sweetened yoghurt. I knew how seriously Uncle Xiao took extending his life, so the first toast was: "Here's to new changes in the New Year for Uncle Xiao!" And to myself, I added: And to no more wrinkles on his intellectual forehead! The second toast was: "Here's to the nanorobots that may soon enter Uncle Xiao's bloodstream to clear out the rubbish, repair his DNA, and begin his journey back to youth!" The third toast was: "May we celebrate New Year's Eve with Uncle Xiao in two hundred years' time!" Uncle Xiao's face was completely relaxed by the time these three toasts were over. After dinner, he sighed and said: "I never expected you two to make me so happy. All my daughter and son-in-law have brought me is worry and regret..."

That New Year's Eve night, Uncle Xiao made an exception and allowed Lü Yiwei to stay the night in Older Sister and Older Brother's old bedroom. Around midnight, he stole quietly into my room, and, although I strictly forbade him from making any kind of noise, there was no way he was going to remember that when he was in the throes of pleasure, and the wretched bed squeaked and rattled endlessly, so if it wasn't one noise it was another. I was sure there was no way Uncle Xiao could not have heard us, so when I got up on New Year's Day morning, I couldn't look him in the eye.

One day, after Spring Festival was over, Uncle Xiao happily thrust a tabloid newspaper at me to read. There was an article in it that said that the world's most widely used anti-diabetes medication, Metformin, had anti-ageing and life-extending properties. It is a drug that promotes the cellular release of oxygen molecules, and thus increases cellular strength and longevity, with a resultant alleviation of the effects of ageing and an increase in life expectancy for the individual as a whole. In 2014, research at the University of Cardiff in the United Kingdom showed that diabetes sufferers who injected Metformin had a longer life expectancy than non-diabetes sufferers. At present, the US Food and Drug Administration has approved further experiments into this, and scientists are already recruiting volunteers to participate in these...

When I had finished reading the article, Uncle Xiao said to me: "I'm taking Metformin every day, aren't I, Xiaoyang? Why don't you double my daily dose!" I was taken aback and replied: "I'm just a nurse; I can only increase medications with a doctor's approval, and it's even less permissible for you to do it yourself. All drugs are effectively poisons, and what would I do if, by some chance, increasing the dose damaged your liver and kidneys? That article doesn't say for sure that Metformin has anti-ageing and life-extending effects; it says that further experiments are being undertaken and that they are recruiting volunteers, so hadn't you better be a little more cautious?" Uncle Xiao wasn't very happy with this and said: "You're young and too conservative in your attitude; if I'm not scared, why should you be? Didn't you see what it said about the results of the experiments at that British university?" I was still very uncomfortable and just said: "Well, let's make a visit to the hospital and see your usual doctor to hear what he has to say." Uncle Xiao reluctantly agreed, so we set off for the hospital. When the rather surprised doctor had heard Uncle Xiao out, he replied brusquely: "No, you can't increase it. You're already on a pretty high dose, and if you add to it, it will be your responsibility if anything happens…"

One day, not long after this, Uncle Xiao called out happily again for me to come and look at an announcement about a set of life-prolonging *qigong* exercises on the internet. It said: *Tortoise Age Gong is a form of life-extending qigong newly compiled by Master Pan Xun, after ten years of dedicated study drawing on the longevity of the tortoise. It is a simple form, easy to learn, and one year of consistent practice can prolong your life by six months. The training venue is beside the North Palace Gate of the Yiheyuan.* Clapping his hands together, Uncle Xiao said delightedly: "Master Fei gave me an extra twenty-eight years, and the patting exercises give me another four months for every year I do them, so if I study Tortoise Age Gong as well, I can add a whole lot more years too, can't I!" Personally, I felt that things announced on the internet weren't that trustworthy, but seeing how excited he was, I couldn't bring myself to object, so I called the telephone number in the announcement to enquire about the fees. These turned out to be 9998 yuan with instruction held every morning, payment in advance. "If it's 9998 yuan, it's 9998 yuan; it's worth it if it gives me several more years of life." Then he told me to have food ready a bit earlier the next morning, and we would take a taxi over there after breakfast.

So that is what we did the next morning, and when we arrived at the North Palace Gate of the Yiheyuan, in the distance we did indeed see a tree with a notice on it reading: *Tortoise Age Gong Instruction Venue.* As we got closer, we could only see a middle-aged man and a young lad sitting there. I asked: "Is this the venue for the Tortoise Age Gong instruction?" "That's right," the lad replied, standing up. "Are you here to take part? You have to pay the fees in full first, then you can join in." I was a little worried by this, so I went on: "Why can't I see any other students here?" The lad nodded in acknowledgement of the question: "We operate a system of train as you come: once you've finished, you go, so there's no hanging around waiting for the students. Longevity is something you have to fight for every minute and every second; if we delay things for an hour, who is to say what illness might not strike our students? We've already trained four students this morning." Uncle Xiao and I exchanged glances, feeling there might be something in what he said, and I continued: "Who is leading the training?" The lad pointed to the middle-aged man, who was sitting under the tree, his eyes tight shut, and replied: "Master Pan himself leads it." On hearing this, Uncle Xiao hurried over to Master Pan and asked: "What is your training method?" But the man didn't reply, and he continued to sit there with his eyes shut. Instead, the young lad replied: "First pay the fees, and then, of course, we will tell you the training method." Uncle Xiao gestured to me to hand over the 9998 yuan he had given me in advance, to the young lad. When he had counted it, the lad indicated that Uncle Xiao should sit on a round stool opposite the middle-aged man, and then he set up a kind of screen made out of plastic sheeting around the two of them. The sheeting was covered in pictures of tortoises. Not knowing what form the training would take, I was worried that Uncle Xiao might come to some harm, so I told the young lad: "I need to go behind the screen too. My uncle has a heart condition, and I need to make sure nothing unexpected happens." The lad didn't reply for a moment, then nodded his head, saying: "All right, but you can only look and listen; you mustn't make a sound, or you'll interfere with the training!"

Once I had permission, I went behind the screen and saw that the middle-aged man had finally opened his eyes, and was saying to Uncle Xiao: "As your trainer, I am first going to introduce myself. I am Pan Xun; I was born on the shores of Lake Dongting, and I am now ninety-five years old. From childhood, I followed my father in catching fish, turtles, shrimp and crabs for a living, from a small island on Lake Dongting, and I often crossed paths with tortoises." Uncle Xiao and I were both astonished to hear his age, and Uncle Xiao asked, in amazement: "Are you really ninety-five?" Master Pan didn't reply directly, but just handed Uncle Xiao his ID card and said: "You can see for yourself!" I couldn't restrain my own curiosity, and bent forward to look. Wow! The date of birth on the ID card did indeed prove he was ninety-five. Great heavens! How could a ninety-five-year-old look that young?! "Are you thinking I don't look any more than forty-five? Are you feeling there is something really strange about how I can have such a youthful attitude and appearance? Well, let me tell you, it is all because of my long practice of Tortoise Age Gong. If you want to rejuvenate yourself and extend your life then coming to learn Tortoise Age Gong with me is your best choice. I have often crossed paths with tortoises, and I have made a careful study of them. Although it is a reptile, the tortoise displays remarkable characteristics absent in other reptiles. It has a thick, hard shell that can protect its internal organs, head, tail and four limbs when it encounters a predator, depriving that predator of any opportunity without having to expend any effort itself. This drastically reduces any possibility of it being harmed, so naturally its life expectancy is extended. Even more importantly, its movements are very slow, not to say lazy. Since its daily exercise is very limited, its energy consumption is extremely low and its metabolism correspondingly very slow. It also loves to sleep, both hibernating and aestivating, and can sleep for more than fifteen hours a day, spending ten months of the year asleep. It avoids the extreme cold of the winter by hibernating, and the searing heat of the summer by aestivating; it can go for several months without eating or drinking, being able to endure both hunger and thirst. This is why it has no trouble living for several hundred years. I have developed this set of Tortoise Age Gong exercises based on my study of and researches into the tortoise. There are three fundamental methods that underpin the exercises, which are sitting, crawling and lying. The most important aims are slowness, quiet and stability. The external effects are to eat less, drink less, see less and hear less. At present, 5556 people have studied and continued to practise these exercises, and their average age is 88.996. So, here are the statistics regarding our students, and you can see for yourself how old they are. They are all still alive, and the oldest is one hundred and two." Uncle Xiao flicked through several pages before Master Pan took them back and said: "Now you can study the method with me. For the first exercise, you shut your eyes tight, cutting yourself off from the sights and people of the outside world, blinding yourself to everyone around you; for the second exercise, stuff two erasers in your ears, cutting yourself off from the sounds of the outside world, so you are deaf to the noises around you; for the third exercise, you sit in a chair, and keep completely still, slowing your breathing right down; for the fourth exercise, when you need to go to the toilet, go down on your hands and knees and crawl slowly to the bathroom. When you have done your business, crawl back to where you were originally sitting; for the fifth exercise, lie face-up on your bed, as though going to sleep. If you find yourself drifting off, then go to sleep. Make yourself stay lying on the bed for fifteen hours of the day, resisting hunger and thirst. You can have only one meal in the day, and one drink of water, and take no medicines at all, since when did you ever see a tortoise taking medicine..." Uncle Xiao was drinking all this in with great interest, but I was deeply suspicious.

When we got home, I asked Uncle Xiao: "Are you really going to practise Tortoise Age Gong?" He nodded: "Of course I am. I've already learned it, the exercises aren't difficult, and I've spent the money. Why wouldn't I practise it? Besides, there are so many people already doing it, and they've got an average age of 88.996. I'd be stupid not to do it, wouldn't I!?" I shot back: "Those are just the numbers Master Pan told you; no one else has verified them. From my own limited life experience and from what I learned in hospital, there are many shortcomings to this Tortoise Age Gong. Number one, if a person doesn't exercise, of course their metabolism slows down, but their limbs may also atrophy. Number two, if a person lies in bed for fifteen hours a day, they may develop ulcers. Number three, a person can endure hunger to an extent, but if their blood thickens from lack of fluid intake, that can cause thromboses." But Uncle Xiao just laughed and said: "People never believe in the new, but I didn't expect a youngster like you to be like that. We need to have faith: after all, a tortoise is an animal, and so, when you come down to it, is a man, so, since we are all animals, why shouldn't a man imitate a tortoise? This Tortoise Age Gong is a method for a man to do just that, and it is bound to be effective. Even if it is unlikely to let me live to eight hundred like a tortoise, it's quite possible it could give me an extra twenty or thirty years." Hearing him so determined, and remembering Older Sister's instruction to "do everything as he wants it", I didn't resist anymore and just let him get on with his Tortoise Age Gong.

The greatest benefit of Uncle Xiao's Tortoise Age Gong training was that it saved me money. Since I was only buying a very little food, I was able to put aside a lot of the money he gave me for that purpose, and, in addition, I had a lot more free time, so my main activity was making myself nice things to eat. But, after three days, I began to feel that Uncle Xiao's complexion was looking off, and, after five days, his blood pressure and blood sugar were both elevated, he was constipated, and, crucially, his heartbeat was irregular. I was very worried, and urged him to stop the regime he was following, but he just shook his head, saying: "There is a price to everything, and if a man wants to prolong his life, there's going to be a price for that too. My current condition must be that price, and once the adaptation period is over, I'm bound to get better..."

His physical condition was causing me a lot of concern, but there was nothing I could do if he wouldn't listen to me, so I had to call Older Sister in America and get her to try and persuade him. One evening when I phoned, the call went through, but there was no reply. I thought she might be asleep, but then I remembered that it was morning in America, so I kept trying. At the third attempt, the call was answered, and the voice at the other end was Older Sister's, but she didn't seem to know who I was. I told her my name three times, but she just kept asking: "Who's there?" I was astounded that she still didn't recognise me. Perhaps she was still half-asleep and dreaming. I was just about to tell her my name again, when I suddenly heard a thud from Uncle Xiao's room. I hurriedly cut the call and ran over to his door. Heavens! Uncle Xiao had fainted and was lying on the floor by his bed. I quickly felt for his pulse, and my heart leapt into my mouth in fear: I couldn't find a pulse. I immediately called 120. Once he was in the emergency room, they began to resuscitate him. In the end, there was nothing seriously wrong with him, but when the doctor learned that I was Uncle Xiao's carer, given the old man's physical condition, he suspected me of maltreating him and began to interrogate me: "This old man almost died because of this collapse; how did he get so malnourished? What kind of a nurse are you? Haven't you been feeding him properly? Does he live alone? Do his children know what kind of state he's in? You've been very negligent! If anything like this happens again, we will have to call the police!" I had no reply to this harsh reprimand.

Older Sister finally returned my call the next morning and asked whether it was me who had called. "It was!" I said. "How did you not recognise my voice?" She sighed and replied: "I'm really sorry, Xiaoyang, I'd taken a heavy dose of sleeping tablets, and I was lying in bed all dazed. All I knew was that the phone was ringing, but when I picked it up, I couldn't hear anything clearly, and I just ignored you!" This alarmed me, and I asked: "What's a young woman like you doing taking lots of sleeping tablets?" She sighed again: "I've had a few problems, Xiaoyang; give me a few days and I'll explain. But first, tell me why you phoned. Did you not get your salary, or is my dad not well?" I could tell from her voice that she was unhappy, and thought that, with her so far from home, it now wasn't the time to tell her what had happened with her father as it would only upset her and add to her worries. I just told her that it wasn't anything special; I'd just phoned because I was missing her. She gave a bitter little laugh and said: "I miss you too, and I miss my dad even more. Maybe I can find the time to come back and see you..."

After Uncle Xiao came home from hospital, it seemed he had taken the doctors' opinions to heart, and realised how close to being fatal this latest collapse had been, so he didn't mention the Tortoise Age Gong again. I was very attentive to his food and drink, and, within five or six days, his health had returned to normal. After this experience, he was on his guard against any more advertisements about prolonging life and that kind of thing, so when we now went for a stroll in the park, he avoided or dodged out of the way of all the hucksters trying to sell longevity exercises. Although Uncle Xiao didn't mention Tortoise Age Gong again, I hadn't forgotten the two men who had managed the training, and I reckoned they might still be luring other old folk into taking it up. One day, Uncle Xiao had invited an old court friend over, and the two of them were sitting chatting at home, so I took the opportunity to go over to the Western Hills Hospital to look up a friend from back home who was working there. As I was on the bus going past the North Palace Gate of the Yiheyuan, I saw that the placard advertising Tortoise Age Gong was indeed still there, and there were several old folk queuing up to hand over their money. I really wanted to get off the bus and go and stop them, but I was afraid they wouldn't believe me. Besides, those two men would surely have their answers ready to counter any criticism, so in the end, I stayed on the bus...

In the spring of the third year Older Sister was in America, she finally told me she was going to come home to see her father. Over all that time, I can truthfully say that I had been honest and diligent, and had fully discharged my duties as a carer. Of course, Older Sister had kept her word too, and made sure that my salary arrived in my account on the twenty-eighth of every month. The steady work and regular pay made my life in Beijing very easy, and they also meant that I could support my little brother and little sister in their studies back home; more importantly, I could also ensure that my boyfriend, Lü Yiwei, could get his postgraduate degree without having to worry about anything. At this time, he was well settled into his second year of graduate research. I can still remember the morning I received the text from Older Sister, and also what that text said: *Hi Xiaoyang! I'm coming back to Beijing to see you both, but don't tell my father for the moment. I want to surprise him. At midday on the twenty-third, tell him you are going to see your boyfriend, and take a taxi out to Terminal 3 at Capital Airport to meet me. My flight is CA2138 from New York, and it's due in at 13.25.* The reason I remember all this about the text is that, after I received it, my life underwent a major upheaval.

As I was standing at International Arrivals, the board was showing that Flight CA2138 had already landed. I watched the passengers coming out, searching for a sight of Older Sister and feeling rather excited. She was my employer, and meeting her like this was part of my job, so why was I feeling so excited? I thought about it for a moment and decided it was because she never talked down to me as a mere employee, but treated me more like her little sister, and put complete trust in me; moreover, she was never late with my wages and was a woman of her word. There was no sign of her, and at first I thought she was just behind the other passengers, but when pretty well all of them must have come out, I began to get a little worried and called her cell phone. When she answered, I asked her where she was, and she said: "I'm already out. I'm to the left of the Arrivals exit. One of the stewardesses helped me out." I was quite taken aback. I had been watching the Arrivals exit all this time, but somehow I had missed her. How stupid! I turned to look for her and did indeed see a stewardess standing to the left of Arrivals, but there was no sign of Older Sister! I went over to the stewardess and was about to ask her if she had helped a lady off the plane, when I suddenly became aware of someone tugging at my skirt. I looked down and saw a woman I didn't recognise, clearly an invalid, sitting on a luggage trolley. I was taken by surprise, and bent down to ask her: "Can I help you with something?" The woman smiled sadly and said: "Don't you recognise me, Xiaoyang?" I was flabbergasted: the voice was Older Sister's, but how could she have changed so much that I didn't recognise her? First of all, she was thin – so thin she had lost her figure – and apart from her head, it looked as though there was no flesh on her at all; her face was even more extraordinarily gaunt, and there was no sign at all of her former smooth, plump, charming beauty. Moreover, her hair was dry and brittle: it clearly hadn't been properly looked after for a very long time, and resembled a tangled bird's nest. Her body was stooped, with none of a young woman's vitality, and her formerly ample breasts were now totally deflated, and they hung down her chest like two frost-shrivelled aubergines. Looking like that, so I couldn't even recognise her face to face, it was hardly surprising I hadn't spotted her in the sea of people coming out of Arrivals.

As I stared at her dazedly, I was too shocked to speak for a long time. In the end, it was she who spoke first: "Help me stand up, Xiaoyang." I gave her my arm, and when she was up, she said to the stewardess: "Thank you for looking after me on the journey, and thank you especially for escorting me out here. Now my family is here to meet me, you can get back to your work; I know you must be very busy." Her face full of concern, the stewardess told me: "You should take her to hospital for a check-up as soon as possible. She only had a little bit to drink and no food at all on the whole flight, and she's very weak." I hurriedly told her not to worry, and bowed my thanks. As I supported Older Sister out of the terminal and into a taxi, she felt incredibly light, no heavier than a sheet of paper, and as she walked, her legs shook like feathers in the wind. Indeed, as I held tight to her stick-like arms, I was afraid she might be blown away. What illness had reduced a vital, healthy woman like her to this in just three years? She only had one wheelie suitcase with her, and she certainly couldn't have managed any more. But how could her husband Chang Sheng have let her travel home alone in this state? How could he not have been worried for her?

When we were in the taxi, and the driver asked us where to, I was about to give our home address when she nudged my arm and told him the address of the place she and Older Brother had moved out to. I was very surprised and asked her: "Why don't we go home first?" She shook her head, and said with a bitter smile: "I'd scare Dad to death if I went home looking like this, wouldn't I! He's an old man now, and I can't add to his worries. I'm going to stay in my other place for a while, and only go back to see him when I've built myself up a bit." I sighed, inwardly recognising the logic of what she was saying. If I was shocked and pained by seeing her like this, how could Uncle Xiao stand to see this change in her, he who thought about her and worried about her so much, and who treasured her as his precious baby?

She must have warned her landlord she was coming back, as the apartment was very tidy and the rooms were clean. I helped her over to sit on the bed and asked if she wanted to go to the hospital for a check-up. She shook her head and said: "There's no need to go to hospital, I've got clinical depression. I've had a definite diagnosis back in the States. All I need is to take my medication regularly and look after myself, nothing else. I know you've got a hundred questions to ask me, but first please go to the supermarket downstairs and buy me some everyday food and daily necessities. When you get back, you can sit down and hear what I have to tell you." So saying, she shoved a wad of one-hundred-yuan notes at me. I hurried down to the supermarket, then came back to hear the story of how she became so ill. When she first went over to America with her husband, Chang Sheng, the plan was for her to get pregnant and study English so that, by the time the child was born, her language studies would be pretty well complete. Chang Sheng was in complete agreement with this plan, but then, out of the blue, when she was three months into the pregnancy, Older Sister, who had been being so careful to protect the unborn child, miscarried. Deeply upset, she quarrelled with Chang Sheng, whose original thoughtlessness she blamed for causing her succession of miscarriages. In his own anger, Chang Sheng said one particularly vicious thing: "You're just like a useless hen that can't lay eggs, no matter how much your father dotes on you." These words deeply hurt Older Sister's feelings and self-esteem, and in her fury, she cursed him back as a rampant rooster whose constant unwanted attentions had ruined her as a woman. In the course of this quarrel, they both said some deeply damaging and hurtful things. For a long time after the argument, both out of anger and also to protect her own health, she didn't let Chang Sheng near her in bed. At first, Chang Sheng seemed to be concerned for her well-being, but she just ignored him, and in the end, Chang Sheng started finding excuses not to come home. Later on, she discovered that Chang Sheng had formed a friendship with one of the other students who had come over to America with him, and she was pretty sure they were sleeping together, so they quarrelled about that too. The other woman was also a lawyer back home, and, for two lawyers with fluent English, a woman with limited language skills who only knew about Chinese construction and landscape design presented little challenge. Older Sister's first instinct was to get proof of their trysts, then entreat Chang Sheng to stop his infidelities; she certainly didn't want to lose Chang Sheng because she still loved him dearly. But her English comprehension was very limited, so Chang Sheng could arrange his meetings with his girlfriend right in front of her, and she didn't understand what he was saying. So, at that point, all she could do was live with her suspicions, her unsuccessful attempts at tracking him, her hurt and her despair. Her emotional state began to deteriorate from this point on. At first, she couldn't sleep, spending night after night awake; then she began to lose control of her temper, getting angry at the drop of a hat and smashing things; after that, she lost her appetite, which damaged her gastrointestinal system. It was about two years after they had arrived in America that Chang Sheng began seriously to talk about divorce. The reason he gave was: "Your father has never respected me, and that has so seriously damaged my self-respect that I can never enjoy the time we spend together. You have become a shrew and are making our married life intolerable, so I have decided to return you to your father so he can continue to mollycoddle you..." Older Sister was probably already physically and emotionally exhausted, so when she had listened to him telling

her why he wanted a divorce and how there was no prospect of a
reconciliation, she didn't lose her temper or kick up a fuss, but just
said: "Right, good, you're a lawyer, so you just see to all the
formalities." Chang Sheng was indeed a lawyer, so there was no
need to return to China as he just got one of his colleagues back
there to make all the arrangements for the divorce as quickly as
possible. Older Sister told me that she was now paying the rent on
the apartment we were in, and it was paid up for a year, so it was
nothing to do with Chang Sheng anymore. I was dumbfounded. I
didn't really have much life experience, and this was the first time I
had witnessed someone's whole existence being turned upside
down like this in such a short time. She went on to tell me that,
after the divorce, her mental and emotional state just got worse and
worse, and in her confused state, she felt there was simply no point
in learning English or looking for work. Indeed, by the end, she felt
there was no point in eating or sleeping either. She just stayed in
her rented apartment twenty-four hours a day, until another
compatriot from Beijing told her to go to hospital. The doctor there
advised her she was already seriously clinically depressed, and she
needed to be on permanent anti-depressants. Originally, she wanted
to stay in New York so at least she was still comparatively close to
Chang Sheng, but she was too seriously ill, and her Chinese friends
told her to go back to Beijing.

"Coming home's all right," she said with a wry smile. "At least
I'll be able to spend some time with my dad. But for the moment,
you mustn't tell him I'm back already. I'll go and see him once I've
got myself better; I don't want to worry him..." I felt very sad on
my way home. I thought that Uncle Xiao could never have expected
his darling daughter could have met with such a terrible disaster. If
he were to find out, he would be so furious, his blood pressure was
bound to skyrocket, and his heart might not be able to stand any
more problems. To protect his physical and mental health, I could
only do what Older Sister had instructed me, and I didn't tell him
about her return to Beijing. That evening, I waited until Uncle Xiao
was in bed and asleep, then went to my own room. I didn't turn out
the light, but sat by my window, silently looking at the treetops

outside, lit by the street lamps, watching the indistinct shapes of the few crows that were perching there, and looking up at the stars twinkling faintly in the night sky. There was nothing I could do; I just felt sad, sad for Older Sister, sad for Uncle Xiao, sad for the whole household. It was hard to accept that the conventional, admirable life of a man like Uncle Xiao could suddenly be changed like this. I sat by the window for a long time that night, right up until those crows in the treetops began to caw, and only then, my mind in turmoil, did I stand up and go to lie on my bed.

Uncle Xiao certainly had no definite knowledge of Older Sister's return, but maybe telepathy of some kind came into play because, the next morning, he suddenly said to me: "I had a dream last night. I dreamed that I saw your Older Sister Xinxin, and she said she was going to come back home." I gave a wry smile and replied: "It could be; she's sure to be missing you." A few days later, he was still speculating to himself: "I wonder if Xinxin has found herself a job in New York that's keeping her really busy? Otherwise, why hasn't she phoned even once recently?" When I heard this, all I felt I could do was agree: "I'm sure that's it. The pace of life abroad is much more hectic, and I'm sure she can't relax now she's working in an English-speaking environment." One evening a few days later, when I reckoned Older Sister's condition might have improved a bit, I took the initiative and gave her a call, hoping to get her to call her father on her cell phone. That way, Uncle Xiao wouldn't be able to tell she was already back in Beijing, but it would temper how bitterly he was missing her. The phone rang for a long time without her answering, and when she finally did pick up, her voice was just as listless as it had been before. When I told her my suggestion, she sighed and said: "I'm sure Dad will be able to tell what kind of physical and emotional state I'm in, just from the sound of my voice, and that would just add to his concern for me. I'm not going to ring him for the moment, but I'll think about it again in a few days. Now tomorrow, I want you to go to the supermarket and buy me a length of wire, a bit more than a metre should do, and some pliers, then find an excuse to go out and come over here to give me a hand. I've decided to put your salary up again, to six thousand yuan, starting this month." Given her current state, how could I, in all conscience, accept another raise from her? I replied hurriedly but firmly: "I don't want it. I don't want it."

The next morning, after I'd settled Uncle Xiao, I used the excuse of wanting to go and see Lü Yiwei to ask for some time off. Then I took the metro to Older Sister's place, and followed her instructions to buy her the wire and the pliers. When she opened the door, I saw she looked very much as she had several days ago, and there really hadn't been any real change. In fact, if anything, her complexion was worse, the rings round her eyes were darker, and her hair was even more of a mess. I asked her if she had had breakfast, but she said she had absolutely no appetite. Even if she had no appetite, she'd got to eat! Without asking permission, I went straight into the kitchen and made her a bowl of noodles and two poached eggs. I really wanted to get her eating more so she would get better quicker and go home. Uncle Xiao was missing her so much! But from the way she picked up the bowl and lifted the noodles to her mouth, strand by strand, it was clear she was having great difficulty eating, and really did have almost no appetite. As she ate, she sighed and said: "This depression of mine has killed off all desire in me: I've no sex drive, no appetite, no desire for possessions, for power or reputation. All the human desires and aspirations have just mysteriously disappeared. It makes me feel that life is pointless and worthless, and all I can think about is death and dying; I just want to die right now. The wire and pliers I got you to bring today are so you can help me wire shut all the windows, in case I get the sudden urge to throw myself out of one of them. Every day, at the moment, I hear a voice whispering into my ear: 'Kill yourself! Kill yourself! What's the good of living?' I hear it most when the sun is beginning to set in the western sky, and I feel more than ever that life is pointless and meaningless; then I find myself being drawn over to the window with an irresistible urge to open it and put an end to things by throwing myself out." I was terrified when I heard this, and caught her by the arm, saying: "You mustn't do it! Every day, Uncle Xiao is longing for you to come home! He misses you all the time. Spare a thought for him in his old age, and give him the peace of mind he wants, rather than destroying it."

Older Sister replied with a bitter laugh: "Ha! My only concern is about my father, and he is the only reason I don't kill myself. I can't die before him and leave him with no one. Let me tell you, over these evenings I have been back in Beijing, several times I have gone to the window, opened it and taken a chair over there. Once, I got on the chair and was all ready to jump; I'd even thought through the best posture to jump in, but suddenly, my father's face appeared before my eyes, and I asked myself: How will Dad cope if I jump? At the last moment, I got down from the chair and slammed the window shut. I ran back to my bed and lay down. I didn't even dare look at the window in case it drew me back over..." Great heavens! Her words made my blood run cold. I sprang to my feet; I didn't need to hear any more. I wired all the windows in the apartment shut, tightening them as much as my strength allowed. As I was doing this, she kept repeating: "Make sure they're really tight, too tight for me to open." The more she said this, the harder I twisted the pliers, using every last ounce of my strength...

As I was about to leave, I made up a story for Older Sister: "There's some trouble back at my parents' home, so I have to go back there for a visit. It will only be a week at most before I can see you again. If it weren't for the fact you're not willing to go back to your father's apartment, I would be taking ten days, but the state of his health means that there's got to be someone there to look after him." Of course, my reason for saying this was to encourage her feelings of responsibility for her father. I hoped she might pull herself together a bit, start eating better, and begin to repair her health. At first, she got rather agitated, trying to persuade me not to go, but in the end, when she saw I wasn't going to change my mind, she nodded and said: "All right, I'll do my best to go back there in a week's time." I waited for six days, then phoned her to tell her to come back. She sighed and said: "All right, all right! But you mustn't tell him anything about me coming back because I've got divorced. That would just provoke him even more and set him off cursing Chang Sheng again. Who's to say he wouldn't go looking for him to seek some kind of justice for me. You just tell him I've come back from New York because I've been missing him, but that I'm a bit weak because I've not been well recently." I agreed to this, telling her: "Just so long as you come, I'll pretend it's the first time I've seen you."

She phoned me to say that she was on her way home from the airport, and could I go downstairs to meet her. I pretended to be overjoyed as I told Uncle Xiao the news. There was a look of childlike delight on his face as he paced around the room, saying: "We must go and buy some of her favourite things to eat." I told him not to worry and that he should just make a list and I would go out and buy them after Older Sister got there. I went downstairs at around the time I reckoned her taxi would arrive, and when she did get out, I immediately noticed that her complexion had improved, and that although her smile was rather forced, it was at least a smile. I picked up her two suitcases, one of which I had bought for her in the supermarket near her apartment and filled with imported goods from the same source. She followed behind me, carrying her hand luggage. Uncle Xiao already had the apartment door open and was waiting outside it to greet her. I saw surprise spark in his eyes when he saw her, as he had certainly not expected the daughter he hadn't seen for three years to look so thin and sickly. Older Sister threw herself into his arms and hugged him tight, weeping. I knew that these weren't tears of joy, but the grievances of a wronged woman. She needed a good cry to wash away all the unhealthy emotions that had been building up in her for so long; otherwise, they could have destroyed her. As Uncle Xiao wiped away his own tears, I knew that he was both overjoyed and distraught.

Once we were inside, Uncle Xiao could hold out no longer and burst out: "Are you ill, Xin'er?" "Yes, Dad; I couldn't take the American climate, and the pressures of studies and work made me ill all the time, so I kept putting off coming home to see you. You're looking very well though, Dad." "I'm all right. How's Chang Sheng?" Uncle Xiao asked, watching her closely. "He's fine. He's working really hard to establish himself in the American legal profession. Here, Dad, look at the presents I've brought you." Older

Sister clearly didn't want to dwell on the subject of Chang Sheng, and went over and opened the suitcase she had brought with her. She showed her father the gifts she had bought him: clothes, food, gadgets and, especially, life-prolonging health products. Uncle Xiao delightedly took them, one by one, and, at that moment, father's and daughter's smiles were equally dazzling. I thought to myself: If only it could continue like this, then everything would be just fine. I just hoped that the warmth of the atmosphere at home would lift her depression when she went back to her place. Because I had said in advance that I had urgent business back at my parents' home, once I had Older Sister settled in, I asked Uncle Xiao for permission to leave. Quite relaxed, he said: "I've got Xin'er to look after me, so set your mind at ease and go." That afternoon, I went to see my boyfriend, Lü Yiwei, for a while, bought some presents to take home, and, in the evening, took the train back to my hometown of Nanyang.

I hadn't been home for ages, and I was really missing my parents and little brother and sister, so it is hard to convey just how happy and carefree I felt when I got there. In particular, an irresistible feeling of pride surged in my breast as I saw the delighted smiles of my family when they opened my gifts: now I was in a position to repay them for bringing me up. Now a grown-up woman, I owed them such a debt! Yet at the same time as I felt that surge of pride, I couldn't help thinking of Older Sister Xinxin back in Beijing, and how she had been the source of my steady and none-too-demanding job. I owed her a debt of gratitude too.

I had made careful plans for my ten-day leave: the most important tasks for the first three days were to unpick and wash the padded winter clothes and quilts ready for the change in season, and to do a deep clean of the house and courtyard; the next two days were divided between checking my little brother's and little sister's homework and giving them some extra coaching; then two days for helping my father with some outside work; that left two days to go and help out Lü Yiwei's parents, and the last day to get ready for my return to Beijing. But to my surprise, before three days were out, I got a phone call from Older Sister asking me to come back to Beijing. I remember, it was on the third evening, after supper, when I was in the yard, bringing in the washing, that my cell phone rang inside the house. At first, I thought it must be Lü Yiwei, and I decided I could leave it until I'd finished in the yard and then call him back, so I didn't answer it. But the phone just kept ringing, until my rather flustered mother brought it out to me. I was taken aback when I saw Older Sister's number on the display, so I hastened to pick up. Down the line, I heard her agitated voice saying: "You've got to come back to Beijing, Xiaoyang. I'll raise your salary by five hundred yuan a month!"

I laughed and said: "We can talk about any raise later; you just tell me what's going on." She made a little sobbing noise and said: "I'm in no state to look after my dad; I'm too confused, and I can't seem to do anything right. When I'm cooking rice, I cook it down to a paste, and I keep forgetting to season the main dishes; I forget to put the washing liquid in when I do the laundry, and when I do any kind of housework I get dizzy and want to throw up. Dad has seen that I can't cope, and from yesterday he has stopped me doing any housework. So he's looking after me now, but he's just told me that he's feeling dizzy, and when I took his blood pressure it was 190/140." I was very alarmed by this, as a reading that high meant he was very much at risk! I urged her to increase the dose of his anti-hypertensive medication and told her I would go and buy my return ticket the next day.

On the train back to Beijing, as I looked out of the window at the endless procession of fields, roads and irrigation ditches, I felt once again how fickle and changeable life was. When I first met Older Sister three years ago, she had seemed so self-possessed and beautiful, a real young city girl, and I had envied her and taken her as my role model. Who would have thought that now, three years later, things would have changed so much that neither she nor her father could even look after themselves? It was late afternoon by the time I got back to Uncle Xiao's apartment. When I went in, I saw Uncle Xiao in the kitchen, bent over the counter, knife in hand, laboriously chopping vegetables, while Older Sister sat in a daze to one side, staring listlessly out of the window. My heart ached, and, without even stopping to change my shoes, I hurried into the kitchen and set about washing my hands as I said to Uncle Xiao: "I'll do that…"

Uncle Xiao had clearly already realised that Older Sister was seriously ill, and the next day, just after breakfast, he told me: "In normal circumstances, Xiaoyang, since you've just got back from a visit home, you should have the day off to rest, but I can't stop worrying about how ill your Older Sister is, so can I trouble you to take her to hospital for a check-up. We need to find out just what is wrong with her, and get her better as quickly as possible. I'll stay here, and I won't go anywhere, so you don't have to worry about me." Of course, I nodded and said I'd go. But Older Sister didn't want to, saying that she had already been diagnosed in America with severe depression, and it would get better with rest. Uncle Xiao said nothing, but his face darkened, which was always a sign that he was about to lose his temper. Recognising this, Older Sister got reluctantly to her feet, tidied herself up a bit and went out of the door with me.

The way Older Sister saw it, there was no need for the two of us to go to the hospital; all we need do was spend the morning in some teahouse or coffee shop, then go home and tell her dad that she'd had the examination, and all would be fine. But I insisted that we go to the Beijing Xiehe Hospital; firstly because I couldn't break Uncle Xiao's trust, and secondly because I wanted to find out exactly what was wrong with her. Presumably because she was relying on me to look after Uncle Xiao and didn't want to fall out with me, she didn't argue but just said: "All right, all right, let's go and waste some money on their fees. I'm sure they'll just confirm the American doctors' diagnosis." In order to save time, Older Sister bought a specialist consultation ticket from a hospital ticket tout, and it was indeed confirmed – after the head of the psychiatric department at the hospital had asked exhaustive questions about symptoms and inspected the results of relevant tests, he gave the diagnosis: severe clinical depression. At the end, Older Sister said to the specialist: "For my father's peace of mind, can I ask you to write 'severe clinical depression' in Chinese, but use English to record the rest of the diagnosis; I'll be able to reassure my father that way." The specialist hesitated over this, but, in the end, went along with it. But, after we had left the consulting room, he called me back and said, in a low voice: "If I'm not mistaken, you are the younger sister of Ms Xiao Xinxin, the patient. Your sister's condition is very serious; you must make sure she takes her medication regularly, and supervise her very carefully to prevent any accidents." Silently, I nodded my understanding.

When we got home, Uncle Xiao didn't listen to Older Sister's or my account of the consultation but went straight to the consultation report to read the diagnosis. As Older Sister expected, he didn't understand any of the English the doctor had written and just saw the words *severe clinical depression* in Chinese. He stared at them for a long time, before asking, heavily: "Does Chang Sheng know you have this?" "Of course he does!" She kept her tone deliberately light. "He went to the hospital with me several times, but treatment and recovery for this kind of condition are very slow; it's a really long haul." Uncle Xiao continued: "So are you going to stay here until you get better, or go back to America for treatment?" "Of course I'm going back to the States for treatment," she replied firmly. "The hospitals over there are much better than the ones here!" I told myself bitterly: Of course she can't go back to America to live. When she says that she's going back there for treatment, what she actually means is she's going back to the apartment in Chaoyang. But, if that's the case, and if I'm supposed to be caring for Uncle Xiao, how can I keep an eye on her too? When he heard her reply, Uncle Xiao said decisively: "If you're going back to America for treatment, then you won't want to stay here for too long. You should buy a plane ticket and go back in four or five days' time. It's really important you get your treatment. I've got Xiaoyang to look after me, and I haven't got any serious problems, so you can put your mind at rest and go..."

That evening, after Uncle Xiao had gone to sleep, I went into Older Sister's bedroom, and asked her, in an indignant whisper, what she thought she was doing keeping up the pretence of going back to America for treatment: "Wouldn't it be much better for you to stay here at home to take your medications and get treated? That way, I can look after you, and you'll save on the rent." She took my hand and said, gently: "Dear Little Sister, thank you for your good intentions, but the treatment for this condition is long and hard, and it's not going to be possible to show my father any immediate improvement. If I stay here, I'll just have Dad worrying over my condition all the time. I know how much he cares for me: he was forty-two when I was born, his only daughter, and he values my life more than his own. Don't you see, if I stay here to get better, it will just be like hurrying him into his grave." She sighed as she finished, and all I could do was sigh with her. In the end, I was only the household nurse, and it wasn't up to me to make any decision.

When I pretended to be happily taking Older Sister to Capital Airport, I was actually escorting her back to the apartment in Chaoyang. I helped her to clean the place up a bit, as, with the windows wired shut, there was a rather musty smell in the rooms. I took the money she gave me, and the shopping list she had written out, and went to the supermarket to buy her some food and household goods. As I was leaving, I took her by both hands and said: "Older Sister, you've got to follow the doctor's instructions and take your medications regularly, so you can get better quickly, and come back home to be with your father as soon as possible. He loves you so much and needs you so much. I'll come to see you once a week, but if anything happens, you can call me whenever you like, or send me a text." She gripped my hands tightly and said: "Dear Little Sister, I'm so glad I found you in the first place, so that I could be relieved of the burden of care of my father for a while. Later on, you can be sure that I will repay you..."

When I told Uncle Xiao the next day that Older Sister was already back in New York and had started her proper treatment. I could see it was a weight off the old man's mind, and he said with relief: "Medicine in America is very advanced, and although we can treat depressive illnesses like this in Beijing, the process is much easier over there..." All I could do was secretly pray for Older Sister's return to health!

Relieved of his worries for his daughter, Uncle Xiao turned back with enthusiasm to the question of extending his life. Early one day, he told me delightedly that he had heard a seventy-five-year-old man on the internet talking about his experience of taking Thousand Year Paste. After he had taken it for ten days, he could read a newspaper without his glasses; after half a month, a long-standing pain in his knee disappeared; after a month, his weak and painful calf was strong and pain-free; after a month and a half, his grey eyebrows had turned black again; after two months, his chronic insomnia had completely disappeared, so he could go straight to sleep and sleep through the night; after three months, he could walk six kilometres without tiring; and after four months several new teeth had grown where he had lost the old ones.

From the tone of envy and admiration in his voice as he related this tale, I could tell that Uncle Xiao was hooked by this Thousand Year Paste, and I asked him: "So, are you going to buy some to try it out?" He nodded: "I know you can't believe everything you hear in these internet advertisements, but you can't ignore all of them, just in case some brilliant doctor of traditional Chinese medicine has actually discovered a miracle drug that really can prolong life. It would be my loss if I don't look into it, wouldn't it!" "All right," I said. "I'll have a look at it, then we can decide." I visited the web page Uncle Xiao was indicating, and took a note of the cell phone number at the top. Thousand Year Paste: it was a clever name, sure to attract the old folks' attention, as which of them wouldn't want to live a thousand years? I called the number, and a woman's voice answered. When she heard I was enquiring about the Thousand Year Paste, she said, enthusiastically: "We can deliver the product in person so we can tell the old person all about it, and explain its use." Uncle Xiao, who was standing beside me and heard this, replied almost impatiently: "Yes, yes, you'd better come tomorrow morning..."

The next day, a man and a woman did indeed arrive at the door with two carrier bags in their hands. Uncle Xiao invited them in warmly, and before they were properly through the door to the living room, the woman's voice was already ringing out: "You're about the same age as my grandfather, Uncle Xiao, and when I look at you, I might as well be looking at him, you're so similar. You've both got wide foreheads, straight noses, full cheeks and long ears like a Buddha statue: you are images of longevity, the pair of you. If you take our Thousand Year Paste regularly for a whole year, I can't guarantee that you will live a thousand years, but you will have no problem reaching one hundred and fifty. If not, I will take full responsibility and give a complete refund." I thought to myself that this was all just hype, but I didn't dare push back against it at that time, so I just stood silently next to Uncle Xiao as the two of them demonstrated the product to him. The Thousand Year Paste came in two forms, black and white, each beautifully presented in glass bottles. The woman explained how they were used: you took the white version during the day, one spoonful before each meal, and the black one you took in the evening before going to bed, ideally thirty minutes before retiring. "Our Thousand Year Paste has been developed following a secret recipe carefully handed down over thirty generations and is a hundred per cent effective. Today, we will leave you with one box of the black version and one of the white. There is no need to pay anything now; try taking them for a week, and if you notice any definite improvements, you can pay us the next time we come. If you feel there have been any ill effects or no effect at all, then you don't have to pay a cent."

I was rather surprised by this. On the face of it, they clearly had a lot of faith in their product, or they wouldn't make this promise. After they left, Uncle Xiao said with a laugh: "That's quite a sales technique! No money up-front, and a refund if it doesn't work. They really seem to be above board, and not just con artists. Would a con artist make an offer like that? What I said before is right: you can't believe everything you see on the internet, but you can't disbelieve it all either." So, of course, Uncle Xiao began taking the Thousand Year Paste. Ha! Believe it or not, when he started taking it that evening, that unprepossessing, sticky paste had an immediate effect. Normally, he didn't sleep very well, and had particular trouble getting off to sleep, lying there tossing and turning for a long time. But that evening, not long after he had gone to bed, I went in to take his blood pressure, and before I had even finished, he was fast asleep and snoring. I was amazed at this: there really was something magical about the stuff if it got results that quickly!

The next morning, he began taking the white Thousand Year Paste three times a day before meals. On the third day, the effects of that too became apparent. Normally when Uncle Xiao came home from his daily morning walk, he would be feeling tired, and would just sit down on the sofa reading the newspaper or watching TV; he might well doze off too. I didn't feel there was anything unusual about this; after all, even youngsters want to rest after exercise, so why shouldn't a man of over seventy? But from the third day after he started taking the Thousand Year Paste, I noticed how much more energy he had; not only did he not sit on the sofa and nod off when he got back from his walk, he would pace around the living room non-stop, and continually find things to talk to me about. Even after lunch, he stopped having his usual nap, and would sit there, happily sorting through all the material about prolonging life he had gleaned from books and the internet. I was secretly very surprised, realising these must be the effects of the Thousand Year Paste. I really hadn't anticipated that he had chanced upon something that really worked. It was lucky that he had discovered it on the internet, as it would have been a great shame if he had missed out on it. Of course, Uncle Xiao was feeling the benefits for himself and said happily: "You see, this time I made the right decision!"

The Thousand Year Paste Healthcare Company came calling again at the weekend. They telephoned in advance, and it was the same man and woman who came. As soon as the woman was in the apartment, she took Uncle Xiao by the hand and asked: "Well, my dear Uncle Xiao, how do you feel after taking our Thousand Year Paste? Have there been any changes? Are you sleeping a bit better? How are your energy levels?" Of course, he agreed immediately that everything was improved. The woman went on to ask: "So do you want to buy some so you can keep taking it? There is a limit to how much of this medicine we can produce, so if you want to buy more, the most you can have is ten bottles at one time, and each bottle costs one thousand five hundred yuan. You can put in an advance order, but the limit on that is thirty bottles." Uncle Xiao became a little agitated when he heard that the supply was limited like this, and said: "Given my advanced age, can't you let me buy forty bottles, and maybe round the price down a little for me?" The woman seemed very embarrassed: "I'm afraid I can't make that decision myself. I will have to ask our manager for advice."

With that, she went outside to make the call. After a while, she came back in and said: "I asked our manager if he could see his way to making a special exception for you, in view of the great service you did our country as a judge, when you were younger. He agreed, and says you can have the forty bottles of Thousand Year Paste, but, as it's a one-off, you will have to pay full price." Uncle Xiao was delighted and said immediately: "Of course I'll pay full price as a one-off." With that, he went straight to his bedroom for his bank card and gave it to the woman to swipe through her POS machine. At this point, I asked: "Can you give us the medicine now?" The woman turned to her male companion and said: "Go down to the car and get Uncle Xiao his medicine." So it wasn't long before sixty thousand yuan had been swiped away, and the man brought up a cardboard box, full of Thousand Year Paste. As they were about to leave, they told Uncle Xiao: "When you have finished these forty bottles, we guarantee you will live at least three years longer. If you want to continue taking it when you run out, just give us a call." Uncle Xiao's face was wreathed in smiles as he replied immediately: "Thank you, thank you, thank you! Mind how you go..." After they were gone, he happily counted off on his fingers: "Master Fei gave me twenty-eight years, the patting exercises can give me ten, and these forty bottles can give me another three, so that makes forty-one in all. I'm just about going to be able to live until I'm one hundred and seventeen..."

As I saw the beneficial effects on Uncle Xiao of taking the Thousand Year Paste, the improved sleep and raised energy levels, I thought of my own parents. Although they were younger than Uncle Xiao, they were still old, so I really should buy some of this medicine to help them too. By this time, Older Sister was paying me six thousand five hundred yuan a month, and even with supporting Lü Yiwei in his studies and seeing to my own living expenses, I was still able to save quite a bit. Then, just as I was about to contact the Thousand Year Paste Healthcare Company, something happened. One evening, Uncle Xiao was opening a bottle of the black Thousand Year Paste when he accidentally dropped it and the paste spilled out onto the floor. At one thousand five hundred yuan a bottle, you can imagine how upset Uncle Xiao and I were! I snatched up a bowl to collect the spilt paste, but only managed to recover a little of it, as the rest was too dirty. There was nothing I could do, but, rather than waste money completely, I went next door to borrow their pet dog, and let him lick up the remaining paste from the floor. To my astonishment, as soon as the dog had finished off the spilt paste, he just lay down and fell asleep.

Uncle Xiao pretended not to pay it any attention, and just laughed, but it gave me quite a shock: was Thousand Year Paste effective on dogs too? Surely it shouldn't be the case that a human health supplement could work so quickly on an animal! It certainly made me suspicious of the ingredients of Thousand Year Paste. When I took the sleeping dog back next door, the neighbours were also astonished. They said their dog never usually went to sleep at that time of day, nor did he ever sleep that soundly. When they asked me what I had given their dog to eat, and I told them, they were very concerned, and told me to be more careful in future, and not give an old man any old health supplement. That's when I decided I should get the ingredients of Thousand Year Paste analysed.

There was a drug-testing lab in the neighbourhood, and because I walked past it so often, I had got to know one of the men who worked there. So the next day I took some of the black Thousand Year Paste to the lab and told my acquaintance: "The old man I look after has been taking a kind of health supplement recently, which has the same effect on both humans and dogs. Can you analyse its ingredients for me, please, to set my mind at rest?" The man had no objections, and, not long after he had taken the paste inside, he came back out and told me: "This paste has a base of dark brown sugar and contains a large dose of the soporific drug Zolpidem. It only has those two ingredients." I broke out into a cold sweat when I heard this: Great heavens! How could anyone be so wicked?! How could anyone have the nerve to put old people at risk by passing off a sleeping drug as a health supplement!? Who knew what might have happened if I hadn't brought it in to be examined, and had let Uncle Xiao go on taking it in such quantities every evening, for any length of time? Of course, I went home to fetch the daytime white form of the Thousand Year Paste. When the man at the lab had analysed it, he told me the results: the paste consisted of white sugar and very strong caffeine.

I was so angry there was steam coming out of my ears as I ran home and told Uncle Xiao the results of the analysis of the Thousand Year Paste. At first, he stood rooted to the spot in astonishment, then, in a fit of ungovernable anger, he seized the phone and called the Thousand Year Paste Healthcare Company's number. But whoever was at the other end hung up at his first word, and when he dialled again, all he got was the China Mobile recorded announcement: "This phone has been switched off." He paced around the room a few times, then pulled out the business card the woman had left behind, and said: "I'm going to go and find her!" Of course I couldn't let him go alone, as what would happen if they cut up rough? But there was no way Uncle Xiao could stand for this! Following the address on the business card, we took a taxi to the factory where the Thousand Year Paste was manufactured. It was a courtyard property in a village in the Beijing suburb of Daxing, and there was a massive padlock on the gates. I discovered from a neighbour that the landlord in the city had sold the buildings, and rented out the courtyard to a group that opened up the Thousand Year Paste Healthcare Company. A fortnight or so before, the company had been closed down by the Trade and Industry Bureau, but their sales ads on the internet hadn't been taken down, and that's how Uncle Xiao had been cheated once again. "Sixty thousand yuan!" Uncle Xiao cried out in anguish, looking up to the heavens, his body trembling with anger. I helped him back into the taxi, and tried to make him see things differently: "If you think about it, you could look at it as having bought a lesson." "A lesson? At sixty thousand yuan! That's a very expensive lesson!" Uncle Xiao vented his anger on me, and all I could do was smile wryly in return.

The next day, I went to make a complaint at the Public Security Office, since swindling someone out of sixty thousand yuan is not just petty theft, and they should find some way of getting it back for us. The officer I saw heard me out, then picked up a stack of paper and plonked it down in front of me, saying: "There, have a look: that's how many cases of old people being swindled we are dealing with. It may be that we will find a way of getting the money back, but you need to tell the old man you're looking after not to believe anything he reads about extending his life. He's a judge, isn't he? He really shouldn't be duped that easily!"

This whole affair left Uncle Xiao lying on his bed, drumming his fists on his forehead. I knew he was doing this out of remorse, and I too was secretly experiencing the after-effects of the affair: thank heavens for that dog; otherwise, I too might have been tricked out of some of my hard-earned savings by that pair of swindlers. And things only got worse. I had just managed to persuade Uncle Xiao out of his bed and to eat properly, when we were hit by two new pieces of bad news. The first was in an announcement posted up in the neighbourhood by the local police station, which read: *Investigations have discovered that recently, a woman called Pang Ren'ai, claiming to be a representative of the Tian Cheng Corporation, has been using the promise of teaching a set of life-extending patting exercises to gain entry to the homes of old people. She is, in fact, the ringleader of a gang of housebreakers, and is using this pretext of teaching the exercises as an opportunity for burglary. If an old person is alone, she takes whatever she can lay her hands on. There is no such person as Kuang Xiuhua, the woman she claims invented the exercises, which are her own random invention and have absolutely no effect on prolonging life. She is not to be trusted, and if anyone knows her whereabouts, please immediately inform the local police station…*

After we had read this, Uncle Xiao and I stood speechless for a long time. That elegant, eloquent, friendly woman was just another common criminal? The only reason she hadn't stolen anything from Uncle Xiao was that I was there as his carer!

The other piece of bad news was an article in the evening newspaper which said that yesterday in Shunyi, the Public Security had arrested the famous master of avoiding calamities and extending life, Master Fei Wen, on suspicion of fraud. The reporter revealed that, in his earlier life, Fei Wen had been a stage magician, but, dissatisfied with the money he was making, he had decided to earn a new living through his skill at magic. He turned himself into this master of avoiding calamities and extending life, specifically in order to swindle old folk who were anxious to extend their lives, and make them willingly hand over their hard-earned life savings to him. I was even more flabbergasted by this news. Good Lord! Were those things I had seen with my own eyes all false and had Fei Wen just been playing magic tricks on us? How could he treat people who had such faith in him like that? I didn't know whether to tell Uncle Xiao about this or not. If I didn't, he would remain in the dark, still believing his life had been prolonged by twenty-eight years, but, if I did, I was worried this fresh blow would be too much for him. But even as I was hesitating over whether to speak out or not, an old courtroom colleague who knew that Uncle Xiao had been to see Master Fei, took it on himself to telephone him to pass on the news.

Of course, the man's only intention was to stop Uncle Xiao being deceived any longer, but when the call ended, Uncle Xiao collapsed across his bed, which fortunately he was already sitting on to take the call. If he had been standing up, and been surprised like that, he would have crashed to the floor. Of course, I rushed over to him to administer first aid, but fortunately it was just a panic attack, and he had only fainted for a moment without any serious repercussions. When he recovered his senses, he asked me hoarsely: "Tell me, who do I dare believe now? Who can I believe now? Who should I believe now?" What could I say? All I could think of was: "Well perhaps from now on, you won't be so quick to believe everything you read on the internet..."

A few days later, when Uncle Xiao finally made himself get up from his bed, he sighed and said: "At least Xinxin is back in America; if she was here in Beijing and found out about all this, heaven knows how angry she would be, and how much she would reproach me. Ai! It would be all right if I was still a judge; I could order my own investigation into these bastards and get them put in jail..." After being swindled on these occasions, his optimism about and enthusiasm for his future disappeared, and I often heard him muttering to himself: "How much longer have I got to live? What is my life expectancy now? Am I still going to be able to finish my law books?" All his former enthusiasm was gone.

I knew that Uncle Xiao had got himself stuck in an impasse with this business of prolonging his life, and I'd have to find some way of extricating him safely; otherwise, he might keep barging around in there and end up by damaging his health. His greatest desire was to extend his life, so the best way was to tell him about genuine ways of achieving this, as only by doing so could he find some consolation and achieve real peace of mind which would finally draw him out of the impasse. But who was there who could tell him about these genuine ways? Were there, in fact, any such ways? I racked my brain until my head ached. Then I suddenly thought of a place my grandma had told me about: Longevity Village in the Funiu Mountains. I remember, when I was little, often hearing my grandmother say with a sigh: "I wish I could have been born in Longevity Village, deep in the mountains, then I could live to be a hundred, and satisfy my craving to celebrate my hundredth birthday." I remember I once asked my mum: "Is Grandma telling the truth? Is there really such a place as Longevity Village in the Funiu Mountains?" Mum just nodded and said: "It's real enough, but it's too far away. They say there is a village deep in the forests of the Funiu Mountains, where all the villagers live to be more than a hundred, and the oldest to one hundred and ten. But the road is very difficult, and very few people make it there…"

Would it be possible to take Uncle Xiao to that village so he could absorb some of the true spirit of longevity and cure him of his malaise? After I had had this idea, I immediately telephoned my mum, asking if there was some way she could ask around to find out if the villagers there still lived a long time, and if they did, what was the best way to get there. After she had heard my request, Mum was very conscientious in following it up, and immediately contacted relatives all over the place to enquire. So it wasn't long at all before she called me back to say: "The people of the village are still very long-lived: there are more than seventy in their nineties, and more than twenty over a hundred; the way to this village starts from Yakouzhen, but the road is long and very hard-going…" On the basis of this, I told Uncle Xiao that there was a place called Longevity Village, deep in the Funiu Mountains, and I asked him very seriously: "Do you want to go and absorb some of the true spirit of longevity? If you do, then come with me to Longevity Village, and don't listen to any more of these Beijing conmen."

Uncle Xiao showed real interest in Longevity Village, but his previous experiences of being tricked made him hard to persuade: "I've heard of a place in Guangxi called Bama where people live a long time, but I've never heard of this Longevity Village of yours in the Funiu Mountains. Are you sure it's true?" I told him that I'd had the information from my own mother: "She would never try and trick you. If you want to go, I'll start getting ready for the trip. If you don't want to go, that's an end of it, and we'll pretend I never mentioned it." He thought about it for a moment, then came to a decision: "Let's go! Let's go and investigate, and treat it as an expedition into the mountains." I told him that the mountain roads were very difficult, and if we did go, he had to be ready for some hardships. He replied: "What hardships haven't I endured already? Do you think a few difficulties on the road are going to stop me?" Seeing him so determined, and with a view to easing his heartache, I decided I would take him on this trip. When I told Older Sister of my decision on the telephone, she gave me her support, saying:

"Go, by all means, if that's what he wants; even just the travel will do him good. I'll put some extra money in your account. As long as you make careful preparations, and ensure he doesn't get too tired, it's all fine." So I began to make meticulous preparations. As well as Uncle Xiao's normal daily medications, I also got some insect repellent, insect bite cream and several other bits of emergency first aid, along with some easily carried foodstuffs and rainwear. Just before we left, I also went over to Older Sister's rented apartment to stock up on daily necessities for her. It was so sad to have both father and daughter suffering their own heartaches!

Uncle Xiao and I first flew to Nanyang, and then took a taxi to the county town of Neixiang, where we hired a car to drive on to Yakouzhen. A lot of people there had heard of Longevity Village, but very few had actually been there. When we started asking around, we discovered that the village wasn't actually that far away as the crow flies, but the road wound and twisted up and down through the mountains for about one hundred and ten *li* before it reached there. Furthermore, the road was impassable to any vehicle, and the only way was on foot. I got Uncle Xiao settled in a small guesthouse in town to rest, then myself went out to the northwest of the township to investigate the route. As soon as I saw the path, no better than a goat track, winding through the mountain forest, I knew that there was no possibility of Uncle Xiao managing all one hundred and ten *li* of it on foot. When I got back into town, I asked the old owner of a mountain goods store if there were any porters willing to take people out to Longevity Village. He nodded and said that there were, but that they charged a lot of money because the road was so difficult. I told him to find two porters and ask their price. With a quick call on his cell phone, he summoned two young fellows in their late twenties.

As soon as I saw their strapping physiques, I knew they were up to making the trip, and I asked whether either of them had been to Longevity Village. One of them said that the year before last, a research unit had come to the county, and he had helped take them out there; the road was very hard-going, and in some places the trees and undergrowth were so thick that they had to cut their way through with machetes. I asked them whether they could use a bamboo chair to rig up some kind of sedan chair to carry an old man up through the mountains. The fellow grinned and said the two of them would do it for one thousand yuan apiece. I thought this was quite acceptable, and told him: "If you get the old man safely there and back, I will give you each one thousand one hundred yuan, and I will pay for all the food and drink." The two of them were delighted with this, saying: "You are very generous, Older Sister. Let's arrange to set out at five thirty tomorrow morning from the north entrance to the township, so we can get there before dark." I replied: "Please show me both your ID cards so I can take a photo of them to send back to the family in Beijing. I'm also going to tell the local police about our trip. So, if anything happens to the two of us, they'll all hold you responsible." The two young fellows just laughed and handed over their ID cards, saying with a grin: "We're no crooks, and we'll earn your money with the sweat of our brows, so go ahead and take your photo..."

We stayed that night in Yakouzhen. Uncle Xiao wasn't too happy to start with when I told him I had hired two porters to carry him into the mountains, but when we arrived at the north entrance to the township the following morning, and he saw what the path looked like, he got straight into the sedan chair without a murmur. I left our suitcases in the guesthouse, and, before we set out, I did indeed go to the local police station to make my report, just in case the two porters did try something on the way to the village. In my backpack, I carried medicines, bread, hard-boiled eggs, saveloys, cucumbers, mineral water and a pair of scissors for self-defence, and I brought up the rear of the party. One of the porters carried a hunting rifle to guard against wolves, and the other had a wooden-handled machete strapped to his back, as the four of us set off into the forest in the first glimmers of dawn and began our quest for the true spirit of longevity.

Although my own home village is in a mountain area, and I am used to mountain roads, it is not very rugged there, the mountains are not particularly high, and the roads are flat and even. This was the first time I had encountered a track that went up or down at fifty or sixty degrees at the drop of a hat as it rollercoastered its way through the mountains. It wasn't long before I was puffing and panting, out of breath. Even the two porters, robust young men as they were, did not find the going easy along this precipitous track as they carried Uncle Xiao in his sedan chair, and after just a few *li*, they were both sweating buckets. As he listened to the three of us panting away, he called out: "It's too much trouble for you all – let's not go on." One of the porters laughed and said: "You've got to go on, Grandad; we want our two thousand two hundred yuan. We've already told our wives how much we're getting, and if we go back empty-handed, we'll never hear the end of it." When he heard this, Uncle Xiao replied: "All right, all right, on we go! I'll give both of you an extra one hundred yuan." The two men grinned, and one said: "You and your daughter are both very generous. We're all of the same mind, and the two of us guarantee we'll get you safely there and back!" We walked and rested, rested and walked, as the spectacular sights of the Funiu Mountains unfurled before our eyes: dense, lush forest, precipitous waterfalls, brilliantly plumaged birds, monkeys swinging through the trees, mountain grasses as tall as a man, snakes slithering across the track, scurrying herds of wild pigs, crystal clear mountain streams, fantastical mountain mushrooms... we stopped to rest thirty-two times, and reached the famous Longevity Village just as darkness fell.

The village's original name was Yuanyang, and those were the two characters rather sloppily carved on a big marker stone at its entrance, obviously the work of a local craftsman: the characters were pretty much of a scrawl, and clearly written by someone of limited education. The village was situated on the south-facing slope of a mountain, with wood-frame houses arranged haphazardly in little plots of flat land across the mountainside. To the left of the village, there were side- and back-drops of dense forest, and in front of it there was a wide, limpid mountain stream that tinkled as it flowed across the rocks. It was quite evident that few outsiders ever made it there, as the village children looked on us as some great novelty, and clustered round. Automatically, they became our guides as they led us to a courtyard at the top of the village, shouting at the tops of their voices: "Grandpa Wu, Grandpa Wu! Outsiders have come! People have come!" The person who came out in response to their cries was a long-bearded, snowy-eyebrowed old man. He stopped and stared at us in amazement, then bowed and asked: "May I ask if you are looking for somewhere to spend the night?" I hurriedly stepped forward to explain why we were there. When he heard that we had come seeking the true spirit of longevity, he couldn't stop himself laughing, and said: "I don't think there is anything like that in our humble little village, but since you are here, and night is about to fall, you had better stay. Come on, then, come inside with me."

We followed him into the house, and just as we sat down at a big, square, plank table, we heard him call out to the rear courtyard: "Mother! We have guests!" I was amazed: could an old man like him still have a mother alive? He had barely spoken when a clear voice rang out in reply from the rear courtyard: "Tell Xiao Yaya to bring them out some old tea first." Almost immediately, a ruddy-faced woman with totally white hair emerged from the rear courtyard, looked at us, then smiled and said: "I heard a pair of red-tailed magpies calling in the trees a couple of days ago. I was sure something good was going to happen, and here you are!" As we all exchanged greetings, a woman with greying hair came in from the side room, carrying a tray with several cups on it, containing a very dark tea, and put one down in front of each of us. This time, it was the ruddy-faced old woman who spoke: "You've already met my son Wu'er, so let me introduce my grandson's wife Xiao Yaya." As she said this, she indicated the old lady who had brought in the tea. "She's seventy-one. She looks good for her age, doesn't she!" I exchanged an amazed look with Uncle Xiao: Great heavens! A seventy-one-year-old called Xiao Yaya.[1] I was only in my twenties, so what would they call me? "How old are you, Venerable Grandmother?" I couldn't hide my astonishment. "Don't call me Venerable Grandmother, that would mean I'm old at heart. Just call me Grandmother. I'm one hundred and eight this year; I married Wu'er's father when I was eighteen, and gave birth to him the same year. There was a heavy fog the day he was born, shrouding the whole mountain, so that's why he has got the character for fog in his name. Wu'er, take our guests to their room so they can have a wash and a rest; Xiao Yaya, go and get the food ready: our guests have been travelling all day along that mountain track, so we must make sure we give them a decent meal!" "I'm sorry to add to the trouble we're causing, but we need to rent three rooms: one for Grandpa Xiao here, one for our two porters, and one for me. We will pay whatever the going rate is here – we don't expect to stay for free." I felt I needed to get in quickly with that, to put their minds at rest, and also to get the price fixed, so there wouldn't be any trouble when it came to settling up. "Pay? What are you thinking of, young lady? We mountain folk never charge for accommodation! We are all out and about at some time, and when we are, all the villages in the area become our home, and we can stay in any one of them. That's the custom in these mountains. Go on, Wu'er, show them where to go." The old lady was very fierce when she got going, and I held my tongue. Of course, I was also delighted at her generosity because it meant I could save some of my spending money.

We followed Grandpa Wu'er to a small courtyard next door, where the walls of the building were all made out of logs, with roofs of planks and thatch. The beds and chairs inside were made out of wood too, and the rooms were redolent of wood and mountain grasses. Our three rooms were in a row, and they all seemed to be unoccupied. I asked Wu'er if these were purpose-built guest rooms. He nodded and said that they were. He went on to explain that the villages in these mountains were very far apart, and accommodation was often a problem when people went out and about. So every village had to provide several guest rooms to put visitors up. I asked him why the children had brought us to his courtyard instead of this one, and he laughed and said: "Ours is the most senior household in the village, so the villagers chose me as the village chief. My son and I are both carpenters, with some skill in roofing, so we built these extra houses for visitors to stay in." I remembered his mother saying he was born when she was married aged eighteen, so I worked out that meant he was ninety. He must have been the oldest village chief in all of China.

Uncle Xiao had never been in the deep mountains before, and even though he had been exhausted by being tossed to and fro in the sedan chair, he was all fired up to explore this magical village, and not long after we went into the rooms, he was shouting to me to go out with him to walk around. It was full night outside, and the whole of Yuanyang Village was plunged in darkness, with the only light coming from the windows and door frames of some of the houses. Perhaps because we were so high up in the mountains, the star-studded sky seemed very low, as if you could just reach out and touch the stars. Everywhere was silent, except for the barking of a few dogs and the sound of the mountain stream. The road through the middle of the village was laid with flagstones worn smooth and slippery by the passage of time. It was time for supper, and the road was practically deserted. As Uncle Xiao walked along, he was breathing deeply through his nose. I asked him what he was up to, and he replied: "The air here is so clean and fresh…"

We ate supper in the main room of Grandpa Wu'er's home. There were two long wooden tables: at one of them sat Grandpa Wu'er's mother, Grandpa Wu'er, his wife, his son and his son's wife, Xiao Yaya, and the four of us. At the other were Xiao Yaya's two sons, their wives, and her three grandsons and three granddaughters, so there were five generations of one family all in the same room. The seventy-one-year-old Xiao Yaya gave the signal for her two daughters-in-law to bring in the food. There were two large dishes on each table: one was mountain rabbit stewed with white radishes, and the other was hen stewed with mushrooms. Instead of rice, they had steamed sweet potato and boiled sweetcorn; the sweet potatoes were cut into two, and each half was huge but cooked until very soft, and the corn was boiled on the cob and was delicious to gnaw at. The congee was made with sweet corn grits, and was also thick and fragrant. There was a small bowl of wine in front of everyone, except the grandchildren, which Grandpa Wu'er said was made from kiwi fruit, didn't make you drunk, and was very good for your health. When the food and drink were all laid out, Grandpa Wu'er's mother picked up her chopsticks and tapped them on her bowl, which was the signal for everyone to start eating. The children and the men all fell to ravenously, except for Uncle Xiao who didn't quite know how to proceed. I picked up a corn cob and handed it to him, indicating to him that he should set to and gnaw off the kernels.

Although I was a non-drinker, I did drain my little bowl of kiwi fruit wine; it was sweet and tangy, and sat very comfortably in my stomach. As soon as the alcoholic Uncle Xiao saw that I wasn't going to stop him today, he downed his own bowl, then held it out to Xiao Yaya and asked: "Can I have another bowlful?" She laughed and refilled the bowl. As the electric lights in the room dimmed and brightened, I asked Grandpa Wu'er if the electricity supply was unstable. He replied: "Running an electricity supply cable up here would be too expensive, so the village has fixed up a generator. But Su'er, who is in charge of the machine, isn't very well-educated, so the lights in the village are always dimming and surging like that." When dinner was over and I went back to my room, I could hardly keep my eyes open. In all my life, I had never walked such a distance along a mountain track in a single day, and I was so exhausted I forgot to go and supervise Uncle Xiao's night-time medications, and just lay down on my bed and fell asleep. That was the soundest I had ever slept, so sound I don't think I had any dreams at all. It was only when I was woken by the persistent crowing of a rooster that I realised it was already full daylight. Then I remembered that I had forgotten Uncle Xiao's medications the night before, and I hurried over to his room. He was still fast asleep and snoring thunderously. I quickly took his blood pressure and blood sugar. Whew! Surprisingly, his blood sugar was normal!

When he was awake, Uncle Xiao laughed and said: "That was the best sleep I've ever had. Maybe it's just because I was so tired." As the two of us went out to wash in the stream, Grandpa Wu'er came by with a porter's pole on his shoulder and asked with a grin: "You slept well, then? Good, good!" Uncle Xiao nodded: "I slept through without even getting up to relieve myself." This reminded me that the same was true of me. Grandpa Wu'er laughed: "Ha!

Anyone who drinks just one bowl of that fruit wine sleeps like a log, and you had two bowls!" Uncle Xiao and I were both surprised by this: so it was all down to the wine?! "That's the main purpose of our wine, to help people sleep. Most old people have trouble sleeping, but in our village, it doesn't matter how old they are, they all sleep like the dead because of this wine." Wow! Uncle Xiao and I exchanged glances. Sleep is one of the most important elements in maintaining a healthy body. "What is it you've got on your pole?" I asked Grandpa Wu'er, looking at the black stuff on his porter's pole. "Fertiliser. We make it with chicken shit, pig shit and cow shit, mixed with rotting leaves from the forest. We pile it all up and let it ferment. It's better and longer-lasting than chemical fertilisers. It's good for both grains and vegetables; anything grown using this tastes delicious." "Ah, so where are you taking it now?" Uncle Xiao's interest was aroused. "To the vegetable fields. You can come with me if you want to see; there's still a little time to go before breakfast." As he spoke, Grandpa Wu'er was carrying his pole across the stream over a little stone bridge onto the opposite bank. Uncle Xiao and I followed on behind, and watching his steady stride, with the pole over his shoulder, it was really hard to believe he was ninety years old. Once we were across the bridge, we discovered that the land on the other side of the stream consisted of plot after plot of vegetables and crops. We were in mid-autumn, so the vegetables being grown were white radish, red radish, white cabbage and smaller things like edible rape, spinach and coriander. They were all flourishing, and twenty or thirty early-rising villagers were hard at work on their family plots. A couple of them were treading an ancient waterwheel that was drawing up water from the stream onto the vegetable patches, and as he watched the pure, sparkling water irrigating the vegetables, Uncle Xiao said: "If their vegetables are grown using pure spring water like his, they're bound to be tastier and more nourishing than vegetables grown with recycled water in the suburbs…"

After breakfast, Uncle Xiao said to me: "As it took such a big effort to get here, it would be a shame to go back immediately. How about we stay here a couple of nights and head back on the third day? Go and talk to those two porters of ours and see if they'll wait here a couple of days. As well as their food and drink, I'll give them each another one hundred yuan a day." The two men were delighted with this arrangement, and one of them said: "You just stay here and don't worry about us; we're quite happy to rest up here for a couple of days." On that first day, Uncle Xiao and I followed Grandpa Wu'er's guidance that the most important thing was to observe Longevity Village's environment, and what the villagers ate, drank and wore. To start with, we went to look at the spot, about three *li* west of the village, where the two springs, Harmony Spring and Peace Spring, rose. They were about ten metres apart, and each seemed to produce around one large barrelful of water per minute. Their watercourses converged to become the main source of the stream that ran through the village. Grandpa Wu'er told us to taste the water from each of them: the water from the Harmony Spring was faintly sweet, and the water from the Peace Spring, faintly bitter.

Grandpa Wu'er said: "If you only drink the water from the Harmony Spring, you can suffer from excess internal heat, you can get boils and ulcers, and your skin can darken. If you drink only from the Peace Spring, you can get diarrhoea, and your skin can go yellow. It's only if you drink from the two together that you get the health benefits, you don't get sick, and your skin is soft and white. Just look at the women in our village: although every day all they have is plain tea and simple food, their skin is pale and soft, every one of them, just like a lotus root fresh out of the water. Young men from other villages far and wide all send matchmakers here to find a wife." Uncle Xiao grinned at this: "You're right, you're right, I'd noticed that. In the time we've been here, I haven't seen a single ugly or dark-skinned woman."

Next, Grandpa Wu'er told us to go and look at the ancient forest behind the village. For Uncle Xiao, who came from the Wei River plain, and me, who grew up in an area of low mountains, going into the ancient forest was quite alarming. The trees all seemed to be a hundred metres tall with trunks too thick to get your arms around, and their canopies seemed to touch the sky. Grandpa Wu'er said:

"The trees here all have their own spirit, and no villager dares climb them, let alone cuts one down. This is primeval forest, and very few people dare go too deep into it. They are particularly afraid of getting lost and meeting pythons and other giant snakes; there are a lot of wolves in there, and badgers and wild pigs; there is even the occasional tiger. Lion's mane mushrooms grow in there, along with all kinds of other fungi, and this forest provides us with all kinds of mountain delicacies."

After that, Grandpa Wu'er took us to see the place where they wove hemp. This consisted of two long wooden buildings on the east side of the village, below the stream. Each building contained ten old looms at each of which a middle-aged woman sat weaving. I went over and looked at the cloth they were producing, which was very fine, light and breathable. Grandpa Wu'er said: "Clothes made of this cloth repel mosquitoes, houseflies, fleas and other biting insects; you won't get pimples or boils either, whether you're a man or a woman, and your skin will stay very smooth. The cloth is made from a type of mountain hemp that grows in the mountains either side of the village. Our ancestors discovered generations ago that once this hemp has been steeped in water and bleached, it could be woven into material for clothing. In the past, every household wove its own, and the women worked at it in the period between sowing and harvesting in the fields. Later on, people outside the mountains got interested in this cloth, and the young people in the village liked to go out and make money by selling our clothes, so there were fewer and fewer available to do the weaving. Later on again, people in the big city came to hear about the benefits to the skin of this cloth, and they started coming here to buy it. The village elders told us to build a cloth factory and put these twenty looms here in one place; then they selected twenty or so nimble-fingered women to work together, with the main aim of producing cloth to sell outside the mountains." Uncle Xiao picked up some of the cloth and inspected it closely, saying: "I'm beginning to understand the main reason why you all live so long: the soil, air and water here are all so pure; you only eat grain and vegetables harvested the same year, and mountain delicacies, and you only drink water from the

Harmony and Peace Springs, which is much better than the mineral water that we buy in the city; you wear clothes that you make yourselves from mountain hemp that is beneficial to the skin; you live in houses with walls made from logs that still have the fragrance of fresh wood. Everything comes straight from nature, so of course you live a long time." Grandpa Wu'er laughed and said: "There is certainly something in what you say. No one dies from disease in this village; they only die when they are so old they can no longer eat, or meet with some accident, such as falling down a cliff when gathering mountain foodstuffs. It could be that the gods know we are too far from any hospital, and so spare us from any illnesses that would require us to consult a doctor or go to hospital. There are two remedies for people with minor ailments like headaches and low fevers: one is to grin and bear it and let the thing go away by itself, and the other is to use natural remedies to treat it, by making a tea out of herbs, which you drink for a few days and the problem is cured."

The next day, again on the advice of Grandpa Wu'er, we went and visited some of the oldest of the villagers. The first person we saw was Uncle September. Grandpa Wu'er told us: "He is the second oldest person in the village at one hundred and seven, only one year younger than my mother." Uncle Xiao and I assumed that someone that age would be living at home, retired, but when we went into his house and asked for him, his one-hundred-and-two-year-old wife, Aunty September, replied very crossly: "He's gone to help that bitch plant her vegetables." I was completely taken aback and whispered to Grandpa Wu'er: "Who is 'that bitch'?" Grandpa Wu'er motioned for us to leave the courtyard then whispered back: "She means Aunty December who lives at the western end of the village. She's just turned a hundred, and Aunty September suspects Uncle September is having an affair with her." When Uncle Xiao heard this, he gave a great shout of laughter and said: "So you can still get jealous even when you're over a hundred?" Grandpa Wu'er laughed back: "Sure, sure! Aunty September turns green every day…" He led us down to a vegetable plot beside the stream and shouted to an old man who was squatting there working away busily: "Uncle September, there are some comrades from Beijing here who have come to see you." There was clearly nothing wrong with the old man's ears, and when he heard the shout, he stood up and asked back, in ringing tones: "What's up? Do they want me to go to Beijing to be chairman of something or other?" "Now there's a happy thought!" Grandpa Wu'er chuckled back. Uncle September continued: "Of course, you've got to think happy thoughts to get by; it's the only way to get through the day and be happy." Uncle Xiao was laughing too now, and joined in: "So, what kind of happy thoughts do you usually have through the day, my old friend?" Uncle September could see that this was a man who enjoyed a joke, so he went on in a loud voice: "I think that maybe one day the gods will let me marry a beautiful young wife." Uncle Xiao laughed out loud.

Before his laughter had died away, an old woman leaning on a walking stick suddenly appeared from the trees on the banks of the stream and shouted at Uncle September: "There's no point me expecting ivory from a dog's mouth, is there! Just the mention of a young girl and you're all raised eyebrows and silly grins! Haven't you already been enough of a randy old goat in the past? Besides, do you think any young girl is going to give a wrinkled old tortoise like you a second glance? You'd do better to forget all that and concentrate on planting those vegetables!" Grandpa Wu'er hurriedly called out a greeting to the old woman: "So there you are, Aunty!" And from this, I realised that the old woman must be Aunty December. As soon as he saw her, Uncle September gave a crooked grin and said to us, with a comical expression on his face: "Of course! Of course I'll forget all that because my real heart's desire is to be told off and scolded all the time!" "What are you planting here?" Uncle Xiao asked, trying not to laugh. "Leeks! Do you Beijing folk know the benefits of eating leeks? They increase the speed of your circulation and promote fertility. If a man eats leeks twice a day, when he sleeps with a woman, he's much more hard and vigorous. Do you get my meaning, my lad?" My lad?! He was calling Uncle Xiao "my lad"?!

Uncle September's words made me blush, and Aunty December

started to scold him again: "You dirty old man. You can't say three words without bringing that subject into it! Aren't you ashamed of yourself when you can see quite well your nephew Wu'er has a young lady with him? You really are an old reprobate!" "What is there to be ashamed about? There's no point in going on living if a man can't think about that kind of thing!" Uncle September replied with a defensive grin. Speaking more seriously this time, Grandpa Wu'er said to Uncle September: "These two comrades have come here to ask you about the true spirit of longevity. Can you talk to them seriously about it, and not get sidetracked? Their time is precious." "So that's what they're after, is it?" Uncle September laughed again. "Well that's easily told: you just have to think happy thoughts, not upsetting ones. If you are laughing and happy all day, then Yama can't come and get you. Old Grandpa Yama only has one rule, and that is he only takes grumpy old folk who always look miserable..."

The next person we visited was Grandma Qi. Grandma Qi had just had her one hundred and fourth birthday. When we got to her place, she was in front of a full-length mirror, trying on an unlined gown with a rose flower print. Grandpa Wu'er motioned for us to stay silent, and wait for her to finish before speaking. Grandma Qi was turning left and right as she was inspecting herself in the mirror and saying to herself: "It'll do! Very eye-catching, and the flowers are good and big. If you're going to buy anything, then you should buy this kind of thing. It's cool and elegant to wear, and people are bound to notice it. He's a good lad if he knows to buy me this kind of thing..." It was only when Grandma Qi was about to step away from the mirror that Grandpa Wu'er finally spoke: "That's a beautiful gown, Grandma Qi!" "Ah! It's you is it, Grandpa Wu'er! So you like the gown too, do you?" Grandma Qi asked happily in reply. "Of course! These two comrades from Beijing think it's very pretty too." He glanced at us as he said this. Uncle Xiao immediately added his own compliment: "Very pretty indeed!" "Good then! Since you all think it's so pretty, I'll start wearing it from today. Sit down! Sit down! What wind has blown these comrades here from Beijing?" "They have heard that you have lived to be over a hundred, and they have come to learn from you!" Grandpa Wu'er introduced our reason for coming light-heartedly.

"What have I got to teach them? All I do is live each day of my life well, always feel content and not stick my nose into other people's business. All I've done is live a hundred years since I was born. However you live your life, you're still living it, aren't you? You shouldn't envy anyone else's life: just because someone else is a county commissioner, that doesn't mean I should be a county commissioner too. Aren't there enough of them already? Why shouldn't I spend my life growing crops? Other people eat meat every day, and that's their good fortune; I eat sweet potatoes every day, and that's another type of good fortune, isn't it?" As Uncle Xiao and Grandma Qi were talking, I inspected the old woman's three-room house and discovered she didn't have many possessions. The reception room had a wooden table and a few wooden benches, and the full-length mirror hanging on the wall. The eastern room had a wooden bed and two wooden chests for clothes. The western room had another wooden bed and three grain barrels. I asked Grandma Qi: "Where do you keep your valuables?" Grandma Qi waved her hand dismissively: "Everything is in those three rooms. I've got a bed to sleep in, the clothes I keep in those chests, the grain I keep in those barrels, and that's enough. All you need in life is food to eat, clothes to wear and somewhere to sleep, isn't it? What's the point in wanting anything else? If you have a lot of other stuff, you can't take it with you when you die." Uncle Xiao and I exchanged looks, and I could see he was a little surprised by Grandma Qi's reply.

In the course of that day, we saw pretty well all the residents of the village who were over a hundred. When night fell, Uncle Xiao said: "Well, our visit hasn't been in vain. At last, I know the mental attitude of people who want to live a long time, and I've found out the kind of environment you need, too. As far as the environment goes, I have to work with what I've got, but what I can do is change my mental attitude…"

We finally left Yuanyang, the Longevity Village, after breakfast on the fourth day. Before we went, Uncle Xiao told me to fill a plastic flask with a mixture of water from the Harmony and Peace Springs; in my backpack, I had a small bag of green vegetables and sun-dried mountain mushrooms and wood ear. I also bought twenty or so metres of hemp cloth and a small bottle of kiwi fruit wine. Uncle Xiao wanted to give Grandpa Wu'er one thousand yuan, but he said he didn't want anything. After a lot of toing and froing, Uncle Xiao finally said: "If you take it, then I'll know I can come back some time; if you refuse it, then you'll be telling me I can't come back." On hearing this, Grandpa Wu'er finally took the money and said: "All right, all right, I'll look forward to welcoming you back."

As the four of us waved goodbye to Grandpa Wu'er, I heard Uncle Xiao say with a heartfelt sigh: "What a shame we weren't born here." One of the sedan-chair porters said with a grin: "The people we envy are you lot who live in Beijing, not the villagers of Yuanyang. You just try living here for a while with no telephone lines, no cell phone signal, no internet, patchy television signal, intermittent electric light, no restaurants, no bars, no teahouses, no bus stops, no coffee shops; what is more, there is no music, no theatre, no dancing or sports to watch. I'm sure you wouldn't be able to stand it." I found myself agreeing with him: even if people here did live a long time, if I really had to choose, I would rather go back to the noise and bright lights of Beijing. Living here in Yuanyang Village would probably bore me to death. Humans are very strange creatures...

After we got back to Beijing, Uncle Xiao's emotional state was greatly improved, and he seemed pretty much to have put behind him those times he was cheated and swindled. In the morning, he started doing his Grab Fist Combat Form Taiji in the park again, and he also took a leisurely stroll in the afternoon as before. He told me: "I really must learn from the people of Yuanyang Village, and only think good and happy thoughts, not sad and troublesome ones." And, as his emotional state improved, stability returned to

our daily life. It was in this peaceful state that we advanced into
winter. Perhaps it was putting on his down-filled padded jacket that
made me notice it, but I could see that Uncle Xiao looked
significantly older than he had when I first met him three years ago,
and his mobility and posture could not really be compared to those
of Grandpa Wu'er in Yuanyang Village deep in the Funiu
Mountains. His arm and leg movements seemed slower, less
disciplined and less smooth; there was a tremor in his legs when he
walked, and on occasions I saw shakes go through his whole body.
Because of this, I made a special point of buying him a walking stick
to use when he was out and about, but he was very unhappy when
he saw it and asked me rather angrily: "Do you really think I've
reached the point where I need a walking stick? Ninety-year-old
Grandpa Wu in Yuanyang Village is still carrying a porter's pole; are
you trying to push me into old age?" I gave a wry laugh and said:
"I'm just taking precautions for you; it's just in case one day you
want to use a stick, you can have it to hand if I'm not there to
help." He replied coldly: "I don't want to see it again; it will just
annoy me." Seeing how determined he was, I hid the stick and
didn't let him see it again. He also kept urging me to tell Older
Sister about everything we had seen and heard in Yuanyang Village,
so she would know that such good places do still exist in China.
"She really shouldn't think of staying on to live in America, but
should come back here and visit Yuanyang Village." So I did indeed
call her and tell her all about the place. When Uncle Xiao heard
how long I was talking to her, he urgently interrupted me: "Don't
forget that's an international call you're making; don't stay on the
line too long." How was he to know that his daughter was actually
living in Beijing between the Fourth and Fifth Ring Roads, really
close to him.

After that phone call, I also went behind Uncle Xiao's back to go
and see Older Sister in her apartment several times. Every time,
when I saw the wired-shut windows, my heart sank. Sometimes she
was in an upbeat mood, sometimes down, but her physical health
seemed to have improved a bit, and she didn't look as emaciated as
before. I told her that as well as treating herself with her

medications, she should also go out and find something to do, and catch up with her old classmates and friends; it would help both her physical health and her emotional state. She sighed and said: "I'm afraid that if I found a job and it went wrong, it would just make matters worse for me, and make me even more depressed. What is more, if word gets about among my old friends, it will end up with Dad finding out. Let's wait until I'm better." After that, I didn't press her further. Once when I went to see her, she told me to go and wire shut the window on the stairwell. I hesitated over this; it was in a public space after all, and might there not be some objections from her neighbours on the same floor?

She saw my hesitation and sighed: "When I wake up at night, I still often have that urge to open a window and throw myself out. Of course, at the moment, I can still suppress the urge, but I'm worried that one night it might be too strong, and I could lose control..." When I heard her talking like that, I immediately took the pliers and wire to go and seal off that window. As it happened, just as I was twisting away with all my might, a man who lived on the same floor opened his door and saw what I was doing. He was astonished and asked: "What are you up to?" I replied: "My older sister lives opposite you, and this window keeps blowing open during the night. She just asked me to fix it shut." He laughed at this and said: "That window has a bolt, doesn't it? If you're worried about it blowing open, just shoot the bolt, and that will do the trick." After that, I couldn't very well continue without disclosing Older Sister's condition, and that wouldn't do, as she was desperate to keep it secret. So I just nodded and said: "You're right; I'll just shoot the bolt." When I went back into the apartment, Older Sister asked me: "Is it as tight as possible?" I wanted to put her mind at rest, and I didn't think she would actually go and check the window, so I just said, innocently: "Yes it is; as tight as possible."

Inexperienced as I was with clinical depression, I did not anticipate what a serious mistake I had made. I did not understand that if the sufferer becomes fixated on a place, especially a potential suicide spot, they will keep going back to check on it, so I did not realise that my carelessness as good as created an opportunity for

Older Sister to kill herself. After I got home that day, Uncle Xiao asked me: "Why hasn't Xinxin phoned me recently?" I hastily tried to smooth things over: "I expect she's worried she may miss you when you go out to do your *taiji* in the park. When she called me on my cell phone this morning, she asked after your health, and told me she was very well herself, and that you shouldn't worry about her." Uncle Xiao grunted and said: "As long as her mental health is improving, that's fine, but remember to remind her she's got to eradicate the roots of her problem if she wants to get better. She won't if she doesn't. If she phones you again, tell her I'm very well, and she shouldn't worry about me." I nodded promptly.

One evening a week later, probably because I was on my period and it was a bit heavier than usual, I was feeling rather tired. After Uncle Xiao had gone to bed, I got everything ready for the next day's breakfast, then went to bed myself and quickly fell asleep. I was startled awake by the persistent ringing of my cell phone. My first thought was that something had happened with my family back in Nanyang, and I snatched up the phone to look. In fact, the display was showing an unfamiliar number. Assuming it was a nuisance call, I was very annoyed, and answered snappily: "What do you think you're up to? It's the middle of the night!" In reply, I heard a rather rude male voice say: "Are you Xiao Xinxin's younger sister?" When I heard that, I hurriedly replied: "Yes, what's the matter?" "I'm a police officer. Please come to her apartment as soon as possible." His tone made it sound like an order. I wanted to ask him why, but he had already hung up. His tone and manner had me very worried. I got up and got dressed in a hurry, then went over to Uncle Xiao's bedroom door and said in an urgent whisper: "Lü Yiwei is sick, Uncle Xiao. I've got to go and take him to hospital." Uncle Xiao had apparently already been woken up by my cell phone, and answered from the other side of the door: "Go! But don't be too worried; young people often get sick."

I called a taxi and rushed over to Older Sister's apartment. When we were still some distance away, I could see there were several police cars pulled up outside the building, the lights on their roofs flashing. My heart leapt into my mouth. I had a terrible sinking feeling, but I tried not to think the worst. My taxi pulled up in front of the building, and a policeman came running over. He pulled open my door and asked: "Is your name Xiaoyang?" I nodded, and he went on urgently: "Your Older Sister Xiao Xinxin has committed suicide by jumping out of a window. Please follow me to the scene." My legs turned to jelly, my whole body swayed, and I almost collapsed. Great heavens! Seeing my distress, the policeman held me up and pretty much dragged me over to a spot that was surrounded by his colleagues. Before I'd even reached them, I caught a glimpse of Older Sister's clothes. It was her! Those were the clothes she usually wore. I gave a cry and made to go over to her, but the policeman next to me stopped me, whispering: "Don't go any closer; you don't want to see what is left of her, you might not be able to take it..." I remember I looked up at the building. Great heavens! Her body was lying directly underneath that window on the stairwell! I should have wired it shut! I had just told myself that, when suddenly everything went black and I passed out.

When I came to again, I discovered I was lying on the bed in Older Sister's apartment, with two female police officers standing looking down at me. When she saw I was awake, one of them said in a low voice: "Just lie there and don't stir. It's all over now; try not to be too upset. If you want us to help make all the arrangements for your sister's funeral, you can read this." She handed me a sheet of paper. I looked hard at it, but simply couldn't make out the characters written there. I had had such a violent reaction to Older Sister's death that fright had temporarily deprived me of my sight. Although I had known there was a danger of her jumping out of the window, really I had thought her worry about it was just a product of her illness, and I didn't believe it could truly happen. I hoped I had just been having a terrible dream. A terrible dream! That's it, it was all just a nightmare. At that point, I broke down and wept.

I don't know how long I wept. I hoped that the sound of my weeping would drag me out of my dream, but no; however long I wept, the two policewomen were still standing by the bed, and one of them exhorted me: "You can't keep crying forever. Everybody is very sad when this kind of thing happens, but you must calm down and steady yourself. We need you to make some decisions so this affair can be settled." Her words brought it home to me that I was dealing with reality, not a dream. I was currently the only person who could represent the Xiao family, and I had to deal with the matters in hand; the police officers weren't going to wait for me indefinitely. Having thought that far, I sat up and took another look at the piece of paper in my hand. It was a letter Older Sister had left for me:

Little Sister Xiaoyang:

I really don't want you to be reading this letter, but if you are, it is because I couldn't resist that voice any longer. First, I beg you to forgive me for thrusting you, who has no real connection with my family, right into the middle of this trouble and suffering. You must forgive me, as only then will I find peace when I get to heaven.

Little Sister – like it or not, I can only see you now as my little sister, and that is what I will call you: Little Sister! As your Older Sister, I will tell you the truth: I know I should still be alive, and I had no right to seek death. I am an only child; I have an ageing father who needs to be looked after; I should be shouldering my responsibilities as a daughter, but life has become a bitter, bitter burden to me. When the doctor first told me I had clinical depression, I didn't pay it much attention. I thought I could beat it through will power and carrying on as normal. But after going through such a long period of trying to treat it, I realised that this illness is the devil itself, and once it had its claws in me, I would never be free of it.

All those drugs could only temporarily pull me from its devil claws, and once their effect lessened and disappeared, it would drag me back into its grip. When I was under the influence of those drugs, usually for a few hours in the morning and afternoon, my head cleared, I could see things properly and acknowledge my status and responsibilities; I was my true self again, a real person, and I knew what I should be doing. It is in one of those times that I am writing you this letter. But at other times, especially as night begins to fall, the devil grips me again, and begins to crush me. It continuously tells me to remember the past, and the memories make me angry, remorseful and vengeful. It makes me remember how rebellious I was in my youth, it reminds me how blind I was to fall in love with Chang Sheng, and how reckless I was with my health; it makes me regret the concessions I made in my marriage to him, and to hate him for his betrayal; it makes me feel how much my life was ruined, and how no man is to be trusted. It makes me realise that life is hell.

It is an illness that constantly reminds me that life has no meaning; it tells me that the few decades of human life leave no trace in the great river of Time; it shows me that in ten thousand years' time there will be absolutely no sign that I ever existed. It warns me that in the end, Earth itself will be destroyed, that the whole of human history will become just an illusion, with no worth and no meaning. It constantly calls me over to the window, and encourages me to throw myself out of it; it tells me that with just one leap, I can set myself free from all my distress. In these circumstances, time and time again I have gone over to a window, longing to jump, but, because you had wired them all shut, it was too difficult for me to untwist the wire, and time and time again I have had to abandon my plan. This afternoon, I saw that the window in the stairwell wasn't closed tight, and this made me both worried and happy. I was worried that one evening I might make my way over to that window again, and happy that now I still had an opportunity to escape the clutches of that devil.

It is while I am in this conflicted state that I am writing this letter to you, as I think there are some things I have to tell you now, just in case we don't have the opportunity to speak again. I want to raise your salary again to seven thousand yuan a month, which makes it eighty-four thousand yuan per year. In the envelope along with this letter, I have put my ICBC CUP card, in which account there is a deposit of 1.6 million yuan. This is my entire share of the divorce settlement, and should cover your salary for the next twenty years. I am very sorry that there will be no further opportunity to raise your salary. The PIN for that card is 860921, and you can use it to withdraw money from an ATM at any time, with the proviso that you can only withdraw up to twenty thousand in one day. Thus, I am asking you to look after my father for the next twenty years, but there is no obligation on you to do so, nor do I have any right to insist, as our original agreement is only for five years. But there is no one else I can trust with this except you.

I really do not want to pass the buck for caring for my father, but this illness may well drive me out of this world. I have no other relatives I can ask

– only you, the little sister I have truly not known for that long. I know you have your own parents to think about, and your own life to live, and this request of mine can only add to your burden and make your life more difficult. Of course you can refuse, so I would ask you to find a good old people's home in the Beijing area to which to entrust the care of my father, and use that bank card to finance it. If you agree, then the first thing I will do when I come back in my next life will be to repay your kindness. If I am not reincarnated, I will pray for blessings for you from heaven. If you agree, and my father lives for more than twenty more years, and the money in that account runs out and you can't pay your salary, you can take it from my father's pension. I reckon that, when he is over ninety he won't be able to administer his own pension, so you can do it for him until he passes away. I believe he has made arrangements for his own funeral.

If I do indeed depart, I beg you not to alarm anyone. Don't ring any of the numbers on my cell phone, and don't inform any of my classmates or colleagues. Especially, don't tell my father; he absolutely won't be able to stand the shock. You can tell him that I am getting on just fine in America. On my cell phone, I have recorded five short messages for him, and every time he asks after me, you can open the phone and give it to him to listen, so he thinks I'm talking to him. This is the last thing I will be able to do for him. In the middle drawer of my writing desk, there is thirty thousand yuan in cash in a large envelope. That is to help you with my funeral expenses. Hire a car to take me to the crematorium, and just have me cremated. Then buy an urn for my ashes and go to the Tian Shou Cemetery. Ask one of the staff there to put my ashes in my mother's grave, and that will be that. My mother's grave is number fifteen in the third row of the Anxi Garden; the name is Jin Siyu. Poor you! You are still so young, and I am making you help with such solemn stuff. It shouldn't be like this, and you must forgive your Older Sister.

The rent on the apartment is up to date, so all you have to do is return the key to the landlord in Apartment 1609 in this building. Please give him my sincere apologies: I know I will have caused him a lot of concern, but I didn't do anything inside the apartment, so it should not affect his ability to rent it out again. If it does, please apologise again to him on my behalf. There are some clothes in my two suitcases, along with some jewellery and make-up, which I leave to you as something to remember me by. But, of course, if you feel they are unlucky, you are free to throw them all out.

Little Sister Xiaoyang, although you have not been part of our household for very long, and the two of us had personal contact for only a short time, I quickly felt that you were someone who I could trust and confide in. I am so glad that when I put that advertisement up on the internet it brought the two of us together, and I thank heaven that it sent me a little sister like you, even though we are not tied by blood. If you do read this letter, Xiaoyang, it is only in heaven or the next life that we will see each other again.

Thank you...

When I had finished reading this letter, grief racked me to the bottom of my heart. Although she wasn't my real older sister, for her, who I had seen face to face so recently, to leave the world in this awful fashion, cut me like a knife and pierced me like a needle. I forced myself to sit up, do what the policewomen were telling me and carry out the instructions that Older Sister had left me. I impressed on the officers the need not to alarm the deceased's father by releasing any news of the affair. If it was necessary for them to make a statement, they must be sure not to mention any names.

After day broke, when Uncle Xiao was probably already up and about, I used my cell phone to call him from the crematorium. I told him that my boyfriend, Lü Yiwei, was seriously ill, and I asked for the day off. I told him that I had already arranged with a nurse friend in our neighbourhood for her to have some breakfast and lunch sent in from a local restaurant. I also urged him to stay at home and rest that day, and not to go out for a walk by himself. Uncle Xiao replied: "That's fine. You go and see to Yiwei; don't worry about me, I can look after myself for a couple of days."

That morning, after Older Sister's remains had been cremated, I followed her instructions and took a taxi to the Tian Shou Cemetery. I put all her jewellery into the grave with her, keeping only the watch she always wore, as a memento. It seemed to me that listening to the tick of the second hand would be like listening to the beat of her heart. I also kept her cell phone as it held the five messages I was going to use to set Uncle Xiao's mind at rest. I made haste to carry out everything to do with Older Sister's last rites, but it was already dinner time when I got back to Uncle Xiao's apartment. I almost burst into tears when I went in and set eyes on Uncle Xiao, but I forced myself and ran straight into the bathroom, where I turned on a tap to cover the sound of my sobbing. Only when I had cried myself out did I emerge and go and make the dinner. As I was cooking, Uncle Xiao came into the kitchen and looked at me. He seemed to notice my bloodshot eyes and asked quietly: "How is Yiwei?" "He's much better already," I replied. "That's good," he nodded. "Don't worry too much. A young person's resistance is very strong, and they quickly shake off minor illnesses."

When I took his blood pressure that evening, I discovered that it was quite a bit higher than usual, and his heartbeat more rapid. I asked him if he had been out during the day, and whether something had happened. He replied: "I haven't been out at all today. I stayed indoors, reading and watching television. I also did a set of Grab Fist Form and a set of ordinary *taiji*, but for some reason I've felt disturbed and uneasy all day." I thought to myself: Of course Older Sister's departed spirit came to take her leave of her father. Of course Uncle Xiao must have felt something. Since you have to go, Older Sister, go in peace...

The next day, I took advantage of Uncle Xiao's afternoon nap to go downstairs and phone my boyfriend, Lü Yiwei, and tell him what had happened in the Xiao household. I also wanted his advice on what to do next. We had originally decided to get married on the first of May the following year, but if I continued to look after Uncle Xiao, we would undoubtedly have to alter our arrangements, and this was the most important thing I had to discuss with him. Yiwei was very alarmed when he heard what I had to say, and admitted he really hadn't thought Older Sister Xinxin would ever go through with it. But he didn't express any opinion about whether I should keep working for Uncle Xiao after the first of May next year. What he said was: "It's your work, so you have to decide." I wasn't very happy with this: of course it related to my work, but it also affected the economic situation of our future household. "You're soon going

to be my husband, so why won't you give me your opinion?"
Nonetheless, I quickly relented, as I decided that, in not saying
anything, he was thinking of my emotional attachment to Older
Sister and didn't want to upset me.

All was well, and news of Older Sister's suicide didn't appear in
any media, and it had no effect on Uncle Xiao's everyday life. The
time had come for me to decide whether to continue working for
Uncle Xiao. If I did continue, then I would have to divide up the
majority of the money Older Sister left me and put it into one-year,
two-year, three-year and five-year fixed-term deposit accounts for it
to attract a little interest and counteract the constant depreciation
of the Renminbi. I also needed to think about making preparations
to buy or rent an apartment in the neighbourhood. After Yiwei and
I were married, we couldn't keep living in Uncle Xiao's apartment:
given the conflict that arose between him and Older Sister and
Older Brother Chang Sheng, what chance would the two of us
have? Nor did I have any qualms about guaranteeing myself a
permanent salary of seven thousand yuan, as that was simply
honouring the deceased's commitment. If I did decide to stay,
though, it would mean I wouldn't subsequently be able to take up
an offer of earning more elsewhere. I turned the matter over and
over in my head. It seemed to me that if I did commit to looking
after Uncle Xiao right up to his death, I would be taking on a very
heavy responsibility. This was especially true, since, as he got older,
the demands on me as his carer would become greater, and I might
well lose much of my freedom in the prime of my life; after Yiwei
and I were married, we would lose the freedom to travel, the
freedom for me to go out and play with my future children, and the
freedom to go home and visit my own parents and look after them.
I was just a random family carer that Older Sister had found, and
although, of course, some feelings had developed between us, did
that mean I had to put myself in lockdown for her? Of course Uncle
Xiao's circumstances were deserving of sympathy and pity, but I

had no overriding responsibility to look after him and nurse him forever.

After several days of conflicting thoughts, I finally came to a decision: I would wait until the forty-nine days mourning for Older Sister were over, then I would make preparations to leave the Xiao household and find some other way of earning my living. Of course, before I left, I would follow Older Sister's instructions, and find an old people's home for Uncle Xiao, and deposit the money Older Sister left in a bank for him. No matter what, I was determined to live up to the trust that Older Sister put in me. The first thing I did was secretly go online and also telephone the Civil Affairs Department to find out what old people's homes there were in the Beijing area. Then I made some preliminary choices according to what I could glean about Uncle Xiao's preferences from our everyday conversations. Finally, I decided to make a personal inspection of a shortlist I drew up. Because I was choosing on behalf of Uncle Xiao, clearly the place had to suit his preferences, so I told him: "There's a fairly well-off old cadre from my hometown of Nanyang who wants to come to Beijing to find an old people's home here to retire to. He has. asked me to choose one for him. Could you go with me to look at some, so I can make a decision? You're much more experienced and knowledgeable than me, and you'll know better what old folk are looking for."

He didn't seem too keen on the idea, as he said: "He'd do better to come and choose for himself. Everyone has their own preferences, and I don't see how we can do it for him." I did my best to persuade him: "This man used to be a public prosecutor, so he was in a similar line of work to you, and his preferences are probably very like your own. He's bound to like wherever you choose. It really would be best if you help me, as I've never seen any old people's homes before." It was probably the pleading look on my face that made him say, reluctantly: "All right then, I'll help you out."

The first home we went to was beside the Wenyu River in Shunyi, and its environment looked pretty good on the internet. I called a taxi to take us out there. The home's manager welcomed us

warmly and gave us a tour of the residences, the offices, the
common entertainment areas, the dining hall and the garden. I
thought the surroundings and the place itself seemed OK, but when
we left, Uncle Xiao shook his head and said: "All the rules there
treat old people as invalids. If someone isn't sick before he goes in
there, he soon will be." I immediately replied: "Well, if you don't
like this one, let's go on to Changping."

The old people's home in Changping had been established
through the fundraising of a group of charitable middle-aged
people. Because the funding was limited, the buildings and
amenities were quite basic. The old folk's living quarters were all
right, but the entertainment and leisure facilities were distinctly
wanting. Even though the natural surroundings were fine, Uncle
Xiao came out after only a few minutes and said, with a curl of his
lip: "Living there would be like being put into slum housing."
When I heard that, all I could do was leave with him.

The third place was in Tongzhou district. As soon as we went in,
it felt very luxurious. The buildings were all two-storey villas, with
two old people upstairs and two downstairs; each had a bedroom, a
living room, a kitchen, a bathroom, and an exercise and recreation
room: five rooms in all. There was a flower garden in front of each
villa, a lawn behind, and an artificial lake in front of the main
building. There were two nursing staff to each resident. As soon as
he saw it, Uncle Xiao said: "Good! This is what I call an old people's
home. Living here would certainly help you live longer." As soon as
I heard this, I went to enquire about the fees. Great heavens! The
fees were thirty-eight thousand yuan a month, or four hundred and
fifty-six thousand a year. If Uncle Xiao really wanted to live here,
Older Sister's money would only cover three years, and that
wouldn't do. When Uncle Xiao heard the staff member describe the
schedule of fees, he said coldly: "This place is only for rich folk; that
old cadre of yours from back home couldn't live here. Let's go..."

The fourth place was in Xishan, and was, in fact, the same
Biquan Nursing Home that held a promotional event in our own
Longevity Park here. As soon as Uncle Xiao entered the complex
and looked around, he said: "This is all right." When I asked about

the fees, I was told that single occupancy was six thousand eight hundred per month after discount, or eighty-one thousand six hundred per year. If Uncle Xiao came here, Older Sister's money would last for sixteen or seventeen years. Furthermore, if he moved into a retirement home, he could stop paying rent on his apartment, and, with that saving added to his pension, he could be guaranteed twenty years without any problem. I was delighted: Uncle Xiao liked the place, the fees were affordable, so this was definitely the place for him. I immediately put my name down for a single occupancy, and paid the one thousand yuan deposit. All that remained was to persuade Uncle Xiao to move in.

It must have been the third day after we had visited the Biquan Nursing Home, I told Uncle Xiao, with feigned regret: "That old cadre's son and daughter in Nanyang think the Biquan Nursing Home is too expensive and have decided not to let him retire to Beijing. The thing is, I'll have to go back on the reservation I made for that room, and the one thousand yuan deposit I paid is non-refundable. It's a real shame!" Uncle Xiao sighed and said: "If he doesn't want to come, you can't force him. If you can't get the deposit back, too bad. Next time you want to help someone, help someone who sticks to their word."

I asked tentatively: "Would you consider going to live in the Biquan Nursing Home, Uncle Xiao? If you did, then that deposit wouldn't go to waste, would it?" His face immediately fell into a deep frown, and he asked, furiously: "How can you ask me that!? Do you think I've fallen so low as to have to go into an old people's home? People who go into that kind of place to end their days are old folk with no sons or daughters, or with unfilial children. I have the most dutiful daughter and son-in-law, who are earning big money in America, so how am I ever not going to have someone to look after me at home? Let me tell you, my daughter could hire two nurses to look after me. What old people's home would be able to make me as comfortable as I am at home? Do you still want to work here or not? If not, then be off with you; I'll just get on the phone to Xinxin and have her hire me a new nurse!" I was so wounded by what he said, I couldn't speak for a while. He really had no idea of his true circumstances. Just at that moment, I really wanted to say to him: You shouldn't be so sure of yourself, Uncle Xiao! You are really not in a better position than other old folk! But I knew the shock of the truth would be too much for him, and I really didn't want to shatter his self-belief and ruin his health.

Since this was what he thought of old people's homes, and he was so set in his opinion, there was no possibility at all of getting him to go into one. So that just left me with one problem: what exactly was I going to do? Should I stay on and keep looking after him, or make my excuses and leave? If I stayed on, I would be shouldering a heavy burden. If I left, where would I find another carer willing to take on this job with no possibility of ever seeing a salary rise? And if I couldn't find someone to hand over to, and regardless of everything, just laid down my burden, I would know in my heart that I was letting down Older Sister's faith and trust in me. I was caught in this dilemma: if I stayed, life would lose its sweetness, and if I went, I would live in shame. I decided that first I would see if I could find someone who would willingly take over the burden of caring for Uncle Xiao from me. I put an anonymous advertisement on the internet for a nurse-carer for a seventy-seven-year-old at a monthly salary of seven thousand yuan. On the face of it, this was a good salary, and after the ad went up, I had seven or eight telephone enquiries. They were all happy with the salary, but when they heard that the old person had no other family, could not be told that his daughter was dead, and that there would never be a salary increase, none of them wanted to take the job on. I was stuck with it.

So I had to carry on. I couldn't just abruptly and heartlessly up sticks and go; I couldn't let down poor Older Sister Xinxin! It was at this point that we had an alarm with Uncle Xiao's health. This time, it happened on New Year's Eve. A few days before, his old courthouse had sent a gilt-edged invitation to a New Year tea party to be held at the courthouse on the day of New Year's Eve, at which there would also be a special performance. Uncle Xiao was delighted to receive this: "The new people in charge still know how to do things: they still remember us old stagers." When I asked whether he was going to go or not, he replied: "Of course I'm going; it will be a chance to see old friends!"

On the morning of the day of the party, I made a very early breakfast and called a taxi as soon as he had finished eating. I asked if he wanted me to go in with him, but he said not: "You go out and have a nice time looking round the local shops; I'll call your cell phone when the party's over." I nodded and watched him go into the courthouse, then went off window shopping in the local mall.

I was really happy to do this. Although there was nothing I needed to buy, nor could I afford to buy very much anyway, I still wanted to have a good look around. I wanted to see what there was on sale in a high-end mall like this; I wanted to see just how good these top-price clothes, going for thousands of yuan, actually looked on me; I wanted to see how elegant these imported handbags made me look; I wanted to see how stylishly the make-up was packaged; I wanted to find out how comfortable the shoes were to wear. Because I was genuinely free that morning, with no other duties, I happily went from counter to counter in the mall, and took the clothes I liked the look of away to try on, item by item, to my heart's content. Even though I couldn't afford to buy any of them, I was still as happy as could be. The time flew by: it was already twelve o'clock. Was Uncle Xiao having lunch with his old colleagues? Why hadn't he called me yet? The invitation hadn't mentioned lunch.

I hurriedly called his number, but no one picked up, and I began to get worried: had something happened? I ran back to the courthouse, and when I asked at reception, I was told that the New Year party had already finished, and, moreover, Uncle Xiao had left before the end. I immediately hurried home, and as soon as I was through the door, I saw Uncle Xiao pacing the living room with a face like thunder. I thought he must be angry with me, and I said, defensively: "You didn't call me!" He suddenly exploded crudely: "Those fucking bastards!" I realised his anger wasn't directed at me, so I asked softly: "What's happened?" "They sat me behind one of the section heads! When I was at departmental level, that fellow was just an administrative officer! Just because he's a glorified office boy seeing to the comforts of the judges, is that any reason to make out he's someone special?" I began to understand: he had been seated wrongly at the New Year party. "He's just a bully! He just wanted to humiliate me!" Uncle Xiao was still pacing rapidly round the room. "Surely not! Perhaps one of the staff just made a mistake," I said, trying to mollify him. "A mistake!? Any fool knows that's not possible! The office staff there spend all their time arranging seating, busy little monkeys that they are. Every one of them knows quite well who should sit in front and who should be at the back. Today, they put someone who is my inferior in rank and qualifications in front of me, and they did it deliberately to humiliate me! I wasn't going to stay at a party like that, so I left early to show my objections!" "That can't be it! It was just a party, after all. Who's going to remember who sat where now it's over?" I said placatingly. "It was at the courthouse; don't you get it? They set it up like that, so everybody who went to the party would look down on me, would laugh at me to themselves, and would secretly mutter to each other: 'What has Xiao Chengshan been up to that he's been seated behind everybody?' It's a slap in the face! How can I get my dignity back after that? What can I possibly say? Eh!?" "Well, it's all over now, so don't lose your temper. Next time such an occasion comes up, have a word with them in advance." I tried to dissipate his anger, but Uncle Xiao exploded with fury and slammed his fist on the table. "The damage is already done, and it can't be undone. I have to get an apology from them. I'm going to contact the head of the court personally..." As he spoke, he made his way over to the telephone, but as he picked up the receiver, I saw his body tip sideways, and he toppled towards the floor. I was at his side in an instant, propping him up and stopping him collapsing completely. "Sit down, Uncle Xiao!" I thought he must just have lost his balance, but when I looked at his face, I went pale with fright: his eyes were tight shut, and he had passed out. My nursing intuition told me that his anger had caused his blood pressure to skyrocket, and that was why he had fainted. I quickly took his blood pressure and checked his heart rate: his blood pressure was 240/120, and his heart rate was 140. Great heavens! I quickly laid him down on the sofa and carried out emergency first aid, telephoning the emergency room as I did so, asking for an ambulance. Fortunately, by the time it arrived, his condition had begun to improve a little, and his eyes had slowly opened.

But I didn't dare take any risks, and I still sent him off to hospital to be checked over. It was only after a stay of two days that he was completely restored to normal. After his recovery, I told him of my lingering concerns: "You were lucky you didn't have a stroke this time, but with your blood pressure that high you are at real risk of one. If that does happen, you could end up incapacitated and confined to bed." I could tell he didn't really believe me, so I gave the doctor who had seen him a call, and got him to explain how dangerous his condition was. Only then did he begin to accept it, and he sighed and said: "Well, the way I see it, I'd better learn to keep my temper from now on!"

I took the chance to urge him: "In future, you'd better not go to any more workplace parties. I've asked about a bit, and it seems that almost all formal parties like that have seating plans that are organised according to the status of your job, its importance in the organisation, and whether you are currently in post or not. Since you are particularly sensitive to where you are seated, it's really not worth you going and getting so angry again. After all, your health is much more important." He listened to me and nodded: "Very well. What the eye doesn't see, the heart can't grieve over, and I can't lose my temper about. There are so many things to make a person angry these days. When I was in post, administrative level personnel didn't get their own car, but now, every little clerk in the courthouse gets one. Their wives even drive them to go food shopping! It makes me so cross when I see the little bastards..." "All right, all right!" I stopped him there, in case he really lost his temper again.

On the night of the day he came out of hospital, probably because he wasn't in the best of emotional states, he couldn't sleep. At eleven o'clock, he said there was a rat in the apartment, and it had got into his bedroom; it was rustling around and keeping him awake. I didn't really believe him: how could a rat get into the building and climb the stairs to the third floor? But he insisted: "It must have come up the pipes in the bathroom; it's happened before. Go to the janitor's office and ask for some rat poison; he's bound to have some. That's what everyone who's had rats before has done." I could see he was serious, so I did as he said. The janitor was already in bed, but when he heard I was asking for rat poison, he got up and handed me two packets through the window, saying: "I've only got Dushuqiang,[2] and I've heard we're not supposed to use such strong stuff anymore. Be careful how you use it – it can kill people too." I reassured him, and when I got back to the apartment, I put one packet down in Uncle Xiao's room. Only then did he gradually drift off to sleep.

After all this, because Uncle Xiao was so stubborn and strong-willed, I didn't let him go out and take part in any more activities in case he got provoked again. How could I have expected that, once I'd implemented these measures to protect his emotional state, he would go and break his leg while putting on his trousers? From the time I started looking after him, I had warned him time and time again: no matter whether he was taking his trousers off before going to bed, or putting them on when getting up, he should do it sitting down to avoid tripping and falling if he got caught up in a trouser leg; his age meant his coordination was impaired, and he mustn't put his legs into his trousers, or take them out, too quickly, or he might lose his balance and fall over. I also told him that old people fall over very easily, and if they break a bone in doing so, their mobility will be restricted and their quality of life will decline, which can also lead to other internal problems. He didn't show much interest in my warnings, but at least he made a show of nodding and agreeing. Even so, he continued to do things as he was used to, and took his trousers off and put them on standing up. Every night, he hung his outer clothes on a clothes hanger on the back of the bedroom door, and, because the clothes hanger was a little distance from the bed, he decided to save effort by not sitting on the bed, but undressing standing up. Whenever I saw him doing his own thing like that, I would always urge him to sit down. He was never too happy about this, and would admonish me: "You're only a youngster, but you're really just like an old woman, constantly nagging about the smallest things." I didn't dare say any more, for fear of setting off an argument, and just let him get on with it. And that's how it happened.

It happened one evening. I supervised his medications, checked his blood pressure, spread out his quilt, turned on his bedside light, then closed his door and went about my own business. According to his normal bedtime routine, he would sit up reading a newspaper or book for a while, then turn out the light and settle down. I was in the bathroom, brushing my teeth, when I heard the sudden thud of a heavy object falling to the ground. I stopped what I was doing, trying to work out where the noise had come from. At that moment, I heard Uncle Xiao's voice coming from his bedroom and crying out: "Aiyo...!" I threw down my toothbrush, and, with my mouth still full of toothpaste, I ran over and pushed open Uncle Xiao's bedroom door. Great heavens! There was Uncle Xiao lying on the floor with one leg half in and half out of his trousers. I could see at a glance that he had lost his balance taking off his trousers while standing up. I hurried over to help him up, thinking he had just taken a tumble. But as he stood up, he cried out plaintively: "Ahhh..." A shiver of alarm passed through me. After I'd helped him to a chair, I hurriedly examined him and found that I couldn't touch his left lower leg: as soon as I did, he cried out in pain. I reckoned he must have broken it, so I dialled 120 for an ambulance. Luckily, the emergency centre knew Uncle Xiao as a regular customer, and they didn't need to ask the address, but just despatched the ambulance.

At the hospital, an X-ray showed that his lower leg was indeed fractured, and he needed to be admitted. When the doctor questioned him on how the accident happened, Uncle Xiao replied, in some embarrassment: "I was standing up taking my trousers off before going to bed. I wasn't careful enough and lost my balance and fell over." The doctor turned to me and said, critically "You're supposed to be looking after him, why didn't you warn him he should sit down to take his trousers off?" I was almost too upset to speak and could only say with a bitter laugh: "Yes, yes, I wasn't careful enough." Uncle Xiao interrupted, grumbling through his pain: "I've been taking my trousers off like that for decades. Who'd have thought I could break my leg doing it? It was just bloody bad luck." The doctor replied as he treated him: "It wasn't bad luck, it was you not acknowledging you're not as strong as you used to be. When you were young, you could hop on one leg while you took the other one out of your trousers. Can you hop on one leg now?" All Uncle Xiao could say was: "Breaking my leg was… it was a one in a hundred chance!" Uncle Xiao had no choice but to stay in hospital, confined to bed, for a month, and even after he was discharged he couldn't move about as he liked. The walking stick I had bought for him previously now came into play, and, in fact, one stick proved not to be enough, and he asked me to buy him another sturdier one. Then he had to practise walking round the apartment with the two sticks.

To tell the truth, I was very anxious at this time: when would I ever be able to hand over Uncle Xiao's care to someone else, when his health seemed to be constantly deteriorating? Then, during the time I was supervising his recovery from his broken leg, because we were constantly in and out of the fracture clinic at the hospital, I got to know one of the nurses there. I could see that she was very diligent and hard-working, and also very caring, so I told her I was thinking of asking her thoughts on coming to look after Uncle Xiao. As soon as she heard the salary was seven thousand yuan a month, she seemed very enthusiastic, but she didn't agree immediately, saying she would think about it. I was all set to continue to persuade her to take up the offer, when a sudden crisis blew up in my own life. It was something that hadn't occurred to me even in my dreams, and it made me completely change my plan to hand care of Uncle Xiao over to someone else. I had to reckon on continuing to look after him myself for a very long time.

When planning our futures, we all plan for the best, and not for any crises, and that's just how I was. I foresaw for myself a life of

comfort and happiness. The way I saw it, we would wait for Lü
Yiwei to finish his postgraduate degree, get married on our chosen
date, and he would go back to study for his doctorate. I would then
find a hospital that was recruiting nurses, and go and work there as
a regular nurse. To start with, the two of us could rent an
apartment, and, after a few years earning, we would put down a
deposit, buy a small place of our own, and settle down properly in
Beijing. Once we had our apartment, and Lü Yiwei had got his
doctorate, we could establish ourselves and get our residency
permit; then we could start a family and live like proper Beijingers.
Because I had this plan, I could endure any challenges I
encountered, and, also because of it, I did my utmost to keep Lü
Yiwei happy and content.

When he said he wanted to try Henan Daokou roast chicken, I
went to the Golden Lion and Unicorn restaurant, owned by a Henan
celebrity, and bought some for him; when he said he wanted to
wear a Goldlion label tie, I went to the Cuihui Mall and spent
several hundred yuan buying him one; when he said he wanted an
Apple iPhone, I dropped everything to go and queue to buy him
one; when he said he liked my body, I gave it to him without
hesitation, thinking it was going to be his sooner or later, anyway.
Nor was I particularly vigilant in my relations with him. Once, he
came over to the apartment while Uncle Xiao was still out in the
park; he took me in his arms and pulled me down onto the bed.
Seeing how keen he was, I went along with him, but, to my
surprise, after he had taken my clothes off, he felt in his pocket and
exclaimed: "Dammit! I forgot to bring a condom!" When I heard
this, I got up and began to put my clothes back on. This was a risk I
wasn't ready to take: he hadn't graduated yet, I was still living at
Uncle Xiao's for the time being, and if we couldn't get married for a
while, what would I do? But he was very insistent and hugged me,
saying: "We can't stop now; break your rule this once, and let's go
ahead, OK? If I have to hold it all in, it might be bad for my health
and make me impotent. There's no time to run out to the shops to
buy condoms before Uncle Xiao gets back." He fell to his knees in
front of the bed as he spoke. My heart softened at his words, and I

thought to myself: Am I really going to get pregnant if we do it this once? All right, all right, I'll go along with him. So I took my clothes off again and let him have his way. As I watched him losing himself on top of me, my own caution gradually ebbed away, and I joined in with a will...

How was I to know that the thing I feared most was bound to happen? A month after this, my period was late, and I knew that something was up. I bought a pregnancy test, and my suspicions were confirmed. I was so scared that my hair stood on end, and I scrambled to phone Lü Yiwei: "We're screwed. I'm pregnant." He was shocked into silence for a moment, then just asked: "Are you sure? Just like that?" Then he said firmly: "Go to the hospital and get rid of it." I wasn't very happy with this: he hadn't tried to comfort me but just ordered me about. That wasn't how someone who was supposedly head over heels in love with me should act. I replied: "I've heard that if your first pregnancy doesn't go to term, you're more likely to have miscarriages in the future. That's what happened with Older Sister and Chang Sheng. We should learn from them. You're soon going to finish your postgraduate studies, so we can get married very soon. That way, we can have the baby; it's really common in Beijing these days for people to get pregnant first and then get married." He heard me out and then said very sternly: "That's not possible. I'm not intending to get married any time soon; if I get married, I'll be distracted from my doctorate!" I got annoyed at this: we had already talked this through and agreed we would get married after he graduated, so why had he changed his mind now? I was so furious, I hung up on him.

Going by past experience, all I had to do was lose my temper with him, and he would immediately come running to comfort me: one, because he loved me, and two, because I paid all his living expenses and tuition fees. But this time, to my astonishment, not only did he not come running to apologise to me in person, he didn't even telephone. I was very uneasy at this but decided to put him out of my head, thinking secretly that there was still time for him to come round to my way of thinking. A month went by like this during which I neither saw any sign of him nor heard from him. At first, I was worried, thinking maybe he was ill or had met with something unforeseen. As I was hesitating about whether to relent and go round and see him, I had a phone call from an older woman called Lin Taohong. This woman was the cleaner at Lü Yiwei's dormitory block. She was in her forties and had two children. She was from the countryside in Qinghe County in Hebei. I always bumped into her whenever I went to see Lü Yiwei, and, in passing, had got to know her quite well. Because we were both from farming families, and both made our living looking after other people, I felt a kind of kinship with her.

Once we were friends, when I took food over to Lü Yiwei, I often left a little something for her too, maybe an apple or a couple of packs of instant noodles or a few bottles of mineral water, so she had come to view me as surrogate family too. She once said to me, very solicitously: "Little Sister, it's a really good thing that you've been able to find a research student at this famous university as your partner; it's a very auspicious thing, and I'm sure good times await you. But you must make sure to guard him well, and not let someone else snatch him away from you. These days, lots of male and female students get together at university and go away at weekends to play house. You need to be a bit more careful." I remember being amused by this at the time and saying, with a laugh: "Thank you for worrying about me, Older Sister, but I don't think Lü Yiwei will go behind my back!" The no-nonsense Lin Taohong replied: "That's all right, I'll keep a look-out for you, and keep my eye on Lü Yiwei…"

Now, when she phoned me, she said: "You haven't been over to the university for quite some time now, Xiaoyang. There's something I've been thinking about for a few days, but I don't know whether I should tell you or not. But today, I couldn't hold back any longer, and I've decided it's best I do, so you're not kept in the dark, and you don't keep paying for other people's fun with your hard-earned cash; it's not fair on you." As soon as I heard this, I automatically knew it was something to do with Lü Yiwei, so I asked impatiently: "Go on, Older Sister, spit it out. Tell me what's going on." She replied: "It's been a few days now that whenever I've seen Lü Yiwei, he's been with a girl who lives in the female accommodation block behind ours. At first, I thought it was just to do with their studies, but then, when I saw them go into one of the chain hotels outside the main university gates, I knew something was up. They came out together as well. You've always been so good to me, I felt I owed it to you to take up your concerns. So this time I've followed them, and I've seen them go into Room 215 in the Wanjiang chain hotel. I'm at the main entrance to the hotel at the moment, and if you want to keep your Lü Yiwei, you'd better get over here and see that girl off... only with words of course, not your fists, or the police might get involved, and that wouldn't be good for Lü Yiwei." As soon as I heard this, my scalp crawled, and I flung open the door and was about to run out. Then I remembered Uncle Xiao was in the apartment, slowly practising his walking – it was almost three months since he broke his leg, and he could already manage without his walking sticks if he didn't try to go too fast. I just shouted through to him: "Something urgent's come up!" And then I ran out of the door.

When I got to the Wanjiang chain hotel, Older Sister Taohong was still standing at the main entrance. I was almost running as I went into the hotel, and she followed on my heels, urging me repeatedly: "If you still want to spend your life with him, don't quarrel with him; leave him some wiggle room to save face. Just see the girl off." I didn't have time to reply but hurtled up the stairs towards Room 215. I slowed down as I got close and put my ear to the door. The doors in this kind of chain hotel don't close very tight, and I could hear everything that was going on inside. The sounds were all too familiar, and there was no longer any way of putting a kind interpretation on the nature of their relationship. I concentrated all the fury that had been building in me on my way over, in my right foot, and kicked out at the door. It wasn't a door designed to withstand an attack like that, and it flew open. In an instant, the scene in the room was revealed to me: Lü Yiwei and the girl, totally naked, were lying, wrapped in each other's arms, on the bed. The loudness and suddenness of my assault on the door must have frozen them in place.

For a moment, they didn't move, and this gave me the chance to charge in and snatch up a teacup and hurl it at them. Like a crazy person, I picked up every moveable object in the room and threw it at them. They danced around on the bed, trying to dodge my bombardment, and, after I'd exhausted my ammunition, I ran over to the bed, seized the girl by the hair, pinned her down and boxed her ears. Lü Yiwei rushed over to rescue her, so I grabbed him by the balls and squeezed until he squealed like a stuck pig. If Lin Taohong and some of the chambermaids hadn't intervened to prise my hands apart, I think I would have squeezed his balls to a paste that day.

The day's battle was ended by the sound of the girl's yells and curses. The hotel manager and his security staff came running up, yelling that I would have to compensate the hotel for the damage, but when I cursed them for running a knocking shop, they quietened down. I only started to weep after I'd left the hotel and Lin Taohong had sat me down on a bench in a park on the same street. She urged me gently: "Try to accept it and move on..." But how could I? I don't care how much people laugh at me now, but at the time I wailed and bawled so loudly that passers-by stopped in their tracks, and quite a few clustered round me to look. My face was contorted with my weeping, and snot and tears ran down my face, but all I wanted to do was bawl out all my grief and resentment. The pillar that had supported me through all my hardships and exhaustion had collapsed, tumbled down, broken and shattered. How could I accept it and move on, when the man I had given myself to, body and soul, had treated me like this? I felt aggrieved, I felt regretful, I felt wounded, I felt angry: the course I had planned for my life had suddenly caved in, in front of my very eyes, and all that lay ahead of me was darkness... Only when I had cried myself out, did I fall into Lin Taohong's arms...

It was after nine o'clock in the evening by the time I got back to Uncle Xiao's apartment. I suddenly remembered that the old man wouldn't have had any dinner, so I hurriedly called out: "I'm so sorry!" But Uncle Xiao wasn't angry, and he didn't even ask where I'd been. He just said, gently: "I've already had a bowl of noodles, but you make yourself something." How could I have had any appetite? Without even washing, I lay down on my bed, hoping I might go to sleep quickly and forget about everything that had happened that day; but my fury whirled round and round in my head, and kept me awake. I lay, eyes wide open, staring at the ceiling and asking myself, over and over: What should I do? What could I do to rid myself of this burning anger? I must have racked my brain until after midnight before I came to a decision: kill him and go into oblivion with him. Only by killing him could I finally swallow my anger. Kill him! Lü Yiwei, you and I will depart this world together! Don't think you can escape me and go off and live your life with some other woman! Think what you like – I'm not going to let you have your way!

How to kill him? With a knife? Put the kitchen knife I used every day for cutting meat into my belt, go and find Lü Yiwei, then suddenly pull it out and stab him? Which was more certain? Stab him in the heart or in the throat? What would I do if he dodged the knife? What would I do if he grabbed my wrist? He was much stronger than me! Agree to meet him by the Kunyu River, and push him in when he wasn't looking? Was the water deep enough for him to drown in? What if someone saw and rescued him? No good anyway; I'd forgotten he could swim. I had to think of something he had no defence against. I thought and I thought, then suddenly I remembered the rat poison Uncle Xiao had made me get from the janitor. He had given me two packets of Dushuqiang, and that evening, I had only used one, so there was still one left. I remembered Uncle Xiao telling me the next morning: "You've got to be very careful when you use Dushuqiang, it can kill people too." Right, I would kill that mangy dog Lü Yiwei with Dushuqiang. Kill him!

Of course I was going to kill myself as well, so the two of us would go together. I did some research online, and I found a suicide case in which a man used rat poison to kill himself and the other two members of his family. Once I had made my decision, I finally calmed down and slept peacefully for the rest of the night. The next morning, I made Uncle Xiao a late breakfast, and after I had served

it and he had started eating, I went into the bathroom to look for
the Dushuqiang. I remembered that Uncle Xiao had put it in the
bottom drawer of a small cupboard under the bathroom mirror. But
I couldn't find it. Agitated by this, I left the bathroom and asked:
"Uncle, why can't I find the packet of Dushuqiang you didn't use?"
Uncle Xiao didn't appear to be suspicious of what I wanted it for
and replied, as he ate: "I thought the damp air in the bathroom
might make it lose its efficacy if it was in there too long, so I put it
in my bedroom. Why? Is there another rat in the apartment?" "Yes,
I heard one squeaking in my room last night." I had to make up
some kind of story. "I'll get it for you in a moment," he said without
even turning his head.

I ate an uneasy breakfast, weighing up my next steps after I had
got hold of the poison: first, I had to give Lü Yiwei a call, and
arrange to meet him for lunch; during lunch, when he was
distracted by something, I would put the poison in both our rice
bowls, and we would leave this world together... After breakfast, I
had just finished doing the dishes when Uncle Xiao brought out the
packet of Dushuqiang and gave it to me, saying: "I've already
snipped it open, so all you need to do is pour it into a small plate
and put it down wherever you heard the squeaking last night. I took
the packet carefully into my room, rewrapped it in paper, then put
some walnut powder in a saucer, and put it down in place of the
poison." After a while, I went and told Uncle Xiao: "I want to go
and see Lü Yiwei." He didn't ask any questions, but just nodded
and said: "Off you go!"

Once I was downstairs, I gave Lü Yiwei a call, but he didn't pick
up. I kept calling until he finally switched his phone off. I called a
cab and hurried over to his university. How many times had I made
that trip?! In the past, I'd made it every time I took him money, or
clothes or food. In the past, every time I made it, I'd been feeling
blissfully happy. But this time I was filled with despair and the
determination to end our lives together. I made my familiar way
over to the dormitory block, and when Lin Taohong saw me, she
told me that Lü Yiwei hadn't gone to class that day, and was still in
his room. She urged me: "Don't kick up a row here." I nodded and

said: "I've put it behind me. I'm not going to make a fuss today; I just want to talk." She waved me in, and I went up the stairs.

Lü Yiwei was sprawled on his bed, drinking some milk, and when he saw me push the door open and come in, he hurriedly put his cup down on the table and jumped off the bed, saying: "This is a university, Xiaoyang, you can't just come in here and make a scene." I forced a smile and said quietly: "I'm not making a scene – I've just come to say goodbye. Since you're in love with another girl now, I'm not going to force you into anything. There's no sweetness in a force-grown melon, so let's part as happily as we were together." He stood there, only half-believing me, and said, in a low voice: "Once I start work, I'll pay you back all the money you gave me, and a bit more." I made myself smile again and said: "Quite right, you should be paying me interest!" My eye fell on the cup he had been drinking milk out of, and I thought to myself: There's no need to ask him out to lunch; I can do it here and get it over with! He continued: "I'll always remember how good you've been to me. In the future, when I've made it, I'm sure I'll be able to help you in return." I smiled again and replied: "All right, we can talk about that again later. Right now you can boil me some water; I'm thirsty from my trip over here." He picked up the electric kettle that I had bought for him, and left the room to fill it with water.

I seized the moment to open the packet of rat poison and pour half of it into his cup of milk and stir it with a soup spoon. I tipped the rest of the poison into another cup and picked it up. He came back with the full kettle and plugged it in. As we waited for the water to boil, I sighed and said: "I'm sorry, I was all worked up yesterday and got a bit carried away. I hope I haven't got you into trouble." He seemed to take my apology at face value and began to mollify me: "I'm sure you'll find a good husband in the future; there are many better men than me around." I was afraid if the water was too hot it might affect the poison, so I interrupted him at this point, and filled my cup with half-boiled water. "It hasn't boiled yet," he warned me when he saw what I was doing. "I'm too thirsty to wait," I said. I took a gulp of water; it tasted a little sweet, and I said to myself: The people who make the poison must have done that to fool the rats, but it also means Lü Yiwei won't stop drinking his milk because it tastes funny. I took my cup over to stand next to him and said: "Today's the day the two of us go our separate ways, so come on, lets clink cups to the future!"

He turned to look for another cup of water, but I said to him innocently: "You can use your milk." He picked up his cup and clinked it against mine. I drained my water at a gulp, and indicated that he should do the same. Perhaps because I had been so convincing earlier, before he drank his milk, he said: "I'll go with you to the hospital when you have the abortion." That was when I suddenly remembered I was pregnant, and that, as I killed myself, I was killing my child at the same time. I also suddenly understood how cruel I was being: I was killing three people at one stroke! Remorse came to me at the very moment of killing, and I struck the cup of milk out of his hand. But before I could do so, he had already taken a sip, so I yelled at him: "Get to the hospital as quick as you can..." Lü Yiwei stood rooted to the spot at my shout, staring at me, wide-eyed. I pointed at his mouth and yelled: "There's rat poison in your milk..." This time he got the message, and he went white as a sheet, before running headlong for the stairs. At the same time, I turned to go too: I couldn't die here at the university so people could point at my body and curse me as a murderer.

As I staggered away, I didn't think I would make it out of the building. Back home in Henan, I had once seen a rat that had eaten poison lying dead not far from the poison itself, but, as it turned out, I got downstairs with no problem. There was no sign of Lü Yiwei at the bottom of the stairs, and I saw that he had already run quite some distance. "You must live, Lü Yiwei! Go to the hospital and get your stomach pumped. You marry your girlfriend, and I'll die with my child and not cause you any more trouble. My child, we must die together, and you must forgive your mother for harming you. You deserve to live, and it is your mother's foolishness that has harmed you..." "Xiaoyang!" I heard someone shouting my name, and wide-eyed in amazement, I saw Uncle Xiao, leaning on his walking stick, standing in front of me. I thought I must be hallucinating: how could Uncle Xiao be here? It must be the rat poison beginning to take effect. "Xiaoyang, get in the taxi and let's go home." This time, I heard it more clearly. I shook my head, trying to clear the hallucination, but the only result was that the figure of Uncle Xiao was even clearer, standing in front of me, with a taxi stopped behind him. He took me by the hand. "Surely that can't be a hallucination?" I muttered to myself.

"I'm not a hallucination; you're fine!" Uncle Xiao said calmly and reassuringly, then pulled me towards the taxi door. "How can you be here?" I asked, freeing myself from his hand. "I've taken Dushuqiang," I explained, "and I'm going to die." I felt the need to tell Uncle Xiao. "My will is under my pillow; please post it to my mum and dad. I'm so sorry..." Uncle Xiao didn't seem at all alarmed by my words, and just said, coldly: "What you've eaten is brown sugar, not Dushuqiang!" His words were like a slap in the face, and they made me shake my head again. I seemed suddenly to have come to my senses, and there was no hallucination anymore. I grabbed his hand and asked urgently: "What did you say?" "I said you ate brown sugar, not rat poison!" Uncle Xiao's expression was even colder: "Do you think I was a judge for nothing? Did you think I wouldn't discover what you were trying to do? As soon as you asked for the rat poison, I knew what you were planning. So you should know that I replaced the Dushuqiang with brown sugar..." A completely unexpected wave – no, I should say a joyful wave – swept through me, and I fainted dead away. The last thing I heard before I lost consciousness was: "Child, we can go on living..."

When I came to, I was lying in a bed in Peking University Third Hospital. An elderly woman doctor said to me amiably: "Don't worry, you and the baby are both fine." Then she moved aside, and I could see Uncle Xiao standing not far away, leaning on his walking stick, the same stern expression on his face. It was dinner time when we returned to Uncle Xiao's apartment. Full of both apology and gratitude, I said: "Thank you, Uncle! Originally, I came here to look after you, but it has ended up with you looking after me." "Do you know what you did today?" he asked coldly. "At its most serious, it's called attempted murder. Do you understand? If I didn't know the reasons behind the affair, and if it really had been

Dushuqiang that you took with you when you went looking for Lü Yiwei, I would absolutely have taken you straight to the Public Security Bureau. Do you understand? Just because the other party betrayed your love, you were going to kill him. Do you have no understanding of the law? What is more, you were going to kill your own child and a man who didn't love you, at the same time as killing yourself. Was it really worth it?"

Even though those words of Uncle Xiao were spoken in reprimand and reproof, after I heard them I felt an extraordinary warmth spread through me, and my tears flowed unrestrainedly. It was the second time I had wept since I discovered Lü Yiwei had betrayed me. The first time, because my heart was full of hate, its heat quickly evaporated what was left of my tears, but this time, I cried endless tears of regret and of grievance. Uncle Xiao sat down in front of me and said: "I understand your current feelings. I don't have anything to say about how you two handled your feelings for each other, as I have very little experience of such things. But, as a retired judge, I do have an opinion on the financial position between the two of you: you should bring a case against him demanding the return of all the tuition fees you gave him. I know that you scrimped on clothes and other necessities for yourself, and gave him a lot of money, and you have the right to demand its return…"

That night, I passed another almost sleepless night. In the course of it, I made two decisions: the first was to go on living and to have my child and never put it at risk again; the second was to cut off all connection with Lü Yiwei for the rest of this lifetime; let him fly off on his magic steed to a life of happiness, and, as for the money I had given him in the past, that was gone like so much dog food. Dog food! My mother once told me: "People can't help feeling sorry for dogs, and they can never let a dog starve to death…"

I struggled with my grief for a whole month before I considered I had freed myself from it and was able to confront this terrible unforeseen event. In the course of the next month, I continually thought of what those old people in Yuanyang Village in the Funiu Mountains had said: you must think good thoughts and happy thoughts... Although I had lost a lot, I still had my child. That was such a fine thing; how could I let myself wallow in grief and suffering? After that, things returned to normal, and I kept on caring for Uncle Xiao as I had in the past. Every day, I took his blood pressure, checked his heart rate and blood sugar, and every few days, I took him to hospital for blood tests on his cholesterol; I followed his regime for drugs for high blood pressure, diabetes and to clear his arteries, and I encouraged him to use suppositories for his haemorrhoids; I went for walks in the park with him, and I made him the food he liked.

In the past, there had been two reasons I was such an attentive nurse: one was because it was a nurse's duty, and when I started my specialist nursing studies, the creed of being wholehearted, responsible and diligent in one's attention to one's patient was injected directly into the hearts of my fellow students and me by the verbal syringe of our teachers' instruction; the other was because from the start I had made a promise to Older Sister Xinxin, and I liked and sympathised with this woman who had given me the chance of work when I was in difficulties. Now I had two more reasons: one was that Uncle Xiao had saved me and saved my and Lü Yiwei's unborn child, and prevented me from committing murder; the other was that at that time I didn't dare think about leaving Uncle Xiao and looking for other work. I was getting heavier and heavier, and my clothes were gradually no longer able to cover my swelling belly: no one was going to want to recruit me to work for them in my current state, and I had no choice but to view Uncle Xiao's apartment as my long-term place of residence.

After this affair, Uncle Xiao himself also underwent some changes. In the past, he hadn't liked to talk very much, and if he did, it was about his health, or about stuff concerning longevity and extending his life. In particular, when he talked to me, it generally sounded like he was giving me orders. But recently, it often took the form more of exhortations: "Don't carry anything heavy! Mind your belly!" And he would constantly be advising me: "There are always apples in the apartment. You should eat one every day: they're good for the baby." Often, he would try to save me from myself: "You should watch less television; those things give off radiation…" He had turned into something of an old woman, which unnerved me rather. Of course, coming from someone who was supposedly so little concerned for me, all this gave me a warm feeling inside.

As the days stretched on, my belly got bigger and bigger, and this made my work looking after Uncle Xiao rather slower and more laborious. For instance, it took me longer to go to the supermarket to buy food, and to cook it. I was slower cleaning the rooms, and I sometimes forgot to take him for his check-up at the hospital. In the past, he had a temper, and could flare up with anger, but now he didn't. His patience seemed to have increased enormously, and his anger threshold to have been raised much higher. One day, I suddenly felt sick after eating, and I threw up everything that had just gone down. As I sprawled across my bed to recover, he actually went to the kitchen, made me a bowl of tomato and egg soup and brought it in to me. This was an unprecedented event: it was the first time he had ever made me food since I started working there. Right at the start, Older Sister had told me her father very seldom went into the kitchen, and really didn't know how to cook; if there was no one at home to cook for him, he would go out to a restaurant. I never expected I would find myself drinking tomato and egg soup he had made himself! Even though he had put far too much salt in it, I gritted my teeth and drank it to the last drop.

As my due date got closer and closer, there was one urgent matter I had to get to grips with. I remember it was one morning when, after taking Uncle Xiao's blood pressure and checking his blood sugar, I asked hesitantly: "Uncle, can I still live here when I come out of hospital after having the baby? If you say no, I'll have to find somewhere in the neighbourhood to rent in advance." He looked up at me rather crossly and said: "Do you need to ask? You should consider this place your home!" I was delighted to hear this, as it freed me from my worries about the future, for the time being at least. As long as Uncle Xiao didn't object to me bringing the baby back here, even during my month-long lying-in period I would still be able to carry out all my nursing duties apart from accompanying him when he went out. I had no mother to guide me, and no girlfriends to share experiences with, so I was on my own on my journey through my pregnancy. I couldn't tell my mother I was expecting because, in the comparatively closed-in and conservative countryside of Nanyang, an unmarried pregnancy was a family shame, and would mean my parents could never hold their heads high in the village again. Nor did I have, in Beijing, any girlfriends who had been pregnant and become mothers, who could mentor me. I only had myself to rely on. Fortunately, Uncle Xiao understood some of this and was constantly encouraging me to go to the women's health clinic for check-ups, to make sure that there were no problems during my pregnancy.

My moment of greatest fear was when the crunch came, and, according to my own calculations of the day and what was going on with my body, it was time for me to go into hospital for the birth. I already had everything I needed for the hospital ready. Just as I picked up my holdall and was about to go downstairs to take a taxi to the hospital, Uncle Xiao said: "I'm coming too." I was taken aback and asked: "What for?" Looking very serious, he replied: "I think you're going to need a family member with you." At that moment, I almost wept.

It was a good thing Uncle Xiao came with me to the hospital, as, although my prenatal examinations had shown the position of the foetus was fine, and I had said I wanted a normal birth, once I was in the delivery suite, the doctor unexpectedly discovered that my birth canal was unusually narrow, and there was no way I could have a natural delivery. I would have to have a C-section. This meant someone had to sign a consent form. Already weak from all my tossing and turning, I made an effort to reach out for the pen, but the doctor wouldn't let me sign, probably because he was afraid my family would make trouble for the hospital if anything went wrong. He insisted that my husband should sign instead. What husband? Before I could say anything, the doctor, who seemed even more agitated than me, was at the door of the delivery suite calling

out: "Which of you is Zhong Xiaoyang's husband?" I heard Uncle
Xiao scurrying over to the door and asking anxiously: "What's
going on?" "Your wife's birth canal is too narrow, and we have to do
a C-section; can you please sign the consent as quickly as possible!"
"Eh?!" I heard Uncle Xiao exclaim and then say, in a fluster: "All
right, all right, I'll sign." I closed my eyes, and silently cried out to
myself in remorse: "I'm so sorry, Uncle Xiao..."

The operation went off without a hitch, and the doctors took out
of my belly a seven-and-a-half *jin*³ baby boy. Through my baby's
bawling, I could hear the doctor saying: "Even though it's an old
man with a young wife, it's a really healthy baby!" I didn't know
whether to laugh or cry, and in the end just let the tears gradually
come. I stayed eleven days in the hospital, and every day, Uncle
Xiao had the chef at a local restaurant make a pot of chicken soup
for me, which he then brought to my bedside himself. There were
four of us new mothers in the ward together, and the others all had
young husbands looking after them, while I had the slow-moving,
white-haired Uncle Xiao to attend me. As well as directing
suspicious and enquiring looks at us from time to time, the other
mothers and their husbands would also occasionally mutter sneers
and insults at me and Uncle Xiao: "The girl must be his mistress...
that old creature's grazing on young pasture has brought results..."
Uncle Xiao must have heard them because I could see his hand
trembling when he brought me my pot of chicken soup. I knew
what his temper was like, and if we had been anywhere else, he
would quickly have given vent to it. But there in the hospital, for
the baby's and my sake, he held himself in. I was so grateful to him.

After I was discharged and returned to Uncle Xiao's apartment,
the first thing I did was not breastfeed the baby but take Uncle
Xiao's blood pressure and check his blood sugar. This was not
because I particularly wanted to show my gratitude to him but
because I was afraid all his bustling about over the last few days
might have affected his health. The results rather surprised me: his
blood pressure wasn't up, and in fact it was even a bit lower than
before I went into hospital; his blood sugar was stable, and his
pulse and heart rate were normal. When I told him these results, I

couldn't help asking: "Have you been doing any extra exercises over the last few days?" He shook his head and said: "Because I was always running to and from the hospital, and I was afraid something might happen to you, I got very tired, and I fell asleep as soon as my head hit the pillow. Sometimes, I even forgot to take my insulin and anti-cholesterol medication." I thought to myself: Could it be that all the purposeful hard work was actually good for him? Or was it, perhaps, the distraction from obsessing about his own health that had a beneficial effect? I couldn't be sure either way, but as Uncle Xiao's nurse, I was delighted. Of course, if Uncle Xiao's health had suffered from his looking after me while I gave birth, then I would equally have been very sad. With the addition of a baby to the household, and all the crying and general disturbance it brought, I began to worry that Uncle Xiao might get twitchy and cross, and if he got cross, he might turn me and my baby out of the apartment – that was the thing I was most afraid of. If we left Uncle Xiao's apartment, where could we go? How could I take on the rent of a Beijing apartment, on my own and unemployed? If, in the past, it had been my sole preoccupation to find a way to leave the Xiao household, how to give up my job as a nurse, how to throw off the responsibility of looking after this lonely old man, now entirely the reverse was true. What I most feared was that Uncle Xiao would no longer want me as his nurse. How quickly things change in this world! Only now did I come to understand the truth of the old saying: *For thirty years, fortune lies on the east bank of the river, and for thirty years on the west.* Applied to me, it could actually read: *For one year fortune lies on the east bank of the river, and in the next it lies on the west.* Who in this world can safely say that they will always have a following wind?

My past dissatisfactions with Uncle Xiao had quietly melted away, as had the kind of superiority I had felt. I took to stealthily observing his facial expressions for any signs that he was unhappy with me and the baby's being in his apartment. I remember that, on the afternoon of our return, just before eleven o'clock, I put on my apron to go into the kitchen to make lunch. The doctor had said that my body was pretty much back to normal, and that I shouldn't let Uncle Xiao cook for me anymore. But Uncle Xiao disagreed: "How can you start cooking for me when it hasn't even been a month yet? You've just had an operation, haven't you? You must rest! I've already asked the domestic employment agency for a temporary helper to come in and cook three meals a day; she'll be here any moment, so you just sit out your month." I felt another inner glow that he was being so unexpectedly considerate. To tell the truth, in the past his eccentric character had made me think of him just as my patient, but now I felt his status was a little like that of a father, and I felt a real closeness to him.

I gave my son the name Zhong Chengren,[4] in the hope that his passage to adulthood would be a smooth one. When Uncle Xiao heard this, he paced around the room three times with his head down, before saying: "That name is all right as far as it goes, but just growing up smoothly is too humble an aspiration. If you call him Zhong Chengren, there's a slightly jokey feel to it, as though you are wishing him to grow up to be a star of some kind." I thought there was something in what he said, so I replied: "All right, I'll follow your thinking and call him Chengcai."[5]

When Chengcai was a month old, I told Uncle Xiao to dismiss the temporary help, and I would take over. The only money the household had was Uncle Xiao's pension and the funds Older Sister had left, and that wasn't enough to support the three of us and the temporary help. After a month's rest, as well as getting fatter, I had also become stronger. Even though Chengcai sometimes broke my night's sleep with his crying, I didn't find caring for Uncle Xiao and looking after the housework too tiring. During the day, I would take Chengcai in his buggy and accompany Uncle Xiao to the park to take a walk and do his exercises, and acting as carer to one young one and one old one made me feel very fulfilled.

One day as I was pushing Chengcai along behind Uncle Xiao, on the way to the park, I suddenly noticed that Uncle Xiao was stopping to rest every ten metres, and that he was breathing very heavily; he seemed to be more stooped than before, and he looked like a different person from the one I first met. It seemed that the ravages of time were even less merciful on people once they passed the age of seventy. Of course, Uncle Xiao did his best to ignore these changes, and he still would not accept any help going up and down stairs. Whenever he heard anyone refer to him as "old man", his face still darkened and he was very unhappy.

Uncle Xiao had never been good at jokes and light-hearted small talk, and his habitual expression was very serious; because of this, wherever he went, the atmosphere automatically became more sombre. If there was a group of old people in the park laughing and joking with each other, all it took was Uncle Xiao to come up beside them, and the laughter just stopped. But when he was with Chengcai, his smile lit up his face. Usually, when he had finished his exercises in the park, he would go and stand in front of Chengcai's buggy and gently tickle him on the tummy or under his armpits to make him laugh. And as Chengcai saw Uncle Xiao coming to tickle him, he would start gurgling with laughter. As soon as Chengcai started laughing, Uncle Xiao started laughing too. I found the two of them laughing together unexpectedly moving, and it made me very happy.

Once, when the two of them were laughing together, I said to Uncle Xiao: "You've made Chengcai your grandson, Uncle!" Almost before I'd finished speaking, Uncle Xiao's smiles disappeared as quickly as a crow hearing a rifle shot, and I heard him sigh: "I don't even know if Xinxin has had a child or not." I heard this with a start, as I suddenly thought that since I had come out of hospital, I had completely forgotten to make Older Sister's pretend phone calls to Uncle Xiao. He hadn't had any word from his daughter for such a long time, so of course he must be worried about her. I secretly cursed myself for my negligence, and for forgetting about my Older Sister. What was more, what was I thinking of, using such an emotive word as "grandson" in front of him? After dinner that day, as we were waiting for Chengcai to go to sleep, I used the excuse of having to go out to buy some more nappies, to use Older Sister's cell phone to call the landline beside

Uncle Xiao's bed. When he answered, I played him Older Sister's recording.

I had disabled the caller ID function on the landline, and additionally his hearing had already deteriorated, as had his ability to differentiate sounds, so I reckoned he would not be able to tell there was anything odd about what he did hear. Indeed, when I got back to the apartment with the nappies, Uncle Xiao said to me in contented tones: "Your Older Sister Xinxin phoned just now; she said all was well with her and Chang Sheng, so I can relax now. The only thing is, I forgot to ask about children." I pretended to be delighted for him and then said: "I expect Older Sister has been very busy over the last little while, and just forgot to phone before. As for the question of children, I think you're better off not asking. You know Older Sister miscarried twice back here, and if by any chance she still hasn't got pregnant, asking her about it would only upset her." Actually, I said this because there was no mention of children in the messages that Older Sister had left...

My use of Older Sister's cell phone to call Uncle Xiao greatly improved his mood. However, a couple of days later, my own mood took a major turn for the worse. The reason for this was the whole affair of registering Chengcai's birth and applying for his residency permit. Applying for a residency permit is a big thing in China; if you don't have one, everything becomes difficult, and you are excluded from all kinds of benefits. I knew that Chengcai was not qualified for residence in Beijing, so, at first, I decided to register him back in my hometown of Nanyang. But what I hadn't taken into consideration was that our village committee would submit a report to the village. This would inevitably mean that the whole village would get to know that I had had a child outside marriage, and my parents would never be able to hold their heads up there again. I racked my brain and eventually came up with a classmate from a village quite some distance from my own. I told her all about my troubles with Lü Yiwei's betrayal and Chengcai's birth, and asked her to help put Chengcai's registration through the village committee of her own village.

She didn't refuse, but a few days later she got back to me to say that the village registration officer had told her that, other than requests for a child's birth certificate, photocopies of both the mother's and the father's ID cards had to be produced, and just having the mother's was not sufficient. At this point, I was stumped; I definitely did not want to allow any contact between Lü Yiwei and my child, and I most certainly did not want him as my child's father! But without a photocopy of his ID card, I couldn't register Chengcai, so what could I do? I phoned my classmate to ask whether the exchange of a little cash could make this problem melt away, but she replied: "Absolutely not." After that phone call, my spirits dropped like a stone, and, for some reason, perhaps because he was hungry or thirsty, Chengcai chose that moment to start crying and wailing at the top of his voice. I tried to coax him out of it, but he didn't listen. I lost my temper and smacked him hard on his bottom several times. Not understanding what was going on, Chengcai was hurt by my sudden blows, and he began to wail ten times harder and louder. This just annoyed me even more, and I couldn't stop myself giving him several more smacks. His yells were making him hoarse. At this point, Uncle Xiao came out of his bedroom and snatched Chengcai up into his arms: "He's only little. What are you doing smacking him? I can see you're unhappy, but if you're worried about something, you can talk to me about it. What do you think you're doing taking it out on him?" I began to cry myself, and choked out through my sobs: "It's all to do with registering Chengcai back in my village. What can you do about it? It's all my fault! It's my fault for being blind when I met that bastard Lü Yiwei! If I hadn't misjudged him in the first place, I wouldn't be in such trouble now. Registering Chengcai is just the first of my problems; how am I going to be able to take him home to meet my mum and dad? How are the two of us going to survive with everyone looking down their noses at us..." Uncle Xiao listened in silence for a while, then finally asked: "Can't you just borrow Lü Yiwei's ID card?" "You're not suggesting I go and see him, are you? I'd rather die than see him again! If there's nothing else for it, I'll send Chengcai to the children's home!" I said, hardening my heart. "How could you do that?" Uncle Xiao asked, catching hold of me agitatedly. "We have to find another way!" I burst out crying. Of course I didn't want to hand my baby over to anyone else, but I couldn't think of any other options...

After dinner, when I'd soothed Chengcai to sleep, and I'd finished cleaning up in the kitchen, I was about to take Uncle Xiao's blood pressure when he stopped me and said: "Don't worry about that. I want to ask you: have you really not been able to think of any way of registering Chengcai in your home village?" I shook my head: "No, nothing!" He was silent for a moment, then got up and took a turn around the living room, before looking at me and saying: "I have a solution to the impossible, but it really is something to be used only as a very last resort when all else has failed." "What is it?" I was very surprised. "You don't know anyone in my village, do you?" "I'm talking about getting Chengcai registered in Beijing." "How is that possible?" I looked at him in even greater surprise, thinking maybe he had got confused and was babbling. "Getting a resident's permit in Beijing is more difficult than climbing up to heaven, but if Chengcai is registered here, it means, later on, he can go to school here," he said, looking straight at me.

That would be amazing! But for a moment, I was speechless, wondering how such an amazing thing could happen to Chengcai and me. Who had the power to get Chengcai registered in Beijing? "Looking at it from a countryside point of view, even if you found a way of registering Chengcai in your home village, when he went to school, his classmates would taunt him and jeer at him," Uncle Xiao said. "This is what made me pay particular attention to this matter. Of course, that much I understood." Every time I woke up in the middle of the night, I couldn't get back to sleep for ages with this situation foremost in my thoughts, so I kept quiet, waiting for him to go on. "The best thing is to get him registered in Beijing, so later on he can go to school here. Beijing is a big city, and people are more open-minded; there are lots of unmarried mothers and single mothers, and not a few girls who want a child in their lives but not a husband. Everyone accepts this and understands it, so it is much better to grow up in that kind of environment." Of course it was my dream to set up home in Beijing: that was why I had come here in the first place to work to earn money to support Lü Yiwei in his studies. I wanted to settle down in Beijing, so our children could be educated here, and so I could give the next generation of my family a better environment to grow up in. But that dream had been shattered.

"You may find this plan of mine rather surprising and alarming, but please don't get cross. If you don't want to go along with it, just tell me. We'll pretend I never spoke, and you can think up some other ploy. There is nothing in this world that can stifle a person's dreams." Uncle Xiao looked at me very solemnly. "So, what is this plan?" I couldn't stop myself asking him excitedly. "Don't be angry with me, even if you don't agree with it!" he repeated with the utmost seriousness, and I nodded my agreement. "You and I should get married!" I took a step back in amazement, my eyes wide. "It is the only way. If you want Chengcai to be registered in Beijing, this is the only legal way to do it. Of course there are negatives to it: it may be legal, but it is morally suspect and underhand. But it is our last resort if there is no other way." That is how he explained it.

I was dumbfounded for a moment, then began to laugh humourlessly: "Of course that would give Chengcai legal residency, but it would also make me your legal wife and you my legal husband, and you would legally have a hold over me! Oh, Xiao Chengshan! I never thought you had this kind of thing in you! You really know how to take advantage of someone when they're down. I used to think you were an upright honest man, but I was giving you too much honour and respect. It seems I got you all wrong! My eyes have been like chimneys blocking the light out with smoke, and I've lost my powers of discrimination. First I read Lü Yiwei all wrong, and now I've done the same with you. I'm worse than a blind person!" "Of course it would be entirely symbolic, and everything would be exactly the same between us as before. We would be husband and wife in name only. This is the only way round the current Beijing residency regulations, to get you out of your difficulties, to give Chengcai a proper home, and to free his spirit from being harmed. If ever you find someone you really want to marry, we can quickly get divorced, so you are returned to your single status." He continued his explanation in the dispassionate and precise words of a judge.

I didn't say anything for a moment; in fact, I couldn't say anything for a moment, as this was all too sudden for me. I had come up with many plans for staying in Beijing in the past, but nothing like this! I had never considered linking our two lives together, not even for an instant. In my eyes, he was too old, and nothing like the idea of a husband my father had instilled in me so long ago. "Now you can take my blood pressure. You don't have to give me an answer straight away; you can take a month, or even longer, to think it over. Whenever you come to a decision, just tell me. You don't have to worry about me being unhappy with it or finding it hard to accept." He was being very generous and open. I seemed to spend the whole night awake, thinking it over. How could I possibly sleep when I was faced with such a huge problem that affected everything about myself?

My first thought was: Uncle Xiao is my patient; how could he come up with an idea like this? Was he really only thinking of helping me? It didn't seem possible to me; was there really such a noble man on this Earth? Could you ever really trust a man? After the way Lü Yiwei had betrayed me, could I ever trust another man, especially an older man? When I looked on him simply as an old man, I trusted and respected him, but now, when I considered him simply as a man, could I still trust him? There is no such thing as a free lunch, so how can helping me and my child get Beijing residency come without a price tag? It must be my body that Uncle Xiao was after. Hadn't someone said that when men get older, their sex drive increases? Having seen how he had wanted to marry Aunty Ji, I was even more inclined to believe it.

Among the nurses and nannies of the neighbourhood, there were lots of stories about employers wanting to get their nurse or nanny on the cheap, and it seemed that I could now be included in their number. I may have already had a child, but I wasn't ugly, and before Lü Yiwei had taken up with that other girl, he was always saying how sexy I was; how voluptuous my breasts were; how pert my bottom was; how pretty my cheeks were; how long my legs were. It was more than possible Xiao Chengshan liked my young body too. I knew from his comings and goings with Aunty Ji that he was impotent, so what was he doing wanting to marry me? Did he want a bit of a grope and a snog? Maybe that was it! Did I really want to share a bed with an old man like him? Did I really want to hand my body over to his fumblings? Could I stand his wizened old hands sliding over my body?

But I still couldn't help thinking this was definitely the best plan to get me out of my difficulties. This way, Chengcai and I could get our Beijing residencies and become proper Beijingers. Moreover, Chengcai could openly and legally go to school and study in Beijing, right up to the *gaokao*. It was true that the price of following this plan would be my reputation. Everyone in the neighbourhood, and other acquaintances too, would think I was after Xiao Chengshan's property, and that I had deliberately hooked him to cheat him out of it. The next thing was that my mum and dad might find it too humiliating to have a son-in-law even older than themselves. And thirdly, it might well affect my future freedom: if I did indeed become Mrs Xiao, and then wanted to take up with someone else, he would be sure to stop me.

But then again, what did I want so much freedom for? Lü Yiwei's actions had already shown me that love meant less than a dog's fart, something to be cast off like a piece of worn clothing. Why should I want to go looking for love again and just find another man to let me down? I had always found Xiao Chengshan a congenial enough companion. And in any case, what was this body of mine really worth, after Lü Yiwei had had his way with it so often, and it had already borne a child? Wouldn't it be a good deal to exchange it for two Beijing residency permits? All right, all right, all right, if he wants it, he can have it. After this night-long debate with myself, I came to my decision: I would go along with Xiao Chengshan's plan; I would marry him and become his wife, put up with his fumblings, and accept in exchange the Beijing residency permits I wanted, and an assured future for Chengcai.

The next day, after breakfast, and when I had tidied up the

kitchen, I told Xiao Chengshan as he was getting ready to go out for his walk: "I've thought it through, and let's do it!" He looked up sharply at me and said: "Very well. After all, we will be married in name only. Now you've decided, we'll have to find a time to go to the Marriage Registry Office to get that done, then you can go and register Chengcai and yourself for your residency permits. I'll explain all this to Xinxin later, and I'm sure she'll agree." I thought to myself that if Older Sister was still alive, there was no way she would allow this. As I put Chengcai into his buggy, I replied: "Let's go to the Registry Office today. I don't want this thing churning around inside me; the longer it does, the harder I'll find it. The sooner it's done, the sooner I'll stop worrying. This is the simple truth. I'm afraid I'll keep looking at it from different angles and change my mind. This kind of uncertainty is real torture to me." Xiao Chengshan stared at me blankly, as though he suddenly had some doubts, but then he patted his jacket pocket, took out his ID card, looked at it, picked up his walking stick and said: "All right then, if getting it done will set your mind at rest, let's go."

The two of us didn't even change our clothes. With me pushing Chengcai's buggy with one hand, and holding Xiao Chengshan's hand with the other as he leaned on his walking stick, the three of us went into the Registry Office. Once we were inside, the laughing and chattering young couples and members of staff gave a sudden gasp, and they all turned to look at us. One of the staff members came over and asked in low tones: "May I ask what it is you want?" Xiao Chengshan replied in a clear voice: "We want to register our marriage." At first, there was silence, total silence, then a low swell of suppressed laughter swept across the room, and my cheeks burned bright red. I just hoped the ground would open up and swallow me.

After we had finished the formalities and were leaving the Registry Office, behind our backs, I heard the mocking voices and laughter: "Dirty old man..." It was then I understood that the pressure this sham marriage put on Xiao Chengshan was much greater than the pressure it put on me, and that it would do real damage to his reputation. I knew that his hearing was certainly still good enough for him to have heard the mockery and laughter. After we got home, I simply said to him, rather uncomfortably: "I'm so sorry..." He didn't let me finish, but just waved his hand and said: "Tomorrow, you can take the household registration booklet and today's marriage certificate to the police station and have your and Chengcai's residency recorded..."

That evening, when I had performed all my nursing duties for Xiao Chengshan, and lulled Chengcai to sleep, I had a wash and opened a bottle of perfume that Lü Yiwei had given me when he was first courting me. I dabbed some on my body, put on my nightdress and made my way to Xiao Chengshan's bedroom. I had to go and fulfil my duties as a wife. But when I reached his bedroom door, a thread of fear wound through my heart: what was he going to do to me? Just use his hands? What kind of tricks would an old man know? Would he abuse me, or hurt me? At that moment, I was genuinely afraid of going into this bedroom, which I had been in so often as his nurse. But I had to go in; it was his right. For the sake of this marriage, he had allowed his reputation to be harmed and, although we hadn't discussed the question of his property, since I was his wife, Chengcai and I would certainly get a share when he died. He was owed something in return. He had rights over the use of my body. This was a business deal, and it had to be an equal one: tomorrow, Chengcai and I would get our Beijing residency permits, and I couldn't leave him with nothing in return.

He was sure to be expecting me. Suppressing a shudder, I pushed open the door I was so familiar with. To my surprise, when he heard the door, he turned on his bedside light and asked: "Is something wrong?" I knew my body must be trembling because I could hear it in my voice too: "I thought... I thought I should come and sleep next to you." "What do you think you're doing?" His voice had turned very stern. I thought he was just putting on a show of decency and wanted me to take the lead, so I forced myself to say with a little laugh: "You were a judge, so you must know that from today you have legally sanctioned power over me." "Bullshit!" In a towering rage, he reached for the walking stick beside his bed: "If you dare come any closer, I'll break your leg. What do you take me for? Some kind of animal?" I stood rooted to the spot in fear. Could I have guessed wrong? "Go back to your own bed! I'm still your Uncle Xiao!" I could feel the tears springing to my eyes. Had I really guessed wrong? At that moment, I realised I had completely misread Uncle Xiao: he hadn't been taking advantage of me to get me on the cheap, he had really wanted to help me...

I am so sorry, but it's getting late now, and I have to go home to look after my two charges, old and young. The park authorities have arranged for me to come back tomorrow evening and tell the rest of my story. Thank you everybody.

MY DEAR AUNTIES, older sisters and younger sisters, thank you for coming back today to hear the rest of the story of my nursing career. I will pick up from where I left off yesterday evening.

Six months and thirteen days after I became Mrs Xiao, Uncle Xiao's health took a major turn for the worse. I remember very clearly that it was a perfectly normal day. The sun had shone very early through the window to fall on the sleeping Chengcai, and there were a number of birds singing brightly in the trees in front of the building, and all this had made Chengcai wake up earlier than usual. When I heard his cries, I hurried out of the kitchen to get him dressed and into his buggy. I pushed him over to the kitchen door and shoved a couple of toys in his hands so he could watch me making breakfast as he played with them. Uncle Xiao came past after he had finished in the bathroom, and pushed Chengcai in his buggy into his bedroom to play with him. I don't know what games they were playing, but whatever they were, from the kitchen I could hear Chengcai gurgling with laughter, and that made me very happy. I stood there cooking, and humming a folksong from my home village in the Nanyang countryside. Little was I to know that a major disaster was brewing on this beautiful, peaceful day.

As usual, after breakfast, I took a glass tea-flask of weak tea and Chengcai's bottle, and, pushing Chengcai in his buggy, followed

Uncle Xiao towards Longevity Park. Watching him from behind, I thought that Uncle Xiao's gait as he walked along leaning on his stick was just as usual. When I was studying nursing at medical school, one of the teachers once told us that we should always take careful note of the gait of the old people in our care: "If you notice any sudden changes in their gait, you should be particularly on the alert. It could well be an advance warning of a serious medical condition." Since there seemed to be nothing wrong with Uncle Xiao's gait, that indicated there was no problem. If all was well with Uncle Xiao's health, and Chengcai was eating and sleeping, I felt I had nothing to worry about. With my own blunted senses, at that moment I picked up no trace of the strange scent of that monstrous beast, catastrophe, even though, in fact, it was fast bearing down on us, now only a matter of a few hundred paces away.

In two hundred metres or so, as we arrived at the main gate of Longevity Park, by good chance we fell in with a group of old fellows who often went to the park to train. They were old acquaintances of Uncle Xiao; in the early days, they never spoke, but later on, as time passed and they were continually bumping into each other in the park, they became more familiar and always exchanged greetings and asked after each other. This morning, as Uncle Xiao greeted them, I heard him say: "Hello, old fellows! All well?" And they replied: "Hello, Lao Xiao! You well?" One fat old fellow among them said with a grin: "Lao Xiao is best of all. Not only has he married himself a lovely wife, he's had a son as well, at his age. Which of us has done better than that?" I was rather embarrassed when I heard that, and I speeded up with the buggy so I overtook Uncle Xiao to get in front of him. As I passed him, I saw that his expression had also suddenly turned rather stony. The same fat fellow didn't stop talking as I went past, but lowered his voice, even though I could still hear him, and continued to tease Uncle Xiao: "Such a young wife! You must be over the moon! Can you tell us what it's like? You old dog!" I heard Uncle Xiao give a low grunt, and when I turned to look, the fat fellow was still going on: "Don't be cross! Now you know what fresh and tender meat tastes like, so why don't you let us in on it too!"

Uncle Xiao raised his walking stick furiously, looking very much as though he was going to hit the fat chap, who hurriedly took a couple of steps back in alarm. But then I saw Uncle Xiao begin to collapse slowly to the ground. My nursing knowledge told me there was something wrong, and I let go of the buggy and ran over to him. I was too late to catch him, and when I got there he was lying face up on the ground. A bleed to the brain! I seemed to make my diagnosis almost instantly. I went over to prop Uncle Xiao up with one hand while I fished for my cell phone with the other. Then I remembered my phone was in my handbag on the back of Chengcai's buggy, so I yelled: "If anyone's got a cell phone, call 120 now!"

As I sat in the ambulance with Chengcai in my arms, I gave the emergency doctor a brief rundown of Uncle Xiao's medical history, and he gave his opinion: "A sudden emotional upheaval can cause the blood vessels in the brain to rupture if they are already clogged; the question is now how big the bleed is..." The ambulance sped towards the hospital, siren blaring, and as I looked at Uncle Xiao lying there, eyes closed and unconscious, inwardly I cursed myself furiously: In the end, this is your fault. If you hadn't married Uncle Xiao just to get your residency permits, that fat bloke wouldn't have been mocking him, and he might not have had this bleed. You're like a comet bringing Uncle Xiao bad luck. Because I was gripping Uncle Xiao's wrist tightly, taking his pulse with one hand, and clutching Chengcai with the other, Chengcai couldn't have been very comfortable in my embrace, but he didn't cry, and just watched, wide-eyed, what the doctor was doing. Little as he was, he seemed to understand there was something very seriously wrong...

The hospital we were taken to that day was not our usual one, and the resuscitation doctor there told me Uncle Xiao needed immediate brain surgery. I said: "Go ahead!" The doctor continued: "The cost of this kind of operation is very high." I replied: "The cost doesn't matter, just do it." The doctor asked what my status was, and I replied boldly and confidently: "I am the patient's wife!" I put my signature on the consent form and told him that I would go home and get the money when the operation was over.

The operation took close on seven hours. During all that time, my heart felt as though it was skewered on a steel hook. As I stared at the hands of my watch ticking round, I prayed and prayed: "May the gods protect my Uncle Xiao..." During this seven-hour wait, Chengcai ate a piece of cake and had a drink of milk; if it had been a normal day, he would have been making noise non-stop, but on this occasion not a single wail escaped him, and he just kept looking unhappily at my face. I don't know if it was because he was scared by my expression, or because his young child's intuition told him that his Uncle Xiao's life was in the balance. The news from the operating theatre finally came over the intercom: Xiao Chengshan's operation had been successful. With Chengcai in my arms, I bounded up the stairs, two at a time, to get to the doors of the lift used to transport surgical patients. The operation was a success, and Uncle Xiao was alive, but he was very slow coming round from the anaesthetic.

Uncle Xiao was lying in a bed in the ICU as I went home to fetch the money. It was fortunate that the money Older Sister had left behind for Uncle Xiao's nursing care meant that I could pay the fees for the operation. As Uncle Xiao lay unconscious, I went to find the doctor in charge and begged him to bring his patient round, no matter how. The doctor said: "We will do our utmost, but I have to warn you, it could be very expensive." I replied: "Bring him round, whatever it costs. I am responsible for this terrible thing that has happened to him, and I must spare nothing to redeem it." Family members weren't allowed into the ICU, and I could only stand outside the glass doors watching Uncle Xiao's motionless form from a distance. Over the next few days, I hardly seemed to leave that corridor, and, in my arms, Chengcai watched Uncle Xiao's bed, equally as silently as I did. Young as he was, he could understand this was an unusual time, so he neither cried nor made a fuss.

Older Sister's money was fast evaporating, and I was already beginning to try to think of ways of earning more if it ran out completely. If I couldn't think of something, there would be nothing for it but to go cap in hand to my parents. They were already unhappy with me for not having gone home for so long, and if I

went back now, asking for money, they would be very cross, not
least because I knew how financially stretched they were already.
But for Uncle Xiao's sake, I would just have to steel myself and ask
them, as there was no one else I could turn to. Luckily, Uncle Xiao
came round after spending twenty-one days in a coma. As the
hospital nurses and I wheeled Uncle Xiao to the recuperation ward,
I cried tears of happiness. Uncle Xiao looked up at me from his bed
with a rather stunned expression on his face and asked, as if he had
just woken up from being asleep: "What's going on? Did I fall
asleep?" Wiping away my tears, I nodded repeatedly. What was left
now was to nurse him back to full health. By then, I didn't have the
money to hire a nurse, but I wouldn't have been comfortable
handing his care over to someone else anyway. So I brought
Chengcai to the hospital to stay with me, and at night I rented an
armchair to sleep beside Uncle Xiao's bed and put Chengcai in a
cot, so I could watch over the two of them, young and old together.
Those were the most tiring days of my nursing career, but I was
happy to do it all. It was my fault that Uncle Xiao was taken ill, so it
was up to me to restore him to health. Although Uncle Xiao was
awake, he couldn't really move his body or limbs, so I had to give
him his medicines, feed him and give him water; I massaged his
arms, legs and body, and wiped him down all over with a wet cloth.
When I was giving him his bed bath, he only wanted me to do his
arms and legs, and wouldn't let me do below his waist. When I
asked him why, he blushed and wouldn't say why, but I knew that it
was because he was embarrassed. I told him: "You haven't had a
proper wash for ages, and you could get bedsores. The nurses
washed you when you were unconscious in the ICU, so why don't
you just think of me as one of those nurses. After all, I'm really just
your bed nurse, aren't I?" But he still kept his hand over his crotch,
so I had no option but to put my mouth close to his ear and
whisper: "If you don't wash down there, it might start to fester, and
if it does that, then lots more doctors and nurses are going to have
to come and inspect it. I'm your legal wife, and it's quite
appropriate to let your wife wash you down there, both morally and
legally." At that, he finally slowly moved his hand away.

There were three patients in the ward, and I knew he was embarrassed, so when I came to wash him down below, I always first hung up a sheet to form a screen so he and I were hidden from the others. The first time I finished washing him, he screwed up his face in discomfort. I thought I must have hurt him, so I asked him softly if I had. He shook his head and forced himself to say: "It's too ugly!" I didn't understand at first and asked him: "What's too ugly?" He screwed his eyes shut and said, painfully: "The older a man's bits get, the uglier they become…" I got it immediately: he meant that his pubic hair had gone grey and his penis and testicles had shrunk, and it had all become too ugly to look at. "My poor Uncle Xiao! Even at a time like this, you're still worried about a thing like that? You really do need to do something about your ego…"

The first two days we were back on an ordinary ward, he wouldn't let me help him urinate or open his bowels. With the latter, he kept asking one of his neighbours to call a male nurse to help him, and he gave the nurse ten yuan every time. "What's the problem here?" I asked quietly. "Forget I'm your wife, and just look on me as a nurse. You should let me do that! What are you giving other people money for? Why don't you just give me the ten yuan a time?" Holding back his tears, he said: "I never thought I'd come to this, needing you to help me relieve myself. It's too dirty and too embarrassing. I won't have any dignity left in your eyes…" It made me feel so bad to hear him talk like that, and I whispered to him again: "Everyone gets old sometime; today it's you, but in the future it will be my turn. If you can't look on me as your wife, look on me as your daughter…" From then on, he let me help him, but every time, he screwed up his eyes as though he was being tortured.

When the relatives of the other two patients in the ward saw how conscientiously I looked after Uncle Xiao, at first they thought I was his daughter, and when they discovered I was his wife, they gave me some funny looks. The older sister of one of the patients drew me outside the ward and asked me quietly: "What are you being so attentive for? Most young girls married to old men like you are hoping their husbands are going to die quickly. Wouldn't you get your hands on his property if he did?!" I was very unhappy at this and replied: "I'm going to forget you said that because we've only just met and you may have meant well. But let me tell you now, I don't want to hear you talking like that again!" At that, she lowered her head in embarrassment and walked away.

One morning after breakfast, when I had finished washing and drying him off, Uncle Xiao seemed to be in a better mood, so I said: "Since you seem to have turned the corner, let's have a photo together as a souvenir." I gave my cell phone to a nearby nurse and asked him to take the picture for us. To my surprise, Uncle Xiao objected strongly: "No photo! No photo!" I was astonished and asked gently: "Why don't you want your picture taken?" He raised a hand to his hair and whispered: "I'm so thin on top now, it doesn't look good. I don't want to leave behind pictures of me being bald." When I heard that, I quickly took my cell phone back from the nurse. So, Uncle Xiao was still vain about his image! I remembered when I first joined the Xiao household as a carer, how thick Uncle Xiao's dyed hair was, and how fastidiously he kept it combed. Who would have thought that, over the last few years, his hairline would recede so quickly, and his hair would become so sparse? With the additional effects of the operations, and the side effects of medication, there was more and more of his scalp showing through, and the operation itself had left a long scar. Ai! He was so worried about this – I just wished I could give him some of my own abundant locks!

I had studied nursing, but my knowledge of treating cerebral haemorrhage wasn't great. I originally thought that once the patient had woken up, he could gradually return to normal and recover completely, but later I came to understand that the condition almost always had lasting after-effects. Once Uncle Xiao had been transferred to an ordinary ward, he said that he had restricted movement in his right hand, arm and leg. I thought this was because he had been lying in ICU for so long his strength had decreased, so I paid particular attention to the massages I gave him. But no matter how much I pummelled him, it made no difference. I went to ask the doctor in charge of his care what was going on, and he told me: "In the course of the operation, as well as locating the blood vessel that was the source of the bleed, we also discovered that most of the neighbouring vessels were also blocked. We fixed those that we could treat, and just had to leave those that we couldn't." Great heavens! I stood rooted to the spot in alarm, temporarily speechless. How could this be?

In the evening after I got this news from the doctor, when I'd finished giving Uncle Xiao his food and medication, I temporarily gave Chengcai over to the care of Uncle Xiao's male nurse, Qiu Dali. Then I went out of the ward by myself and stood in a daze, considering the question of paralysis. When I thought of how the robust Uncle Xiao would be partially paralysed from now on, I couldn't help putting my head in my hands and weeping. Of course, the main reason I wept was for Uncle Xiao, thinking how harsh Fate had been on someone so strong and proud: first he had lost his wife, then his daughter, leaving him all alone, and now this! It was too unfair! At the same time, I was also weeping for myself: Uncle Xiao had given me a home; he had let me and my son stay on there, in the expectation of many happy years. Who would have thought that, in the twinkling of an eye, disaster would strike? How could I, singlehandedly, look after Uncle Xiao, lying paralysed in bed, and Chengcai, who was not even walking yet!?

I wept for a while, then dried my eyes, washed my face, put on a smile and went back into the ward. I couldn't let Uncle Xiao see how upset I was. I was his only support, and if he saw me upset, it would certainly worsen his condition. Nor could I let Chengcai see my tears, for although he was only little, he could already read my face, and if he saw I was unhappy, he would look at me wide-eyed in alarm and distress. I couldn't let that happen and make a little child lose his peace of mind. I had to carry the burden by myself.

Around this time, the high-ups at Uncle Xiao's courthouse heard that he was ill and kept coming to see him. It was then I learned that, because of Uncle Xiao's seniority, I could send all the hospital medical and accommodation expenses for reimbursement. The court obtained a refund for me of all the money I had already paid out, which relieved me of all my financial worries for the time being. I secretly went out and bought Uncle Xiao a wheelchair, as he would need one when he was discharged from hospital. But I didn't dare take it into the ward straight away, as I knew that his temper would make it difficult to get him to accept it. I hoped that the doctor would break the news to him.

The time came to leave the hospital. Uncle Xiao asked the doctor, very unhappily: "My right arm, side and leg are still not better; they're so weak I can't move them, so why am I being discharged?" The doctor replied: "At your age, Mr Xiao, recovery from a brain haemorrhage can be like this, and you have already far exceeded my original expectations. This is an exceptionally good result, but medical science doesn't yet have the answer to restoring function to your right side. Once you're home, make sure you continue your exercises with the appropriate apparatus, and you might find there is some improvement. But you have to prepare yourself mentally for the fact that you will never get back the function you had before you fell ill. You are not a young man, after all." At first, Uncle Xiao just looked at the doctor in a daze, and then he turned to me, eyes full of shock and helplessness. I hurried to take his hands, and gently stroked the backs of them, hoping he might find that soothing. I felt his hands trembling; after he had come round, he and I alike had both expected him to be returning home just as before, and we were not to know that events had already taken a different turn. As Uncle Xiao gradually recovered his poise, I went out of the ward and pushed the wheelchair in. Uncle Xiao began to weep at the sight of it. I wanted to help him into the chair by myself, but after two attempts, I couldn't budge him. The nurse, Qiu Dali, saw what was going on and came over to help. "How are you going to manage when you get home?" he asked. "Are you going to be able to get him back into bed? How about this? I'm just about to go on my break, so I could use the time to go home with you." I thought about it for a moment and could see that he was right: I wouldn't be able to budge Uncle Xiao at home either. So I said: "If you come home with us, I'll give you twenty yuan for your trouble." He just laughed and said: "You shouldn't be so quick to talk about money; who doesn't get into difficulties sometimes?"

From then on, I realised that I needed to build up my arm strength so that, as soon as possible, I could move Uncle Xiao by myself.

That day, Qiu Dali pushed Uncle Xiao in his wheelchair, while I pushed Chengcai in his buggy, with everything Uncle Xiao had needed in hospital on my back. As we made our way home, we looked like a family of refugees...

When Uncle Xiao returned home from hospital this time, it marked for me the beginning of life the like of which I had never experienced before. I got up early every morning to make breakfast. When I had done that, I went to help Uncle Xiao out of bed. Because he was paralysed down his right side, it was very difficult for Uncle Xiao to dress himself. First, I had to help him off with his pyjamas, and on with his underclothes and outer things. After that, I exerted all my strength to move him into his wheelchair, and wheeled him into the bathroom to wash. Slowly, he had taught himself to brush his teeth with his left hand. After Uncle Xiao had finished his ablutions, I went to wake up Chengcai, and after I had got him dressed and washed his face, I put him in his buggy, and then it was time for breakfast. I pushed both Uncle Xiao and Chengcai over to the dining table, brought in the food and began to feed the two of them. As I fed Uncle Xiao with a spoon in my right hand, and Chengcai with a spoon in my left hand, watching them eating, mouthful by mouthful, under my supervision, gave me a feeling of quiet contentment. In Beijing, these were the two people, one old, one young, who were closest to me: Uncle Xiao had given me a home, and Chengcai had made me a mother. The thought that they couldn't leave me, and that they needed me, made me feel that there was still some meaning to life. I had no greater expectations and ambitions at that time, and I felt that this was more than good enough for me.

After breakfast, I might take them to Longevity Park for something to do. I used a leash to attach Chengcai's buggy to my belt, so I had both hands free to push Uncle Xiao in his wheelchair and could pull Chengcai along with the leash, so the three of us formed a little group that became something of a local attraction. Every time the three of us went out, all the people in the neighbourhood would turn to look at us, and Uncle Xiao would hang his head in great embarrassment. But Chengcai was delighted and would wave his arms in his buggy, shouting and laughing. Sometimes, when we crossed the road, taxi drivers would stop of their own accord to let us pass. If we were going up a slope, it became really hard work as I bent my back into pulling Chengcai behind me, and pushing Uncle Xiao's wheelchair in front, but passers-by always hurried over to help, which gave me a warm feeling.

After lunch, I put the two of them, young and old alike, down for a nap, while I went out to the supermarket or the food market to buy all the food and other stuff we needed, getting back around the time they woke up. In the afternoon, if the weather was fine, I would take them to the park again for Uncle Xiao to join his old cronies in *taiji*, chess and cards; Chengcai could play in the sandpit in the Kiddies Corner. If the weather was bad, I let the two of them play together at home. After we got home from the hospital, Uncle Xiao couldn't come to terms with his paralysis and would spend the whole day frowning; his appetite fell off as well. After a while, I discovered that whenever Chengcai was messing around in front of him in his wheelchair, his frown would gradually lift. And when Chengcai could finally totter along on his own two feet and burble a few simple words, he could even get Uncle Xiao to break into a smile.

One day, I was sewing up some torn seams in Chengcai's clothes, and Uncle Xiao was sitting dozing in the living room, when Chengcai wobbled over to him, leaned on his knees and said: "Grinpa, how hold are you?" – I had originally wanted Chengcai to call Uncle Xiao "Daddy", but Uncle Xiao had glared and corrected me: "He should call me 'Grandpa'" – so Chengcai called him "Grinpa". When Uncle Xiao heard Chengcai calling him, he came out of his doze and asked him: "What does 'hold' mean?" Chengcai laughed: "Mummy days I'm two years hold. How hold are you?"

Uncle Xiao laughed when he understood, and said: "This year, Grandpa will be eighty years hold." "How many is eighty years hold?" Chengcai asked. "Eighty years hold means I've been holding on for a very long time!" Uncle Xiao replied with a grin. "Is it more than the sweeties Mummy gave me?" "Yes, yes, a lot more!" There was another wide grin on Uncle Xiao's face as he replied. It was then I realised that Chengcai could lift Uncle Xiao's depression where I couldn't. The old one and the young one were the best matched of companions.

After dinner, I usually turned on the television so Uncle Xiao could watch the news. I was aware that he didn't like to watch TV soaps but particularly enjoyed big national events, and he watched the news with great pleasure. While he was watching television, I would give Chengcai his bath. Bath over, I would put Chengcai to bed, then go and turn off the television and take Uncle Xiao to the bathroom to wash him. To begin with, I had great difficulty washing him. The reason it was so difficult was that he didn't want me to help him, and he had suggested that I ask one of the male nurses from the hospital to come over and wash him three times a week, and pay him fifty yuan a time. I did a swift calculation which told me that at that rate we would be adding six hundred yuan a month to our outgoings, so I pretended that I had been over to the hospital, but none of the nurses had been willing to undertake the return trip to do the job. When he heard this, he then suggested that I just wheel him into the bathroom, and he would wash himself. I knew that he didn't want me seeing his body because he thought it was old and wizened and too ugly. I said: "I saw your body when I was giving you bed baths at the hospital, didn't I? And there's nothing to worry about. I didn't find it ugly; quite the opposite, in fact; I thought you're much better looking than most old people, so why don't you let me wash you?" Since there didn't seem to be anything else for it, he heard me out and effectively gave me his tacit agreement.

The next problem was that when I moved Uncle Xiao out of his wheelchair onto the small round stool under the shower, the floor was very slippery, and I was always in danger of falling over. In the end, I came up with a solution: I went out and bought a small, lightweight plastic wheelchair, in which I could push Uncle Xiao directly under the shower to wash, and when he was finished I could dry him off with a towel and push him out. When I had settled him down in bed after he had finished washing, and closed the bedroom door on him, my day's work was well and truly over. Then it was my turn in the bathroom, and by the time I was finished, both young and old were asleep. At this point, I often turned on the little portable stereo that I had bought myself when I first arrived in Beijing, put in the earphones, and listened to some Henan opera like *Hua Mulan Joins the Army*, or *Mu Guiying Takes Command*, or *Striking the Golden Branch*, or *Qin Xuemei* – under my father's influence, ever since I was little, I have loved to listen to opera, and in junior high school, I wanted to be a star of the Nanyang Opera Troupe. Every night as I listened quietly to these excerpts of opera, with Uncle Xiao snoring and Chengcai breathing through his nose in the background, I felt very contented and satisfied, thinking that my life really wasn't too bad at all.

I was constantly coming up with ideas about what to do about Uncle Xiao's right-sided paralysis. Once I took him to a rehabilitation centre in the west of Beijing. The rehabilitation doctor asked about his age and medical history, and after a careful examination of his reflexes down his right side, he told me quietly that there was no possibility of further improvement and that I shouldn't waste any more money on it. But I wasn't going to stop trying, just in case he could get back some kind of function that could have a positive effect on his quality of life.

Children normally start at kindergarten when they are three, but I started sending Chengcai when he was two and a half. After that, I took Uncle Xiao to several other rehabilitation centres in the city, asking them whether there was any way of improving Uncle Xiao's condition. But, one after the other, they all replied that there was no such possibility. Once back home, I didn't lose heart but went out to visit a specialist bicycle repairman and paid him to make me a rectangular stainless-steel frame a little less than a metre high. I took it home and put it in the living room. I told Uncle Xiao: "I'm going to help you over to stand beside this stainless-steel frame, and I want you to try to hold it with both hands and then move along it, step by step, to see if we can't get some function back into your right arm and leg." He looked at the frame, thought about it for a while, then nodded his head and said: "All right."

By the look of it, Uncle Xiao's desire to be able to stand up and walk again was very strong. With my support, he made himself stand at the metal frame, and tried, with gritted teeth, to walk forwards. But having lost his strength down one side, even a single step seemed to sap all his strength, and he couldn't manage it. I saw that he was gnawing his lip so ferociously that he drew blood, and I hurriedly said: "Don't get worked up; it's the first time you've tried. Let's see what happens later." But he was gripping the frame tightly with his left hand and wouldn't let go; clearly he wanted to keep trying. There was nothing for it but to keep supporting him as he stood next to the frame, panting for breath. Once he had got his breath back, he tried again to extend his right leg, but his whole right side was so weak it had no control over his leg, which simply would not do as it was being asked. Then he tried to extend his left leg, but because his right leg had no purchase, it wouldn't move either. He was so worked up, his whole body was dripping with sweat, and because he was putting his entire weight on me as I supported him, I was getting exhausted too.

After this first, failed attempt at rehabilitation, I helped Uncle Xiao try again many times without any progress. If there had only been a little, it would have boosted our morale, but God wouldn't give us even the slightest sign of improvement. Every time, Uncle Xiao was just the same when he left the stainless-steel frame as he had arrived at it. All this time, Uncle Xiao kept repeating: "I don't believe I can't manage a single step! In my whole life, I've never encountered a difficulty like this. I can't believe it's got me beaten..." But he simply couldn't manage a single step. The last time we tried, Uncle Xiao sighed in despair: "I'm finished..." And with that, he burst into tears. I was devastated. There really was nothing I could do to help him. There was not even a speck of hope left for us: God had made his decision.

The evening of the day he decided to give up, when I was checking his heart rate and blood pressure, he suddenly gripped my elbow with his left hand and asked: "Is it because when I spent so long as a judge, I offended someone's spirit, and now they are paying me back by making me a prisoner in my own room? I know that there are some individuals who I sent to prison, whose cases were reviewed, and the evidence against them proved to be false. Do you think it could be their spirits who have come back after death to take revenge on me?" I replied with a laugh: "How can you have such foolish thoughts, Uncle? No one wants to harm you. It's just the nature of the illness, and you're not the only person it's happened to..." I didn't feel I could blindly persist with the attempted rehabilitation, as that would only add to his emotional torture and physical pain. Perhaps it is the case that when you reach a certain age, there are certain conditions that can't be reversed; God has already taken away your resistance to an ailment, and all you can do is endure it, confront it and learn to live with it.

When I took that steel frame out of the apartment, I noticed how Uncle Xiao looked at it regretfully but resignedly: it had represented hope to the two of us, but that hope was now gone. After this, Uncle Xiao's mood remained constantly dispirited, his appetite seemed to lessen, and he spoke even less. One morning, I found him writing the same four words, over and over again in pencil on a sheet of paper: "I won't accept it!" When I saw this, I thought it meant he wasn't satisfied with the doctors' treatment, so I urged him: "The doctors absolutely did their very best!" He shook his head and said: "I'm not dissatisfied with the doctors – I'm angry with God. Why has He played this dirty trick on me? There are plenty of people in their seventies, eighties and even nineties in Beijing, all in good health. Why is it me He has left all messed up like this? It's not fair!" I didn't know what to say to him.

One afternoon, as I was just getting back from doing some food shopping and had reached the front door, I heard an ear-piercing noise from inside the apartment. It sounded like grinding meal, and it really alarmed me. There was only Uncle Xiao in the house at the time, and how could he make a noise like that? I threw open the door, and then I understood: there he was brandishing his old walking stick in his functioning left hand, and bringing it crashing down on his wheelchair and cursing as he did so: "You bastard! Why are you squeezing the life out of me? Why?" I stood motionless in the doorway, silently watching him until he was exhausted and disconsolately dropped the walking stick. Only then did I go in and gently stroke his back.

He became more and more dejected, and I thought to myself I had better find some way of reversing this as quickly as possible. Luckily, as I was racking my brain unsuccessfully, the wife of a fellow section chief from his old courthouse telephoned to tell him that her husband had had a stroke a few days ago and was very depressed. She had heard that Uncle Xiao was in quite good spirits after his brain haemorrhage, and wondered if she could wheel her husband round for the two of them to meet, so Uncle Xiao could have an encouraging word with him. When I heard this, I thought it was a good idea. Although Uncle Xiao himself really wasn't in a good state, and might not actually be able to do much encouraging, the two of them, sitting together, both suffering from similar conditions, would at least have something to talk about. Having someone else to share their own suffering with might be a consolation. I immediately invited the couple over the next day. That evening, I told Uncle Xiao that his old colleague was coming over the next day to see how he was getting on. I didn't tell him the fellow was also ill, as I thought he might refuse, as indeed he did at first, saying: "Just look at the state of me: I can't even move without a wheelchair; just the sight of me will upset him. Ask him not to come." I tried to persuade him: "He's an old court colleague, and he really wants to see you. It would be rude to refuse. Besides, there's nothing to be ashamed about being ill; who knows who it might happen to next?" At this, he dropped his objections, which I took as agreement.

The next morning, I tidied up and cleaned the living room, put out fresh flowers and fruit, then massaged Uncle Xiao's right arm and leg as I waited patiently for our visitors to arrive. There was a knock at the door, and I hurried over to answer it. When I opened the door, even though I was expecting to see a man who had had a stroke, his condition still alarmed me: he was sprawled in a wheelchair, his mouth crooked, his eyes drooping, unable to move by himself, and with saliva dribbling constantly from the corner of his mouth. When his wife, who was pushing the wheelchair, saw me, her eyes went red, and she looked as though she was about to cry. I shot her a meaningful look to stop her from crying and led the pair of them over to where Uncle Xiao was. He was sitting dejectedly in his wheelchair, but when he saw his old colleague, he gave a great start, forced himself upright and cried out: "Xiao Wu Kui! Don't tell me you've had a stroke too!" When the man he called Xiao Wu Kui heard this, he babbled something, but I couldn't make out a single distinct word. Uncle Xiao used his left hand to turn his wheelchair a little closer, then reached out and stroked the other man's hair, saying: "Don't upset yourself! Don't upset yourself! I understand! You're saying you've had a bit to drink, aren't you? You used to be able to drink more than anyone else in the court. Do you still remember the time you drank me under the table?" Xiao Wu Kui babbled some more, and his wife interpreted this time: "He says that if he had known, back then, that drink was going to lay him out like this, he wouldn't have drunk so much!" Uncle Xiao laughed – he actually laughed: "All right, we won't talk about the past; we can't change it, after all. The most important thing is to come to terms with the present. Illness has come for us, and there's nothing we can do about it but accept it."

What Uncle Xiao said to Xiao Wu Kui that day was exactly what I wanted to say to Uncle Xiao. Heavens! It turned out that Uncle Xiao understood all these principles and could explain them to someone else, but he hadn't been able to accept them for himself. I was right: after Uncle Wu Kui left that day, there was a major change in his mood. He stopped frowning all the time and rattled around the living room in his wheelchair. His appetite gradually increased, his complexion improved, and he stopped flying off the handle at the least provocation. I guessed the reason for his new-found equanimity was that he had now seen someone from his own social circle with the same condition and knew that Fate hadn't just picked on him alone. It was also only then that I myself understood that humans are creatures that like to make comparisons because that is the only way to discover that others are worse off than yourself and then come to accept your own circumstances. This is an attitude that we nurses need to incorporate into our armoury when we are trying to comfort our patients.

After this, Uncle Xiao became resigned to his life in a wheelchair. He stopped grumbling and losing his temper. He stopped bottling up his anger and began truly to become one with his wheelchair. Every morning when he got up, he would let me put him in his chair without a murmur, push him into the bathroom to urinate and open his bowels, let him wash his face and rinse his mouth, and then have breakfast. After breakfast, he would wait for me to take Chengcai to the kindergarten, then let me push him to the park for some fresh air. As he was chatting to the other old folk, I would massage his right arm and leg. As it got close to noon, I would push him back home and turn on the television to watch the news while I made lunch. After lunch, I would lift him out of his wheelchair – the constant lifting had made me a lot stronger, and I could now do it without any great effort – and put him into bed for his nap. After his nap, I would push him back to the park to meet up with some other old folk in wheelchairs and shoot the breeze. After dinner, he watched some more news, waited for me to settle Chengcai, and then I gave him a wash and put him to bed. Apart from when he was asleep, he spent his whole day in his wheelchair. For a martial artist with an uncertain temper and a high self-regard, this was not a life that was easy to accept, but Uncle Xiao had finally knuckled down and done just that.

In order to improve Uncle Xiao's wheelchair-bound life a little, I began to investigate different types of chair and their capabilities. There were two main types of wheelchair on the market: one was hand-driven, and the other was electric. Because Uncle Xiao had no strength on one side of his body, an electric chair would be difficult for him to control and would be prone to accidents, so would not be too suitable for him. I therefore paid particular attention to the different types and models of manual wheelchair. In the end, I bought four manual chairs: one had a wide, comfortable seat that could recline, and a tray in front for a water cup and other necessities. It was suitable for outside use in spring, autumn and winter. Another was an all-purpose plastic model with a hole in the middle of the seat, to allow him to relieve himself and wash himself. Another had high arms and a comparatively narrow seat, and was for him to sit at the dining table to eat. The last one was made out of real wood and was for use in hot weather. I couldn't get rid of his need for a wheelchair, but I could make sure he could spend his days a little more comfortably.

Time is a formidable character, and it finally allowed Uncle Xiao to get used to the idea of spending the rest of his life in a wheelchair. By the time Chengcai reached the age to go to primary school, Uncle Xiao was completely comfortable in his chair, eating, drinking, relieving himself, washing and getting dressed. He could even quite happily joke about it. I remember on Chengcai's first day at school, Uncle Xiao said to him: "Well, my little man, make sure you study hard at school, so one day you can go to law school and become a judge. Then Grandpa can pass on to you all his own experience of being a judge." Chengcai chuckled and said with a bright smile: "All right, Grandpa! But that overseas Chinese chap downstairs says he's going to go to study in America. Do you think I should go too?" I was washing vegetables at the time, and when I heard this, I tried to change the subject, but it was too late. Uncle Xiao had already made the association with his own daughter, and his expression immediately darkened. I thought to myself: I'm going to have to make a call on Older Sister's behalf this evening! It had been quite a time since I'd last called because I'd been busy with Chengcai starting school, and had forgotten about it.

That evening after dinner, when I had finished the washing-up, I secretly took out the cell phone that Older Sister had left me, and went outside to call the landline at Uncle Xiao's bedside. When he answered, I played him the second of the recordings Older Sister had made. As I eavesdropped, this time I didn't hear Uncle Xiao say anything. I thought this was a little unusual, but I didn't really pay it any attention at the time, and just thought that Uncle Xiao must have been cheered up by hearing his daughter's voice. To my astonishment, as soon as I got back into the apartment, Uncle Xiao said to me abruptly: "You're not to do that again!" I was completely taken aback, not understanding what he meant, so I just stared blankly at him. He lowered his voice and said: "A few days ago, when you were out shopping, Chengcai took Xinxin's cell phone out of your handbag. I recognised it because I had bought it for her. I was very surprised at the time but thought she must have left it behind for you to use. Then, when I turned it on, I accidentally opened the voicemail and heard the messages she had left on it. I had never understood why she hadn't come back to see me for so long, and the fact that whenever she called me, no matter what I said, she always just said the same things, had made me suspicious. Then I finally understood that whenever I thought I was talking to her on the telephone, it was actually you playing those recordings." I had never expected him to discover this secret, and I didn't know what to say. All I could manage was to stutter: "Unc... Uncle... I..." "Tell me what's happened to her!" Uncle Xiao looked at me intensely. "I held off asking you over the last few days because I was afraid of hearing the truth, but please tell me now!" "Nothing... nothing's happened..." For the moment I couldn't think of any story that he would believe.

"Xinxin did this to comfort me, so just answer me one thing: she's dead, isn't she?" Uncle Xiao looked at me, eyes unblinking. I didn't know what to say, and desperately tried to think of some way of alleviating his fear, but for the moment, nothing came to me. The way that Older Sister died was so pitiful, he would never be able to deal with it. "Were she and Chang Sheng in a car accident in America?" he asked intently. My heart aching, I thought to myself that maybe saying there had been a car crash would lessen the blow. "If they weren't both in the accident, then surely the other one would have come back home to explain to me what had happened? And if Xinxin died of some illness, then Chang Sheng would surely come home too, wouldn't he?" I just nodded my head and softly repeated the two words: "Car crash." It seemed to me at the time that this was the only way of lessening the impact on him. Besides, I couldn't think of anything else. When Uncle Xiao saw me nod, a tremor went through his body, and he raised his left hand, as though he was about to grasp something, and his eyes looked blankly into the distance. Seeing this, I hurried forward to support him and whispered: "Uncle..." "When did it happen?" His voice trembled with emotion. "A while ago." I didn't want to be specific because I wouldn't be able to give any details convincingly.

"I should never have let them leave the country..." Uncle Xiao suddenly began to wail, and the tears coursed down his cheeks. "There are so many cars in America. It must have been Chang Sheng who was driving. He's so stubborn and opinionated, always thinking he's right and not listening to other people's advice. He's so careless and reckless; he must have been driving too fast and caused the accident... what it boils down to is that Xinxin should never have gone with that man. I've let her mother down and not looked after her daughter properly. I deserve to die... I should never have let them get married..." I didn't try to console him because I didn't know what to say. I just kept stroking his back, hoping it might help somehow.

I could feel how taut his back was, and I was worried that his ageing heart wouldn't be able to take this grinding anguish. That evening, when Uncle Xiao had finally settled down, I put him to bed, but I myself didn't seem to sleep at all that night, as I listened out for his movements next door. In the end, it was all right, as he calmed down, and apart from him being in low spirits with little appetite for the next few days, his health didn't seem to have suffered significantly. I remember that, on the fifth day, I took the bank card Older Sister had left me and a list of the money I had spent, and gave them to Uncle Xiao, saying: "Because our side was responsible for the accident and couldn't get the cost of a new car off the insurance, we didn't get any money back. These are all the savings Older Sister and Chang Sheng left behind." Uncle Xiao just glanced at the card and the list, and pushed them back at me, saying: "I don't want to look at them. I'll leave them with you, and you can take care of how you use them..."

Once Older Sister's death was out in the open, my emotional burden was lifted as I didn't have to keep pretending to Uncle Xiao that she was still alive, and inventing lies to tell him. Although at first Uncle Xiao didn't say anything and just kept his hurt to himself, by this time he seemed to have put it all behind him. Even so, he had, of course, suffered a major blow, and the heartache was acute. But what had happened had happened, and no one can turn back time. Uncle Xiao had already suffered the loss of his wife, and he knew that the only way to deal with the heartache was to confront it. For two days, he just sat in the apartment, constantly staring at the photograph of Older Sister he held in his hand. All I could do was sit quietly, keeping him company. On the third day, he finally motioned to me to take him out to the park. Before all this happened, his hair and eyebrows still had some traces of black, but now I noticed that this was all gone, and his hair, eyebrows and even the fine hairs on his neck were all snowy white. Of course, it was the grief that had done this.

When acute heartache passes, you are left with a dull ache; after the dull ache comes numbness, and only after the numbness goes can you forget the pain. It was only after about two and a half months had passed that it could be said Uncle Xiao was gradually emerging from the shadows of his grief. After breakfast one morning, having wheeled him to Longevity Park for some fresh air, he said to me: "There is only one thing in this world I am still worried about, Xiaoyang, and that is that I don't know if there is going to be time before I die for me to finish writing those three legal volumes and get them published." "Of course there will be!" I replied encouragingly. "Lots of people type one-handed on a computer, and you can certainly do that too. But if you think typing one-handed is too laborious, then you can dictate and I'll write it down, and we'll get it done that way. I may not be that well-educated, but I can certainly cope with taking your dictation." At the time, he didn't say yes or no, but two days later, when it was raining too hard to go to the park, he handed me a sheaf of paper and said: "Come on then! We'll make a start today." I realised he wanted to dictate, so I hurried over to the table, opened the sheaf of paper and turned on the recorder on my cell phone.

"Today, I'm going to dictate the principal content of the third volume, which is called *A History of Human Criminality*." He spoke very slowly to make it easier for me to get it all down. "...When humans first emerged as social beings, no matter under what system a country was governed, great importance was always placed on law and legislation from the outset. The total number of legal and legislative statutes passed up to now in all countries across the world is enormous. Why does human society take such pains to establish this legal and legislative framework? Because, right from the very start of human society, humans have committed crimes. Humans, both male and female, have the instinct to commit crimes: they instinctively want more wealth and possessions; they are instinctively drawn to vice; they are instinctively drawn to violence. Without the constraints of law and legislation, society would inevitably descend into chaos, leaving people with no way of living a normal life." The way he explained this, even someone like me with no knowledge of the law could relate to it. He continued: "Looking back on the history of human criminality, we can see that the reason why people offend is entirely because they lose control of their desires, and those desires are strange and various..."

In the course of that day, Uncle Xiao also incorporated many of the cases of corruption and fraud he had collected over the years, to illustrate the importance of controlling desire. I wrote them all down. Three of these made a particular impression on me. One involved the head of a national government department who was in charge of overseeing national construction projects. This man was born into a very influential family, and his mother and father were both important officials. From his childhood, he had met all kinds of important people, witnessed all kinds of important events, and knew all about the good things in life. Because of this, he was very aloof as a person, disdainful of wealth and possessions, and seldom accepted other people's invitations to celebrations. After being made head of department, he never accepted gifts of food or clothing, let alone money, from any of his subordinates. If anyone tried to give him anything, gifts or money, just the look of disdain on his face was enough to put them completely out of countenance, and in this way, he was able to keep a spotless reputation. However, thanks to the influence of a maternal uncle who was a professor of archaeology, he had one particular hobby: collecting antique porcelain. Whenever he saw a fine piece of porcelain, he wanted to buy it to add to his collection for him and his friends to admire. There was a provincial project officer up in Beijing on an errand who heard about this hobby. Instead of simply presenting him with a valuable piece of porcelain, he went out and paid top price of three hundred thousand yuan for a piece of Ming porcelain. When he went to visit the department head, feigning disinterest, he said: "My family has a porcelain bowl that my maternal grandmother gave my parents as a wedding present. I don't know whether it has any value as a collectable, and I wanted to ask you to help me authenticate it." With that, he took the bowl, wrapped in old paper, out of his bag. When he saw it, the head of department exclaimed: "Good heavens! This isn't any old antique – this is a genuine Ming blue-and-white large brush washer, the kind scholars used. It is immensely collectable!" The project officer saw how unwilling the man was to let go of the bowl and said: "If you like it, I'll sell it to you for fifty yuan. After all, my mother only uses it to wash her hands in. She'll be better off if I buy her an enamel basin anyway." The head of department agreed immediately, and quickly handed over fifty yuan. The two men developed a friendship after this, and the department head was happy to accept the other's invitation to banquets. For his part, the project officer eagerly kept bringing all different kinds of antique porcelain to sell cheaply, and subsequently all the projects he wanted to develop were approved. Inevitably, the department head came to grief. The court recovered from the head of department's house more than twenty pieces of antique porcelain, including a small Song dynasty *ru* ware dish from the Guan kiln, which would have fetched more than three hundred thousand yuan at a China Guardian auction...

Another case involved the director of an art school who was

born into the arts world. He was a handsome man and had been a theatre actor in his youth. As an official, he had a very artistic temperament and was a connoisseur of beauty. The greatest danger for a man in a senior position in an educational establishment like his is how easy it is to get entangled with female students. And it was certainly the case that the girl students in this school were very beautiful. However, he felt that girls who had been moulded and modelled by modern life lost something of their innocent beauty. He didn't spare a second look for any of his female students, he didn't have any unchaperoned contact with any of them, and he didn't let any of them worm their way into his affections, or give them any opportunity to suck up to him. He kept himself scrupulously clean financially and never accepted any gifts or money. He did have very lofty ambitions and hoped to make an even bigger mark in government circles. So that was the kind of man he was, until, one day, he bumped into a female cleaner in one of the corridors, and stopped dead in his tracks in astonishment. Later, he confessed in court, that the instant he laid eyes on that girl dressed in a cleaner's uniform and wearing absolutely no make-up, he felt as though an electric shock had run through his body, and he thought he was looking at an immortal descended from the realm of the clouds. Everything about this girl, her face, her eyes, her body, was guileless and genuine. Moreover, her facial features and body shape had a kind of ultimate harmony: a natural beauty without any artifice. He felt that, in every respect except her clothing, this girl was exactly like the goddesses he had always pictured in his head. He started to interrogate this naïve young girl and discovered that she came from the deep mountains of Xiangxi and had graduated from high school but not gone on to university. She was eighteen, and, because she didn't want to be a burden on her parents, and in order to support herself, a few days ago she had followed some of her fellows from the countryside and taken a job as a cleaner at the art school. The director was delighted at this and immediately telephoned the school's property management office, and told them, henceforward, to make this girl responsible for cleaning his office and the meeting room next door. From then on, he and the girl were in close contact. He took the initiative to go out and buy clothes he liked, for her to wear. He felt that just watching her moving about was a thing of great beauty. He bought her lots of the kind of jewellery he liked, to enjoy the sight of her wearing it. The girl herself couldn't understand why she was receiving such favours from a superior.

Finally, on one occasion when he asked her out to dinner, he couldn't help himself telling her what he wanted: to see her naked. The girl was aghast, but, after all he had done for her, there was nothing she could say. So, in a hotel room, with incredible shyness, the girl took off all her clothes. At first, the director just looked her up and down, wide-eyed with astonished delight, but then he found he couldn't resist taking her in his arms. The girl began to tremble with fear, but he didn't force her into doing anything, and just helped her back into her clothes. He said he had a kind of infatuation with beauty, and after the first time he saw this girl naked, he couldn't control his desire to see her again. Not long after, he asked her again. The fifth time this happened, the girl threw herself at him and gave him her body. He said he had never before seen such pure beauty in a naked girl, and it filled him with joy. His salary was not enough to support his wife and son, and to satisfy the girl's every whim. There was nothing for it but for him to start embezzling public funds. By the time his crime was uncovered, he had already embezzled one hundred thousand yuan...

The third case involved a local mayor. Uncle Xiao said that this mayor was from farming stock in the countryside around Xinyang in Henan, and was the sixth in a family of seven brothers and sisters. During the famine of 1960, his parents had no food to eat and were afraid he would starve to death. So, when he was just four years old, they reluctantly put him at a crossroads outside the local township to see whether some benefactor might take him away. It was just after dawn when his father put him there. He was already so hungry, he was too weak to stand up or cry out, nor could he understand why his father was doing this. All he could do was sit there, not making a sound. He waited the whole day, as person after person walked past him. It was late evening, and he had passed out from hunger, when, finally, a man picked him up. That man became his foster father, and he grew up with him and his foster mother. Even at four years old, he always remembered this act of kindness, and because of it he loved his foster parents dearly and made sure he worked hard at school. In the end, he made it into Peking University and stayed on in Beijing to work in the city administration. He knew that he was of humble origins and could not rely on others to help him rise in society, and he would have to make his way through hard work and his own abilities. This indeed is what he did, rising rank by rank to a leadership role. Throughout this time, he remained most filially devoted to his foster parents and wanted to provide them with everything they wanted; his desire to repay them for his nurture and education was very strong. He also greatly valued his own achievements and had no desire to ruin his reputation by accepting gifts or money. His self-discipline and self-awareness were exceptional, and he was considered the most upright of officials.

After he rose to be a local mayor, he had authority over land transfers in his district, so many property developers tried everything to get him in their pocket. They used every trick in the book, including beautiful girls and gold bars, but he was quick-witted enough to avoid them all. In the end, it was his devotion to his foster parents that caused his downfall. One day, his foster father suddenly appeared at his home in Beijing and said: "Son, your father has something to ask you. There is a builder in our county who has his eye on a plot of land in your district. He says you can grant him permission to build on it, and I'm asking you to give him that permission. This man is a good fellow and very generous; even though he does not know us very well, the first time he came to our house, he gave us one hundred thousand yuan. He is a man worth knowing." The mayor became very agitated when he heard this and asked: "Did you take the money, Dad?" His foster father nodded and said: "Yes, I did. He was so respectful towards us, how could I not? Besides, your younger sister and her husband have already used it to build a piggery..." The mayor looked at him, wide-eyed with alarm, but he managed to hold back the reprimand that sprang to his lips. He couldn't lose his temper and hurt the father who had brought him up, so, after a night of mental turmoil, he ended up by giving the developer his permit. Because of this, the developer could claim a connection with him and built up a friendship. Every few days, he would go round to the mayor's house, or to his parents, and he never arrived empty-handed, bringing all kinds of household goods, and, of course, hard cash. Because the mayor had acquiesced this first time, he felt it would be churlish to refuse now, so he squared it with himself and accepted the gifts. After a few years, the things he received were really quite a sight. When he was arrested, the gifts and money he had accepted were more than enough to secure a conviction...

I wrote out these cases Uncle Xiao described, one by one, and, if sometimes I couldn't recall them accurately, during the night, after Uncle Xiao and Chengcai had gone to sleep, I could refer to the recording on my cell phone and correct any mistakes. After I had done that, I would hand my records over to Uncle Xiao to look through. He proofread them very thoroughly, correcting them, here and there, with a pen he held in his left hand. Once we had the final version, I would type it out on Uncle Xiao's computer, print it, and that was that.

Other than getting Chengcai off to school, over this period, Uncle Xiao's and my daily programme went like this: take him to the park to get out of the apartment for a bit, go back home, take down the dictation of his book, then tidy it up in the quiet of the night. As the days passed like this, exercising, dictating and correcting, calm returned to the household. During this time, a peaceful feeling filled my heart, making me forget all the things that had happened to us in the past. I would often say a little prayer to myself: please may we go on like this. But this prayer was not to be answered.

Around noon one day, before I went into the kitchen to make lunch, I turned on the television and gave Uncle Xiao the remote control so he could watch TV for a while. He usually watched the

CCTV news at this time. I had just about finished the lunch when I heard the sound of the television suddenly being turned up to a shattering volume, so loud it almost split my eardrums. Alarmed, I ran out of the kitchen into the living room, but, before I had even opened my mouth to ask what was going on, Uncle Xiao got in first: "Why is there suddenly no sound from the television? Is it a problem with the transmission, or is our remote control broken?" At first, I just laughed and said: "How can you say it's not working when it's this loud?" But then I suddenly thought: Has Uncle Xiao got a problem with his hearing? I hurriedly took the remote control out of his hand, turned the sound down, then asked him, in my normal voice: "Are you hungry yet?" But Uncle Xiao didn't answer and went on: "Is it the television station's fault?" My heart lurched: there must be something wrong with his hearing. But I wasn't willing to accept that such a change could have taken place so suddenly. Surely I had been talking to him quite normally before I went to make lunch, so how could something so dramatic have happened in such a short space of time? I decided to make sure and asked, still in my normal voice: "Shall I bring you your lunch?" He was watching my lips move and replied: "Are you sure it's the remote control that's broken?" I nodded. He seemed not yet to be aware there was a major problem with his ears, and I didn't want to alarm him. I turned the television off, then called Chengcai, who was doing his homework in his room. I gave him his lunch and told him to eat up then go back to his homework – his school had a half-holiday that day, and I wanted to take Uncle Xiao to the hospital.

Uncle Xiao looked at me suspiciously as I wheeled him out of the door, but it was only when we were getting into a taxi that he asked: "Where are we going now?" "To the hospital!" I said loudly into his ear. First he just muttered to himself: "Why is the street so quiet today?" Then, as though the light had suddenly dawned on him, he turned to me and asked: "Is there something wrong with my ears?" I forced a smile and said: "We're going to the hospital to find out."

The ENT doctor at the hospital was very quick with his diagnosis after he had examined Uncle Xiao: sudden-onset anacusis. Both Uncle Xiao and I were unfamiliar with the medical terminology. When I passed it on to Uncle Xiao at the top of my voice, he asked disbelievingly: "How can I have this sudden anacusis thing?" The doctor laughed and said: "It's a common condition in people of your age." "Why?" I was amazed. "There is a normal progression with deafness in people. As they deteriorate with age, some of the blood vessels and nerves in the ear can just stop working." The doctor explained in layman's terms for my benefit. I asked anxiously: "What's the cure?" The middle-aged, male doctor smiled and said: "There may not be one. Hearing loss because of old age is something that happens to all old people sooner or later. Of course, if you insist on a cure, there is a possibility. You need to unblock all the blood vessels in the ear and eliminate any inflammation. It takes anywhere from a couple of weeks to a month, and there's no guarantee the hearing will be restored at the end of it. In addition, this treatment can also cause damage to other internal organs." "Are there any old people who have got their hearing back using this method?" I persisted. "There are, but very few of his age and with ears in the same state as his." I glanced at Uncle Xiao, but he appeared not to have heard our conversation and was still just looking at me confusedly. At that moment, I realised that his life was now out of his own hands, and control of it had gradually slipped into my own. All I had to say was "Don't treat him", and he would lose his hearing forever. "Do it!" I told the doctor. If there was the faintest hope, I couldn't give up on it. Hearing is the most important way an individual senses and engages with the world, and I couldn't let Uncle Xiao lose it completely without putting up a fight. "If we're going to treat it, then we need to set up an IV. The sooner we start the treatment, the better the results." So saying, the doctor got the IV drugs going. While he was doing that, I took the opportunity to phone Chengcai, telling him to amuse himself at home when he had finished his homework. Thank heavens that, having grown up in our extraordinary household, little Chengcai was very quick on the uptake and could already tell when a situation was urgent. He just said: "Don't worry, Mum. You just look after Grandpa, and I can look after myself here. If anyone knocks on the door, I won't answer." I heaved a sigh of relief and went to look after Uncle Xiao's infusion.

It was already dark when we got home. Chengcai had tired himself out and was asleep in bed. On the coffee table in front of the sofa was a message he had written just before he went to bed: *Grandpa, Mummy – I made myself some instant noodles to eat. I'm tired and I'm going to bed. Good night!* After Uncle Xiao had read the note, I saw a faint smile play on his exhausted, teary-eyed face. He insisted on wheeling himself over to Chengcai's bedside, stroking the sleeping boy gently on his cheek, then wheeling himself back to his bedroom.

After that first day, there were another twenty or so days of ongoing treatment. As it turned out, what that doctor had told me proved to be correct, and the results of the treatment weren't great. After one course of it, Uncle Xiao's left ear had regained a little hearing, but his right one showed no improvement at all on how it had been before we had consulted the doctor. There was no possibility of continuing the treatment, as using more of the powerful anti-inflammatory drugs could damage other of his internal organs. The afternoon we decided to stop the treatment, Uncle Xiao looked at me in consternation and said: "Are we stopping the treatment, even though I haven't got my hearing back?" I nodded, then put my mouth to his ear and said loudly: "If we went on, it could damage some of your other organs." Uncle Xiao looked at me dazedly. I saw despair creep into his eyes until they completely clouded over. Finally, he lowered his head, unable to accept yet another blow to his health like this. I sighed soundlessly and couldn't stop myself patting him on the shoulders. It seemed that God was deliberately taking back all the gifts he had given at birth, one by one. This time it was Uncle Xiao's hearing.

Needless to say, this all had an effect on Uncle Xiao's mood, and he became very depressed. He had no interest in going to Longevity Park anymore, and his appetite disappeared. He didn't want to eat or drink, he wouldn't wash, and he even stopped speaking. I let Chengcai try to comfort him, but sadly, no matter how loud

Chengcai made his voice, he couldn't hear anything, and his face remained expressionless. There was nothing Chengcai could do except hold his Grandpa's hand tight and show his love and concern for him that way. I made enquiries everywhere about which were the best hearing aids, visited countless shops that sold them, until I finally bought him one made by the German company Siemens, specifically for old people. The moment I fitted him with it, he could immediately hear everything around him, and a look of pure joy spread across his face. However, quite soon, the hearing aid, which had no automatic noise-reduction system, began occasionally to emit a really piercing noise into Uncle Xiao's ear, causing him extreme discomfort. In the end, he just stopped using it.

Once again, I became very worried about his emotional state and asked everywhere about ways of comforting old people suffering from sudden-onset deafness. One day, by chance, I saw some news on the internet reporting that the Disabled Persons' Association had established a concert hall especially for deaf people who still retained a little hearing. Every seat in the hall was equipped with a device that could automatically regulate the sound of the music to suit listeners who only had minimal hearing, and there was a performance like this very week. I immediately contacted the concert hall to buy two tickets. After I had secured the tickets, I told Uncle Xiao about it all, in a loud voice, and, in case he hadn't heard me clearly, I also wrote it down for him. But he just shook his head and said decisively: "I'm not going!" Annoyed, I told him: "Each ticket cost more than four hundred yuan, and there are no refunds. Wouldn't it be a waste of money not to go?" It was probably the words "waste of money" that hit home, and he stopped protesting. So, the next evening, after I had settled Chengcai, I took Uncle Xiao in a taxi to the concert hall for the hard of hearing.

After I had pushed Uncle Xiao into the hall, I discovered that, apart from nurses and carers, almost all the audience were old people. Probably the high price of the tickets meant that younger people with hearing impairment couldn't afford them. It seemed that almost half the old people in the audience were in wheelchairs, so the seats in the hall had been very carefully designed. Beside each seat, there was a collapsible one that allowed a wheelchair to be wheeled into the space it left. After we had found our allotted seat, I saw that Uncle Xiao was looking all around him in wonder, as though he had never imagined there could be so many other deaf old people like him. I heard him mutter to himself: "Good heavens, they're all deaf..." That evening, I too fully understood that loss of hearing was probably a feature of growing old common to everyone.

Not far into the concert, I discovered that everything I had read about the concert hall in that advertisement on the internet was true. The decibel level of the sound sent to each member of the audience's hearing aid was automatically adjusted by computer according to hearing ability and then transmitted for individual adjustment. I noticed that Uncle Xiao was listening very attentively, so I took his hearing aid to see what the music sounded like to him: it nearly blasted my ears off! After the concert, as I pushed Uncle Xiao out of the hall, I saw that much of the gloom that had built up over the last few days had lifted from his face. That's the power of music, I thought to myself. Outside, I heard Uncle Xiao say: "So it seems that the hearing all old people enjoy is just about the same." It was then I suddenly saw that the real reason he had cheered up this evening was that seeing so many deaf old people had made him realise that God hadn't been picking on him alone in taking away his hearing. This kind of equality of treatment had restored his emotional equilibrium.

About three and a half months after the onset of Uncle Xiao's deafness, he finally, jokingly, told his cronies in Longevity Park: "It's all right being deaf: you don't have to listen to so much irritating nonsense." It was only then that I felt I could relax: Uncle Xiao had accepted the major change of his deafness.

When my son, Chengcai, went into second grade, my own love life revived. That is to say, I was willing to let a man into my life. Because this matter is interconnected with the rest of my story, I'll tell you all a little about it now.

The man in question was none other than Qiu Dali, who I have mentioned before as the young male nurse of about my age I met when Uncle Xiao was in hospital being treated for his paralysis. At that time, Uncle Xiao had just suffered his right-sided paralysis, and he hadn't lost any weight, nor had my arm strength been built up yet, so I had great difficulty lifting him in and out of bed. Our attending nurse then was Qiu Dali, and when he saw how things were, he came over to help. During Uncle Xiao's stay in hospital, whenever I wanted to get something to eat, do some shopping, go to the toilet or go and see to Chengcai, I always asked Qiu Dali to keep an eye on Uncle Xiao, and in that way, we became quite friendly. On top of that, he was from Henan too, so I felt a kind of kinship with him. When Uncle Xiao was discharged from hospital, Qiu Dali also helped me take him home. After that, because he knew where we lived, when he was off duty, he took to looking in on us from time to time, and sometimes he would bring Uncle Xiao some fruit, or give Chengcai a little toy.

I didn't give this much thought and just took it as him giving a fellow countrywoman a helping hand. Until one day, he sent me a text: *I can see how hard your life is looking after both an old person and a young child, and I'm sure you'd like someone to help you with it.* I was quite taken aback: so that's how he saw things, was it? You've already heard me talk about the first chapter of my love life, so you'll understand why I didn't have much faith in young men. I certainly didn't want to get involved with him at that point, so I replied to his text: *I'm a married woman; please behave with some decorum!* At first, I felt rather pleased with myself when I sent that text: you dare to have designs on a married woman do you? Ha! But then I began to feel uneasy. When all was said and done, since Chengcai was born, Qiu Dali was the first man to show me any warmth and affection, and hadn't he been really helpful too? Wasn't my reply a little over the top? Might it not hurt his feelings? Besides, I was still young, and during the long nights, was it so wrong to want a little male attention? Supposing he really was a decent man? Had I made a mistake?

The surprising thing was, Qiu Dali wasn't scared away by my

text, but replied to it the next day, saying: *I wasn't saying I wanted to do anything about it now, I was just expressing a little of my hopes for the future. Don't be angry!* Ha! He was certainly thick-skinned, and after this, he simply continued as before, dropping in occasionally to see how we were. He hadn't become at all distant in his manner when he came to help out, and he behaved just as I would expect a fellow countryman to do. Even so, at that time I was still afraid he might try and take advantage of my situation and overstep the mark, so I couldn't bring myself to give him any encouragement. Whenever I opened the door to him, I looked at him quite indifferently, but he just went on as before, ignoring my expression, and got on with doing what he could to help, just as before. I thought to myself: If you want to try and ingratiate yourself with me, go ahead! But if you think you're going to worm your way into my affections, think again! That was the theory at least, but every time I saw him scrubbing out our toilet bowl or washing our basin, I couldn't help feeling something; when I saw him voluntarily helping me wash Uncle Xiao and getting splashed with water from head to toe, my heart softened; when I saw him crawling on the floor, playing with Chengcai and making him chortle, I felt a kind of happiness. As my heart was wavering like this, there was another development with Uncle Xiao's health.

It happened one bright, clear morning. The sun seemed to have risen even earlier than usual that morning, and Chengcai's school was organising a spring excursion, so I was taking him there, admiring the morning sun as we went. The fine weather had put me in a good mood, and as I was wheeling Uncle Xiao to the dining table, I said to him in a loud voice: "When you've finished your breakfast, I'm going to take you to look around the Qianda Plaza. I saw on the internet that there are thousands and thousands of tulips on display there; my internet pals say it's a fabulous display. Let's go and give our eyes a treat!" I had hardly finished speaking when Uncle Xiao said faintly: "How can we go and look at flowers in such threatening weather? The clouds are so low, there's bound to be a spring thunderstorm!" I looked at him in amazement. How could he say that when he could see the weather for himself? There wasn't a cloud in the sky, and the sun was blazing down! How could he say there was going to be a thunderstorm? Was it because he was in a bad mood? Was it because he didn't want to go to the Qianda Plaza to view the tulips. "Don't you want to see the flowers, Uncle?" I tried probing him, not wanting to make him cross. "Of course I do! But how can we, with the weather like this?" He didn't look cross, and spoke quite mildly. This made me realise he really did think the sky was overcast, and my heart lurched, as I immediately thought: Maybe there's something wrong with his eyes now! I remembered that he had been rubbing his eyes a lot over the last few days, and I had warned him: "It's not good to be always rubbing your eyes." "They're a bit uncomfortable," he replied, "and rubbing them helps." I hadn't paid it any more attention at the time, but now it seemed not to be a very good sign. To test my suspicions, I hurriedly fetched a white china flowerpot I had bought the day before. It was decorated with a pattern of brightly coloured lotus flowers. I put it down in front of Uncle Xiao and asked: "What do you think this is?" "Is it a lump of Chengcai's clay? I can't see it very clearly." As he spoke, he reached out his left hand to feel. I hastily grabbed hold of his hand, saying: "We need to go to the hospital, Uncle!" I snatched up my cell phone and dialled 120.

We got to the hospital without delay, and the ophthalmic doctor immediately examined both Uncle Xiao's eyes. It didn't take him more than ten minutes or so to come up with a diagnosis: thrombosis in the central artery of the retina. The doctor said: "This is a particularly rapidly developing eye condition, and the sight can be lost in an instant. The main cause of this condition is hardening of the arteries: the artery walls thicken, and their aperture narrows, so the blood flows through them more slowly and forms clots. The process takes place without the patient noticing anything, until the clot blocks the central artery of the retina, causing blindness." Uncle Xiao had been fine when he got up that morning, and the reason he had suddenly thought the sky had gone dark was that a clot that had already formed had suddenly blocked his retinal artery.

Blood vessels again! Most of Uncle Xiao's health problems stemmed from his blood vessels. In my youthful ignorance, I had never thought that blood vessels were so important. The doctor explained to me: "The blood vessels in our bodies are enormously long: in an adult, if you joined them all together, they would stretch more than one hundred and fifty thousand kilometres. As blood vessels get older, like water pipes, they can get blocked by rubbish – blood clots. When they become blocked, this is detrimental to our health. A blocked carotid artery can cause serious problems in the brain stem. If a blood clot enters the kidneys, it affects renal function and can cause uraemia. A blood clot in the retinal artery can damage the eyesight. It's a great pity!" The doctor put a fast-acting vasodilator, amyl nitrite, under Uncle Xiao's nose for him to sniff, then set up an intravenous drip. The results were quite quick: his left eye gradually regained its vision, but he still couldn't see anything out of his right eye. The treatment continued, and neither the doctor nor I gave up hope. Uncle Xiao was getting agitated, constantly holding his left hand in front of his eyes to test his vision. But after five days, the doctor called me to his office and told me that the vision in Uncle Xiao's right eye was already gone, and there was nothing more they could do to restore it. It really was a bolt from the blue.

I stared blankly at the doctor's mouth: why was it always bad news? I was totally bewildered: why did that doctor's mouth never have any good news to tell me? Was Uncle Xiao ill-fated? Had I chosen the wrong hospital? I dragged myself back to the ward. Uncle Xiao seemed to know that the doctor had summoned me to discuss his eye condition, so he used his left eye, which had had some of its vision restored, to look at me urgently but pitifully, like a little child who has been naughty, waiting for a grown-up to tell him his punishment. I didn't know how to break the news to him. Too many things had happened to him recently, one after the other. Did he have the stamina to bear up under this latest blow? Supposing the emotional turmoil after I told him caused problems with some other blood vessel? What would we do? As I was hesitating, his expression suddenly changed. The stubborn expression I knew from when I first joined his household re-emerged, and I heard him say: "They don't want to treat me, do they! Do they want me out of the hospital? If they can't treat me, they can't treat me. If the worst comes to the worst and I'm blind in my right eye, what's so extraordinary about that? How much do doctors today care about their patients? Come on, let's go. Let's go home. I'm not going to beg!" I grasped him by the hand and explained, urgently: "It's not that doctor doesn't want to treat you, it just there's nothing he can do…"

When I woke up in the night that night, I went by force of habit to Uncle Xiao's bedroom to see how he was sleeping, but, to my surprise, just as I had my hand on the doorknob, I heard him talking to himself: "I'm over eighty now, and lots of ninety-year-olds live decent lives, so why are you always picking on me? Grandpa Wu'er in the Funiu Mountains can take on the job of mayor in his nineties, so what have I done to offend you? First you paralysed me, then you made me deaf; do you want to blind me now? Do you dare tell me you're being fair? You've been so cruel to me, I hate you…" When I heard this, I hurriedly took my hand off the doorknob. It was going to be Uncle Xiao's eighty-sixth birthday, and to cheer him up, I decided to throw him a birthday party.

A few days later, I secretly told several of his old cronies from Longevity Park that I wanted them to come to the apartment on Uncle Xiao's birthday for a celebration meal, and to have a bit of a party. I was afraid he might not want this kind of thing, so I was very secretive about bringing in all the stuff I needed for it. I wanted it to be a nice surprise for him: so many rotten things had happened to him recently. He was so preoccupied with all the things that were wrong with him that he forgot his birthday. That morning, when he saw me steaming and frying away in the kitchen, he asked: "It's not the New Year or any other festival, so what are you doing making so much food?" I just laughed and said: "Chengcai thought it might cheer things up a bit." It was a Sunday, so Chengcai was at home. When Uncle Xiao heard it was all at Chengcai's request, he didn't say any more.

As half past eleven approached, I told Chengcai to stand by the lift doors to welcome the guests. There were four of them in all, carefully chosen by me because they were over eighty, and so would have things in common to talk about. When I was at nursing school, our teachers told us that after people pass sixty, every ten years marks a distinct period in their lives. From sixty to sixty-nine, the things that preoccupy them are different from those of people aged seventy to seventy-nine. Equally, people aged eighty to eighty-nine are concerned about and like to discuss different things from people aged seventy to seventy-nine. The four old chaps that I chose were sure to have things to talk about with Uncle Xiao. The first to arrive was eighty-two-year-old Uncle Qin, carrying a piece of his own calligraphy. When he came into the living room, he cupped his hands in a gesture of respect and said: "Happy birthday, honoured brother Chengshan!" Then he unrolled the calligraphy couplet he had written and declaimed: "We do not complain the world no longer wants us as judges; all we want is a quiet life, and new judges will appear." The next to arrive was eighty-one-year-old Uncle Shan, who was carrying a small red lantern, which he opened out when he came into the room to show Uncle Xiao. There was a cautionary saying written on each of its three sides: *Dawn is the most dangerous time of day, when it is easiest to suffer a paralysing stroke; the middle day of the month is the most life-threatening day, when you are most likely to suffer a heart attack; the last month of the year is the scariest month when chronic diseases are at their worst.* The third to arrive was eighty-six-year-old Uncle Wei, who was carrying a small cake. He went to stand in front of Uncle Xiao and said: "Happy Birthday, Brother Xiao! I've brought you a sugar-free cake and would like to remind you of my formula for a long life: Go to bed at exactly ten o'clock; when you wake up in the morning, have a five-minute lie-in." The fourth guest to arrive was eighty-seven-year-old Uncle Lang. He came in and said: "Young Xiao, I have just brought you some advice: we live in a world that worships youth and a society that scorns the elderly, so there is a very close connection between the speed of deterioration with age and cues taken from our social environment; so never think of yourself as old." As Uncle Xiao had forgotten that it was, in fact, his birthday, he had had no idea that so many of his friends from Longevity Park would suddenly appear to congratulate him. Laughing happily, he kept saying: "Thank you, brothers... thank you... thank you..." I had chosen easy-to-chew dishes for the celebration lunch to suit several of the old fellows whose teeth weren't too good. I had also poured each of them a glass of red wine, which I told them to drink slowly. I said they would only get one glass, and however great their capacity was, I wouldn't pour any more.

They all grinned at this and said: "All right, all right, we know you're not being stingy; you're just worried about what might happen if we have too much." They sat round the dining table, wearing their hearing aids, laughing and joking so volubly it sounded like a conference with simultaneous translators. Watching them from outside the group, their main topic of conversation seemed to be how to master the art of passing water. I heard Uncle Qin, who had studied medicine say: "If you live as long as we have, the most important thing is to master pissing, because how big or small our prostates grow, and how much elasticity our bladders lose, affect urination; and as our mobility gets worse with age, quite often we can't make it to the toilet in time. The first thing to remember is to go to the toilet as soon as you get the urge to piss, and whatever you do, don't try to hold it in. If you let it all gush out after holding it in, your vagus nerve can be over-stimulated, and you can die from a sudden cardiac arrhythmia; too much pressure on the bladder can reduce the metabolic function of the kidneys in eliminating waste, and if too much water and waste material build up in the body, that can cause kidney failure and uraemia. The second thing is to piss completely, and not stop before you've finished; if you stop short too often, that can cause urethritis which can spread to the kidneys and turn into nephritis; if kidney function is impaired, the whole urinary system is adversely affected." Eighty-six-year-old Uncle Wei nodded and said: "That's right, that's right. I never manage to finish completely. I'm sure I've got it all out, but when I put the old man back in my trousers, some more always comes out, and it makes my trousers and underpants all wet. I have to rely on my body warmth to dry them out. You can't change your trousers and underpants every time you take a leak, so I'm really suffering." Uncle Shan said: "I've been incontinent at night since last year, and I can't help myself wetting the bed. When I was young it was wet dreams; now it's incontinence. I always have to get my daughter-in-law to help me dry the quilt, and it makes me feel really ashamed." Eighty-seven-year-old Uncle Lang chimed in: "I've had all of those problems you've had, and I won't lie to you, I'm incontinent during the day now as well. I'll tell you what it's like: it's like being a little kid again, always wearing a disposable nappy. If I've got a nappy on, it doesn't matter when the piss wants to come out, I just let it flow. I don't have to worry about it at all; I change my nappy once at midday and once at night, and that's it…"

During this celebration lunch, I was in charge of everything that needed to be done in the kitchen, and Chengcai was in charge of taking the bowls and dishes into the dining room. Although it was quite tiring work, the laughter coming from Uncle Xiao and his old friends made us both very happy. The lunch seemed to have lifted Uncle Xiao's mood. That night, when I went to supervise his bedtime, Uncle Xiao sighed contentedly: "The problems we meet with when we pass eighty really aren't that different. I may be a bit worse off than the others with my eyesight, but I'm better off than them when it comes to pissing…" I silently gave a sigh of relief as I reckoned this meant that I had navigated Uncle Xiao safely past some dangerous shoals. I thought that the water ahead would be plain sailing, and I could relax and have a bit of a rest. Little did I know that there were shoal after shoal in those waters, and we were fast bearing down on the next one.

It must have been about twenty days after the birthday party that I began to notice how quickly Uncle Xiao's memory was fading, and how many things he was forgetting. I knew that old people's memory could deteriorate, and they could become forgetful, so when, in the past, Uncle Xiao had happened to forget something I had told him, I wasn't too alarmed. But more recently, this tendency had rapidly become more advanced. As an example, when it was time for his night-time medications, I poured him a glass of boiled water, put the pills in his mouth, and when I had seen him swallow some water, I went off to get on with other stuff. Half an hour later, he shouted out to me: "Come and pour me some water, Xiaoyang, I haven't had my medications yet!" All I could do was tell him: "You've already had them!" Another example was our morning routine when I would get him out of bed and put him in his wheelchair. Then he could wheel himself to the bathroom where he shaved with his electric razor. But one morning, after he had got to the bathroom and was sitting in front of the mirror, he called me in and asked in bewilderment: "What did I come to the bathroom for?" "To shave." My heart lurched as I answered him and put the electric razor in his hand. Even more serious, one dinnertime, perhaps because he had been playing basketball, Chengcai was particularly hungry and was wolfing his food down. Carelessly, he got a few grains of rice stuck to his cheek. Uncle Xiao couldn't help laughing at the sight of this, and he couldn't stop. He laughed until he shook all over, which delighted me because he seldom laughed. But after I'd pointed out what had happened to Chengcai, and he had wiped the rice off his face, Uncle Xiao suddenly turned to me, still laughing, and asked: "What is it I'm laughing at?" I was dumbstruck. How could he have forgotten so quickly? That wasn't normal! Uncle Xiao himself noticed that his memory was failing him severely and asked me: "Is there something wrong with my memory?" I realised that we needed to go to the hospital for a doctor's opinion. We never seemed to be out of the hospital! It also dawned on me at that time why so many old people wanted to live near a hospital.

I decided to go to hospital the following day. I wasn't to know that, the same day, a terrifying event was going to occur. After breakfast, I got together everything I needed and pushed Uncle Xiao down to the main gate of our residential compound. Just as I raised my hand to flag down a taxi, I felt a sharp pain in my lower abdomen. I realised I must have picked up some bug or other the night before, and I had the runs. I hastily instructed Uncle Xiao: "You just wait here in your wheelchair. I'm going to the toilet, and then I'll be back." He nodded and said: "All right. Off you go then!"

As quickly as I could, I turned back and went into one of the public toilets in the compound. When I came out after I'd finished and washed my hands, there was absolutely no sign of Uncle Xiao out on the street. Where could he have got to? The wheelchair he was in was the kind he could push himself along in with one hand, so I assumed he had started off, by himself, in the direction of the hospital. I set off in the same direction, but, to my surprise, after two blocks, I still couldn't see him.

I began to panic. He surely couldn't push himself that fast! I turned back and looked in the other direction, and found there was still no sign of him at the gates to our estate. I ran another three blocks that way, but still no sign. I was completely at a loss. Where could he have got to? Could he have gone back to the apartment? I ran back there, but there was no one inside. I was so upset, I began to cry. How could someone just disappear? I ran back to the main gates and asked anyone passing by if they had seen him, but they all just shook their heads. I was at my wit's end when my cell phone rang. I got it out and saw a number I didn't recognise. I answered it, and heard a man's voice at the other end: "Is that Zhong Xiaoyang? I'm the security guard on the doors of the vegetable market. Your charge, Xiao Chengshan, has come here looking for you. I found your nursing registration card in the canvas bag on the back of his wheelchair, and saw your cell phone number on it, so I called you. Please come and collect him as soon as possible." As soon as I heard this, I flew across the road towards the vegetable market. When I got there and saw Uncle Xiao, I threw myself at him and began to cry. I scolded him as I wept: "Didn't I tell you to wait for me? Why have you come to the vegetable market?" He mumbled: "I forgot what you told me. I thought you'd come here to do some shopping, so I wheeled myself over as quickly as I could..." I couldn't bring myself to scold him anymore, so I just hailed a taxi and took him to the hospital.

Having been there so often, I was very familiar with the hospital and knew quite a few of the medical and nursing staff, so once I'd checked in, everything was very straightforward. The results of the tests were quite alarming. The temporal lobes of Uncle Xiao's brain displayed clear signs of atrophy, there were starchy patches, caused by old age, on the myelin sheaths of the neurons; the nerve fibres themselves were tangled, and half the colloid matter from the glial cells had been lost. The doctor said: "With this on top of everything else that is wrong with him, we can already say for certain that he has Alzheimer's Disease, what we commonly call senile dementia." He also told me that about twenty-three per cent of people over eighty-five got this disease; at the end of 2015, 46.8 million people across the world were suffering from senile dementia, and in 2016 there were more than nine million new cases, so it was increasing at a rate of one new patient every three seconds. Its prevalence meant that there was no need to be too alarmed about it.

The doctor went on to tell me that the causes and mechanisms of the onset of this kind of disease are not yet clear. Moreover, the onset of the disease is insidious, and the changes in the patient's vitality are masked, so early diagnosis is difficult. Uncle Xiao's condition was already well-advanced. There are many known causes of the disease: for example, damage to the brain cells by free radicals; or damage caused by blocked blood vessels starving the brain cells of nutrition; or mental disorder caused by the endocrine system and so on. He went on to say that going by the speed of deterioration in Uncle Xiao's current state, he could lose his memory completely in six to ten months. His brain "eraser" would continuously wipe clean his memory of the past, sometimes whole chunks at a time, until he reached the point of total imbecility. The doctor added: "We don't currently have any effective treatment for this disease, and the results of drug therapy are far from perfect. Of course, I will write you a prescription for the drugs he should be taking." Dazed and frightened, I leaned against a wall, unable to move for a while. When we arrived, I had thought that the doctor would examine Uncle Xiao, then write out a prescription for drugs that would alleviate his memory loss. I had never anticipated such a dismal outcome. I couldn't contemplate the fact that Uncle Xiao, who still wanted to write three great legal works, could become an imbecile with no memory of anything. Good Lord! I couldn't stop my tears. Even though Uncle Xiao and I were not connected by blood, even though our marriage was a sham, the pain was like a hammer blow. God shouldn't treat a lonely old man like this! He had already lost his mobility, most of his hearing and his sight, so why should he have this disease heaped on him as well.

Probably because he saw I was taking so much time in there, Uncle Xiao, who had been waiting outside, wheeled himself into the consulting room. I hastily wiped away my tears, but I was too late, and he saw their tracks streaking my face. He fished out the hearing aid that he seldom wore, adjusted it in place, then wheeled himself over to the doctor, who was now examining another patient. The doctor turned and asked: "Is there something else, sir?" "I need to know my real condition!" He fixed the doctor with his stare as he made this solemn request. The doctor looked over at me, apparently asking whether he should tell Uncle Xiao the true situation or not. Before I could open my mouth, Uncle Xiao said: "You don't need to ask her, she's just my nurse, not a real family member. I'm the only one who has the right to know the truth about my condition! I am a retired judge, and if you try to hide anything from me, it will end with you feeling the full weight of the law!" Seeing how forceful Uncle Xiao was, the doctor looked at me helplessly and told him what he had just told me. Uncle Xiao heard him out without apparent shock or distress, and just said: "Thank you!" Then he said to me, quite normally: "Let's go."

When we got home that day, Uncle Xiao still seemed quite calm, with none of the grumbling or anger he had shown in the past. This surprised me. In the evening, I found him alone in his bedroom, making phone calls, but I couldn't hear what he was saying. At that time, I still hadn't recovered my balance from the blow of the results of the examination, and I was lost in thought, trying to consider the matter from every angle. Why did so many things have to go wrong with people when they grow old? One thing after another, without even time to draw breath!

The next morning, after I came back from taking Chengcai to school, I was surprised to see a man sitting in the living room with Uncle Xiao, who was wearing his hearing aid and talking to him. I was rather startled by this sight because, for a long time now, whenever Uncle Xiao saw somebody, it was me who arranged it, but I had had no warning of this man's arrival. When Uncle Xiao saw I was back, he beckoned me over and made the introduction: "This is Lawyer Geng, who I have invited over to help with the divorce formalities." "Divorce? Whose divorce?" I didn't understand what he meant. "Ours. Yours and mine." I stood rooted to the spot. "It's best if we separate," he said simply. I thought I understood his intention: he was worried that after he became mentally incapacitated, I might claim that our sham marriage was actually genuine, and Chengcai and I could legally make claim to all his property. He didn't want that to happen, so he intended to sever the marital connection and make his own arrangements for the disposal of his property in advance. I knew that I had nothing to complain about if this went through, as Uncle Xiao had already helped me by marrying me when I was in the utmost difficulties, and making it possible for Chengcai and me to establish ourselves in Beijing. One should never expect too much, and what Uncle Xiao was doing was entirely as it should be. I didn't make any objections then, and just nodded and asked: "When are we going to do it?" "Now!" Uncle Xiao replied. "Get our marriage certificate, and we'll be off!" Even though our marriage was in name only, when I heard it was going to be broken up immediately, I did find it a little hard to take. Once the divorce was formalised, Chengcai and I would return to being outsiders in this household. But I didn't let any of this show on my face, went over to my bedroom to fetch the marriage certificate, then wheeled Uncle Xiao out of the door. How could I force an old man not to do what he wanted to do? When Lawyer Geng saw me compliantly pushing Uncle Xiao off to see to the formalities, he left us alone. Uncle Xiao had probably asked him over because he didn't think I would agree to the divorce so easily.

There were lots of people waiting to file divorces that day, and we had to queue before it was our turn. When the official asked the reason for our divorce, Uncle Xiao, who was used to talking in a loud voice because of his hearing problem, replied at great volume: "My wife and I both feel that continuing our marriage would be torture for both of us." All the people waiting in the hall to register either marriages or divorces heard him and stopped talking. The whole hall fell silent, and everyone could hear Uncle Xiao's laboured breathing. They all turned to look at us. Probably because I looked so young, all their expressions carried the same look of comprehension, and even the official showed that he understood what Uncle Xiao's words meant. He didn't ask Uncle Xiao anything else, and he didn't ask me anything at all, but just nodded knowingly at me and began to fill out the divorce certificate. I am sure that what all those people thought Uncle Xiao meant was that he couldn't make love to me anymore, and that was leaving me unsatisfied. I doubt there was anyone who guessed the real reason for our divorce, or understood the whole story of our marriage. It is very difficult for anyone fully to understand someone else's affairs. None of us can honestly say: "I understand that person."

After the divorce formalities were over, I once again became just a nurse-carer in the Xiao household. Of course, I still ran the household; nothing had changed about that. The other people in the neighbourhood all soon knew about the divorce, and there were two old biddies who wanted to introduce me to a new partner. This all annoyed me rather, and I didn't know who had set the news circulating. After this affair was over, I noticed that Uncle Xiao called Lawyer Geng over to the apartment again. I didn't know what he wanted to discuss, but as a simple hired nurse, it wasn't my place to ask.

One evening, when I got back from school with Chengcai, as we came in through the gates of the estate, we bumped into Lao Dong, the janitor. He asked me: "Ah, Xiao Zhong, your apartment is on the third floor, so how can you have rats? Have they come up the water pipes from the floor below." I was taken aback and asked: "Who says we've got rats?" "Judge Xiao! He's just phoned me. He said there was a rat in the apartment, and could he have some rat poison. The only stuff I've got is Dushuqiang, and that's illegal now. I only had one packet left, and I sent it up to him." I was shocked. I knew only too well the uses of Dushuqiang!

The first thing I asked when I got back home was: "Did you bring some Dushuqiang into the apartment, Uncle Xiao?" He seemed not to have heard me and took no notice. I went over and put on his hearing aid for him, then asked again: "Is there any Dushuqiang in here?" Looking a little uncomfortable, he nodded and said: "I saw a rat scuttling out of the bathroom. It must have come up the water pipes from downstairs." "Did you ask for some Dushuqiang?" I fixed him with a stare. He wouldn't look at me and just gave a sort of mumbled grunt. "Where did you put it?" Reluctantly, he pointed to his bedside cabinet: "I thought I'd put it down under my bed before I go to sleep tonight. When you've got a moment, can you help by just opening the packet for me?" I opened the door of the cabinet and found that the packet of Dushuqiang was indeed there in the top drawer. I didn't say any more at the time, but this business had roused my suspicions on two counts.

Firstly, if there was a rat in the apartment, normally Uncle Xiao would have told me about it, and I would have handled it. But he hadn't said a word. Secondly, if he wanted to put down rat poison, it was also me who should have looked it out or gone out to buy some, and he shouldn't have phoned the janitor himself. These suspicions put me on my guard: after all, Uncle Xiao wasn't in a good way, either physically or emotionally, so could he, out of despair, be contemplating doing the same as I had done when I discovered my boyfriend was cheating on me, and poisoning himself? A shudder went through me at the thought of it. I thought I should nip this thing in the bud, and take pre-emptive action. After dinner, when Uncle Xiao was in the bathroom having his evening wash, I hurried into his bedroom and made some adjustments to the Dushuqiang in his bedside cabinet.

My suspicions and surmises proved correct. In the middle of that night, I was startled awake by the shrilling of the alarm next to my bed. I turned over and leapt out of bed. Without even putting anything on my feet, I ran to Uncle Xiao's bedroom. I had specially installed the button beside his bed, which connected to the alarm beside mine, so he could alert me if he got into any difficulties. When I ran into his bedroom, I saw that all the lights were on, and he was lying fully dressed, face up on his bed with his clothes and hat just so. When he saw me come in, he said solemnly: "I'm sorry for using the alarm to wake you up in the middle of the night. I have used up all my strength getting dressed, and I want to say my goodbyes to you." "What goodbyes?" I already had a pretty good idea what he was going to say, but I deliberately asked the question anyway. Uncle Xiao said calmly: "I have already swallowed that packet of Dushuqiang, and it will take effect in a few minutes. I think you already know how powerful this drug is, and quite soon I will be dead. Before I go, I particularly want to tell you how grateful I am to you for nursing me and looking after me for so long. If you want to enjoy the rest of your life, and raise Chengcai to adulthood, then find yourself a husband to pass the days with. I think that male nurse, Qiu Dali, is a decent fellow. The reason I divorced you was so that you would be a divorcee, not a widow. Being a widow doesn't sound so good, and it wouldn't help you get remarried. That is how it's always been. A surge of heat has just gone through my heart. Here, take these two sheets of paper." He used his good hand to pass me two pieces of paper. I glanced at them and saw, written at the top of the first one: *Explanation of My Suicide*.

I didn't hurl myself at him weeping piteously, but just asked: "Why do you want to do this? You used to say you wanted to live forever. If you go like this, what will people say about me? They are bound to say that I didn't look after you properly, and some will go so far as to say that it was my mistreatment of you that drove you to do it. Why do you want to rob me of my reputation? Do you want me never to be able to find a job in nursing ever again?" He looked at me shamefaced. "You know you can't do this, don't you?!" I urged him. He was silent for a moment, then said: "The main thing for me is fear. I'm afraid that after I lose my memory, I will sink into dementia. I've seen people like that in the past, and I don't want to become one myself. I'm afraid that other people will call me an imbecile! And at the same time, I will bring you all sorts of problems, and I will become an intolerable burden that you will have no way of putting down. That's why I must die before it happens. After I am dead, the police are bound to investigate, and they may even suspect you of harming me. With this document to explain, and with our previous divorce, they can no longer have any suspicions of you or cause you any trouble." He had obviously thought this all through very carefully. "If you look at the second sheet, you will see that is my will!" He indicated that I should go on reading.

It was then that I saw the words at the top of the other sheet of paper were *Will and Testament*. I read on. *My name is Xiao Chengshan, and I currently reside at Apartment 302, Building No. 16, Qirui Garden Court, Haidian District, Beijing. After my death, I leave Apartment 302, Building 16, Qirui Garden Court, my savings in the bank and all the furniture and fittings in the apartment, to Ms Zhong Xiaoyang and her son, Chengcai. No distant relatives of myself or my late wife, nor my daughter's relations by marriage may make any counterclaim...* Before I had finished reading, tears had sprung to my eyes, and I sobbed: "Uncle Xiao, thank you for your care and concern for me and my son, but there is no need to do this at this time. There are no problems with your health, and you can continue to live a long life. You are sure to live until 2029. Several expert forecasters have said, by that time, they foresee that scientific and technological methods will be able considerably to extend life expectancy. You really shouldn't be thinking of doing such a hurtful thing now."

Uncle Xiao listened to me through his hearing aid, then smiled faintly and said: "The will has been formally drawn up, in triplicate, by Lawyer Geng's respected law firm. It has already been witnessed, and there is one copy for you, one copy at the lawyers, and one copy lodged with the Public Notary. I am no longer concerned with living forever. That is not to be my good fortune, and very soon I will be taking my leave of you forever." I replied quite calmly: "You can't abandon life like this! I am certainly not going to let you go." Uncle Xiao said: "You can't stop it. The poison is probably already eating away at my internal organs, and I'll soon be gone. Please go into the other room now, so you won't be scared. After I have died, remember to cover my body with a sheet until the undertakers come, and, whatever you do, don't let Chengcai see it, or he will have nightmares." When he had finished, he closed his eyes firmly, as though he wished to have no more to do with this world. I opened my mouth and said, very clearly: "A few years ago, Uncle

Xiao, you taught me we couldn't abandon our lives. You threw the poison away and saved not only Lü Yiwei, but Chengcai and myself as well. This time, I have followed your instruction and thrown away the rat poison you were going to kill yourself with. What you swallowed was only walnut powder. You are not going to die, after all. Get up, take your clothes off and go to sleep!"

"What!?" Uncle Xiao glared at me. "While I am alive, I can't let you kill yourself!" "Who gave you that right?" I hadn't expected him to explode like that, so he was almost howling with rage. "How dare you go against my wishes and stop me from handling my own life? Don't you know that most people with dementia can't recognise anyone, can't understand anything and just stare blankly at the world like a two-year-old child? Don't you know that dementia sufferers can't do anything for themselves and their movements are just mechanical? Don't you know that even though they are doubly incontinent, they are not aware enough to stay away from people, and don't understand about the stench and are often smeared with faeces and urine? Do you want people to make fun of me and call me an imbecile to my face? Do you want people to look pityingly at me all day, and help wipe away my snot and drool? Do you want all my friends and neighbours to look down on me, to hate me and be disgusted by me? What gave you the right to make this decision for me? You're my fake wife and my real nurse; how dare you be so brazen?"

I hadn't known he could be so fierce. I was deeply wounded, but I held back my tears and said: "Uncle, I may only be a fake wife and a real nurse, but I am also a woman who has devoted her life to you. As long as I am alive, even if you lose your memory completely and become totally incapacitated, I will never let you be covered in faeces and urine. I will treat you just the same as I do today when you are alert and clear-headed. You will live your life clean and dignified, preserving all your self-respect. I won't let anyone bully you or humiliate you. My helping you to live is not to punish you, but to help you wait – wait until medical science finds a cure for atrophy of the cerebellum and senile dementia. You know that medical science has made great strides over the last few years.

Haven't they defeated the Ebola virus and slowed down the progress of breast cancer? Haven't they slowed down the infection rate of AIDS? Why should they not find a cure for atrophy of the cerebellum and senile dementia? All we need now is time, don't you see? You have to keep on living, living until God decides otherwise, and then we'll see. I'm certainly not going to let you go before your time. I want you to live to see the last day of your natural life!" Tears were flowing down Uncle Xiao's face as he listened to me. I heard him sob: "How could I not want to live a few more days? How can I not be afraid of death? When I think that I might have eaten the Dushuqiang and could be entering the realms of eternal darkness, it makes me shudder. But I am even more afraid of what it will be like when dementia sets in. When it does get a grip on me, I won't know anything and will be at anyone's mercy! You are just my nurse, so what will happen when you get tired of it and have had enough? Open my computer over there on the table, and find the stories of the family members of dementia sufferers that I saved. Read them carefully, and then you'll understand what a terrifying thing it is to have someone with dementia in the family!"

I turned and opened the computer. I found the stuff Uncle Xiao had saved, and there indeed were the stories of family members with a senile dementia sufferer. One was written by someone called Liu Fang and read: *Since my mother developed senile dementia, it takes seventy minutes to feed her a single meal, and I am so tired I feel I might as well be dead...* Fang Jianyan wrote: *My father, who has senile dementia, keeps taking everything in the house outside to dry in the sun, even pots and pans and bowls. He does it at least three times a day. Lord! The good times of my life are well and truly over!* Someone called Jin Chuan wrote: *For the last five nights in a row, Granny has got out of bed at around two o'clock and knocked on every door in the house, in a panic, saying that there's a murderer in the house and we should all find sticks and cudgels to beat him off. We're all being driven mad by it...* Lian Jie wrote: *Today, some of my classmates came over for coffee and a chat. My grandad, who has senile dementia, smeared himself all over with his own shit. My friends all just ran away in alarm. Why can't he just die...* Another person calling themselves Older Sister Ms Liang wrote: *After my husband contracted senile dementia, if I take my eye*

off him for a second, he runs away saying he's taking cover from artillery
shells. He does this practically every day, and I have to go and find him. I've
thought of tying him up, but if I do, outsiders will say I'm maltreating him.
But then, if I don't, he may run out into the road and get run over and
killed... "Have you read them?" Uncle Xiao asked from his bed.
"What do you think of how they have to pass their days?" "As your
nurse, I will accept any circumstances that we encounter!" "And will
you not regret saying that when we get to the point when you are
praying for me to die, but I just keep on living?" I seized his hand
and said: "I understand. You believe that I will not be able to care
for you right to the end of your life's journey, and are afraid that I
will abandon you halfway through. It is not an unreasonable fear, as
you and I are not related by blood and have no physical
relationship. We were brought together by chance, and I only came
to help you to earn a living. You only let me stay because you
needed a nurse, but after so many things have happened while we
have been together, I have come to think of you as family, my
closest family apart from my mum, dad, little sister and little
brother. And now, I swear to you before God: if I abandon you after
your senile dementia takes over, may I die a terrible death, and may
God strike me down!" When Uncle Xiao heard this, he gripped my
hand tight and didn't say any more.

From that night on, I moved into Uncle Xiao's room so he would no
longer be able to take his own life. Truth be told, there are many
opportunities for someone who really wants to kill himself, and I
had to take every precaution to ensure that a tragedy was not played
out in our household. Uncle Xiao slept in a double bed, and there
was enough room for me just to bring in my own quilt. When he
saw me bringing the quilt in, he cried out in alarm: "What are you
doing? I'm not used to having someone else sleeping in my bed!" I
smiled deliberately and said: "It doesn't matter whether you're used
to it or not, I'm still going to sleep there. Besides, I'm your ex-wife.
Everyone thinks I slept here before, so what's odd about me going

on doing so?" "You!?" Uncle Xiao glared at me for a moment, then shut his eyes tight. He didn't have the strength to throw me out.

From then on, I never left Uncle Xiao's side, or, even if he strayed away a little, he was always in my line of sight. I once told him, half-jokingly: "You'd better forget any thoughts of killing yourself; I'm not going to let anything but a natural death happen on my watch. I need to protect my reputation as a nurse, and if you do kill yourself, everyone will think I tormented you to death so I could get my hands on your property sooner. You can't let me live the rest of my life with that shadow hanging over my good name. Besides, medical science seems to be advancing so rapidly, why should we let our pessimism get the better of us?" It was probably three weeks or so after this that Uncle Xiao finally said to me: "All right, all right, I guarantee you I won't try to kill myself, but you have to promise me one thing in return." "Go on. What is it?" "Find someone who loves you and marry him!" I was rather taken aback and asked: "Why have you brought that up?" He sighed and said: "After dementia takes hold, I don't know how long I will have to live. I've seen people on the internet say that, because dementia sufferers have nothing on their minds, they aren't tormented by worries, and sometimes live longer because of it. If that is true, you can't just keep living your life as a widow. That wouldn't be fair on you. You must remarry. You must put all that stuff with Lü Yiwei behind you and believe that there are lots of decent men on this Earth. Getting married again wouldn't just be good for you, it would be good for me too because you'd have another pair of hands to help look after me." So that was what he thought, was it? Of course, I immediately replied: "Firstly, I've no intention of getting married again. I have absolutely no faith in young men. Secondly, since I'm not letting you kill yourself, and I'm already mentally prepared to look after you for the long term, you don't have to think of anything else."

When he heard me talking like that, his expression changed and he said: "If you don't make me that promise, I'm telling you now that I will kill myself! If I give up on life, there are lots of ways for me to do it, and there's no way you'll be able to stop me." I knew he was right. I couldn't possibly keep up the highest level of vigilance all the time, and always have my eye on him. Throwing himself from the window, gassing himself, hanging himself: there were lots of ways for him to do it. Ha! So that was how he was going to force me to remarry! All I could do was respond, with a bitter laugh: "And what do you think is so easy about remarrying? Where am I supposed to go to find someone who loves me and who I love?" He just shook his head and said: "You can't stay away from the well for ten years just because a snake bit you there one morning. You found one bad apple, and you think the whole barrel is full of them. The truth is there are lots of good men out there. I've mentioned him before – what about your young countryman, the nurse at the hospital, Qiu Dali? He's all right, and I could see that he fancies you. I think you should get in touch with him. Of course, when it comes to picking a partner, you have to be choosy, but not too choosy. Life isn't so long that you can afford to hang back forever over this." Laughing, I replied: "I quite like that Qiu Dali fellow, and he's made it clear in the past that he fancies me, but I think we're a long way from talking about marriage. Once bitten, twice shy!" "Then ask him over for a chat and a meal. You can say I invited him. How are you going to get to know each other better if you don't even meet?" Uncle Xiao kept on at me. Just for his peace of mind, and to stop him doing anything stupid, I promised I would let Qiu Dali come over for a visit. Really I was just being pragmatic and letting Uncle Xiao know that Qiu Dali and I were still in contact, and nothing more. How was I to know that I was going to lose control of the matter?

Qiu Dali seemed to be more than pleasantly surprised when I phoned him to ask him over. This was because I had kept him at a distance in all our previous interactions, and I had paid no attention to his protestations of affection. He didn't ask any questions, but just said: "I'll be right over." I thought I'd better find some chore that needed doing, or what would we talk about when he got here? I went into the bathroom and broke the flush on the toilet. When he arrived, I told him: "The flush on the toilet is broken. The compound's sanitation engineer isn't on duty at the moment, so

I've had to bother you to come over and help." "That's easily fixed," he said. He said a quick hello to Uncle Xiao and then got busy in the bathroom. When he had finished, I said my thank-yous, stuffed some leftover steamed pork buns in a plastic bag for him to take home and eat later, poured him some tea and said: "Go and keep Uncle Xiao company. I've got to go to the supermarket for a few things. If you're on duty at the hospital, just go when you have to and don't wait for me to get back." "All right," he said nodding. I left the apartment, thinking: "Well, at least we've met. That's my part of the deal with Uncle Xiao."

After I'd got what I needed at the supermarket that morning, I went on to browse in a few other shops just to spin out the time before I went back to the apartment. Around eleven o'clock, I thought he must have left by now, and made my way back. To my surprise, when I opened the front door, he was still there, sitting beside Uncle Xiao's bed, giving the old man a massage. I was taken aback, and my expression must have been a little cool and unwelcoming. He noticed this and explained hastily: "The old fellow wouldn't let me leave, and I didn't want to go against his will." Uncle Xiao said, in a loud voice: "Ah, Xiaoyang! Go and cook up a few dishes. We need to thank Dali for helping us out." I couldn't really refuse, so I just replied: "All right, I'll go and do it now." When the food was cooked and on the table, Qiu Dali shot me a look and immediately picked up a bowl and some chopsticks and began to feed Uncle Xiao. Uncle Xiao said, between mouthfuls: "There's something I want to tell you, Qiu Dali. Xiaoyang and I are divorced now. She has gone through hell looking after me over the last few years, and I wanted to give her her freedom back." "Eh!?" Qiu Dali was clearly taken aback, but then he looked at me for a moment, and there was something very like delight in his expression. I glared at Uncle Xiao, showing I was not at all happy that he had mentioned the matter at this point. It was a pity Uncle Xiao only had one good eye, so he didn't see my expression clearly, and he just continued, blatantly: "Men, eh? If they see a girl they like, they should go after her; otherwise, she might get snapped up by someone else..." "Eat up, eat up..." I had to say something to interrupt Uncle Xiao's sales pitch, and if it had been anyone but him talking like that, I would have been furious. Qiu Dali clearly caught the encouraging tone in what Uncle Xiao was saying, and, as he was helping me take the plates and dishes back to the kitchen, he seized the chance to say to me, ardently: "I always wanted to say to you in the past that I would wait for you. But now the time has come when the waiting is over, and you've got to give me a chance!" "What chance?" I looked hard at him. "A chance to look after you and your son!" he replied with a grin. I told him coldly: "There are two reasons I let you have lunch here today. One is because the old man wanted you to stay, and the other is because I wanted to thank you for everything you've done for us in the past. Nothing else. You mustn't get the wrong idea. I'm sure you are very busy at the hospital and should be getting back there. I don't want us to get in the way of your work." When he heard me giving him his marching orders, all he could do was look embarrassed and take his leave. I thought that would be the end of the matter, and Uncle Xiao could stop worrying. But to my surprise, Qiu Dali invited himself over the next day too. It was a Saturday, so Chengcai wasn't at school, and it was he who answered the door. As soon as he did, Qiu Dali thrust a kite into his hands. Chengcai was delighted and kept shouting out happily: "Thank you, Uncle! Thank you, Uncle!" He took Qiu Dali by the hand and pulled him into the living room.

When Qiu Dali saw Uncle Xiao sitting there, he went over and greeted him, bowing respectfully, and handed him a bag of bananas he had brought along, saying: "I look after invalids all the time at the hospital, and I know that eating a banana every day helps gut motility and acts as a laxative. You should remember to eat one every day too!" Uncle Xiao laughed and said: "Thank you, thank you!" Seeing how happy both young and old were to see him, there was nothing really I could say. I couldn't ask him to leave immediately, so I just nodded curtly to him by way of greeting, and went and busied myself in the kitchen. When I came out again, he was pushing Uncle Xiao over to the front door, saying he was taking him and Chengcai to Longevity Park to fly the kite. I opened my mouth to veto the idea but only got as far as asking: "Fly what

kite?" when Chengcai burst out: "Let's go, let's go, let's go!" I saw
there was nothing for it but to let them go. The apartment was
instantly very quiet after the three of them left, and for the first
time in a long time, I felt myself relax.

Qiu Dali stayed until after dinner that day, and before we knew
it, it was past eight o'clock. He showed no sign of wanting to leave,
and even suggested he might stay to help wash Uncle Xiao. I could
see the situation was getting a bit desperate from my point of view,
so I urged him: "You've been helping out all day, and we're very
grateful, but you should leave now. I can see to washing Uncle
Xiao." But I had scarcely finished speaking when Chengcai began to
shout: "Don't let Uncle Qiu go! Let him sleep here so we can fly the
kite together again tomorrow!" I glared at Chengcai and told him:
"That's not possible!" To my surprise, though, Uncle Xiao chimed
in: "What's not possible about it? We have a guest room don't we?
He can sleep there!" Qiu Dali took advantage of the situation and
said firmly: "All right, all right, I'll stay in the guest room." With the
three of them all of the same mind, I was too embarrassed to insist
on him leaving, so I went, unwillingly, to make up the guest room.

When I had settled both Uncle Xiao and Chengcai, I went to the
bathroom myself, and it was then that Qiu Dali, who had retired to
the guest room, suddenly pushed open the bathroom door. I gave a
great start, spat out the water in my mouth and asked him what
the matter was. He didn't reply but suddenly fell to his knees in
front of me. I took a step back in horrified amazement, with no
idea what to do. The next instant, he put his arms tightly round my
calves and murmured: "Let me look after you all..." I hastily bent
down to release my legs from his grasp, not at all expecting that he
would immediately clasp hold of my arms. The bathroom was quite
a tight space, and I tried to struggle free of his embrace. As I
struggled, I bumped into the wash basin and my tooth cleaning
equipment, which fell with a clatter. I immediately stopped
struggling in case I woke Chengcai. My hesitation just encouraged
Qiu Dali, and gradually, inch by inch, he pulled me down to the
floor in his embrace. Still not wanting to make a noise, all I could
do was hammer on his back with my fists, but the harder I

hammered, the tighter he held me, as he brought his face down next to mine.

Well, all you aunties, older sisters and younger sisters here today, I'll tell you what happened next, and I don't mind how much you mock me. That evening, I was really angry with him, and I was willing to fight him to the end. I pounded him on the back with a tooth mug. Our relationship certainly hadn't reached this point yet! But after all was said and done, I was a girl who had been without male contact for many years, and as he kept pressing closer to me in that confined space, the closer he got, the more he was touching me, so in the end there was nothing else for it. I didn't have the strength anymore, and I didn't actually hate him, so why not just go along with him? In the end, I let him have his way...

The next morning when I got up to make breakfast, he followed me into the kitchen and said: "Why don't we just go to the Marriage Registry Office and register our marriage so we can be a proper husband and wife!" I just thought to myself: Well, I've already given him my body, so why not!? But then, when I looked at his rather smug expression, I wasn't quite so happy with the idea. "Ha! So, do we just do everything on your say-so?" I gave him a look. "What's the rush? Can't we be together if we don't get married?" He could see that I was upset, and hurriedly nodded and said: "All right, all right, let's get together first and then get married." After that, Qiu Dali was effectively living in our apartment. When he moved in, he took over many of the things that had to be done for Uncle Xiao, and my own burden got a lot lighter, so I actually had some time to rest.

The doctor's original predictions for the course of Uncle Xiao's conditions proved correct. My own observations told me that his memory and powers of discrimination were deteriorating, day by day. At first, he couldn't remember clearly things that had happened the same day, but it wasn't long before he began to forget what day it was, and couldn't add up simple items on water and electricity bills; then, after a while, he began to forget the route back to the apartment from the park; a fortnight later, he failed to recognise familiar neighbours as he went up and down in the lift. Two months later, there came an evening when he asked Chengcai: "Whose family are you from?" Of course, he did remember that pretty quickly, and slapped his forehead, angry with himself: "How could I be so stupid? How could I not recognise Chengcai?" He began to travel a path between memory and forgetfulness, with only an intermittent barrier between the two. I was extremely worried.

I had to find someone who could think of some way of arresting this deterioration, or at least slowing down its progress, and allow him to retain at least a little clarity of thought and improve his quality of life. First, I sought out specialists in Western medicine. On the internet, I found what must have been nearly all the top experts in psychiatry and neurosurgery, and picked out several with the best reputations. I went to the hospitals where they worked, and quizzed them in person about the means of treating senile dementia. Sad to say, they all told me the same thing: this is a degenerative disease of the central nervous system; it is a disease whose progress can't be halted; at present, there is no effective treatment even to slow down that progress. All they could do was recommend some therapies and write prescriptions for some drugs to improve mental acuity and memory and limit the psychological effects, but not to address the roots of the problem.

In a panic, I sought out specialists in traditional Chinese medicine as I transferred all my hopes to that. After I had questioned a large number of families of senile dementia sufferers online, I took Uncle Xiao in his wheelchair to see an old Chinese doctor who specialised in this condition. After he had taken Uncle Xiao's pulses, this doctor wrote out a prescription. I treated this like a treasured possession, and even now, I can still remember its contents: fifteen grams of angelica, twelve grams of Chinese peony, nine grams of atractylodes rhizome, twelve grams of *fuling* fungus, twelve grams of water plantain rhizome, fifteen grams of *chuanxiong* rhizome, all prepared by boiling in water. One course of treatment lasted fifteen days, and the patient should take three courses. After I got home and settled Uncle Xiao, I went back out to the Tong Ren Tang pharmacy to buy the ingredients. That evening, I boiled them up and gave the medicine to Uncle Xiao to drink. Before I gave it to him, I tasted it myself. It was extremely bitter, but Uncle Xiao seemed to hold out hope for its efficacy and drank it down without even raising an eyebrow. Over the following days, I boiled up the medicine every day, and every day he drank it. The apartment was filled with the smell of traditional Chinese medicine, which, to us, was also the smell of hope. The problem was that, after a month and a half, Uncle's Xiao's deterioration was showing no signs of stopping, and what was more, he was also becoming delusional.

One morning, after Chengcai had gone to school, and Qiu Dali had gone for his shift at the hospital, I was preparing to take Uncle Xiao out in his wheelchair for a breath of fresh air in the park. Out of the blue, Uncle Xiao pointed at an open window and yelled: "There's a thief!" I gave a great start of fear and surprise, snatched up a rolling pin and went over to the window to look. There was no one there. I wasn't completely reassured, and went and checked in every room: still no sign of anyone. As I was puzzling over this, Uncle Xiao started shouting again, pointing at the front door: "There he is, there he is! Catch the thief!" The front door was shut tight, and there was no chance of a thief getting in that way. I turned to look at Uncle Xiao and asked doubtfully: "Where is this thief?" Uncle Xiao didn't reply but pointed at the sofa and suddenly exclaimed: "Please sit down, Judge Yao!" It was only then that it dawned on me that Uncle Xiao was talking nonsense. I shouted at him: "Stop imagining things, Uncle Xiao. No one has come into the apartment." Uncle Xiao blinked when he heard this, like someone coming back to his senses, and gave a long groan. A feeling of hopelessness flooded through me. Uncle Xiao's remaining powers of memory and recognition were finally failing and were in danger of forcing his descent into full dementia. After dinner that evening, he put in his hearing aid and called me over to him. "While I'm still clear-headed, there are three things I need to tell you. First, the PIN for my bank account is 825673. Eighty-two is the number of years since I deposited my first ten cents, fifty-six is the number of yuan that ten cents is now worth, seventy-three is Xinxin's birthday, the third of July." With that, he put an open bankbook in my hand, and when I looked, I saw that the account held six hundred and eighty thousand yuan. He continued: "My single person's retirement pension is deposited into this account every month. From now on, this household is entirely in your hands." He used his good left hand to grasp my own hand and shook it firmly. I couldn't hold back my tears.

"The second thing is, if, after I have descended into full dementia, I have a heart attack, you must remember to tell the doctors absolutely not to defibrillate me, not to resuscitate me, and absolutely not to intubate me or perform a tracheotomy, but to let me go quickly. The third thing is the guiding principle that you must absolutely not use up all the money in that account seeking treatment for me or trying to improve my quality of life. Draw a red line at two hundred thousand yuan, and when you reach that red line, stop spending money on me, and use the remainder to support Chengcai's education. These are my dying wishes, and it will be showing me the greatest disrespect if you don't follow them. If, in future, Chengcai is successful in his studies, then, up in heaven, I will feel my life has been given extra meaning." I began to sob. To stop him abandoning all thoughts of a cure, and to keep my own hope alive, I reminded him: "You still haven't finished your books!" He gave a wry laugh and said: "It seems likely God doesn't enjoy reading my books, and he doesn't want me to become an academic lawyer. That's why he sent me this disease. So, I'll follow his orders, not write those books and settle for being just a retired judge…"

Not even a month after that evening, Uncle Xiao lost his memory completely. He couldn't remember things he should have been very familiar with, and he didn't even know where the toilet in the apartment was. When I took him to the bathroom, he couldn't remember the way back to his bedroom. After another month, he didn't even recognise me and often asked: "Who are you? Where have you come from?" When a group of his old colleagues came over to visit him, he didn't know who they were. He even thought they had come to hurt him, pointing at one of them and saying:

"What are you doing? Why are you holding a gun? You're not a bailiff, so why are you carrying a weapon? Is court going into session? I don't believe it. I bet you made some excuse to draw it from the bailiffs' gun store, and you're planning some crime! Is it because I sentenced you too harshly? You killed two people, so of course I sentenced you to death! If you're not happy about it, you can appeal, but if you kill me, it will just make your sentence worse! Worse, I say! I know there are bullets in your gun. They're 7.62 rounds, a lot of stopping power. They make a big exit wound. I can tell you've already got a round in the chamber, and your finger is on the trigger. Are you trying to scare me? Are you testing my nerve? Do you want to see if I'm a real man? Go on then, shoot! Shoot, and if the worst comes to the worst, and I die, what does it matter how? When you're dead, you're dead, aren't you? Everyone dies in the end. If I die at your hand, all the better! Good! Good!" He was laughing bitterly as he said all this to his former colleague. As the group of them said their goodbyes and left, they were all shaking their heads and sighing.

A few days later, I found him arguing with an invisible antagonist, protesting: "Why are you forcing me to eat chilli peppers? Because they're good for me? Hah! What's good about eating chilli peppers? They stimulate the appetite, do they? I don't see it! Anyway, there's nothing wrong with my appetite! They help get rid of excess moisture in the body, do they? I don't think so! Besides, how much moisture is there in the body to get rid of? To increase the circulation? Bullshit! Still, bullshit doesn't cost anything, so bullshit away as much as you like! I think eating spicy food isn't good for your stomach, and most importantly, it really burns your arsehole when you take a shit. Of course they don't hurt you! You're the one making me eat them, so they hurt me all right! I'm really sore!..."

On another day, he seemed to be having an argument about parking his bicycle with some invisible antagonist: "Why won't you let me park my bicycle here? Are you deliberately trying to provoke me? Do you live on this side of the street? I'm telling you, I'll go straight to the court and swear out a case against you! You don't believe I will? Let's go and see, shall we? And I'll be sure to make you compensate me for my lost time! I'll make you apologise, and I'll make you regret your behaviour today for the rest of your life! You don't believe me? All right, you just wait till our case comes up! You just wait..."

Sometimes he would keep ranting for up to two hours at a time, and nothing could stop him. The more you tried, the more he ranted, especially in the middle of the night. Once he started, there was nothing for it but to hear him out until he got so exhausted he went to sleep. Another time, a few days later, he seemed to think someone was scratching his chest. He kept using his good left hand to fend off the invisible hand, making swatting motions and saying to himself: "Go away! Take your hand away! If I'm really itchy, that's my problem. Stop messing me about, I'm getting bored with it! Go away! I don't want to see you anymore!" In the end, he stopped talking and just kept making the fending off motions until he was exhausted and gasping for breath, his face white as a sheet. I had no choice but to seize hold of his hand, in case he did himself a mischief.

As his symptoms progressed, his speech became jumbled and incoherent, his voice going up and down, and the words just tumbling out so you really couldn't make out what he was saying. Chengcai was the person closest to him, and in the past, the first thing he did when he got home from school was to run over and greet his Grandpa, and tell him what had happened at school. Uncle Xiao always used to pat him on the head and tell him to go and do his homework. But now, he looked at Chengcai as though he was a complete stranger, and all he did was mutter incomprehensibly. Chengcai was afraid of him now, too, and would go into the room and look at him from a distance, not daring to go any closer. He asked me in tears: "What's wrong with Grandpa? Why don't you do something for him? Do something for him!" It broke my heart that I couldn't think of anything to do.

The scariest thing happened one morning. Chengcai was going on a school outing, and I had to take him down myself to meet the coach at the main gates of our compound, so I was a little later than normal waking Uncle Xiao up. When I got back to the apartment from seeing Chengcai off, I hastily pushed open Uncle Xiao's bedroom door, all ready to wake him. As soon as I opened the door, I was hit by a terrible stench, so powerful I had to hold my breath. When I looked properly, I saw that Uncle Xiao must have opened his bowels before he was out of bed, and, in his demented state, feeling uncomfortable, he must have reached down and scooped up his own faeces and smeared them on his body, handful after handful, until he was covered in them right up to his neck. Great heavens! This was the worst thing I had ever had to deal with in my whole nursing career. Panicking, I hurled open the window, hurriedly stopped him from smearing himself with any more of the stuff, tore off his pyjamas any old how, shovelled him into the plastic bathroom wheelchair and pushed him down to the bathroom for a shower. Once I had scrubbed him clean, I put him into clean clothes, then washed myself, gave the bedroom a thorough clean, and changed all the bedding. I was so exhausted I thought I was going to collapse. As I sat beside the bewildered Uncle Xiao, gasping for breath, I just wanted to weep and wail. Good Lord! How could such a fastidious person, as Uncle Xiao had been, turn into this? It was then I remembered the words he had said to me after I had stopped him from killing himself: "The day will come when you can't take it anymore." He was right. I had thought of all the difficulties, all the symptoms he might develop, but I had never ever thought he would be reduced to this. It terrified me that a person's mental state could deteriorate to this extent, and it made me infinitely sadder than before. Even in their declining years, Fate still had this trick to play on people. Lord, is this what you have in store for me too when I grow old?

A month after this, he stopped talking completely. He showed absolutely no interest in his surroundings, to the extent that he didn't even look at anything. He spent the whole day staring vacantly at the wall, or at a certain spot, not moving at all, and without even a flicker of his eyes. It didn't matter what strange noises came in from outside, or whether the lights were on or off in the apartment, he simply didn't register a thing. The sights, smells and sounds of the outside world meant nothing to him, and he had no understanding of anything at all. Gradually, he even forgot how to eat and drink. If you put food to his lips, he swallowed it like an automaton, but if you didn't, he didn't know to call out if he was hungry. If you gave him water, he drank it, but if you didn't, he had nothing to drink and didn't know if he was thirsty or not. He had lost all control of his bladder and bowels, and when I put an adult nappy on him, as often as not he just tore it off. At least he still did as he was told, like a puppet, and made no move to resist.

He had become like a one-year-old child, without the ability to respond to life or the world around him. Although I had given a lot of thought to preparing for this stage of the disease, Uncle Xiao's condition caused me untold heartache. Nonetheless, even then, I did not abandon all hope of being able to treat Uncle Xiao, and I still hoped his condition might take a turn for the better. Since neither formal Western medicine nor traditional Chinese medicine had had any results, I hoped I might discover some remedy in folk medicine. I secretly prayed I might find some wise man among the people who could alleviate Uncle Xiao's condition. There is a little copse in the northwest corner of Longevity Park, inside which there is a patch of grass that is a meeting place for the family members of senile dementia sufferers in the neighbourhood. They often take their invalids there for a rest, and exchange news with each other about possible cures.

One day, I heard one of these family members say that food therapy could be useful in improving the sufferer's condition, so I asked him: "What kind of food therapy?" "Congee," he replied. "Get them to eat hot congee if their condition allows." I immediately went home and made two types of congee according to the man's instructions. One was haricot bean congee, made with twenty grams of haricot beans and fifty grams of round-grain rice. First you wash the haricot beans, then put them in a pot with half a litre of pure water and add the rice. You boil it over a fast flame for five minutes, then reduce the heat and simmer for thirty minutes until it turns into congee. I gave it to Uncle Xiao while it was still hot. The other sort was called walnut and pearl barley congee. You take fifty grams of walnuts, thirty grams of pearl barley, ten grams of round-grain rice, five grams of red dates, and twenty grams of goji berries. You wash all the ingredients, stone the red dates, pound the walnuts into small pieces, put them all in a clay pot, add water and boil into congee. I fed Uncle Xiao this too. In fact, I fed him both kinds of congee for close on three months, but I didn't see any results. Of course, Uncle Xiao didn't notice that the treatment had been ineffective, and he just continued to sit listlessly in his wheelchair, indifferent to everything. The person who wasn't indifferent was me! When Qiu Dali saw that I was so worried I had no appetite, he urged me to try to take a step back from things, saying: "It's not that we are not treating him, it's that there simply is no treatment." I urgently wanted to find some other method, but the only place to look was in folk medicine because at the moment, formal Western medicine certainly had no way of turning the situation round. I asked for help from my circle of friends on WeChat. It wasn't a large circle of friends, but a lot of them wanted to offer answers, sadly none of which proved to be of genuine use.

One early evening as I was despondently pushing Uncle Xiao back home from Longevity Park, we chanced to meet a white-haired old man, who was still mobile with the aid of a stick. When he saw Uncle Xiao, drooped with lifeless eyes in his wheelchair, he stopped in his tracks and said: "Has he got senile dementia?" I nodded. He went on: "Has he stopped recognising anyone at all?" I nodded again. He asked yet again: "Do you want him to improve a little?" I came to life at that and answered eagerly: "Of course! Do you have some method, sir?" He shook his head and said: "No, I don't, but I do know someone who does. Would you like to give it a try?" "Of course I would, of course I would!" I almost babbled. The old man looked at me, stroking his beard and asked me: "What relation are you to him? His daughter?" I hurriedly said that I was. He went on, softening his tone: "Well, as you're his daughter, I think you should be making a bit more of an effort. Deep in the Lüliang Mountains in

Shanxi, there's a place called Qingyang Ridge, and on top of the ridge here is a tiny Daoist temple. Its abbot, Wu Mei, is a former professor of psychology at Yanjing University. I have heard that he has a method of curing this disease. A friend of mine in Handan also had this condition. He used the abbot's method and has already shown significant improvement. Of course, I can't say whether it will have the same effect on your father, but if you want to give it a try, then go and see. But if it doesn't work, I don't want you blaming me for sending you on a wild goose chase." "Of course, of course!" I bowed my thanks to him and asked the best way to get to the Lüliang Mountains in Shanxi. That evening, I discussed it with Qiu Dali, asking him to request a few days' leave so he could stay at home and look after Uncle Xiao and Chengcai, while I made the trip, coming back after five days. He was very happy to agree: "All right. The important thing is that you go without having to worry about them."

Very early the next day, I made sure Qiu Dali knew all about what had to be done for the household, including feeding and toileting Uncle Xiao, and getting Chengcai to and from school. Then I put my bag on my back, and set out. It was early evening the next day when I got to the little Daoist temple on Qingyang Ridge in the Lüliang Mountains. It was, indeed, tiny; just a five-alcove shrine to the three Daoist deities, consecrated to the Primeval Lord of Heaven, the Heavenly Lord of Numinous Treasure and the Heavenly Lord of Dao and Virtue. Above the main door to the shrine was written a couplet that read: *To stamp out evil things, you must brandish the precious three-foot sword to crush them; to dispel things that anger you, you must unfurl towards the clouds the protection of the Seven-starred Banner.* I went into the shrine and kowtowed to the Three Divinities, and laid before them the selection of offerings I had brought with me. Then I turned and clasped my hands in respect to the little Daoist monk who was sitting beside the door, and said: "Reverend sir, can you please take me to see Abbot Wu? I have a seriously ill friend whom I'd like him to treat." The little monk nodded and said: "My master is an old man, and he has many things to attend to in the temple; I will take you to see him, but you must be sure not to take up too much of his time. Please follow me to the hut behind the temple."

Inside the hut behind the shrine, I saw the white-bearded, thin-faced, frail-bodied Abbot Wu. He was sitting in the lamplight turning the pages of a book of some kind. When he saw me come in, he put down the book and looked at me calmly. I knelt down in front of him, and then urgently explained to him the reason for my visit. He heard me out, then said in a weak voice: "A Daoist temple is a place for followers of the Dao to practise asceticism; it is not a clinic to treat people. But we do watch the movements of the heavens, and study the lay of the Earth; we sit in meditation apart from physical boundaries, and we consider that treating the body and treating the country are the same thing, and we take delight in extending human life. For these reasons, we have some knowledge of medicine and the use of medicines. This disease of senile dementia is a bitterness in human life, and whether you taste it or not is ordained by heaven; those who do taste it should not complain of its bitterness, and those who don't should not rejoice. I recognise that you have spared no effort in journeying such a long distance from the capital city to this little shrine deep in the mountains to seek a way one may be freed from this bitterness. So this poor Daoist will teach you a method that you can take away and try. If it is not effective, then that will show you that the sufferer's bitterness has not yet been tasted to the full, and heaven is not yet ready to release him from it. If it does have some effect, then you must remember your debt to the Three Divinities."

I hurriedly kowtowed again in acknowledgement, and eagerly awaited his next words. He said: "Daoism pays particular attention to the living of a joyful life, so this poor Daoist has made some researches into medical matters. From this poor Daoist's point of view, medicine is an endless and endlessly beautiful science, but all it raises are possibilities; any illness may afflict any person, and each has its particular characteristics. You cannot use the conclusions of existing medical science to cover everything, nor can you say that because medical textbooks say it cannot be cured, that means it definitely cannot be cured. In the case of senile dementia, no matter what stage the patient is at, there always remains intact the thinnest of threads of sanity. It is not all completely dark in the depths of their consciousness; there is always a glimmer of awareness. Western medicine holds that this disease can be neither arrested nor reversed, but this poor Daoist does not agree. This poor Daoist's medicine can strengthen that slender thread of sanity, and help expand his consciousness to fill the void." So saying, he turned to open a cupboard beside him, which I saw was full of medicinal herbs. He rummaged in a drawer for a moment and took out a big packet of medicine, which he handed to me, with the instructions: "This is a medicinal powder. The patient should take two spoonfuls every day, one after breakfast and one after dinner. It should be taken with warm boiled water, to soften its pungency. When you get it home, it would be best to store it in a glass jar so it does not lose its flavour."

I took the medicine and asked pleadingly: "Beijing is a very long way from here, and it is not an easy journey. Would you be able to give me a written prescription, so when this packet is finished, I can get it made up in Beijing?" The abbot shook his head: "It is not that I don't want to help, the fact is that some of the ingredients you would not be able to buy in any traditional Chinese pharmacy in Beijing. Moreover, some of the processes used in making this medicine are beyond the ability of anyone there too." The little monk, who was standing to one side, chimed in: "Some of the ingredients aren't even in any medical dictionary; they were discovered by my master in these Lüliang Mountains, and the methods used to process them are very complicated. If you use it up, you'll just have to come back for some more." I hastily nodded in acknowledgement and took out my money to pay. But the abbot stopped me, saying: "There is no payment for this medicine. It is a small representation of the benevolence of this shrine, and we simply hope that it may be of some use in treating your father's illness. However, I must make it clear that this medicine is a supplementary treatment; the main medicine is Woman." "Woman?!" I exclaimed in astonishment.

The abbot continued, softly: "If you want to reawaken the

remaining consciousness in a man's heart and allow it gradually to expand, of course you need the action of medicines, but the most important part of the process is to allow it to be in contact with young womanhood. The power of the love between the sexes is one of the greatest, most fundamental powers. It is the only thing that can break through the thick wall of lost awareness and penetrate through to the layers of remaining consciousness. Do you understand what I mean?" I nodded, only half understanding and hurriedly asked: "How do you bring about that contact?" "By the patient drinking the woman's milk." This time, I took a step back in amazement, thinking I must have heard wrong. "Drinking her milk?" "That's right!" He nodded. "Let the patient put a young woman's nipple in his mouth. Drinking milk from the breast is the first action a person learns after emerging from their mother's womb. Within this kind of instinctive action is encompassed everything about life and living. A man repeats this action many times in his life: first of all with his mother, and later with his loved one. Its memory enters deep into every man's bones, profoundly deep, and reviving the memory of this action has the greatest potential. It can bring back memories of being born, and, from there, other memories can gradually increase, layer by layer." "What!?" I looked into his unblinking eyes. "How can you doubt the principle behind these words. Do you have something else to ask? If not, the day is getting on, so please go down to the village at the bottom of the mountain and find some farmer's house to stay the night in, as we do not have sufficient space here at the shrine to offer you accommodation." "Thank you, Master Abbot!" "Go now!" He gestured to the little monk, indicating the audience was over.

On the way home the next day, I decided to try out the abbot's method. If it didn't work, there would be nothing lost; if by any chance it did, it would be an important step for Uncle Xiao. Of course, this peculiar method of treatment required me to overcome a considerable mental barrier: it was asking me to hand over something comparable to my virginity. Was that acceptable? Indeed, I was certainly not without misgivings about telling you all about this matter today. But, in the end, I thought that it was worth giving it a try if there was any chance of it bringing some improvement to Uncle Xiao's memory and his quality of life. There is always a price for any kind of treatment. If a Daoist abbot, who had never even met us before, could give Uncle Xiao the treatment he himself developed, completely free of charge, could I really not be prepared to pay something myself?

When Qiu Dali asked me about the treatment, I only showed him the packet of herbal medicine powder the abbot had given me, and didn't mention the rest of it. I felt I would have to do too much fast talking to get him to believe in it. After breakfast the next morning, I waited for Qiu Dali and Chengcai to leave the apartment for work and school respectively, then gave Uncle Xiao a spoonful of the supplementary medicine. After that, I made sure the front door was locked, then, first of all, carefully washed my nipples and went over to where Uncle Xiao was sitting in his wheelchair. Although I knew he didn't understand anything that was said to him, I thought it best to explain to him first, and said: "We are going to try a new method of treatment today, Uncle. Ordinary people might not understand this method, and it may be going against your own principles, but if we don't try it, we will never know if it works or not." With that, I unbuttoned the top of my dress and put one of my nipples in Uncle Xiao's mouth. It was the first time I had been bare-breasted in front of him, and if you say that I must have been nervous and agitated about it, you are forgetting that, fortunately, Uncle Xiao was totally unaware of anything that was going on around him. His good left eye swivelling aimlessly around, he just sat there, completely unmoving as he allowed me to put my nipple between his lips. But I could feel that those lips were totally unresponsive, and it was like putting my nipple between two planks of wood. I used my hand to make my nipple twitch between his lips a few times, but there was absolutely no reaction. I pulled his head into my chest, so his head was right up against my breasts, but still nothing. It was only then I remembered I hadn't asked Abbot Wu how long each period of contact should last. I stood in front of Uncle Xiao's wheelchair for forty minutes that day, and by the time I took my nipple out of his mouth, I was exhausted and drenched with sweat. As I sat there, catching my breath, a mournful question flashed through my head: when God first created man, had he done so reluctantly? If not, why had he racked his brain to come up with this kind of ending for some of them?

Of course, in my heart I understood that even if this kind of treatment brought results, they would not be immediate, and now I had started it, I would just have to wait. Every day from then on, morning and afternoon before I pushed Uncle Xiao to the park, I let him suckle for about forty minutes each time. Around a month passed without seeing any results. At that point, it occurred to me that perhaps I had chosen the wrong time of day for the procedure, and maybe night-time would be better. So then, every evening after I had settled Chengcai, I told Qiu Dali that I was going to spend some time with Uncle Xiao, and he should go to bed and get some rest. Then I would go to Uncle Xiao's bedroom, lock the door, pull Uncle Xiao over to me and put my nipple into his mouth for forty minutes. Every time I did it, I silently prayed to the gods that we would get some results. But the gods didn't seem to hear my prayers, and they showed me not even the slightest manifestation of their concern.

One evening, I forgot to lock the door after going into Uncle Xiao's bedroom, and just as I pulled him over to me and put my nipple into his mouth, Qiu Dali suddenly pushed open the door and came in. The light in the room was still on, so Qiu Dali could see exactly what was happening. He was flabbergasted. Of course, his entrance took me completely unawares, and when I made to try to explain, before I could even open my mouth, it was clear that he had put another interpretation on the scene. I heard him say, icily: "I never thought you could be so perverted! It's not enough for you to have me suck your nipples, you have to let this imbecile old man do it too!" I bellowed at him: "Fuck off! Just fuck off, will you!" He clearly thought he was the one being wronged, and he said to me, even more viciously: "In the past, you told me that the relationship between you and Xiao Chengshan was innocent and that you were not a true husband and wife. Well, that was a fucking lie, wasn't it! Even with him in this state, you still want to keep this kind of relationship going; you want to let him suck your milk! Is that how you normally made love before he got dementia? So, now I know! Zhong Chengcai is Xiao Chengshan's son after all! You two bastards made up a story to fool people, to show how virtuous you are. Well, no one will believe you now!" I was speechless with anger at this. In a flash, I took my nipple out of Uncle Xiao's mouth, rolled off the bed, seized a *taiji* sword that Uncle Xiao had used to train with in the past, drew it out of its scabbard with a *whoosh* and pointed it at Qiu Dali's chest, growling: "Fuck off out of this room right now, or I'll skewer you! What do I care what you think?!" Shocked by my sudden action, he retreated, step by step, saying: "All right, all right, I'm going. But what about all the stuff I've got here?" Through gritted teeth, I said: "I'll pack up everything you have here, and at seven o'clock exactly tomorrow morning, I'll put it all outside the door. You can come and collect it then. From now on, you're not going to set foot in this apartment again!"

I used the point of the sword to force him out of the front door, and only when I had shut it did I let my tears come. So that was the kind of man I had given myself to! I didn't even have the discrimination of a dog, and always thought bastards were decent men. I hated it that he could think me so unbearable and that he could wound me so deeply with his poisonous words. What a lucky escape it was that I hadn't gone with him to register our marriage when he wanted to; otherwise, I would have had to get another divorce. If I had made the mistake of committing myself to living with such a wicked man, wouldn't that have been a sheer living hell? The good thing was that Chengcai had slept soundly through all this, and knew nothing about it. Only Qiu Dali and I did. Also, he hadn't yet been able to worm his way any further into our lives, nor did I have any deep affection for him, so I would be able to heal my own wounds. Looking at it now, I think this affair actually relieved my emotional pressure at a stroke. But now, let's get back to our original topic.

As time passed, day by day, so my hopes diminished, bit by bit. Soon, three months had passed, and I couldn't detect any change in the way Uncle Xiao's lips felt on my nipple. Soon the packet of the

supplementary medicine Abbot Wu had given me would be
finished, and I thought to myself: There are two reasons for going
back to that little Daoist temple on Qingyang Ridge. One is to ask
for some more of the supplementary medicine, and the other is to
ask Abbot Wu if there is something wrong with my method. I took
Uncle Xiao to a senior citizens centre, paid over some money, and
asked them to look after him for five days. I asked a neighbour to
take Chengcai to school and collect him, gave him a front door key
and some money to buy food at the compound's dining hall,
instructed him on when to open the door and when to keep it shut,
and when to go to bed and get up, then left him to look after
himself and set off with all speed on my journey.

Flurries of afternoon snow were falling as, once again, I entered
Abbot Wu's hut at the little temple on Qingyang Ridge. The abbot
was sick, and was half leaning against the little Daoist monk as he
listened to my questions. In a weak voice, struggling for breath, he
replied: "Try to summon up... the feelings... you had... when you
first breastfed your own child... there's nothing wrong... with what
you are doing... it's just your emotions are... not strong enough...
it has only been a short time... not enough to stir up such powerful
things... persevere... the God of the Three Pure Divinities is
watching you... and it is up to Him when to manifest his spirit..." I
was too concerned for the abbot's health to bother him anymore,
so, after the little monk had given me the medicine, I made my way
down the mountain to find somewhere to stay the night.

After I got back this time, when I put my nipple between Uncle
Xiao's lips, I imagined him completely as a little child, a child who
needed my care, and I no longer thought of him as an invalid or an
old man. In truth, by this time, Uncle Xiao surely was just like a
little child, relying on you to do everything for him, knowing
nothing and understanding nothing. Sometimes at night, as I held
him to my bosom, and looked at his totally uncomprehending
expression, I would remember how proud and strong-willed he had

once been. My heart ached, and I wept silently to myself. Humankind! We should never think of ourselves as invincible, since which of us knows in what extremities we might find ourselves when we grow old? When my tears fell as I put my nipple in his mouth, he truly became my other child. It was during one such night that the miracle happened.

I was exhausted because I had spent the whole day giving the apartment a thorough clean. After I had settled Chengcai, I went into Uncle Xiao's bedroom, locked the door, got onto the bed as usual, put my nipple in his mouth, and fell asleep. I don't know what time it was when I felt a sucking on my nipple. I was still half-asleep, and I thought it must be Chengcai, so I made to stroke him as I always had done. But what I felt when I reached out my hand brought me fully to my senses, as Chengcai's body and Uncle Xiao's felt nothing the same. As I came properly awake, I gave a great start: previously, when my nipple had been in Uncle Xiao's mouth, his lips had remained motionless, or with only automatic reaction, like a puppet, so how was it that now he was quite clearly sucking quickly and independently, like a little child? I didn't dare move but just looked at his face in a shaft of electric light. What I saw amazed me: his previously expressionless face was full of animation, the wrinkles on it moving as if they were alive, giving every indication of eagerness. As I was wondering to myself whether all this was a good sign or a bad omen, I suddenly heard Uncle Xiao confusedly cry out the single word:

"...Mummy..."

This cry made me realise immediately that the treatment was showing results, and Uncle Xiao was showing some slight memory of what it was to be alive. He had remembered the thing he loved most: his mother. Just as I had come to this conclusion, Uncle Xiao cried out again:

"...Mummy..."

It was clearer this time, and as he cried out, his two eyes, which had been tight shut, slowly opened. His good left eye and his sightless right eye looked at me, blank and unfocused. I was rooted to the spot, not knowing whether to reply. Abbot Wu hadn't told me what to do if the patient began to recover his memory. I didn't dare encourage him, in case I said the wrong thing and scared away the memory that was coming back. All I could do was lie there, motionless, watching him. He spat out my nipple. He looked at me steadily, but still without focus, then, the next instant, he had buried his head, sobbing, in my bosom, asking:

"Where are you going? Why don't you want me?"

This was the complaint of a true child. Almost without thinking, I folded him back into my arms and gently stroked his back, just as I had once comforted Chengcai when he was upset.

"...sugar cane..." he said vaguely from the depths of my embrace.

Sugar cane? What was it about sugar cane that he had remembered, I asked myself.

"...big sister..." he continued.

I remembered that when I first arrived in the Xiao household, Older Sister Xinxin once told me that her father had had two older sisters, but that sadly, they had fallen ill and died, one after the other, ten years before. Perhaps he had remembered one of his sisters.

"...I've left you some..."

He was speaking very indistinctly, and I had to strain to make out the words.

"...thought I'd eaten it all..." he went on, as though explaining something. "...you were cross with me..."

Although these were all just broken sentences, I thought I understood what he was saying. He was explaining to his mother that he hadn't eaten all the sugar cane, and had left some for his older sister. None of you here in the audience can imagine how happy I was to hear all this. It was clear proof that the method Abbot Wu had told me wasn't just empty talk but could get real results. Before that night, Uncle Xiao had been a complete imbecile, unable to speak even a single word. But now, he could actually remember something from his childhood, and even explain it to his mother. At that time, I felt I should help him to clarify this memory, so I reached out and took his hearing aid from the bedside table. He was lying on his side, facing me, so I put the hearing aid into his good ear, and said softly into it:

"Mummy isn't angry."

"...then why did you turn away from me..." he asked from my embrace.

"Mummy is going to buy something else."

I gave this reply because I thought he must think he was somewhere he didn't know; otherwise, he wouldn't be worried about his mummy leaving him alone, and not wanting him. They were probably in a country market, and his mother had bought him some sugar cane. He had turned away to eat it, and when he turned back, he couldn't see her.

"...are you buying beancurd..."

"Yes, beancurd," I whispered reassuringly in his ear.

"...Third Uncle..."

"I know you bumped into Third Uncle." All I could do was guess.

"...Third Uncle said you don't want me..."

"Third Uncle was just joking with you! How could your mummy not want you? You're Mummy's little treasure." I stroked his back soothingly.

"...beancurd..."

He mumbled this word, then fell back asleep and began to snore. Only then did I sit up, very carefully, get off the bed and turn on a sidelight. Now I could see more clearly: the imbecile expression on his face really had changed. This was the happiest night I had had for a very long time.

When he woke up the next morning, his memory seemed to have retained the improvements it had made during the night. When he opened his eyes, he no longer stared blankly at nothing, but looked at me and asked:

"Third Uncle?"

I adjusted his hearing aid for him, and told him gently:

"I've told Third Uncle he shouldn't frighten you like that."

"Big sister..." he mumbled again.

"Your big sister has gone to your grandmother's house." I said this to try to extend his memory.

"Grandmother?" He stared at me.

"Grandmother likes you too."

"...yes..." He nodded his head, then followed on with the single word: "...dates..."

I didn't know what he meant by that. Did he remember his grandmother buying him dates to eat, or had he climbed a tree to pick some? Afraid of getting it wrong, I just mumbled back:

"Dates"

"Date tree..." he continued.

There was probably a date tree at his grandmother's house, so I went on:

"Your grandmother says she's going to take you to climb the date tree to pick some dates."

He laughed like a little child. I had guessed right.

After breakfast, I took Chengcai to school, then, when I got home, I gave Uncle Xiao the supplementary medicine, and, just as before, put my nipple between his lips. As soon as I did so, I felt the difference. He began to suck eagerly, so hard, in fact, it even hurt a little, but just as I gritted my teeth to get through it, he released my nipple and cried out the single word:

"Mummy..."

I quickly replied:

"Yes?"

He looked at me rather sadly and said:

"Daddy..."

I was delighted that he had remembered another relative. I reckoned he must be asking where his daddy was. I knew that Uncle Xiao grew up in a village, and a village boy's father would probably be working in the fields, so I told him:

"Your daddy's gone to work in the fields!"

"...work..." he repeated to himself.

"Your daddy's gone to harvest the sweetcorn."

I thought I'd use some country terminology to try to stimulate his memory further.

"...sweetcorn..." he repeated.

It seemed I had got it right, and they called maize "sweetcorn" in the part of Shaanxi where his home village was.

"...rabbit..." he suddenly exclaimed, and even waved his functioning left arm.

I had no idea what he meant, so had no reply.

"...ran..."

He sounded rather annoyed. His memory was jumping around randomly, so could it be that when he was young, he was picking maize with his father one day, and they saw a rabbit which they chased, but it escaped. I tried this guess out on him.

"You can catch it later."

He laughed; actually laughed. I was delighted; a few months ago, he couldn't laugh.

For the rest of that day, no matter whether we were at home or on our way to and from Longevity Park, I talked to him non-stop, drawing out of him as many memories of the past as he could manage. Although he only spoke in broken bits and pieces, I felt that his recollecting was like a little chicken foraging for food, running hither and thither in the remembered fields of his youth, continually expanding his activities and the scope of his searching, as it was his childhood and youth that were etched most deeply in his brain.

It must have been five or six days after that night that his memory took another leap forward. This time, it was during the night, some time around ten o'clock, I think. I had finished washing him, changed his disposable nappy, and given him a few sips of water. I arranged him so he was lying on his side, put my nipple in his mouth, and then I slowly closed my eyes and prepared to go to sleep. I was just slipping into deep sleep when I felt him spit my nipple out. After his fragmented recollection of his childhood and youth, this had become a common occurrence, so I didn't pay much attention and just thought vaguely to myself: He probably wants to go to sleep himself. Well, if that's what he wants, let him. Then, to my surprise, he called out:

"Summer willow..."

This startled me, so I opened my eyes properly, although I didn't understand what it meant. I decided he had just remembered some other event from his youth, so I blearily closed my eyes to go back to sleep. But, just at that moment, he cried out again:

"Summer willow..."

I opened my eyes again, put his hearing aid in his good ear, and asked:

"What do you mean 'summer willow'?"

He just repeated the same two words, leaving me none the wiser.

"Summer willow!"

He looked at me through the darkness, repeating the words yet again.

I didn't reply but wondered whether he had remembered something that had happened under a willow tree one summer.

"I'm so sorry!"

He said it suddenly, and reached out with his good hand to stroke my hair. Then I understood. He was calling out to someone, and that person's name was Xialiu Summer Willow. From the sound of it, it was almost certainly a girl!

"I'm so sorry..." he repeated, stroking my hair again.

That convinced me he had remembered a girl, and he thought that I was that girl.

This Xialiu clearly was not Older Sister Xinxin's mother because there was a wedding photograph of Uncle Xiao and Older Sister's mother hanging on the bedroom wall, under which was clearly written: *Memento of the marriage of Xiao Chengshan and Jin Siyu.* I had looked at it countless times in the past.

"I'm so grateful for what you gave me..."

His voice was very low, but I could make out what he was saying quite clearly. I was completely awake now. I felt I ought to reply, as this was clearly a sign that he had remembered some episode from his youth. This Xialiu must have been his girlfriend, and I ought to encourage this expansion of his memory. So, I gave a little grunt, as much as to say "think nothing of it".

"You gave me too much..."

He stroked my hair again, and I worked out what I thought he was actually talking about. Had this girl let him fondle her and kiss her breasts? But no, a man wouldn't think of that as "giving too much". More likely she had given him her whole body.

"I promised to marry you..." he went on.

This seemed to me to confirm my suspicions. This girl was his girlfriend before Older Sister Xinxin's mother, and the relationship had got as far as them talking about marriage.

"Of course we should have! I made my intentions clear. But your family's status..." he mumbled.

Status? That must mean something to do with her family background. Perhaps she was from one of those "rich, landlord farmer" families, so her social standing was not favourable, and, when Uncle Xiao was young, that would have been a major obstacle. I had heard old people say that, at that time, revolutionary fervour was particularly strong, and marrying someone from the wrong social background could cause a whole lot of trouble.

"I can't choose who my mother and father are," I replied boldly on behalf of the girl.

"If we'd got married, I might have been thrown out of the Party," he said, weakly.

He was probably telling her what the Party bigwigs had told him when they had a word with him.

"And you didn't think anything about my situation?!"

I was still trying to draw out his memory.

"What would my mum and dad have done?" He was trying to justify his excuses for not marrying her.

"What was I supposed to do?" I pushed back at him, on behalf of that girl from so long ago. I thought if I did so, I might force him to remember even more.

"I'm so sorry!" He was almost sobbing with emotion.

"So all I get is a 'so sorry', and that's it?" I continued to goad him.

"My mother said she would drown herself in the river," he said, choking on his own voice.

I could guess the meaning of all this. After his mother had

learned of the possible impact on his future life that marrying Xialiu could have, had she adamantly opposed it, and even tried to stop him by threatening to throw herself in the river? I asked, tentatively:

"You just wanted to be rid of me. All for the best of reasons, of course!"

"I really am so sorry!"

"Pah!" I exclaimed in disgust on her behalf.

"You must hate me..."

"Of course I hate you!"

In the gleam of the night light, I could see a tear gathering in the corner of his eye.

"I'm so sorry... when you did get married, I sent you... fifty yuan..."

"And that was the value you put on my body, was it?"

I thought that was the kind of attitude Xialiu would have had.

"It was... just a token."

"And that set you free to throw yourself at another woman, did it? To go after that Jin Siyu?"

I was following my instincts and airing Xialiu's grievances for her.

"Jin Siyu knew about you..."

"I suppose you were boasting about your prowess, and how you'd had your way with some girl called Xialiu, weren't you!?" I said, sarcastically.

"It was because I said your name in my sleep..."

Ai! He really had been in love with this Xialiu. He even talked about her in his sleep.

"She questioned me about you..."

So, he had had to tell Jin Siyu all about his past affairs. What a mess! That night as I drew him out about his affair with the girl, Xialiu, he remembered lots of things, until finally he was worn out and closed his eyes and went to sleep.

Two months later, he began to remember his daughter Xinxin, and the time she started at middle school.

Three months or so later, he came close to recognising me. I can still remember the circumstances. It was afternoon, and I was getting on with the daily routine. First I took Chengcai to school, and then I gave Uncle Xiao his supplementary medicine. After that, I took him in my arms and let him suckle at my breast. After about ten minutes, he suddenly spat out my breast, lifted his head from my bosom and asked:

"Could the child come home unexpectedly?"

I was taken aback: the child? What did he mean by that question?

"I'm afraid Xinxin might burst in on us... Xinxin might burst in..."

Was there a hint of embarrassment in what he was saying? Either way, I was delighted.

"Daytime is no good..." he went on.

At that moment, I realised that he thought I was his wife, Jin Siyu, and he thought she was getting frisky with him in broad daylight. I laughed with delight. He had mistaken the things I was doing to treat his illness for his wife getting intimate with him. This told me his awareness was increasing even more. To my surprise, my laugh made him suddenly suspicious:

"Who are you?"

"I'm your wife, Jin Siyu!" I said with a smile.

"No, you're not!" he broke in.

"How do you know?" I asked him back.

"Jin Siyu wouldn't laugh at this; she'd be embarrassed."

What? He could remember Jin Siyu's embarrassment about their intimate relations back then.

"Just think about it." I looked him in the eyes.

He blinked sightlessly, as though straining to search through his mental archives.

"Someone employed me," I prompted him.

"Jin Siyu..."

He was talking to himself as he furrowed his brows in the struggle to remember. He was silent for ten minutes or more, then, just as I thought he would never work out who I was, he suddenly pointed at me and exclaimed:

"Xiao Gong!"

I looked at him in surprise. Xiao Gong?!

"You'd better get out of here quick!" He pointed agitatedly at the door. "Quickly! You mustn't let Siyu see you!"

I understood. This was another of the women in his life, and he was afraid he'd be found out by his wife, Jin Siyu.

"I'm not leaving!" I pretended to be angry.

"I'm begging you!" he said, piteously.

I grinned. He had remembered someone else...

From that day on, he would no longer let me put my nipple in his mouth, and he kept urging me to leave. Right up to today, his memory has been stuck on Xiao Gong. I have no idea when he will eventually recognise me. I am eagerly looking forward to it.

This evening, I have asked my son, Chengcai, to push his Uncle Xiao to the main gates of this open-air auditorium, so you would all have a chance to meet him. Could I ask one of the attendants to open the doors, please! Chengcai, bring Uncle Xiao in. Can everybody see him? I would ask you not to alarm him. Please don't all surround him, talking to him, as I'm afraid that might have a detrimental effect on the recovery of his memory. I don't know to what degree his memory will eventually be able to return, or whether the senile dementia will ever be driven out of his body, but I do know that I will continue to care for him, regardless. So that is the story of my nursing career. Thank you all very much for spending three evenings listening to me babbling on. Once again, thank you.

"You'd better get out of here quick, Xiao Gong!"

You see, he is still urging me.

"All right, I'm going now..."

NOTES

TUESDAY

1. *Shanghan Zabing Lun* (Treatise on Cold Pathogenic and Miscellaneous Diseases) was written by Zhang Zhongjing (c150-c219 CE). Zhang is one of the most important doctors in the history of Chinese medicine. The book was lost not long after his death, but reconstructed in two volumes by Song dynasty physicians. They deal with infectious fevers and internal medicine respectively and are still consulted in traditional Chinese medicine today.
2. The Anshi Rebellion (755-763 CE) occurred in the middle of the Tang dynasty (618-907 CE) when the silk trade was at its height and Chang'an (the Tang capital) was the biggest city in the world. Its leader, An Lushan, was a non-Chinese general in the Tang army. Sent to Chang'an for punishment, he rebelled instead. His rebellion sparked others, and the Tang never regained the stability and prosperity of its early years.

FRIDAY

1. *Gaokao*: the standardised, nationwide examinations for university entry.
2. Until May 1995, China had a six-day standard working week, with only Sunday off.
3. *Quchi* and *sanyinjiao* are acupressure points at the elbow and the calf respectively.
4. Li Shizhen (1518-1593) was a Ming botanist, pharmacologist and author of *Compendium of Medical Herbs*.
5. Prince of Yan: this refers to Zhu Di, fourth son of the first Ming Emperor, who rebelled against his nephew, the second Ming Emperor, Jianwen, and usurped the throne as the Yongle Emperor.

SATURDAY

1. *Xiao yaya* literally means "little girl".
2. *Dushuqiang* (literally "strong rat poison") is a rodenticide containing the compound Tetramethylenedisulfotetramine (TETS) which is banned worldwide. It is illegal in China but still widely available because of its ease of production.
3. *Jin*: traditional unit of weight equivalent to 500g.
4. The characters 承人 (*chéng rén*) mean something like "be a man" or "succeed as a man".
5. The characters 承才 (*chéng cái*) mean something like "be talented".

ABOUT THE AUTHOR

Zhou Daxin is a contemporary Chinese author and winner of several major literary honours including China's highest award for fiction, the Mao Dun Prize.

Across his body of work – more than thirty novels and short stories – Zhou has made piercing observations of Chinese society by setting his characters in rural, urban and even allegorical environments and touching upon challenging, often intimate humanitarian questions seldom dealt with by other authors of his generation.

ABOUT THE TRANSLATOR

James Trapp has published China-related books on language, astrology, science and technology. His translation works include new versions of *The Art of War* and *The Daodejing*. Much of his work revolves around integrating the study of Chinese language and culture, and breaking down barriers of cultural misunderstanding that still persist.